HAG NIGHT

TIM CURRAN

PART ONE: SNOWBOUND

1

There was a blizzard waiting in the wings threatening to dump another three to four feet of snow, but Morris was unconcerned because he figured they could outrun it. He was a TV producer for godsake. The sort of guy that squeezed extra dollars from emaciated budgets and fought scheduling and uppity suits from the front office. He and deadlines were old enemies: they had met on the field of battle again and again and he'd always come out victorious. This time would be no different. To him, the blizzard was just another deadline and he would beat it.

"I don't like the looks of this," Wenda told him, studying the frozen white world through the windows. Now that it was night it looked even more threatening than it had an hour before.

"Just a quick shoot," Morris told her, "and we're out of here."

From the front of the bus, Burt said, "She's getting rough out there, people. This keeps up we're going to need skis."

"More driving, less commentary," Morris told him.

But he was right and Wenda knew it.

The snow was flying thick in the headlights of the bus. It was piling up heavy on the road before them in snaking currents of white. Drifts were pushing in from both sides and they hadn't seen anything resembling a town in well over an hour now since they'd cut off the main highway and onto the secondary road. A city girl born and bred, Wenda did not like the idea of being trapped in a blizzard out here in this godawful desolation. Hell, there wasn't even a Starbucks within sixty miles, she joked to the others, and she wasn't much without a hot Caffè Misto. But, all kidding aside, if they got stuck out here with that blizzard raging they'd be buried alive.

"Are we lost?" Bailey said from the back.

There was an aggravated sigh from Megga. "Nobody gets lost these days, princess. They call it OnStar...*hello.*"

Mole and Reg ignored it all, both of them obsessively toying about with their equipment: the DAT unit, HD video, light meters, laptops, and peripherals. They were in their own techie fantasy zone and oblivious to the world around them. Doc was snoozing.

Wenda knew the logical, practical thing was to call this off and make for the main highway while they still could, but there was no way Morris would admit defeat. The ghost town shoot was too important to him. More so, it was important for the network and the sponsors who'd already paid big bucks.

Burt had the radio on and the National Weather Service was still broadcasting its alerts, which had become warnings and traveler's advisories now. They were calling for an unprecedented 36 inches of snow in the next twenty-four hours with gale force winds blowing at fifty-miles-an-hour which would push the wind chill down into the single digits. Back in the city, Manhattan was already getting nailed with blowing and drifting snow and they were closing Fifth Avenue, which was pretty much like cutting the throat of Midtown.

Yeah, great day for a fucking location shoot, Wenda thought.

"We're getting close now," Burt announced as the shadows grew long. "About five minutes we should see it."

"This is the shits," Mole said. "No service on my cell, no internet for my laptop. Damn, it's like the Middle Ages here."

"So you'll be porn-free for a couple hours. Do you some good," Morris said.

That got laughs from Reg and Bailey.

Megga saw it as an opportunity. "He's right, Mole-Man. Maybe if you gently wean yourself from chickswithdicks.com you might learn to appreciate the real thing."

"Oh, I know all about the real thing," he told her.

She chuckled. "As if."

Wenda sighed. On your average day of shooting, she knew, things could get a little tense with this crew...but out here, in the confined spaces of the bus, there would be blood in the offing. Although Bailey was sweet-natured and vacuous, Megga had an evil streak in her a mile wide and was not above putting it to work against Reg and Mole, particularly Mole. There was nothing she enjoyed better than demeaning his maleness at every opportunity with a constant string of barbs concerning his sexual preference or lack thereof. She would keep at him until he got pissed and then Reg would come to his defense and Bailey would get upset and Doc would try to counsel them with sage advice until Morris lost it and yelled at all of them.

It was coming, oh yes.

Wenda could sense the venom welling up inside Megga and it was only a matter of time before she sank her fangs in someone. This group was almost comically dysfunctional on the best of days, but trapped in the bus with that storm descending on them, things were more tense than usual.

"We gotta almost be on top of your ghost town right now," Burt said over his shoulder to Morris. The bus lurched as it moved up a hill. The road was zigzagging and Burt slowed, cut to the left then to the right. Everyone seemed to be holding on tight. The snow in the headlights was thick as drifting silt in the belly of a sunken ship. As he banked another turn, the headlights swept over a hilltop crowded with leaning monuments and old tombs jutting from the snowpack. For one brief second, Wenda thought she saw someone standing in the darkness just inside the stone wall that encircled it. Someone whose eyes shined yellow in the bus lights.

"Hey…did you see that?" Burt said. "Now that was weird."

"What?" Megga said, always in search of the weird wherever she could find it.

"I saw someone standing there by the graves," Burt told her.

"Out here?" Morris said. "In the storm?"

"Maybe I just imagined it," Burt admitted, but from the tone of his voice it was obvious he did not believe that at all.

"I saw it, too," Wenda said. "Its eyes were yellow."

Morris swallowed. "Now listen, kid, this horror-thing is our bread-and-butter, but let's not go believing it ourselves. C'mon already. Remember, Cobton, our ghost town, is damn old. What you saw was probably one of them statues people used to put up. You know, an angel or something."

"Yes, a Death Angel. Sometimes they're statues and sometimes they're not," Megga said, notching things up as she always did.

Wenda did not bother defending her position. She had seen it. The gooseflesh that spread over her arms and up her spine was testament to that, and statues did not have eyes. Shining eyes.

It seemed like at that moment everyone tapped into what she was feeling. They went silent and the atmosphere was thick and ominous. The only sounds were the rumble of the bus's engine, the frantic *swish-swash* of the wipers, and the sound of the wind throwing snow against the windows.

Burt lit a cigarette, breaking the anxiety. "What a drive," he said.

"Hey!" Morris said. "No smoking. This a rental for chrissake."

"My union contract clearly states that I get a fifteen minute break for every three hours I work," Burt explained, the cigarette smoldering in the corner of his mouth. "I been driving for closer to four. Besides, my nerves ain't for shit right now. I been staring through this windshield for too fucking long. I'm seeing shit."

"What sort of shit?" Megga asked him.

"The sort of shit that ain't there, honey."

Bailey was getting scared and Megga held her hand. Reg and Mole had completely forgotten about their gadgets. Morris was staring at the windshield, clicking his pen. The snow seemed heavier, the wind making a low moaning sound like death exhaled from the belly of the graveyard they had just passed. More twists and turns in the road. The bus bumped over drifts and potholes.

"There..." Burt said, blowing smoke out his nose. "Your ghost town is down in the hollow below, Morris. I just saw it. Looks pitch black. Ain't a light to be seen."

"The caretakers should be there," Morris said. "They better be: I'm paying them."

"Well, if they are," Burt offered, "then they sure as hell ain't afraid of the dark."

2

As Burt moved the bus carefully down towards Cobton, Doc Blood came awake, yawned and stretched, then smiled. "Ah, a refreshing little *siesta,*" he said. "It does a body good."

"You can sleep anywhere," Reg said.

"It's a gift he has," Morris said.

"More than a gift," Doc told them, "it's a matter of discipline. When I was in 'Nam we barely got any sleep. Dexies to get you going and Bennies to take you down. We'd come in off patrol and three hours later we were going back out again. We were lucky if we got in a solid eight hours of rack-time a week. That's when I learned to turn all my down time into refreshing sleep. I nodded off

4

between firefights, on choppers, during briefings. I became a master of slumber. I practice it to this day."

"You should teach me," Megga said. "Most nights I wander from one end of my apartment to the other in daze."

"Kinda like she does all day," Mole said.

"Piss off," Megga told him.

"You should eat more fruits and vegetables," Bailey suggested. "I sleep like a baby every night."

Megga rolled her eyes.

Doc reached in his coat for a pack of Marlboros and lit up much to Morris's chagrin. "Do you have troubling dreams?" he asked her, running a hand through his thick white locks. "Often dreams are the seat of trouble. Look at me. For years I had a continuing nightmare that I was going about my day clad only in underwear. It's true. I stopped wearing them and the dreams faded. Often, when I'm alone, I go about my day entirely unclothed. There's nothing like a nice fire, a good book, and your own nakedness."

It was Wenda's turn to roll her eyes.

Before anyone could comment on what he'd said, Megga began telling him in detail about her own reoccurring dreams which involved rusty sawblades, impaled kittens, and plastic baby doll heads in her closet that could be heard licking their lips in the dead of night. Doc listened, then searched for a root cause.

"Hmm, most unusual," he said, pulling off his cigarette. "Baby doll heads."

"Her closet's probably full of them," Mole said.

"It is. She collects them," Bailey put in.

They're all fucking whackos, Wenda thought.

Playing the horror bit was one thing, but Megga lived it. Wenda had gone to her place once for dinner and it was absolutely disturbing...much like Megga herself who slept in a room painted black with two beds—one for her and one for the mannequin she called Missy Creep. Wenda was pretty sure Doc wasn't going to be able to do a three-minute analysis on this girl; it would take months to sift through her shocking array of psychological baggage.

Megga, Megga, Megga.

Wenda could never be a hundred percent sure whether Megga was just the consummate actress or the real thing. On set, she was professional. Incredibly professional. She never missed a cue, never dropped a line. But what about the real Megga? That was hard to know. She was so good at role-playing that it was nearly impossible to get a glimpse of the real her. Wenda was never sure whether she was just an unbelievably good, natural actress or a thing that sucked blood by night.

Don't put it past her. Don't put anything past her.

In the headlights, Wenda could just make out bits of the town below—a steeple, a jagged roofline, a crooked chimney. The sight of it made something move in her belly with a slow crawl.

"Lots of drifts over the road going in," Burt said. "Hang on tight, I'm going to have to give her some speed to punch our way through."

"I wonder why the caretakers have all the lights off," Bailey mused, mostly to herself.

Megga laughed wickedly.

"That," Doc said, "is what we'll find out very soon now, for better or worse."

3

Chamber of Horrors. Fridays at Midnight.

That was it. That was Wenda's ticket. And that was also why she was out in the bus with the crew in the middle of the blizzard of the century (as it was being called). Maybe her mom and her sister and her next door neighbor knew her as Wenda Keegan, but to the rest of the world she was Vultura, the host of *Chamber of Horrors*. In high school, there had been a few plays—*Our Town* and *The Corn is Green*—followed by some community theater and stagework in college, but it never led anywhere. She was a good strong alto, but she didn't have the force to headline anything. Her dramatic skills were "stilted" as her drama coach told her at Stony Brook U. Upon advice from her mom—*it's a pipe dream, Wenny, a girl like you working on the stage*—she switched to marketing and shortly after graduation landed a job at WKKX Channel 5 in Albany. It was a good position. She worked hard. Within four years, she was number two in the department selling air time and programming spots.

That's when Morris discovered her.

Or discovered my legs and tits, she decided later. Morris was a producer and director who had just moved from Manhattan to Albany and was overseeing shows like *Morning Edition* and *Cooking with Granny,* which, despite the title or maybe because of it, owned its time slot in the Capital District-Schenectady-Troy metro area. Granny was Miriam Clayton, a sixties-something farm woman with a razor-sharp wit, reams of down-home advice, and a collection of recipes that had made her not only a star but the author of two cookbooks. Morris was riding high at the station. The station manager, Lou Phelps, asked him to take on the Friday midnight timeslot. He wanted something young and wild and hip. And Morris, having grown up with Zacherley's *Chiller Theater* and *Creature Features* hosted by "The Creep", knew exactly what he wanted. Drawing upon WKKX's extensive catalog of old movies, he created Vultura and *Chamber of Horrors*.

All he lacked was Vultura herself.

Enter Wenda Keegan, WKKX assistant marketing director. A somewhat shy and high-strung young woman with bright red hair and sparkling green eyes, who had the legs and the impressive bosom to pull in the Friday night male viewership.

"But a horror movie host?" Lou Phelps said. "I don't know. That kind of stuff went out in seventies."

"Which is why it has to be re-introduced. Retro, man, everything's retro. We've got the movies. Why play 'em late at night or on Saturday afternoons? Why not repackage them with *Chamber of Horrors* hosted by Vultura? We're not talking Zacherley or Svengoolie or Dr. Paul Bearer here, we're leaning towards Elvira, Vampira. We're selling sex here, Lou. It's the only thing that *does* sell."

"Who do you got for the girl?"

Morris told him. "This lady is a knock-out. Model pretty, she's got the legs and tits and flirty eyes to keep the boys coming back. She belongs in front of a camera, not behind a desk hawking air space for Burger King and Pennzoil Quik-Lube. She has the look. She's a little uncomfortable with it, but I'll bring her around."

And Morris did just that.

Forcing her to watch hours of 1950's horror host Vampira and her later-day imitator, Elvira, Morris created Vultura from whole cloth...with a little help from Kansas City's Ghostess with the Mostess, Crematia Mortem, and the all-too hilarious Ivonna Cadaver from LA. Wearing a ragged black dress cut thigh-high with a plunging neckline that showed Wenda's charms to full effect, Morris had the makeup people paint her face ghost-white and lips midnight-black. The first color test shots weren't grabbing him, though. That's when he decided to do the entire thing in stark black-and-white, which would mirror a lot of the old scare flicks they were playing. A cobwebby set was built, lots of candelabras and faux-stone walls, an alternate graveyard set, and Vultura was off and running. With the long black braids and the makeup, Wenda lost herself in the character. Maybe as Wenda Keegan she was somewhat shy and unsure of herself despite her looks (again, maybe *because* of them), but when she morphed into Vultura and saw herself on the monitor in the shifting grays and guttering candlelight of black-and-white, she suddenly knew the character and had no trouble pouring on the juice in her low seductive voice. Unlike Elvira, Vultura took her movies and herself absolutely seriously, laying on the sex hot and heavy reminiscing about her favorite dank tombs and coffins she'd laid (or *been* laid) in while discussing movies like *Curse of the Living Corpse* and *The Four Skulls of Jonathan Drake* as if they were artistic masterpieces of mood and subtlety and not low-brow creaky late show fare.

It worked.

It worked 100%.

In six months her salary doubled, then tripled. Advertisers lined up. There were remote shoots at record stores and nite clubs, live feeds from cemeteries on Halloween night. They started with old late-night standbys from Universal—*The Ghost of Frankenstein* and *Creature from the Black Lagoon*—and Technicolor Hammer classics—*Plague of the Zombies* and *The Brides of Dracula*—but soon enough Morris realized the movies were absolutely secondary so they started running Grade-Z programmers like *The Bride of the Gorilla, Frankenstein's Daughter,* and *Zontar: The Thing from Venus*.

Morris was right.

It mattered naught.

Most of the stuff they showed was easily available on DVD, what *wasn't* available was *Chamber of Horrors* and Vultura herself. The movies got worse and the ratings got higher. Go figure. They spent more air-time in the dungeon with Vultura and her cohorts, assembling dozens of subplots amongst the renovated dungeon complete with the stretching rack (where Vultura was to be found at the opening of each show, lots of leg and heaving cleavage, tied down and being stretched, screaming out her joy), hanging cage, and Diabolical Den (which sounded like a 1970's Aurora monster kit). It was this latter set that was the home of the Graveyard Girls (Megga and Bailey), two strumpet vampiresses seething with barely concealed lust who spent a lot of time talking about sucking things—*I'd like to sink my teeth into that*—and licking other things—*Mmmm, I can practically taste it now*. In their low-cut

8

vampire girl gowns with ample charms on display (breasts often pressed up against one another), they became an instant hit, sleeping together in the same coffin and practically tonguing each other on camera…and launching a hundred masturbatory fantasies.

As *Chamber of Horrors* moved into its second season, it was programming gold. It was syndicated on twenty-three stations across New York, New England, and the Midwest. The month of October was always busy, Vultura and her crew showing up at costume stores and haunted houses and Halloween-themed parties. They made the horror con and comic book con circuit, always promoting, promoting, promoting. The cons were fun and fans lined up to see them. They all wanted their pictures taken with Vultura or Doc Blood or sandwiched in-between the Graveyard Girls. Wenda always had fun and played it to the hilt…the only fans that bothered her were the ones that panted on her and had sticky fingers, other than that it was a riot.

The format was set. Every episode started with Vultura stretched on the rack, writhing and screaming to a Goth metal soundtrack. Then came the Graveyard Girls, who were practically a soft-core lesbo act by that point. And finally, Doc Blood. Doc, formerly "Sawbones McCord", was a stage magician whose credentials included weatherman, Shakespearean summer stock, college drama instructor, juggler, and a corny magic act straight out of the old midnight spookshows. But he had something and Morris saw it. Before long, Doc Blood was a popular part of the show as he regularly staked the Graveyard Girls (a lot of gasping and orgasmic cries during the obligatory penetration), sawed them in half, or took off his own hands with a meat cleaver, popped his eyeballs out, and yanked strings of bloody razor blades from his mouth. It was cheap stage horror, cheese sliced thick, that might have appeared ludicrous and cornball in color…but in black-and-white, it was oddly effective.

That was the show.

And that was why they were going to the ghost town of Cobton. They had a ski lodge in the Adirondacks lined up to sponsor a month's worth of shows. They wanted some snow scenes. Next week it would be at the lodge, this week the ghost town. Morris had searched high and low for the latter. There were dozens up in the Catskills, but most were nothing but overgrown foundations, rusting mine works, or a still-standing chimney or two. Few had roads leading to them anymore and nearly all were impassable in the winter without snowshoes. Then he found Cobton: a fully restored village from the 18th century that was a tourist trap of sorts—and, unfortunately, one not much visited—during the summer. The family that owned it was more than happy to rent it out to *Chamber of Horrors.* They even supplied a pair of caretakers. Of course, it cost WKKX an arm and a leg to get the roads leading to it plowed open. They were all secondary roads closed in the winter. But it would be worth it because the ski lodge was picking up the tab.

"Maybe an hour's work," Morris had said. "A few exteriors, some interiors. We'll splice it together back at the studio."

Originally, they had tried to do it the cheap way, filming a few test shots at the studio with fake snow but the whole thing came off looking like an outtake from an Ed Wood movie, footage from *Plan 9 from Outer Space* that had hit the cutting room floor. Shit even old one-shot Eddie wouldn't use.

Morris wasn't about to try and sell that off to the ski lodge. *They'd fucking laugh,* he said. No, they had to do a location shoot and that's all there was to it. Some good shots in the old town by night, lots of shadows, lots of atmosphere. Let Jekyll and Hyde—his pet names for Bailey and Megga—do their thing and get the testosterone rising while Doc Blood crept about with Vultura holding center stage, deadpan ghoul to the last, showing lots of skin while she discussed the merits—or lack of the same—concerning the movie, which would either be *Snow Creature* or *Half-Human,* both of them Grade-Z abominable snowmen flicks from the 1950's (this keeping with the snow theme of the ski lodge itself, of course).

"Location, location, location," Morris had said, finding himself amusing as always.

Wenda hadn't been crazy about it from the start and that feeling worsened with the blizzard, but she was contracted and she had no choice. Dressed in her Vultura costume—more flesh than costume—she figured if she didn't catch pneumonia or take out somebody's eye with a stray nipple in the cold, it would be fairly easy.

And that's what brought them to Cobton.

The ghost town in the hollow below that was pitch black in the night.

4

Burt opened the bus up gradually, picking up speed to meet the first of many snowdrifts that had blown across the road. Everyone gripped their seats and waited for it. The winding road that fed down into the hollow was maybe two city blocks in length, twisting and turning, the cemetery they had seen earlier clinging to a high hillside off to the right now. If they'd have been able to walk straight from there to Cobton, they would have been in the town fifteen minutes ago. It wasn't far as the crow flies, but the road seemed to carry them farther away from the town before bringing them in closer.

Here it comes, Wenda thought, *I can just about feel it.*

The thing was, she was not sure what she was waiting for. She was tensed like a cat, her fingers gripping the seat like claws. Her heart was pounding hard but it didn't seem to be in her chest but from somewhere much lower like it had dropped down into a well. She could hear it in her ears—distant, muffled—kind of like the heart of the old man in Poe's story: the dull, quick sound of a watch enveloped in cotton. This was the way she felt before they shot *Chamber of Horrors* each week. Nervous, her heartbeat fluttery, her hands shaking just a bit. Threaded with an anxiety that was pure apprehension that only faded when she got into her Vultura get-up. Realistically, she knew, she should have been more panicky and self-conscious scantily clad as Vultura, but it was never that way. In character, she was calm, resolute, and confident, things she never was as herself. The reason being that she was no longer Wenda Keegan. No longer a walking basket of nervous tics and indecision and petty angst, she was someone else and that person—even if they happened to be a ghoul—was perfectly comfortable within their own skin.

"Some of these fucking drifts are heavy," Burt said, 'we're going to have to punch through them. Hang on tight."

"Christ, and here I thought we'd do this thing without a fatality," Morris said.

"Such is the nature of existence," Doc Blood mused.

Wenda tried to unwind, but she was as tense as a spring. She gripped the seat, trying to control her breathing. She felt like she was on the spiky edge of a panic attack. The bus jerked as it plowed through first one drift then veered slightly off to the right as it plowed through another. Snow enveloped the vehicle like sea fog, whirling and white, sounding like blowing sand against the windows.

"Take it easy," Morris said.

Bailey was close to freaking out and once again, her voice got that shrill squeak to it that went right up Wenda's spine like the tines of a fork. Megga was speaking quietly and soothingly to her, holding her hand. It was so out of character for Megga, who was not very different from the character she played on TV. She was just as morbid, just as cruel, just as twisted, maybe a little less horny, but that was about it. But Bailey and she had bonded. They were just as close off-screen as on. Geometric opposites in every way…but they were like sisters. Go figure. Megga had very little sympathy for anyone or anything, but she was more than sisterly with Bailey, almost motherly.

And maybe a little more than that, Wenda often thought.

The bus moved on down the road, which was greasy with the snow lying over sheets of blue ice. The tires were having trouble getting traction. Burt was swearing as he tried to get it under control, but the bus seemed to be moving of its own volition now—hydroplaning over the road and getting far too close to the encroaching snowbanks.

"Shit," Morris said.

Bailey muttered, "Oh God, oh God."

"YEAH!" Reg cried out. "POUR IT ON, MAN! WOO-HOO!"

Morris told him to shut the hell up. Doc Blood mused on the fragility of life on the earthly plane. Wenda gripped her seat like it was the bucket of a Ferris wheel coming over the big loop and careening earthward. The bus jerked and thumped, bursting through drifts and each one made it swerve uneasily while Burt fought to get it under control. Nobody was saying a thing as they punched through another drift and the windshield was covered in snow. The bus began to swerve again, Burt swearing as it started to go sideways into a spin and they all were thinking the same thing: *we're going to roll, we're going to roll right over and be trapped in this goddamn iron coffin.*

But, as before, Burt got it under control so they were moving in a straight line. The only problem being that the road was so slippery coming down the caning hillside that the brakes were pretty much useless to slow it down, its own weight pushing it forward and making it gather speed.

Then the road leveled out and the bus slowed incrementally and Burt sighed. "Jesus H. Christ, that was close," he said.

Everyone took a deep breath, held it, let it out slowly, deciding that they might indeed live through this one. The town was maybe a half a block away now and they were honest-to-God going to make it. The tension bled off them like steam from a pressure cooker.

And then Burt cried out: *"HOLY SHIT! WHAT THE FUCK IS THAT?"*

No time for speculation: the bus hit it, whatever it was.

The bumper smashed into it and there rose up a manic, unearthly squealing of rage and agony as it was dragged beneath them, the tires thumping over it.

Bailey let out a short, sharp, economical sort of scream.

And Burt lost control of the bus.

Trying to pump the brakes and work the wheel at the same time, the bus swung to the left and right, bumped off one snow bank then the other, spinning around and throwing anyone not belted in. Cameras and equipment not packed away went airborne, clattering to the floor. People were shouting. The bus did a complete 360°, then blasted through a snow bank in an eruption of white, found a ditch, and came to a jarring rest.

"Is anyone hurt?" Morris said as he got out of his belt.

"No, just banged around," Doc Blood said.

"We're okay," Megga announced, speaking for herself and Bailey.

"What a fucking rush, man!" Reg said.

Mole didn't think it was much of a rush because his laptop had taken a good beating and it appeared as if its days of surfing were over. Burt was digging under the dashboard for the emergency kit, which was about the size of a suitcase. He got a flashlight out.

"What did we hit?" Wenda asked.

"Some kind of animal," he said.

"Can we be more specific?" Doc put to him.

Burt just shook his head. "Don't ask me. I grew up in fucking Brooklyn. What do I know of animals? I don't know tit about nature."

"It wasn't an animal," Megga said.

Everyone looked at her. In the dim overhead light her eyes were almond-shaped, wet and dark. "I saw it. It came running across the road. It was a woman."

Bailey gasped.

"It weren't no fucking woman," Burt said. "It was running on all fours. It had a mane like a fucking wolf. That's all I saw...before we hit it."

"Then it could be manslaughter," Mole said.

Reg whistled. "Whoa."

Burt glared at him, but before he could say a thing, Morris intervened. "You shut the fuck up with that talk," he warned Mole.

"It was a woman," Megga maintained.

"It was a fucking animal," Burt said, getting red in the face and ready to start swinging.

Morris stepped in front of him. "You just thought it was a woman."

Megga shook her head. "No, it was a woman and she was running on all fours."

5

Burt did not like where any of this was going and if they thought they were going to hang him for running down some fucking animal, then they had another thing coming. But he *was* scared. He was scared bone-deep. He was sure it had been an animal. He'd only seen it for a second or two, maybe less, but it had been an animal. It had hair like an animal and right before the bus hit it, he had seen its eyes flash up at him in the headlights, silver and feral. No, he had not hit any woman regardless of what that fucking hot-shit little whore said.

Yet, he was scared.

He was confused, mixed-up, doubting what he had seen and he could see the others were, too. And that scared him. Scared him because when he was nineteen he'd been involved in a hit-and-run and almost went to prison because of it. The guy he'd run down— some shit worthless drunk who staggered out into the street—had been all right. Leg broken but that was about it. The only thing that had gotten Burt in trouble was the fact that he'd panicked and drove off. Three hours later, he turned himself in. The bulls at the precinct had not gone real easy on him about it, telling him he'd be doing hard time and that was because Burt had half a dozen traffic violations on his record by that point.

But, hell, his driving record had been spotless since then.

He knew he had to calm down. He got funny when he was put up against the wall like this. He got pissed-off and irrational and his first instinct was to take a poke at somebody.

Just cool off, take it easy. That was no woman and you know it.

He slapped the flashlight against his leg. "Listen, Miss," he said to Megga, keeping his voice modulated, his tone even. "I don't know what you saw, but I saw an animal. People don't run on all fours."

"Normal people anyway," Morris put it.

And Burt could see it in Megga's eyes: *Who said it was normal?*

"Dude," Reg said, "why the fuck are we debating this? Whatever it was, it ran out in front of us. It's nobody's fault. Just an accident."

"Ah, the voice of reason," Doc said.

Wenda nodded. "Let's just go look for godsake. This is stupid."

Morris opened his mouth to concur with that, but he never said a word because it was at that moment that a wailing rose up…eerie and unnatural, not the sound of an animal or a woman, but maybe— as incredulous as it sounded—the wailing of an animal *imitating* a woman. Whatever it was, it was in pain, shrieking out its death throes. The sound was hysterical and piercing, chilling. The last sort of thing anyone wanted to hear in the desolation of a blizzard now that night had come on.

Burt was shaking.

It was warm in the bus, but he was still shaking. The sound of that…that *thing* out there was getting down inside him and filling him with brittle white ice. His flesh was creeping from his belly to his throat and he figured the last thing he wanted to do was go out there and look at something that made sounds like that.

"C'mon," Morris said, stepping towards the door. "Let's go see. Whatever it is, it's still alive."

Everyone pushed towards the door with him and that keening cry rose up again, echoing off into the desertion of the storm.

6

"What the hell?"

Megga was staring at it, the thing they had not only hit, but dragged and stretched over the road. She had been at Morris's side as they climbed up out of the snowy ditch and onto the icy pavement. She was one of the first to see it.

"Damn," Reg said.

"Oh my God," Bailey said, turning away, making gagging sounds like she might throw up.

The rest of them were not too far from that themselves.

They stood in a loose semi-circle, the wind moaning and blowing snow down the road and into their faces, biting and cold, bleaching the color from their cheeks. The road itself was like a long tunnel with the snowbanks rising up six feet or more to either side.

What the bus had hit was spread out an easy thirty feet. The snow was red with blood and it was easy to see the point of original impact where the *animal* had gotten struck, then caught under the bus, pulled apart, dragged, and finally released to die on the icy road. The blood patterns were very specific. Already, the falling snow was covering them, but there was a lot of it, plenty to raise the gorge of the staunchest stomachs.

What they had hit should have been dead.

But it did not appear to be as close to death as it should have been: in fact, despite the degree of mutilation, it was unpleasantly alive, filled with a shuddering diabolic vitality.

Bailey had to hang back as did Mole.

Morris and Megga, Doc and Wenda stepped forward with Burt right behind them. He was hesitant, as if he simultaneously wanted to see and he wanted anything but. Reg came pounding up behind them, brushing snow off himself. When he had caught sight of the thing he had jogged back to the bus for his HD camcorder. This, in his thinking, had to be captured for posterity.

As Wenda looked at the creature, bile coming up the back of her throat, she could only think: *What in the fuck is that?*

She saw the furry hindquarters of what looked to be a dog, a very *large* dog. Its legs were still kicking with reflexive action, tail slapping the snow with jerking motions. The fur was patchy and silver, almost threadbare in places and she could see skin beneath that…a smooth alabaster skin that looked very un-dog like. But what disturbed her most, made something in her head feel like it wanted to take wing and fly right out of her skull, were the hind paws. They didn't look much like paws at all but feet, human feet…they were too long to be the paws of a dog and the black talons seemed to be sprouting from what could be nothing but human toes. Or something quite similar.

Morris swept the light up and they saw that the dog just ended above those hindquarters. It had been cut in half like someone had taken a scissors to it and snipped it neatly. There was an explosion of gore that had soaked into the snow and splattered in all directions, creating something like cherry ice. The flashlight beam revealed that the hindquarters, though sheared from the rest of the animal, were not disconnected. Slimy, bloody ropes of tissue and bowel connected them to the rest of the creature a good distance away. The snow was dyed red, bone and organ and assorted meat tossed about. Morris followed the train of tissue to the front quarters of the animal and it was even worse.

This can't be, Wenda thought, as the light revealed a ladder of spinal vertebrae that had been broken and scattered like a child's blocks. *I can't be seeing this...I can't be.*

She kept staring. Her eyes felt like they were painted on and she couldn't have blinked if she wanted to.

The front quarters looked much like the rear—the same patchy silver fur, the white skin showing through—but the paws were absolutely hairless and they ended in very human fingers that clawed in the snow.

The rest of the carcass was not dog, it was human...it was a woman. It was a thing that had been severed at the waist, the anatomy tangled up with the kicking animal hindquarters farther back. Her flesh was perfectly white, tufts of fur greased with frozen blood standing up like clocksprings.

The left side of her ribcage was smashed flat, the right set with a small round breast with a jutting nipple.

Her shoulders were broad, almost athletic, the neckline sweeping almost elegantly to a head that was not completely human and not completely canine, but a combination of both.

The glassy silver-red eyes were human...or nearly...but the nose was a snout, the mouth hanging open and revealing a dentition of spike-like canine teeth and incisors that looked like they were designed to tear out throats and bring down prey.

Even the ears were pointed and laid back flat against the skull. Strands of silver-white hair fell over the blood-splattered face ...

7

Megga felt her whole body go tense as a pain that was sharp and cutting seemed to slice through her brain. In a purely subjective sense, it felt like a steel wedge had split her skull open and some great hammer was driving it deeper and deeper into her gray matter.

She gasped.

Her knees went weak.

And up inside her head, in that ever-widening, ever-splitting fissure, she felt something cold and invasive like a slow-oozing, chill jelly seep into her mind. It was something dark, something horrible, living or semi-living, a monstrous *other* that sank its needle-like teeth right into the meat of her brain.

It had a voice: *YOU,* it said. *YOU, WE RECOGNIZE YOU, WE KNOW YOU BECAUSE YOU ARE PART OF US.*

She wanted to thrash her head violently side to side and tell that voice, that invading *other*, that no, no, no, she wasn't part of whatever it was and whatever tenebrous, envenomed evil it represented. But her mouth would not speak and her mind would not think and that was because...*because* it was a lie, a great, stinking, bald-faced lie and she knew it. God, how she knew it. The thing crawling through her psyche was the mind of the wolf-woman. In its death throes, it was throwing out feelers, casting for scent, searching for safe harbor and it found it quite instinctively in Megga.

And that was because Megga had been suckling the swollen breast of the dark side since she was a schoolgirl.

But now that some creeping malevolence from the dark side had found her, called to her, recognized her as its own, and slithered into her head uninvited...all the morbid flirting and teasing and adolescent dark fantasy left a bitter taste in her mouth.

One that made her want to gag on the bile of her own soul.

No, no, no...leave me alone...please just go away...I don't want this...

At that moment—bare seconds into it—it felt like something snapped in her brain. Like that thing had grabbed her free will and cracked it wide open like a walnut.

This is exactly what you wanted, you silly little twat. You've been begging for it your whole life and now you're getting it. The bait has drawn US in and we'll never, ever let you go now. Like calls to like.

No.

This could not be.

She would not accept the possibility.

Her mind was overburdened, stressed, pushed beyond all acceptable limits by what she had seen tonight. Couple that with a highly-excitable, highly-imaginative, downright neurotic personality poisoned by a mordant death obsession, and hallucinations of the worst order weren't really too surprising.

Yet...even in her denial...she could feel that *thing* inside her head. It was weakening some because it was dying, but its intellect, its will was still dominant and quite possibly strong enough to squash her like a green-juiced insect.

YOU BELONG TO US, LITTLE GIRL.

No!

NO!

NO! NO! NO!

Get the fuck out of my head! Get out! Get out! Leave me be!

But it wasn't going to leave her be. It had made contact, it had uplinked, it had planted its dark and festering seed deep in the shivering marrow of her brain and already that seed was bearing flower, bursting with midnight-black, coiling rootlets and petals of cemetery lace.

She could not deny it.

It showed her the agony of refusal and defiance, igniting a neural firestorm of agony in her brain, a sizzling white-hot electrical discharge that made her nerve endings blaze with such heat and fury and dizzying pain that she not only wanted to scream, she needed to scream. As the agony thundered inside her, her voice shrieked with madness and despair, echoing through the hollows of her skull but never quite reaching her lips, which were pressed in a trembling pink line.

And for a moment there, just one terrifying, nightmarish moment, the world disappeared from view, blotted out by the rising, consuming blackness of the thing that had invaded her, the thing whose dominating, discarnate mind was like a black expanding thunder cloud throwing out white, jagged bolts of sheer kinetic energy.

GET THE FUCK OUT OF MY HEAD!

And then…yes, Megga could see again. The world swam back into view and it was a harsh, cold, and unforgiving world of blowing snow, bone-deep chill, and an ever-circling darkness pressing in from all sides as she stared down at the freakshow wreckage of the wolf-woman spread over the snowy pavement. She saw it. She smelled it. It filled her head with a slaughterhouse musk, making her reel and shiver with a weird, hypnopompic vertigo inspired by the still-trembling roadkill smear right before her, an anatomical waste heap sinking into its own toxic red sludge.

The thing was dying, oh yes, to be certain it was.

But even as its lights winked out one by one, even though it was beyond the point now of regenerating its flesh, it still reached out to her, gripping her mind with tenacious fingers.

US.

PART OF US.

YOU BELONG TO US.

And then, just as surely as it had filled her head, it drained away and there was nothing but a cool white buzzing in her head. Megga blinked and then blinked again. It was delirium. It was stress and the onset of neurosis, that's all it was. Good God, she'd been half out of her mind for years, a dark little fallen angel drowning in the whirlpool of her own angst and morbidity, feeding on the gravy train of pop culture horror…so was it really any surprise?

Was it really?

8

Snap out of it.

Wenda opened her eyes.

For a moment there, it was like her mind had been sucked into some surreal, completely subjective black hole, a blank and evil universe where there was only her and the hideous remains of the wolf-woman…or whatever in the Christ she was.

She had completely zoned and she had no idea why. Looking over at Megga, she had a pretty good idea she was not the only one.

There's a power to this thing and you felt it.

As Morris put the light on it, it jerked, the jaws opening wide with a bloody froth of bile. It snapped its teeth, it glared at them with a black hatred that was vast and bottomless. It made growling and snapping sounds, fingers scraping in the snow with hooked black talons.

And Wenda thought: *It looks like like like—*

9

"A fucking werewolf," Mole said.

Werewolf, werewolf, werewolf.

Megga heard the words and why, yes, of course, that's what this thing was. A simple, positively medieval term that seemed to have very little place in the modern world…but oh how descriptive it was on this black and blowing night.

Werewolf. Fucking shapeshifter…skinwalker.

Megga was breathless, absolutely breathless. It was cold and the snow was blowing into her face, pinching her cheeks with very icy fingers. But that was nothing. That was fucking pedestrian compared to what she was feeling in the aftermath of her (hallucination) little mind-trip, for lack of a better word. She felt…well, *airless* inside like a deflated balloon or a can of Fix-A-Flat that had been emptied into a tire.

"Are you all right?" Wenda said to her, picking up on it as she always picked up on such things.

Megga ignored her because she simply had to. There was no way she could lie, so avoidance was the best strategy. "I always knew there were such things."

"It would seem there is relevance in the tales of old wives," Doc put in.

Doc…God, but Megga loved Doc. How he put things and the way his voice sounded…she admired how his mouth and brain always seemed to be so perfectly wired together in a dynamic fusion. Always so cool. Cool? *No, man, that dude is fucking ice, baby, ice, ice, ice.* He just had a way about him. She stared at him and had a perfectly crazy idea that she loved him. Oh, she'd always had a thing for older men, especially intellectual sages. Guys her own age bored her with their whining, angst, and narrow world views and if there was going to be any whining, angst, or narrowness in a relationship then it was going to be coming from her end, thank you very much. She loved Doc's voice. It was the voice she would have liked to hear reading her a bedtime story when she was a little girl—*The Witches* by Roald Dahl was her favorite—or whispering hot-blooded desires into her ear as a woman. She saw him by candlelight and she was on top of him, riding him hard, devouring him with the heat between her legs and—

Holy shit, what was that about?

Her mind was flying in all directions at the same time. She wasn't even making sense to herself. That hallucination—she was telling herself it had been nothing more—was still weirding her out, all kinds of things crawling out of her subconscious.

One of them was this:

She was nine-years old and the mad dog was after her.

For years, the memory haunted her, a cruel incursion into her dreams, and now she was living it again…the horror, the pain, the sheer terror of it all. The dog came out of the vacant lot, a big hulking black lab whose shaggy coat was threadbare, patches of open flesh set with scars and pustulant wounds. Its eyes were pink and runny, its left ear torn off, its jaws foaming and fanged.

Megga backed away from it.

Had she just kept going, it might have ignored her in its suffering which was immense and total. Instead, she stopped right there on the sidewalk where the thorny weeds thrust up through the cracks. She froze up in a dizzying moment of paralytic fear…and screamed.

It came from the terrified core of her being: sharp, shrill, and godawful LOUD.

The tone of it pierced the lab's ears, slicing through its diseased brain and echoing endlessly with volume, bouncing around in its skull with painful reverberations that at first made it whimper then howl with absolute, atavistic rage…a sound that was eerie, hurting, and nightmarish.

What happened then was a given.

Before Megga could hope to flee, the beast—for it surely was that, not a dog but a diabolical hell-hound with glowing eyes and white-slavering jaws—came charging out at her with almost hallucinogenic speed, a primeval blur, a savage missile of bunching muscle, bared fangs, and bad attitude driven by a raging, cutting agony in its dying brain.

At the last moment, just before the beast hit her, she hoped beyond hope that it would run right past her, but it did not. Its movements were clumsy and confused, but it located the sound of the shrilling noise and hit it. Megga went down. The convulsive weight of the beast pinned her to the sidewalk as its wild, flaying claws tore at her, its teeth snapping at her, foul ropes of saliva spraying in her face.

She fought against the beast, pounding and pummeling it with her fists, clawing at its oily hide with her nails.

But this only enraged it.

It seized her right calf in its bloody jaws.

Nine-year old Megga was screaming and fighting, kicking out with her left leg while pain threaded through her right in hot waves. The dog just wasn't biting her…it was chewing, tearing, rending. Her pantleg was shredded, her calf muscle punctured as those teeth came down again and again and again.

Then running feet and a voice booming: "GET OFF MY DAUGHTER, YOU MANGY FUCKING MUTT!"

The lab released her calf and turned on this latest intruder, who screamed and shouted, driving burning blades of pain deeper and deeper into the dog's brain. It had no choice: it attacked. The man who came at it had no fear. A dog was a dog was a dog and he would fucking kick it to death for touching his daughter, he'd shoot *its guts out. But then...yes, he saw the foaming jaws, the slimy snot-ribbons of contaminated saliva swinging back and forth as it charged and he called out: "MAD DOG! MAD DOG! MAD GODDAMN DOG!"*

The beast got within striking distance and leaped.

As it did, the man brought up his gun, a 12-gauge pump, and fired. The sound of it was like thunder and to the dog it was an axe that split its head open...which wasn't too far from the truth because the buckshot hit it straight on, macerating its muzzle and blowing its head apart into a red-gray-pink shrapnel of bone matter, spinning teeth, and splashing brain jelly.

The beast was literally dead before its carcass thumped to the sidewalk.

Later...was it that day or the next?...Megga was barely conscious, lying in a hospital bed, hearing a doctor's cool, calm voice saying, "I'm sorry, honey, but the dog was rabid. We don't want you getting like that, now do we?" And as a nurse and her father held her down, the first of many needles was inserted into her belly.

Rabies vaccine.

The cure is worse than the curse, they say.

The needles felt red-hot as they pierced her stomach lining...

Megga came out it, trembling minutely and muttering under her breath.

The wolf-woman snarled as Reg videoed her, teeth gnashing from blackened gums as a speckled and very dog-like tongue licked away the blood and discharge that came bubbling up its throat. It growled at him, making guttural noises that were not exactly bestial but more like a wolf attempting speech. Its eyes locked with Burt's and it growled out a string of garbled, phlegmy-sounding utterances.

"She said my name," Burt said, nearly out of his mind with it. He began to back away. *"She said my fucking name."*

By this point, everyone but Reg and his camera had backed well away from the thing.

"It can't speak," Morris told him. "It's a...it's a...it ain't fucking human."

Megga could have disagreed, but she didn't.

She didn't have the heart to.

Maybe what came out of the thing's mouth was choked and garbled with the fluids filling its throat, but she had heard words, too. She was nearly certain of it. *Burt,* it had said. *Burt, Burt...BUUUUURRRRT.* If she needed more reason to come apart there it was.

The wolf-woman looked at her again.

And there was no denying it this time around: her mind, however briefly, brushed against Megga's own and the pain was gigantic and terrible...it was not so much psychic invasion this time as a seam of pure, almost electric agony drilling right into her head. It felt like a cat had entrenched its claws in her brain and drawn them over the surface of her dura mater. The pain was beyond anything she had ever known or imagined could exist.

This time she did scream.

Involuntarily, her mouth sprang open and a shrill, piercing cry came out and by the time it did, it was simply too late to stop it. The others momentarily forgot about Burt's panic attack and the horror in the snow and turned their attention to her.

"Dude...take it easy," Reg said.

Wenda and Doc were holding onto her.

"It's okay," Wenda said. "Really."

What a consummate bullshit artist. Okay? Okay?

"There are things in this world and those out of it," Doc said as he gripped her firmly. "We have seen the latter. We might consider ourselves fortunate this night to see something very few have ever seen."

Oh, that voice. That golden voice. Whatever weird psychic trip she'd gone on this time evaporated as Doc spoke. She felt immediately better, stronger, her legs sturdy beneath her. She shrugged off Wenda, but not Doc.

"I'm sorry," she said. "Really...I don't know...I freaked out or something."

The wolf-woman flattened her ears against her skull and let go with a shriek of her own that was nearly hysterical in tone...not a human scream exactly, but more like that of a cat heard squealing in the dead of night. Megga knew it was directed at her. The thing was mocking her. It stared at her with lunatic hatred, its eyes huge and glistening.

Burt was standing there, swaying from side to side.

He had stuffed a fist into his mouth so maybe he, too, would not scream. The wolf-woman reached out a semi-human hand in his direction as if she wanted to sink her claws into him and tear him apart like an especially juicy slab of liver. He took two steps backward, tottering and weak. A gagging sound came from his throat that was thick and suffocating in tone. He looked, if anything, like a little boy paralyzed with fright. His fist fell away from his mouth and he looked at everyone there with glazed, tear-filled eyes.

Then he broke free and ran off in the direction of the bus.

The creature was chewing on its own tongue in its death throes by that point, the head whipping from side to side and spraying gouts of pink saliva and blood into the air.

She's dying and you felt her pain, Megga thought.

Burt was shouting as he stumbled away.

Nobody tried to stop him. They had nearly forgotten about him. They simply, almost casually, backed away from the thing. The snow was coming down heavier by then and visibility was down to fifteen feet at most and the creature faded into the storm, letting loose with a pained howling as they abandoned it. The wind was blowing so hard that they were bunched together now. Maybe fear had a little something to do with it. Maybe the stark desolation fused them together.

"We gotta get back to the bus," Morris said. "We gotta use the OnStar and call in some help here. Somebody's got to deal with…with that thing."

They moved off towards the bus, still staying together, Reg tagging along behind and that's when he hit the ground. *"FUCK IS THAT?"* he cried out.

Everyone stopped. They were looking in all directions, knowing not what they might see next.

Mole and Doc got Reg to his feet, helping him stand in the wind that was beginning to take on the roaring sound of a freight train. He brushed snow from his face. "Something flew over me," he said. "I mean right fucking *over* me. Like a big bird or something."

He was panicked, his eyes wide and unblinking as he tried to look in every direction at the same time.

"There's nothing," Morris said.

"I SAW IT!" Reg shouted into the storm. "I FUCKING SAW IT!"

Megga hugged herself against the cold. She knew without a doubt that he had seen something. Pure imagination does not inspire panic like that and Reg, a real easy-going calm sort of guy, was nearly coming out of his skin.

Mole picked up his camera and handed it to him.

"We're going back to the bus to wait this out," Morris announced. "We'll get the OnStar going and get the State Police out here. I'm not dealing with any more of this shit and neither are any of you."

Megga almost laughed. *As if we have a choice.*

10

"Burt! Hey, Burt, come back! Come back!"

He heard the voice calling him out in the storm, but he was no longer listening. In blind panic, he was running...or attempting to. Slipping and sliding, the wind punching into him, his boots skating on the snow-covered ice, he fell down, got up, fell down again and just started crawling. He didn't give a shit. Forward momentum was forward momentum in his book.

He had to get away.

Let those idiots sit around and look at that thing from hell all they wanted, but not him. No way. No goddamn way.

He heard the voice call to him again and he thought it might be Doc, but fuck Doc and fuck the lot of them. *Chambers of Horrors.* Jesus Christ, it sure was that. That's what this whole damn night had turned into.

Breathing hard, the icy wind seeming to crawl right down his spine, Burt pulled himself to his feet, standing uneasily in the storm. He couldn't even see the others now. The blizzard was throwing snow in every direction, surrounding him in a rushing glacial whirlwind of white.

Fuck.

He couldn't even be sure where the bus was.

Despite his panic, he waited. No sense wandering blindly in the storm. It would be so very, very easy to get lost in it.

The voices of the others were gone.

He was alone.

He waited there for what seemed minutes, though, realistically, it had only been brief seconds. And as he waited...he heard something that was absolutely impossible: the buzzing of flies. Well, maybe it wasn't flies. No, not that stupid and directionless. This was angry and directed. More like the buzzing of hornets. It was there and then it was gone.

A voice in the back of his head told him, *The wind, it was just the fucking wind because it could not be anything else. Not in this storm. Not in the cold.*

26

He had to move but the blizzard was raging.

He had the most unpleasant notion that it was toying with him. That the storm itself was not just the elemental wrath of nature blowing cold and fierce, but something more. Something sentient.

There was a sudden inexplicable blast of hot reeking air that swallowed him in a pungent envelope of heat. It brought a nauseating stink of sweet decay. A concentrated stench like that of a woodchuck trapped in a dry well, rotting to hair and bones in dark, warm silence. The stink covered him. It was sucked into his nose and crawled down his throat like an engorged brown-gray carrion worm.

It was horrible.

Unbelievably horrible.

Burt tried to fight free of it, but it surrounded him, filling his head and pushing him down to his knees where he vomited into the snow, a hot steam blowing back into his face. He regurgitated until there was nothing left, dry heaves making his abdomen jerk like it had been kicked. Then it passed. The smell thickened, grew almost moist and gamey in the air, then it, too, was gone as if it never was in the first place.

What the hell?

Before he could properly wrap his mind around it or try to make sense of it, he heard that buzzing again. It was the low, rising drone of hundreds of hornets coming at him out of the storm. And that was bad enough...but as he listened, it seemed to become a wavering, shrilling voice...a voice that was the buzzing of thousands of insect's wings: *Burt...over here, Burt...I'm waiting for you—*

And with a breaking hysterical terror, he looked in the direction of that loathsome voice and he saw a figure...a gray figure at the perimeter of the wind-driven snow. He thought at first it was a woman, because despite the buzzing tone of the voice there was some very unnatural female caliber to it. And the shape...the gray, leaning shape...it looked like a woman. A wraith that was blowing and billowing and fragmenting, the wind blowing right through it and making it flap and flutter.

Here I am, Burt...right...here...

He let out a scream and ran towards where he thought the bus was. For all he knew, he was charging deeper into the storm. Then he tripped, lost his footing, and the ground fell out from under him…and he was rolling down into the ditch, the shape of the bus appearing before him, tail lights blazing red like huge, hungry eyes.

11

Morris was the voice of reason as always.

And that was something that was badly needed, Wenda knew, because everyone was scared, everyone was quite near to freaking out (all except Megga who not only *had* freaked out but seemed to be fascinated by it all), and they had to get it together. Because regardless of what Reg had seen or *thought* he'd seen and regardless of the horror in the road, with the storm kicking up its heels they were very much in a survival situation now. They were trapped and they wouldn't survive it by losing control.

Oh, listen to you. You have panic attacks like other people have gas. Since when are you so calm? Since when are you the rational one?

Wenda did not know, but she felt somehow empowered at that moment. As if all the wild, arcing, nervous energy that had always caused so many problems—and only subsided when she was Vultura—had been waiting for something like this. Waiting for something to direct itself against. She was scared, but steady. Her mind was clear and her thoughts were solid. Yes, it was like within the last thirty minutes the world had broken free of its axis and was no longer spinning but wobbling out of control. And yet…she felt oddly focused.

"Morris is right," she told the others. "Time to act rationally here."

Megga giggled at that.

And then she screamed.

Several of them did because whatever Reg had seen came swooping out of the storm at them, veering right over their heads. A huge, black, formless shape that came and went quickly. Reg had said it was like a big bird. But that's not what Wenda saw out of the corner of her eye as it swooped over them. She saw something much more like the wing of a bat, black and shining and almost membranous.

It came again and they all went down to their knees.

Reg crazily tried to get it on video but it was way too fast for that.

Wenda caught its backdraft full in the face and the smell of the thing had been revolting. It stank the way she imagined the satin lining of a buried casket must stink: like dank rot and corpse drainage. Everyone scrambled to their feet.

"Look," Doc said. "Good God, look!"

They all did and Morris put the flashlight beam out there. There were forms out in the storm. They could not be seen in the heavy snowfall and blowing drift as anything more than shadows, but there were many of them and they were closing in. Their eyes reflected back yellow in the light.

"RUN!" Morris said. "EVERYONE RUN FOR THE BUS!"

They jogged up the road, slipping and sliding, trying to hold one another up as they came within sight of the bus. The wind threw drift into their faces and knocked several of them down. Wenda was one of the first to find her feet. Sheets of snow obscured the bus, rising and falling, whipping away over the snowpack. When it cleared for one brief moment, she saw something standing atop the bus. It looked like a man…the very gaunt shadow of a man that was darker than the shadows around it. It was narrow, leaning, almost skeletal. Like a locust pole mimicking a man. Then…she couldn't be sure it happened so fast…but it was like that shadow lifted its arms and became something like a billowing black sheet that jumped up into the storm.

Everyone slid and scrambled down into the ditch as the blizzard raged, throwing snow around in spinning tempests. Doc led the way up the steps, calling for Burt, feeling the warmth reaching out to him. Wenda was right behind him. That's when the windshield exploded inward, breaking apart into a sheet of glass that blew into flying bits. Then the side windows shattered and the rear. A howling tempest of snow and cold and fragmented safety glass came whipping through the bus. Wenda stumbled back into the others and Doc fell on her and they all went down in a heap.

By the time they got to their feet, the bus made a creaking, groaning sound as it was lifted up five or six feet and then dropped, more glass shattering, thin metal bulkheads collapsing. It was lifted again and dropped, more breakage from within.

"THE TOWN!" Morris called out. "EVERYONE! RUN FOR THE TOWN!"

They clawed their way up from the ditch, trying to run in the heavy snow and arching drifts. Falling, getting up, falling again. The town was maybe two hundred feet from them, the houses and buildings clustered together like toadstools under a tree.

Nobody asked questions. This was pure mainlined survival instinct and nothing more.

Wenda raced forward with the herd, trying not to think about what she had seen when she followed Doc up the steps into the bus: the sight of the windshield shattering inward.

She had seen what had caused it.

A single white human hand whose fingers were long and spidery.

It had slapped against the glass until it came apart.

Then whatever it was connected to crawled inside.

12

They were moving too fast and Morris could barely keep up with them.

Even Doc Blood who had fifteen years on him if he had a day was unbelievably spry as he vaulted through the snow like a hare. It was amazing. Morris worked out three days a week, watched what he ate, jogged on the weekends...and Doc was leaving him in the dust. Doc who smoked two packs a day, had a potbelly, considered napping a competitive sport and bacon to be a condiment, was kicking *his* ass in a footrace. Jesus.

But it wasn't just him.

It was the others, too.

He wasn't surprised at Megga or Bailey or Wenda: they were young and in tip-top shape. But Reg was pulling out into the lead, too. Reg who was nothing more than a rack of bones that lived on Doritos, Coke, Red Bull, and take-out pizza, whatever was easiest to consume while he plugged himself into Xbox.

Quit thinking. Run! Run!

Yes, the rational man had no place in a situation like this.

This was survival.

Make sense of it later, for now...*run!*

Yes, yes, yes, rumination was for later when you were somewhere safe and warm, cozied up by the fire in a good chair with a beer in your hand. So he thought no more about any of it, about the insanity of the entire situation—which was far too much like the movies they showed on *Chamber of Horrors* for his liking. He kept an eye on the others, though, because he was in charge and these were his people and he didn't want anything to happen to them...though how much of a taste for midnight horror shows they'd have after this ordeal was open to speculation.

The bus was at their backs.

That was a good thing. Despite the pounding it had taken, the battery was still working and the engine was still running and the headlights were directed at the ghost town. That was something. The lights let him see the others, throwing loping, elongated shadows of them over the snowpack.

Morris ran, the others pulling ahead.

Something swooped over his head again and he felt like a rabbit in a field waiting for an owl to descend. The comparison was apt, he knew. He ran and tried to leap a drift, but it was too high and his boots tangled together and he went face-first into it.

Dammit!

He brushed snow out of his eyes and began to run again and something hit him, putting him down and stripping his hat from his head. He pulled himself out of the snow, feeling around to make sure the back of his head was still there. It was. Running again, a sluggish forward jog. Already his legs were tiring. It was like trying to sprint through slush. The cold wasn't helping. He had no feeling in his face and his limbs felt rubbery and numb.

He tripped over another snowdrift.

Got up, slipped again.

That's when he knew he was going to die. He just wasn't going to make it and the realization of that seemed to sap his strength and he fell into the snow, trying to rise, but crawling forward like a child with little inertia.

This is how it ends.

Out here.

At the perimeter of this fucking ghost town.

He stood up, stumbling along, just waiting for death to take him.

13

Above Bailey's screams and the manic shouting of the others, Wenda somehow heard Morris cry out for help: his voice was shrill and almost childlike. She wanted badly to ignore it, to make for those buildings and get under some cover, but she slowed and turned her head back, looking over her right shoulder.

Shit.

Morris was trying valiantly to pull himself out of a drift. He'd rise, stumble along, fall again like a toddler learning the fine art of balance. A dark shape that looked oddly like an immense black kite in the wind-driven snow soared just over his head and she got the ugly feeling that whatever it was, it was toying with him and that it could take him any time it so chose.

"Please!" he called out. *"Someone...someone, please..."*

Wenda knew the proper thing to do was to help him just as she knew the realistic thing to do was to run and save herself. None of the others were slowing or even looking back. Maybe they didn't hear Morris...but she didn't believe that. And if they survived this, it was a point of contention she was going to ram down their throats.

Because right then, as afraid as she was, she was much less Wenda Keegan—who turned the other cheek and wouldn't spit if her mouth were filled with shit—and much more Vultura.

You know all the nice toys you have, Wenda? The new Corvette in the garage? The cabin out at Lake George? The trips to Aruba and St. Croix? Well, you have them courtesy of Morris. He created the gravy train you now feed upon. He invented Vultura and all the rest—you just stepped into the job via genetics and circumstance. You just happened to have the looks and were handy so you got it. He's done everything for you, by God, so don't you dare turn your back on him now.

She raced over the snow towards him, swearing under her breath.

The wind was trying to drive her towards the ghost town but she leaned into it and fought her way back to Morris who was moving slower and slower now. She tried to keep her head down so what was diving at him wouldn't take her.

"MORRIS!" she shouted into the wind when she got within feet of him. "RUN! RUN!"

He saw her, maybe realizing he wasn't the last person on Earth, and jogged over to her. She hooked her arm around his and pulled him forward, making him run whether he wanted to or not. Towing him, she was moving much slower, but she refused to give in. He was dead weight but she was strong from doing an hour of laps in the pool at the Y every day and she would not give up. Something in her demanded that she fight harder now than she ever had in her life. She felt energized and—God help her—really alive, really strong for the first time.

They broke through the last of the big drifts and the running was easier now because the wind had stripped most of the snow away and the pack was less than a foot deep as they neared the drive that circled around the perimeter of Cobton.

They were going to make it and she knew it.

Unless those doors are all locked. Because if they are, you're fucked and you know it.

The others were already nearing the buildings and they would be with them in a matter of seconds now. Morris started to pour it on, sensing shelter ahead and they ran with renewed vigor. And then something hit them from behind, slamming them both face-first to the ground.

They scrambled to their feet quickly, taking no time to ascertain if they were wounded or missing anything vital.

They ran.

"OVER HERE!" Reg shouted, standing before a tall Georgian house. "DOOR'S OPEN!"

Doc and Bailey were running for the safety it provided. But Megga had already located another house two doors down, a Colonial Saltbox, and she had the door open. She saw Wenda half-dragging Morris and came running over. She shouted something to Wenda but it was lost in the moaning of the wind. She hooked Morris's other elbow and towed him towards the open doorway. Mole came over to help, slid on the ice, and pulled himself back up again. By then, they had Morris almost to the door.

Behind them, Mole slipped again, shouted something. The wind took him and slid him back another five feet.

"Shit!" Wenda said. "We have to get him!"

Megga got Morris to the door and Wenda called out to Mole. She turned to look at him and he was running in her direction.

But he never quite made it.

A wall of snow was blown over him, making him teeter and take a few fumbling steps off to the side...and then a black form came out of the storm and took him. Took him fast. It seized him and flew up into the blizzard with him.

They heard him scream and a spray of blood spattered the front of the Saltbox, droplets of it splashing Wenda's face.

He was gone.

"MOLE!" Wenda screamed. *"MOLE!"*

Then a torrent of snow blinded her and she could see nothing. The force of it knocked her into the doorway and her feet went out from under her. The storm was worsening, filled with wrath and anger, it seemed. Visibility was down to maybe ten feet by then. Wenda wiped snow from her face and she saw luminous yellow eyes watching from the blizzard.

And then Megga yanked her through the door.

That was when the impact of the situation really hit her: their little group had been separated, split into two parties.

She wondered if that was by accident or on purpose.

14

Megga got the door closed and searched around for a lock of some sort as Wenda searched around for a light switch. Morris was kneeling on the floor, breathing hard, trying to get his wind back and his mind working again.

"So fucking cold," he said.

"We're all cold," Megga told him.

Though in a snowstorm it was never completely dark, not the way it was most nights, they needed light. The inside of the house was lit by that weird backlight common in a blizzard, but it was still dim and hard to see anything.

"Morris," Wenda said. "Where's the flashlight?"

"I had it," he said.

Stripping off his gloves, he tried to work warmth back into his fingers. Slowly, very slowly, he began to search around for the flaps of his pockets. But it wasn't fast enough for Wenda. She knelt by him, brushing his hands aside and started digging in the deep pockets of his leather coat.

"Nothing," she said.

"I had it…I don't know. Maybe I dropped it."

"Good going," Megga said.

"All right," Wenda said, glaring at her in the dimness.

"Luckily I was a Girl Scout," Megga said. "I'm always prepared."

She dug a penlight from her pocket. It wasn't much, but in the gloom it was like a searchlight. There was no lock on the door. There was only a bracket to either side of the frame. She searched around and found a plank. It was heavy and solid. She slid it into the bracket.

"Christ, like frontier days," she said.

She looked for a light switch but there was none just like there were no fixtures on the ceiling that she could see. But why would there be? This town was supposed to be period in every way, a colonial village. If lights had been installed at some point they would have been taken out when the buildings were restored to their original state. And come to think of it, she had not seen any telephone poles or electrical lines on the drive in.

"You see a light switch?" she asked.

Wenda shook her head. "I rather doubt there will be one."

"No," Morris said. "There's no juice out here. No lines within a mile or two of this place." He breathed onto his hands to warm them. "The caretaker I spoke with said they have a generator in his shack behind the village, but that's just to run cords so they can use lights and power tools in the buildings. This place is only open in the daytime and only in the summer. But…"

"But what?" Megga said.

"But the caretakers were supposed to have lights rigged for us. For the shoot."

"Maybe something got to them before they could do it."

Megga went up to one of the multi-paned windows and looked out into the night. She could see the eyes out there. They were closer than they were before. Whatever was out there was in no hurry; it—or more precisely, *they*—had all night and knew it.

"Well, we can't sit around in the dark," Wenda announced.

She was right and Megga began looking around. She took a door off to the left that led into a sitting room. Everything was period from the oval braided rugs to the wide plank floors, the Windsor chairs to the candlestick lamps. The good thing being that there was a fireplace and a nice stack of wood. If it wasn't just for show, then they were in luck.

"In here," she called to the others.

By the time they got there, Wenda pretty much towing Morris behind her, Megga had her penlight in her mouth and was setting up some kindling—strips of pine so dry they nearly broke apart in her hands. Tearing some pages out of a book on the shelf, she lit them with her cigarette lighter and the kindling caught almost immediately. When it was going good, she fed a few birch logs into the blaze. Everything was so dry it caught immediately. The warmth and glow of the fire was encouraging, but she knew they were a long way from easy street.

"That's better," Morris said. "It's handy to have a Girl Scout around."

"Are they still out there?" Megga asked.

Wenda nodded. "Closer."

Morris warmed himself at the fire. He shook his head. "I…I don't understand any of this. It's all so crazy. That thing…that thing in the road…shapes flying around. I don't get it. It's not right."

Megga sympathized with him on that point: it wasn't right and it shouldn't have been, but it *was*. And as she paused to think of it, and there hadn't been much time up to that point to do much of that, it hit her with full force. She should have been terrified at the possibility of what was out there, what would want to come in after them...but she wasn't. In some way, it was thrilling, in another it was vindication of her belief that somewhere, somehow, such creatures existed.

"What the hell are they?" Morris asked. He sounded desperate.

"Vampires," Megga told him.

"Oh, come on! *Vampires!* I'm serious here."

"So am I. Can you think of anything else they *can* be?" she put to him. "What else can become a wolf? What else can fly like a bat? There's no doubt what they are and you better accept it whether you like it or not. If you don't, you won't make it through the night."

He made a choking sound like he could barely breathe.

It was not easy for him. It would not be easy for any sane mind.

But reality was reality, regardless of how twisted.

Vampires, Megga thought. *Freaking vampires. The undead. Sweet.*

It was absolutely insane, but she figured in many ways she was better suited to deal with the reality of it than the others. The shock of it would hold them back. Their own disbelief would trip them up, make them vulnerable. Their rational twenty-first century minds would not be able to accept it. *Vampires.* Silly shit from movies, from books, from old wives tales. But with her, belief came easily. Maybe too easily.

But isn't this what it has always been about? The obsession with the macabre and the morbid? The black candles and skulls and shelves crowded with Poe and Lovecraft? Isn't this what you've been waiting for your entire life? To see these things? To know they exist despite what enlightened science might say to the contrary? That there are dark spaces and dark holes in the world, cracks in the floor of reality where nightmare things can crawl free?

She had the fire going good so she looked over at Wenda who had not said a damn thing. "Well, Vultura?" she said, falling into her Graveyard Girl persona. "What sayeth thee?"

Wenda sighed. "I'd say it's bullshit...but *something's* out there. *Something* was on that road, half-woman and half-wolf. And something took Mole. Something grabbed him and yanked him into the sky." She touched the bloodstains on her parka. They were real enough. "And something is gathering outside this house right now. If they're not vampires, then they're close enough. The question is: what do we do about it?"

"Yeah, what *are* we going to do about it?" Morris said.

Hmm. Megga was sensing a lot of things at that moment as she studied both Morris and Wenda in the flickering orange light of the fire. Morris was losing his grip on reality. He was a get-it-done kind of guy, ambitious, domineering, relentless in his pursuit of the almighty buck. A force of nature to be reckoned with. Megga had never known him to be anything less than dynamic and in charge...but now he was limp as a noodle. Empty. And Wenda? Well, that was interesting, too. Wenda only came out of her shell when she was Vultura and then she was completely confident, so confident sometimes that the shift of personalities was almost frightening. But something had changed there, too. She didn't seem so mousy and confused and indecisive as she normally was.

"Do?" Megga said. "What we're going to do is survive until dawn. If they're traditional vampires, they'll have to crawl back into their graves then."

She gave them a quick primer on the undead, though it was hardly necessary. Both Morris and Wenda had screened the movies they played on *Chamber of Horrors*. At least, Wenda had. Megga knew that for sure. Wenda not only screened them but she took extensive notes on them. She was studious by nature. She took notes and she studied them before the crew went to conventions so that if a fanboy asked who was a better Dracula, Bela Lugosi or Christopher Lee, she'd have some kind of opinion and if they started assailing her with questions about Max Shreck's ratlike persona in *Nosferatu* or Barbara Steele's performance in *Black Sunday,* she would be informed and not an outsider, a nub.

Regardless, Megga went over it. "They can become bats or bat-*like* things. They might be able to become patches of mist. They might fear holy objects, but that might depend on their religious orientation when they were alive. If they were an atheist in life, the cross will mean nothing to them. What most people know about vampires comes from movies and most movies draw from a single source: Bram Stoker's *Dracula.* But not everything in there is in keeping with the folklore of the vampire. We need to remember that," she explained to them. "Some of it was dramatic invention. The erotic, sensual thing is hardly ever referred to in the old folktales. Stoker might have made that stuff up, basing it on early tales like Le Fanu's *Carmilla*. I guess what I'm saying is those things out there are monsters. I kind of doubt we'll see Robert Pattinson among them. But they'll use any means to get at our blood. Nothing should surprise us. If the old tales are true, they must be invited in."

Morris was staring into the fire. "Then we don't invite them in."

But Megga shook her head. "You don't get it. We don't know what their association is with Cobton. Have they been here before? Were they lying dormant until recently? Did they turn this place into a ghost town in the first place? For all we know, they may have been invited into every fucking house in this village."

"Oh, Christ," he said.

Wenda had been listening, but she had no comment. "Let's not worry about that shit. Let's go and make sure all the doors are bolted, the windows locked. This house is a Colonial Saltbox. That means it has a central chimney. There's bound to be another fireplace in the kitchen, on the other side of this room, and a couple more upstairs. My bet is that there's wood laid out for them so they look nice and authentic. Let's get it all in here. Then we lock ourselves in and wait it out."

The new take-charge Wenda was as dynamic, it seemed, as Morris had been once upon a time. *Interesting*, Megga thought.

"All right," she said. "Let's start with that. You coming, Morris?"

"I'm not leaving this fire. No way."

There was a kerosene lamp on the mantle. Megga picked it up. It was full of fuel. "What are the chances this works?" She pulled off the glass chimney and lit the wick. It caught and held the flame. "Well, I'll be damned."

Leaving Morris at the fire, they went back towards the front door. Together, they looked out the window and did not like what they saw. There were dozens of people standing out in the blowing snow. They couldn't see them very well, only their lupine eyes staring at the house.

15

"It might be a good idea to keep away from the windows," Doc suggested. "No sense enticing what's out there."

Reg was trying to get some video on the things and not having much luck. Thus far, they were hanging back in the squall of snow. Even when it cleared and he focused in on them, they almost appeared misty as if they were breaking apart like the snow blowing around them.

Like Wenda's group, Doc and the others had quickly built a fire and taken advantage of the numerous kerosene lamps, most of which were in working order. They had sequestered themselves in what might have been a parlor. There was a large flagstone fireplace that was now blazing away, chasing off the chill of the night…or as much of it as possible. The room was period from the slate-gray walls hung with grapevine wreaths and samplers to the spinning wheel, wing chairs, and camelback sofa.

Yes, authentic in every way, Doc thought. *So authentic that it's all too easy to believe that there is no longer such a thing as the current century. That we have been tossed back in time to the 17th or 18th century when belief in those things outside was probably commonplace in much of the world. To a time before the age of reason and good, hard science had proven such things could not be. A time of ghosts, spirits, and witches.*

He was trying not to think about it.

He was trying to remain rational about it all because through rationality there was strength. But even as he tried, primitive superstitious terror flitted about in the dark corners of his mind, weakening his resolve. As Doc Blood—or Sawbones McCord or any of his previous theatrical incarnations—he had cultivated the same character, that of a somewhat uppity, elitist, pretentious magician. Through the years, he became so good at playing the role that eventually there was very little differentiation between himself and the character. Doc Blood was a sage. He was calm and philosophic and generally annoying to those in his company. For the others—Megga excepted—their characters were just *characters*. They shed them like they shed their costumes.

But not so with Doc Blood.

The character was everything. If he let go of that and became himself—Leonard Creese—he would be nothing but a temperamental drunk that was of little use to anyone, including himself. No, he maintained the character for without it, he was nothing. And there was no earthly way old Leo Creese—Jim Beam in the morning, Jim Beam in the evening, Jim Beam at suppertime—could handle this situation. Only Doc Blood could. And these people needed someone with a head on their shoulders to guide them.

Burt was pacing back and forth like an angry old bear that wanted out of its cage. Doc figured that was *apropos*, for there was something very dark and almost threatening brewing in their bus driver. This was a time of tension and anxiety and fear, obviously, and things suppressed in the human psyche had a way of externalizing themselves when the pressure was on. He'd seen it himself in the war: stress made the biggest, meanest grunts imaginable become docile and harmless, while the reserved, bookish types became kill-happy monsters. Things would happen this night, he was certain, and not all of them would be because of what waited outside.

Reg was trying to get Bailey to talk, but she would not even look at him.

A frightened little colt, Doc thought. *Without Megga to lead her and tell her how to think and how to feel and respond, she's entirely directionless.*

She was sitting on the sofa, still wearing her parka, hat, and gloves. Her legs were drawn up, arms encircling them, chin resting in the V of her knees. Her blue eyes were wide and wet, her lips pulled in a straight line. A lock of blonde hair had fallen over her face and she did not bother to brush it aside.

Doc sighed. "Bailey…listen to me. Nothing's going to happen to you. I won't allow it. *We* won't allow it. We're safe in here and we're going to stay safe in here. In the morning we'll get out. In a matter of hours, the State Police will be looking for us. So try to keep your chin up. All is not lost."

Her eyes blinked a few times and she looked over at him. She smiled slightly.

"There, that's better."

"Sure, dude," Reg said. "We just gotta wait for sunrise and shit. Then we'll be outta this chiz. That's all."

"Sure, that's all," Burt said with about as much sarcasm as he could muster.

"That'll do," Doc told him.

Burt turned towards him and it was obvious he was going to say something unpleasant, but at the last moment he simply closed his mouth. Which was probably a wise move, Doc decided, because he was not about to put up with that sort of thing. He would have been the last person to threaten anyone with violence, but if it came down to it…well, he'd pulled two tours in the jungle as a paratrooper and had seen things that would have made guys like Burt piss their pants. Maybe all that was forty years ago, but Doc figured he still had a few moves left and he would use them if it came to it. God yes, he would.

He lit a cigarette. "It is said that war brings out the best in people and the worst. And our situation might be comparable to war. Having been in a war, I can say that it is. Now, we can stand together and support one another and make it through this or we can act childish and selfish and we can die. I don't see much of a choice, do you?"

"Hell no," Reg said.

Bailey said nothing.

Burt was chewing at his lower lip, his eyes directed at Doc. Doc was baiting him, pushing his buttons and he knew it. Finally, unable to intimidate him with his dark eyes and searing look, Burt turned away. He stared into the fire.

And Doc thought: *Feel free to commence hostilities at any time, you little chimp. You won't be the last man standing.*

"Well, there's no way out until dawn so we just have to make the best of it," Reg said.

Burt laughed low in his throat. "No way out for *you,* but maybe I've got other plans."

"We'd love to hear them," Doc said.

Burt ignored him.

Reg said, "But what are those things? I mean, like vampires or werewolves or something? Shit, they gotta be something."

"If they're not, then they're close enough, I'd say." Doc pulled off his cigarette. "The question would be: why now? Why here? How could they be in the first place and what is their connection to this town? Questions we'll probably never answer."

Reg was checking over the woodpile. "We've got an axe," he said, "and this thing." He held up a fireplace poker that looked like something used to skewer hogs. It was wrought-iron silverplate, heavy, and lethal-looking. "Whatever it is."

Doc nodded, checking the blade of the broadhead axe and seeing it was indeed sharp. "So we have a few weapons then. Now, my knowledge of the supernal is more literary than folkloric...but am I wrong in thinking that such creatures fear fire?"

"Yeah. I think so."

"So, we have an arsenal at our disposal. That's a plus."

"You don't know tit," Burt said.

"Ah, jeers from the cheap seats," Doc said. "Well, maybe not, but I do think fire will work to our advantage. Let's gather every stick we can find in case of a siege. Does that sound reasonable to you, Burt?"

"I guess."

"Good, then. Two of us will go, one stays with Bailey."

"Me and Reg'll do it," Burt said.

As they went to the door, Doc said, "Remember something, Burt. It's not just your life now, but all of ours. We survive by cooperating. We need each other. If we support and watch over each other, we're going to survive. You may want to keep that in mind."

He gave Reg a look and they understood each other.

Burt went out into the corridor with a kerosene lantern. "You're just fucking full of yourself," he muttered.

That I am, Doc thought as he secured the door after them.

Seeing the despairing look on Bailey's face, he sat down by her and said, "Did I ever tell you of my experiences in experimental nudist free-form theater in California? I didn't? Well, imagine if you can: the lights going down, a full house packed with swinging penises and jiggling breasts. I step onto the stage, glistening and naked, as King Lear…"

16

"I'm just saying that asshole is full of his own shit," Burt said to Reg as they climbed the stairs to the second floor to harvest more wood. "And I'm getting a little sick of it."

"Man, just relax. You don't have to love him or anything. All we have to do is make it until dawn. Now just quit worrying about that stuff. *Damn.*"

Reg knew it was going to start soon as they left Doc and Bailey. He knew Burt was going to start with his shit, trying to splinter things, divide and conquer. That's the kind of guy he was and Reg didn't have a lot of patience for that shit on a good day—it reminded him of all the assholes he'd went to school with, their cliques and divisions—let alone tonight. Things had happened that he couldn't sufficiently wrap his brain around. It was all so unreal, so freaky and warped, he couldn't even begin to make sense of it. *Vampires.* Shit. It was all too much. He kept expecting Morris to come through the front door, telling everyone it was a gag, hidden cameras and behind-the-scenes chiz for some Halloween episode of

Chamber of Horrors. Some whacked-out *Blair Witch Project* kind of thing.

He kept waiting for it and hoping for it.

But he knew by that point it just wasn't going to happen.

Mole was dead. *Fucking Mole.* They were like best friends and all. Reg kept telling himself not to think about it and what had gotten him or things were going to get ugly and he was going to have some real problems.

So he was fighting. Fighting to keep it together and not go to pieces and crawl into some shadowy corner within himself where it was calm, cool, and safe.

Burt led the way up the stairs, holding the lantern out in front of him.

Reg was a few steps behind with the fireplace poker.

He could hear the wind moaning out there and he hoped to God that's all it was, just the wind and not *them*, not those things out there because he just wanted them to go away.

At the top of the stairs, Burt paused. He cocked his head. The lantern threw crazy shadows around them, making everything that much worse. *No wonder people used to believe in ghosts,* Reg thought. He couldn't imagine living like this…by firelight and lantern light. Just the idea of it was spooky.

"What is it?" he asked Burt.

"Thought I heard something."

Reg licked his lips and gripped the poker. "Like what?"

"I don't know. It was faint. Probably nothing."

He stepped onto the landing and into the corridor. Reg made an effort to regulate his own breathing. *Probably nothing.* That's what Burt said but, of course, he didn't really mean it. That was the kind of shit scriptwriters threw in horror movies. *It was probably nothing.* One of those not-so subtle little hints to the audience that would get their imaginations rolling. He wondered if that's what Burt was doing. Playing a game. Reg didn't know much about Burt beyond the fact that he was pretty much a driver and a gopher around the studio. He'd never really talked with him outside of going on location shoots. He couldn't say he'd heard anything bad about the guy, or good, for that matter.

But he was remembering some of those cliques in school.

If they couldn't get you one way, they'd try another.

Was that what Burt was doing? Doc had his number and he knew it and he couldn't get Reg to come around to his way of thinking and turn on Doc, so he was trying something else. Maybe trying to put a scare into him. Was he that low? Would he do something like that?

"I don't hear a damn thing," Reg said, moving into the corridor.

"Like I said, kid, it was probably nothing."

They found the master bedroom and its attendant brick fireplace, which looked big enough to step into. There was a log rack and a nice pile of birch there. Reg hauled the logs out into the corridor while Burt looked around.

"You gonna help?" Reg asked him.

"You're doing just fine, kid."

"Shit."

Once he had the logs out in the hallway they went into the bedroom next door, which faced on the other side chimney, and got the wood from its rack. Reg figured it would take two or three trips to get downstairs with it all and if Burt thought he was doing that by himself, too, then he was—

"I heard it again," Burt said.

Reg felt tense inside. If this guy was messing with him, playing some game, then he was going to get his ass kicked because there was absolutely nothing funny about this.

Reg set his logs out in the hallway. "What did you hear?"

"Not sure...sort of like a tapping."

Reg listened now, too, forgetting that maybe he was being played. In the darkness with nothing but the lantern light flickering and the shadows coiling thick in the corners of the room, the snow whispering at the windows...it was all too easy to believe in unknown sounds and maybe even the hungry shades gathering outside the old house. The situation reduced him to a childlike state of fear where every shadow was a threat that adult logic could not dispel. It grew inside him in a swelling black mass of pure rising terror and he felt sick with it, physically sick.

Burt made his way over to the window.

He set the lantern on the nightstand, then carefully pulled open the heavy curtains. Reg was right next to him. There was nothing out there looking back in at them, just the ever-present storm circling the house, throwing snow at the window and whistling around the eaves. The old house creaked and groaned in the onslaught. Reg peered closer to the glass. It was dark out, but backlit by that weird pink illumination of blizzards. He could see the road below, a few of the other buildings of Cobton, but nothing else. The lights of the bus had gone out.

"I don't see them out there," he said.

"Me either."

It was weird how they put together old towns like this, Reg got to thinking. Everything so crowded, wedged together in an unbroken mass like animals pressing together to keep warm…or huddled out of fear. The roof overhang of one house intruding above the one next door, some of them touching and overlapping, spires and crooked chimneys pushing up to fill any available space. It was like the town was designed to accentuate shadow rather than light. He figured you could tour the entire village from up there, leapfrogging from one roof to the next.

"Wait a minute," he said, his face pressed to the multi-paned glass so he could get a look at the saltbox house where Wenda and the others were hiding out.

"What?"

The storm rose up again and blotted it out, but he knew he had seen it. Then the snow thinned momentarily and he saw it again: a shape crawling up the wall over there. A human shape…or something quite like one moving straight up the side of the house like some white mutant ape. But it was no ape. It was a woman. He was sure of it. A woman going up the side of the house like a climbing beetle.

Burt finally shoved him out of the way so he could see but the snow was too heavy.

"Well?" he finally said.

Reg told him.

"You're imagining shit, kid."

They went out into the hallway and, instead of going down the stairs with the wood, Burt went on down the corridor to look around.

"We better get back," Reg told him.

"Keep your shirt on."

Burt was holding the lantern up, finding first a broom closet, then a staircase leading to the attic, then another room at the end. He went in there and over to the windows past the ornate canopy bed. They looked out of the back of the house. He pulled the curtains aside quickly and Reg jumped. Maybe it was done for effect and maybe not.

They looked out the window and could see more of Cobton whenever the snow eased up and quit blowing in sheets: a crowded intersecting maze of colonial houses cut by crooked, narrow streets no wider than alleys; steep-pitched gabled roofs white with snow rising up sharp against the sky, jutting dormers and stacked chimneys, vanes and steeples and ridgepoles high above like reaching skeletal digits. You could almost feel the antiquity of Cobton rising on black, malefic wings…an antiquity of evil.

The town formed sort of a quadrangle, they saw, with a village square in the middle. And parked down there in great contrast to the town itself, was a station wagon: a Subaru Outback.

"Must belong to the caretakers," Burt said. "Four-wheel drive. It could get us out of here."

"If you don't die getting to it."

"Worth the chance."

But Reg wasn't so sure. He wanted nothing more than to get out of Cobton…but a blind run out into the storm and darkness with those things out there…it seemed too risky. Only an absolute suicidal idiot would even contemplate making it to the car.

"I'm going to make a try for it," Burt announced. "When we get back downstairs, I'm going to try it. The back of this house butts the square. I'll slip through a window or something and pull up in front. You guys get in, we all get out."

"Maybe," Reg said.

Burt was going to argue it, but he stopped. His mouth hung open. "I hear that sound again," he whispered.

This time, Reg heard it, too: *tap, tap, tap-tap-tap.*

Burt led him from the room.

The sound did not fade this time; it increased. They went into the room at the far end of the corridor, which was much smaller than the others and looked to be some kind of nursery with antique dolls and wooden blocks, a wicker basinet. The tapping was coming from the window. Burt handed the lantern to Reg and approached it soundlessly. Reg waited there, his heart thudding in his chest, his stomach squeezed up tight his throat. It felt like every nerve ending was standing taut inside him like electric wires.

Burt gripped the heavy curtain.

He let out a low, long breath.

He swallowed.

Then he pulled it open.

17

There was a woman outside the window.

She was hovering there like some great death's-head moth, her hands up against the glass like white blossoms, fingers splayed, her body extending straight out into midair as if she were riding on a raft. She was naked, her pallid flesh blending in with the blowing snow, her face milk-white, her eyes venomous yellow and set with split red veins. She had no pupils. Just those luminous orbs like autumn moons. She was grinning, sharp teeth hanging over her juicy red lips.

Burt fell backward and hit the floor.

Her mouth opened and closed as if she were speaking...and Reg was almost sure that she was. He could hear her voice in his head. It was silver and sharp like a cutting blade, tinkling like expensive crystal, the hot breath of a lover and the cold voice from a buried box.

It was sweet.

It was foul.

It was beauty and depravity...a series of ethereal contradictions that confused and weakened him and finally owned him. He only knew one thing: he wanted to lay with her in a silken box and sink into her.

"REG!" Burt cried. "REG! JESUS CHRIST!"

There was no subtlety from Burt. When that goofy, dreamy look did not fade from Reg's eyes, Burt slapped him across the face and dragged him from the room. The last thing he saw before Burt slammed the door was the woman's black and glistening tongue licking the glass.

18

Bailey was at the point where she was afraid to keep her eyes open and afraid to close them. She did not want to see what was going to happen next so she closed her eyes. But when she did, she saw Mole's death and that made them open again.

Shut it out, close it down, block it, block it.

Oh so much easier said than done. The images were burned inside her mind and the video loop just kept playing and re-playing like she was on some kind of continual feed that could not be shut off.

It tormented her, it haunted her.

She saw Mole get taken by a titanic blur that hit him with slashing claws. They were surgical knives that peeled his scalp back in a bloody flap and then he was in the air, screaming and writhing, towed to fantastic glacial heights and then deposited, dumped, in the snow atop a gambrel roof. The thing that took him squatted over him, some human vulture, a winged night-hag spreading midnight-black plumage...but when he wiped the blood from his eyes with jerking fingers he saw it was no bird, no carrion-hag, but a rawboned woman. She was stick-limbed, crooked, and naked, a viscid steam rising from her pores. She said something to him in a language he had never heard before, her face like cracking white glass, her eyes swirling balls of hot blood-red gas that burned into his skull. Grinning like a dead snake, lips pulled back from rusting needle teeth, she took hold of him and shook him, at first playfully and then with rage. He heard a sound like cracking knuckles and realized it was his own bones dislocating.

When he started to scream again, she made a squealing sound and enveloped his mouth with her own which was like the maw of a lamprey. He could feel the terrible suction macerating his lips and popping fillings from his molars and tearing teeth loose by the roots. When she pulled her mouth away, she spit a bloody phlegm at him and he felt his own teeth speckle his face.

By the time she battened her lips to his neck and began to feed, his mind was long gone. When she was finished, she removed his head with a quick twisting motion like pulling the cork from a wine bottle, and tossed it off into space. Then she leapt up into the night, no longer a woman but something like a million tiny shards of twinkling glass that drew themselves into a whirlwind that spun across the rooftops and was no more.

This is what Bailey kept seeing.

This is what she could not shut out.

And this is what she knew waited for all of them in the darkness.

But it's not real. It can't be real. You can't know how he died. You weren't there.

True, true, and true. Yet...she did not doubt what she saw. The images were far too vivid. This was not sheer imagination, it was something beyond imagination. She had somehow channeled his death, tapped into some psychic video feed of his last moments. She had seen him die. She had witnessed the horror of it and felt the pain of the claws, the sucking mouth, and the teeth in her throat. She did not know how this could be, but it was and she knew it.

They would all die like Mole.

One by one.

And there wasn't a damn thing they could do about it.

19

The sounds came again and Wenda felt tense to her core.

The first time she heard them after they left the sitting room, both Megga and she stopped dead in their tracks. It sounded like someone was walking around above them, moving slowly and deliberately across the floor. Except she thought it was not some*one* but some*thing*.

The sounds were coming from upstairs and as much as she wanted to turn back and hide in the sitting room with Morris, she knew she couldn't. The wood they needed was up there. They had to have it. There really was no choice in the matter and she knew it.

Still, standing at the bottom of the stairs with Megga, she hesitated.

"Well?" Megga said. "Do we investigate, Vultura?"

"I suppose we don't have a choice."

"No, we don't."

In the glow of the lantern, Megga's eyes were huge and wet-looking. Wenda thought she looked excited. More so, she looked turned on like she was very close to an orgasm, which was absolutely absurd under the circumstances, but with Megga you just never knew. There were things with that girl that were downright scary.

Wenda had a knife from the kitchen with her: a huge antique thing with a white bone handle and a shiny silver blade. A carving knife that looked like it was made for gutting and hacking. She gripped it tightly, staring at her companion. "You don't need to act so eager about it," she said. "What's up there might kill us."

"I know," Megga breathed.

There was no doubt then: Megga *was* excited.

"Maybe now would be a good time to quit living your life like you were trapped in a Poe story."

Megga shrugged. "If there's one of them up there, I want to see it."

"Why?"

"Because I *have* to. I have to see it."

"You're crazy."

Megga smiled at that. It was a Graveyard Girl smile—seductive, cruel, hungry. She got in so close that Wenda thought she was going to kiss her on the mouth. But a few inches away, she said, "If I'm crazy, so are you. Because you're coming with me." Her breath smelled dark and sweet and something about it made Wenda's face flush.

Megga turned and started up the steps. "C'mon," she said in that same salacious tone, her words nearly dripping with lewd innuendo. "I can't do this without you. It takes two."

Wenda wasn't sure at that moment what she was more afraid of: what might be upstairs or what Megga might want to *do* upstairs. She followed her up there and the scariest thing, she thought, was that Megga was enjoying this. She was probably scared, too, but mostly she was living out her dark fantasies. This was a movie or a story to her. She was going to meet some hideous thing from beyond and she was thrilled by the idea.

It's an act. It's gotta be an act. Maybe this smooth, urbane, Goth thing ala the Graveyard Girls is the only thing that's keeping her together. She's different and you know it. She's macabre by nature. A morbid sort. Didn't Doc once say during one of his impromptu analysis sessions with Megga that morbid personalities often mask an absolute fear of death and dying? Necrophobia?

She knew one thing for sure: she was going to be on her guard because she fully expected Megga to do something stupid to validate her own morbidity. And maybe, in the twisted labyrinth of her mind, she might not really even have a choice.

Wenda followed her up the stairs much as Reg followed Burt and, like him, expecting trouble. At the top, they waited but heard no sounds.

"Maybe it was just the house," Wenda said, listening to it creak and settle in the wind. "Maybe that's all it was."

Megga smiled at her. "Do you really think so?"

They moved down the corridor and into the first bedroom they saw. There was some wood at the hearth. Wenda quickly bundled it in her arms. There. They had wood.

"Let's check that other room and then we're out of here," she said. "There should be wood in there, too."

But Megga was already heading towards it, drawn to it like a needle pointing to magnetic north. Wenda was feeling something bad inside her like an icy wind around her heart, forever circling. As she approached the door she could sense something in the

50

atmosphere souring like milk. It grew heavy and ominous, almost suffocating, hostile. It was like the charge of the air itself had gone negative and she could feel it at her spine and along the back of her neck. The shadows seemed to be crawling around them, bunching as if they were getting ready to spring.

"Here goes," Megga whispered.

She went to the plank door and grabbed the handle, pushing it inwards. It opened without so much as a squeak. She pushed it in slowly, maybe to heighten the effect. Wenda felt her heart drop in her chest, the atmosphere not just soured now but spiritually rancid. Then the door was open and a smell of dry and noxious corruption blew out at them.

Megga held up the lantern.

The room beyond was like a lagoon of perfect blackness and the lantern light cast nary a ripple over its surface. Megga stepped in there with Wenda right behind her. It seemed colder inside, their breath coming out in great rolling clouds. Gaunt shadows slid around them, the darkness impossibly thick and impenetrable. It was nearly palpable, a heavy weave that tried to push them back. The air was like an envelope of venom.

Megga gasped.

Someone was on the bed.

20

There was a sheeted form lying there, unmoving, and the malignancy in the room was issuing from it, practically dripping from it.

Wenda was very much aware at that moment that the only weapon they really had was the knife she carried and it felt positively weak, impotent in her fist. She had the weirdest sense of anxiety and utter defeat. Something inside her wanted to curl up and play dead, make a blood offering of itself to whatever was under the sheet.

There was a noise like congested breathing.

The sheet rustled.

A crackling sound like dry leaves.

The form sat up and they both saw it crane its neck and look at them with its blank, sheeted face. Wenda took one, then two faltering steps back, the room seeming huge and cavernous around her like physical reality had suddenly been distorted. A stark terror flooded over her and she did not feel cold with it, but hot. A moist prickly heat enveloped her and she felt woozy, like she might go right over. Her scalp was greasy with sweat.

The sheeted form rose up, not so much standing but rising like a wind had taken hold of it, inflating it, making it flap like a blanket on a clothesline. And then whatever that thing was, it drifted off the bed and came down again mere feet from Megga who stood absolutely still, her mouth hanging open and her eyes glazed like dusty windows in a deserted house.

"Megga!" Wenda heard her own voice say. *"Get back! Get away from it!"*

But Megga just stood there, still as the death that was coming for her.

"GET THE FUCK AWAY FROM IT!"

The shrouded thing raised its sheeted arms like a Halloween ghost and—it seemed—made to strike. The hot sweat covering Wenda went cold and she charged in, raising the knife to strike. And a single gray hand snaked free of the shroud and seized her by the throat. Its touch was like thawing meat. It lifted her off her feet and tossed her. She landed on the bed, heard the knife strike the wall, and then she fell to the floor. She lay there, dazed, her breath locked in her throat as she tried to get some air into her lungs.

As she used the bed to pull herself up, she saw images in her mind that did not or could not belong.

She saw the cemetery.

The Cobton cemetery they'd seen on the way in.

For the thing under the sheet, that's where it had begun.

Beneath the churchyard...that's where it had come from and she could see it in her mind. From nighted catacombs and secret tombs beneath those ancient, twisted oaks and the marble forest of tombstones, there came a thrusting and panting from deep within the frozen black earth. The wind that blew was turned in upon itself and was sucked down into that subterraneous frozen soil, filling one nitrous oblong box with morbid, straining life. There was an agonized, uneasy thudding. A heartbeat, a papery rustling like rats nesting in a bone pile. Down below in that noisome narrow house, that midnight womb, the labor pains gathered volume and urgency. Graveyard dirt was parted and forking roots split asunder as the birth canal widened and pressed and propelled its progeny up through rank depths. Up, up, up, until woodrot fingers broke the membrane of yellowed grasses and clawed through October leaves, breaking the crust of snow above.

There was a smothering black wail of a newborn.

And the crone was free, summoned forth like all the others. And this was the thing they had seen watching them with yellow eyes from amongst the old graves and shattered crypts.

Wenda scrambled on all fours, searching for the knife, listening to her own heart pounding. She heard Megga make a pathetic, moaning sound…then the rustling, straw-dry noise of the thing that reached out for her.

The knife.

Wenda gripped it and ran around the bed, the blade held out before her. The lantern was on the floor where Megga had dropped it. Thank God it still burned. The crone had Megga in its embrace, her head flopping limply on her neck, her throat exposed.

"NO!" Wenda shouted, going right at the ghost with her knife, slashing and hacking and succeeding only in fraying the shroud.

The thing turned to look at her.

Wenda saw a ruined face of seamed gray flesh that was threaded with cobwebs, a waxen mask whose huge selenic eyes were cinerary urns glowing with ashes. What stood before her was more than a mere cadaverous husk, but a living mold-encrusted graveyard angel filled with hunger, need, and a cold appetite that was galvanic like electricity bleeding from the severed arteries of high-tension lines. Still gripping Megga, it reached out for her. It would sate itself on her, too, drain her dry.

And it would not be the first time tonight.

Again, Wenda saw the cemetery.

She saw the hunched, tenebrous form making its way amongst moss-covered slabs and leaning headstones, gliding through the blowing snow. It had been a woman before the ravages of interment, before the cold and flat dormancy of its sleep. But it was no longer a woman. It was an appetite. And this was its primary motivation, the candle that still burned and flickered in the hollowed mortuary of its flesh. It glowed with an even, hungry light like a black taper seen through a frosted window. And it was this hunger that would renew it, remake it, rekindle its pestilential spirit, transform it from a sculpture of mausoleum dust and drifting web into the semblance of a woman again.

An odorous and dry breath from a burial vault, it dragged itself forward amongst funerary crosses and ivy-covered sepulchers, seeking the grim shadow of the Cobton church steeple and the town itself. Its winding sheet flapped and frayed, becoming a tempest of confetti. Strands of it were drifting and blowing like deep-sea grasses as the thing moved down the hillside to feed.

But a voice: "You, you there," it said. "You there…"

It stopped.

The apprehensive form of a caretaker, yanked from a greasy paperback world of frontiers and gunfights like a tooth plucked from sagging gums. He approached the scarecrow whirlwind, his fingers clutching the scepter of a long-barreled flashlight, dread waking in the pit of his belly with a nightmare shrieking.

And the crone was on him.

The caretaker screamed as snaking tentacles of shroud crept over him like graveworms. As his fingers pressed through the cerecloth and scratched over the dusty slats of rib and scapula, he felt the crawling, squirming things that nested within the folds of that winding sheet. And then those deadwood lips found his throat, kissing his life away, and he was emptied, leeched, dropped like a bundle of sticks to cool in the snow.

This is what it would do to Megga.

This is what it would do to Wenda, too, and she knew it.

The crone was a snake and they were the eggs she would suck dry and drop empty at her gray and flaking feet. Megga was beyond resistance; she was a sacrifice laid at the feet of horror. A greased pig made ready for the disemboweling.

But Wenda was not about to give in.

As those black thorny claws reached out for her, she let out a manic cry and vaulted forward with the knife, slashing the crone across the face with the blade. Her flesh bisected almost too easily, opening like a split seam, like gray lips parting and revealing something beneath that was not flesh and blood exactly but a fibrous yellow, seedy pulp like the guts of a pumpkin. It was practically luminous. The crone screamed with a howling sound of wind blown through low places. She became a squalling, gusting charnel storm of crematory ash, ossuary dust, and pulverized bone grit. A stuffed effigy fragmenting into a cyclone of spinning, churning debris.

It moved through the room with a whistling, sucking sound and Wenda was tossed to the floor, right on top of Megga. She covered her head as that blizzard of bones, leaves, dust, and wind-flowing cerements raged…and then, the hurricane subsided. It changed swiftly into a magnetic, oscillating stream of shimmering white ectoplasm upon which the crone's howling ghost face was indelibly stamped. It dove at the window…and passed through it.

Wenda pulled herself up, panting and dizzy.

She wanted nothing better than to curl up into a ball and cry like a baby, but there wasn't time for that. She stumbled over to the window and could see nothing out there but the blowing snowstorm. A single square pane was missing from the window. It was about the size of a small paperback book, but it did not look broken out so much as *melted*. The frame was burnt, the glass having oozed in streams and globs.

Wenda pulled Megga to her feet. "Are you all right?" she asked her.

Megga still had that vacant, dopy look on her face. She blinked, smiled, and then did something Wenda never saw coming: she reached out and took hold of her and kissed her hard on the mouth, sliding her tongue in past her lips. Wenda shoved her away and she stumbled drunkenly to the floor, giggling.

21

"You asked for my opinion and I'm giving it," Doc said. "Going out there is foolish, suicidal, and reckless."

Burt just glared at him. "Well, I'm willing to try. I'm willing to get our asses out of here or die trying. I'm not going to sit here and wait for it. Maybe that's okay for you, but I have other plans."

He was set on doing it and Doc knew he could not talk him out of it. Burt was trying very hard to make them think he was doing it for the benefit of the group but Doc knew better. Burt was selfish by nature. He didn't give a damn about the rest of them and, chances were, if he indeed made it to the car out there and got it going, he would probably drive away and leave everyone else stranded. That's the kind of guy he was.

"Okay, dude," Reg said. "Suppose you make it to the car and there's no keys in it?"

Burt smiled and pulled a multitool from the inside of his coat. "I hotwire it. I did it plenty of times when I was a teenager. I used to be able to do it in three minutes or less."

Ah, Doc thought, *now the true face of Burt shows itself. A little criminal.*

Reg nodded. "Sweet, but the steering wheel will still be locked."

"There's ways around that for a guy with imagination," Burt told him.

Reg looked at Doc and all Doc could do was shrug.

"You realize you're probably going to die out there," he said. "If those creatures out there get to you, there's nothing we can do to assist you. You realize that, of course."

"I wouldn't expect help from you."

"You can't expect help from any of us."

Burt grunted as if it was no news to him.

Reg went over to the window. Doc joined him. The storm was blowing hard out there and visibility was down to a few feet. The snow was coming down in sheets, the wind turning it into a churning maelstrom of absolute elemental wrath. The house shook as it blasted into the walls, the glass rattling in the windows. The sound of the storm was a near-constant howling that sometimes rose into a whining shriek and then fell to a low and pained moaning. It was death out there and they both knew it. You could get lost in ten feet in a blow like that. Even if Burt went out there with a flashlight, it would do him little good. The light would be reflected off the flying snow, creating wild leaping shapes all around him, blurring distance and making him see things that weren't there and hiding others that were. And some of those things would have long white fingers and grinning red mouths.

Doc felt a stab of yellow fear in his belly as he imagined himself lost in the howling white vortex, long-armed shapes moving in from all sides.

"At least be sensible," he told Burt. "At least give it another twenty or thirty minutes, let the storm die down a bit."

Burt looked out the window. "Okay. But no more. We can't afford to wait much more than that."

On that point, Doc had to agree.

Those things were still out there, waiting. They had pulled back into the storm for the time being but he knew they were there. He could feel them as he felt the low and distant throb of his heart. They were just waiting for an opportunity to slake their thirst. He planned on doing everything in his power to deny them that opportunity. But as far as Burt went, there was nothing he could do to stop him. His mind was clearly set and he was going.

Doc went over and sat by Bailey.

He had tried just about every trick in his vast repertoire to draw her out of her shell but to no avail. It was just too much for her. He and the others were having trouble with the situation they were in, of course, all three of them dancing precariously close to the pit of madness, but they had not given in. Bailey, however, would not even put up a fight. She had sunk away to some place where she could escape it all. He held her hand. It was cool and limp. He wondered if she was in shock and figured she had every right to be.

Doc had refused to give those things out there a proper name until Reg and Burt came busting in with the wood, telling him what they had seen at the window upstairs. Now there was no getting around it. His mind kept trying to avoid the word, but it was there as it had been from the beginning: *vampires*. An old, shop-worn term that had little place in this world of laptops and cell phones and Skype, but it was real and being who and what he was, his mind searched through the old literature page by page. If they were anything like their fictional counterparts, then they would have wild talents, shapeshifting abilities—he could attest to that one—and hypnotic powers. They would be stealthy, drifting shades and patches of mist. You would never hear them coming for they would be silent as falling leaves or moon-shadows creeping across a summer lawn. They would have to be invited in and once invited, they could slide under locked doors and come in through keyholes and ooze through cracks in walls. Hungry ghosts with flesh like fog…yet, at other times, they would be as physically real as a living human being and, come sunrise, absolutely helpless.

That is, if the things he had read had any basis in fact.

He squeezed Bailey's hand but there was no response. He might as well have been trying to illicit a response from the hand of a mannequin or a rubber glove. *I'm scared, too, my dear. Believe that. I'm scared to death because despite my bluster and blow and my stage persona, I'm old and I know it. I'm far too old to have my world turned on its head like this and reality crumble about me. I'm afraid I'm just not up to the challenge and that scares me to death.* He thought these things because he would never admit them aloud any more than most men would. So he held Bailey's hand and listened to his voice tell her that it would be over at sunrise and the world would start spinning again, that they were merely trapped in some pocket of shadow that would dissipate in the warm light of day and the cold light of reason. This was a fever dream but it would pass as all things must pass.

But even as he said these things, he had to wonder.

He had to wonder if this was only a localized thing or an ancient pestilence the world had once known and forgotten about (save in the tales of old wives) and would now know again.

If these things started rising up everywhere, then the world would have to cease their petty wars and jealousy and greed. The lovemaking, merrymaking, money-making, and life-taking would come to an end in the face of this new—thought quite old—enemy. Communally, there would be a new voice on the wind, one that was ancient and malignant calling out of the darkness. The voice of the hunt and mankind would be its prey. Nightfall would become a time of terror, a time when every last man, woman, and child would huddle like frightened rabbits in their warrens, fearing the hungry pestilent shadows of the night that would creep through the cities and towns...all of which would be mortuaries and graveyards, gutted tombs and bone-strewn cathedrals of rat-scrabbling survivors and the hollow-eyed undead which preyed upon them.

Doc shook his head, refusing to think anymore.

"I heard something," Burt said. "Out there...I just fucking heard something."

Lost in the tangles of his thoughts, mired in them, Doc hadn't heard a thing, but it was obvious from the look on Reg's face that he had heard it, too. Then it came again: a skittering sort of sound beyond the door, as if some immense and fleshy rat were scratching about out there.

Reg picked up the poker from the fire.

Burt grabbed the broadhead axe.

They were both pale and shaking as Doc rose to his feet. There were two ways to handle this. They could either ignore the sounds or face them. Facing them could be deadly, but ignoring them was only going to notch up imaginations and they were already running at a high, delusory pitch.

"Do it," Reg said. "I can't handle this fucking waiting..."

Doc reached for the door handle, feeling the weight of the lantern as he listened to the sounds out there, which had increased in fury. Bailey had pulled up tight in a ball and the tension was strung thickly in the air.

He opened the door.

22

Wenda kept a tight eye on Megga because she did not trust her or have any faith in her ability to resist the call of the undead outside. What had happened upstairs was devastating and terrifying. She could not get the images of the crone out of her mind, but what bothered her more than anything about it was Megga.

She did not fight.

She did not even attempt defiance.

Which made things only that much worse, because Morris was becoming increasingly withdrawn and frightened, and with Megga being weak it meant that Wenda had to stand on her own and watch over the both of them. Not good, not good.

You should've let that crone take her. Megga's always wanted something like that. Why fight it? Let her become one of them. Let her be some crawling undead thing.

But Wenda knew she couldn't do that.

When they'd gotten back with what wood they could grab and grab quickly, Morris had been huddled by the fire. Despite the sounds from upstairs, he had not moved. He obviously couldn't deal with any of it. He was used to being in charge, used to making things happen by sheer force of will and his own dominating personality. But his talents for management were useless against what they were facing. He could not control this scenario. It was too big to grasp and too dangerous to manhandle. So, he pulled into himself and became what he'd probably always been beneath the visage of the big, tough, can-do businessman: a frightened little boy.

Wenda tried to sympathize with him, but as things stood she needed everyone to stand tall and he had shrunk to an almost infantile stage. Things were desperate and there was no room for weakness like that, simply no room.

What amazed her most was that she had stood up against that creature upstairs. Such a thing would have been unthinkable yesterday…then she supposed everything about tonight was unthinkable. Still, she was amazed. She went after that thing when the sane reaction would have been to run from the room and curl up by the fire with Morris.

But she'd fought.

She'd slashed that evil witch and sent her fleeing from the room.

At first she didn't understand the mechanics of it, but when they got downstairs Megga said, "Good thinking, bringing that blade."

"Why?"

"Because of the blade. It's sterling silver. They don't like silver."

Even now Wenda was trying to make sense of that, applying the only logic she had which had been gleaned from the old movies she had screened for *Chamber of Horrors:* everything from *Taste the Blood of Dracula* to *The Vampire Lovers* and *Curse of the Undead.*

Silver? She didn't recall the silver thing. Silver was useful against werewolves…but vampires?

Megga, of course, would have had the answers but Wenda's patience with her was pretty much used up. She was standing over near the curtains, peering out through a slit.

"Are they out there?" Morris said.

"No. All I see is the storm." She sounded almost disappointed.

"Maybe they went away."

Megga rolled her eyes at that. "I wonder how the others are doing."

"Better than us, I imagine," Wenda said.

Megga didn't comment on that. "I hope…I hope Bailey's okay."

There. The only strand of humanity in her: Bailey. The only connection she had to the real world. They hammed it up on the show as lesbo vampires, but sometimes Wenda wondered if that didn't carry over into the real world. She'd never seen any direct evidence of it…yet, they were both attractive girls and both were single and seemed happy staying that way.

You're single, too.

Sure, but as she liked to tell herself, it was easier that way. Less complicated and she didn't see where she had time to balance a relationship *and* the show. She figured she'd never know what the true nature of the relationship between Bailey and Megga was, but she didn't think they were in love as such. It was almost a co-dependency. Megga provided the aggression and fearlessness that Bailey lacked; and Bailey represented the warmth and solid, steady parental background that Megga never had.

Together, they were a whole.

Wenda fed a few logs into the fire. She sat back on the sofa and waited. She still held the knife and she was pretty sure she would not let it go before daylight.

Megga was staring at her, pulling off a cigarette. "You're not too happy with me, are you?"

Wenda said nothing.

"You think I fell apart up there."

Wenda looked over at her. "You *did* fall apart up there. I always thought you were tough. I always believed that…but when it came down to it, you were weak. If I hadn't been there, you'd be outside with them now."

Megga looked toward the doorway. "Maybe that's what I want. Maybe that's what I've *always* wanted. To be them. To be like them. To be a creature of the night."

"To what end?"

"To be different, I guess."

Wenda suppressed a peal of sarcastic laughter. "Oh, you're different, all right."

Megga just sneered. "You don't understand."

"Maybe you're the one that doesn't understand. Maybe your head's all fucked-up from reading Anne Rice and watching silly vampire romances on TV. Well, let me clue you into something: that's all fantasy. There's nothing sexy or uber-cool about those things. You saw that crone up there. You saw what she was. Did she look happy to you? She was nothing but a walking pestilence. I don't think those things are anything more than hunger. But if they feel anything at all, it sure as hell isn't contentment. That woman looked like she was in agony, she looked...*defiled*. Is that what you want?"

"Maybe it is," Megga said. "Maybe I want the despair and the self-loathing."

"You've already got that, in case you haven't noticed."

Megga shook her head. "I've always wanted death."

Wenda just sighed. "What you need is a good psychiatrist."

"Fuck you."

"Whatever. All I know is that I've got enough problems without your morbid fantasies."

"Oh yeah? And who put you in charge?"

Wenda sat forward. "I'm in charge because Morris is absolutely useless—"

"What?" Morris said.

"—and you're not much better. I've got the only clear head in this room. We're not going to survive unless we stand strong against what's out there and stand together. Don't you understand that? Can't you let go of your teenage Goth fantasies long enough to see that?"

Megga laughed at her. In fact, her whole face and body laughed at her. Everything got in the act as if to show Wenda the absurdity of what she had just said like it was some naïve, childlike notion that you could possibly fight against them or stand strong against what they represented.

"Okay, Megga. If you don't want to be a normal living, breathing human being, then get out of here. You're no good to us," Wenda told her. "Pack up your plastic fangs and your Wal-Mart Dracula cape and get the fuck out of here. Go outside. Let them have you. Go see just how *content* they are."

When Megga made to open her mouth, Wenda said, "But understand one thing and understand it good: if you go out there and you come back trying to spread that plague to us, I'll kill you. I'll ram a fucking stake right through you."

Megga just glared at her.

Wenda glared back. She picked up a length of oak from the woodpile. It was about sixteen or seventeen inches long, thick around as a bedpost. It would do nicely. So as she watched Megga watching her, she took the knife and began to sharpen it into a stake.

23

The bitch is serious. She's absolutely fucking serious.

Little Miss Perfect, wouldn't-swat-a fucking-fly Wenda who only came to life when she was Vultura had now morphed into the primo queen bitch, the cock-of-the-fucking-walk. She was large and in charge and even threatening…something Megga did not care for because *she* was the threatening one. It was the way it was supposed to work.

But…*damn,* look at her over there sharpening that stake. It wasn't just threat posturing or some simple defensive mechanism, no, old Wenda was making a stake and she looked determined enough to use it. That gleam in her eye was steely, resolute, and bold. She'd already attacked one vampire tonight and Megga got the unpleasant feeling she was just warming up. That harmless Wenda Keegan was coming into her own, that at heart she was a fucking alpha warrior maiden that would kill vampires without hesitation and maybe even Van Helsing could learn a trick or two from her.

Interesting.

Megga felt threatened by her and feeling so, she wanted to yell at her, to tear her house down, to go up one side of Miss Wenda Keegan and down the other, screaming obscenities at her until she crawled back into the pretty pink box she'd come out of.

But part of her didn't dare.

Wenda was beginning to look positively…*predatory.*

"You better make sure I'm one of those things before you go using that," Megga said to her.

Wenda kept sharpening the stake. "I'm not a killer. I don't get off on death and pain. I leave that to people like you and the rest of the McVampire groupies of the wet-panty brigade. Unlike you and the rest of those deluded idiots, I know badness when I see it. I know what evil looks like and how it smells. I won't be killing anyone. But I will destroy those things. If you want to give yourself up to them, go ahead, but I'll get you and when I ram this through your chest, it won't be out of hate, Megga, it'll be because it's the right thing to do. That crone might have blinded you to her true nature, but I saw it just fine. Do what you want. But before you find a coffin to sleep in, think about Bailey. Think about how she needs you. Think about what a disappointment you'll be to her when she learns how weak you really are."

"Fuck you," Megga snarled.

But that didn't even move Wenda. Christ, the way she was it was like trying to insult a rattlesnake that was going to bite you.

Megga turned away from her, pissed off and hating. Why in the hell did she mention Bailey? *She did it because it has power over you and she knows it. You can expect her to rub it into your face again and again if you don't step off the train to the graveyard here and reassess you're thinking. She's simply trying to goad you into realism.*

Megga wondered if Wenda was still pissed because she'd tried to kiss her…well, she *had* kissed her. Funny, that. She'd never had any feelings for her. A co-worker. That was about it. She was friendly with her, cooperative, but she harbored no romantic impulses. Yet…after Wenda had slashed the crone upstairs, she had wanted her like she'd never wanted anyone, male or female, before. She told herself it was just some weird hypnotic aftereffect.

But was it?

She didn't know.

In fact, other than feeling a mad hot-blooded desire for Wenda, she couldn't really remember a lot of what happened up there. They'd gone into the room. There'd been someone on the bed under a sheet…then it got a little grainy and distorted like a dream recalled half way through the day. Images of Wenda. Images of a woman. A strange woman who was beautiful and alluring with crystal blue eyes and platinum hair that hung in a long braid over one shoulder in the European style. She remembered the woman had been smiling...a sweet, friendly, harmless sort of smile that made her feel at ease. In her mind, only the image of the smile remained like that of the storied cat: a huge smile of gleaming white teeth.

You saw that crone up there. You saw what she was.

Wenda's words. And to Megga they were incomprehensible. *Crone? What crone?* There had been no crone, just that beautiful blonde woman holding her arms out to her, wanting to embrace her. Megga had even heard her speak. She said something about how glad she was that Megga was safe, that those awful things outside had not gotten to her. That she needed to be wary of them. And that she—the woman herself—could protect her if only she came into her arms.

She was nothing but a walking pestilence.

No, no, no, Wenda, you're wrong. It wasn't like that...but as Megga began to remember she was no longer seeing the beautiful European woman. She was just seeing those blue eyes, which were deep and fathomless like drowning pools. In their depths, she saw dark mountains capped by black impenetrable forests rising above little villages tucked in remote valleys. Deserted villages where the wind blew dust devils up empty avenues and winding cobblestone streets were edged by silent half-timber houses falling to ruin and doorways pooled with sinister shadows. And as darkness fell over the rooftops like oil, she could hear the strident giggling of unseen children and the sound of chattering teeth from the overgrown churchyard on the hill, and see white hungry faces peering through rotting shutters.

Megga shook her head, trying to push that awful imagery from her mind, but like a leech it clung, it held on, it fed on the darkness of her mind, bloating itself. Those villages...none were Cobton. These were in a far-away place where the crops had withered in the fields and the houses stood like leaning monoliths.

That woman looked like she was in agony, she looked...defiled.

Now it was invading Megga's mind, the truth of what she had seen up there. The memory crowded in, filling her with unease. In that woman's eyes she had seen the spectral darkness of alien lands laid empty by a creeping pestilence and she could hear the woman's voice...a strange tongue, thick and guttural, Slavonic. She could not understand the words spoken, but the malevolence and spiritual decay behind them was all too evident.

Then Megga could remember herself standing there as that…that *woman* moved in at her and, no, she was not beautiful at all. Her face was gray and fissured like an old root, the eyes a sullen sickly yellow, and the smile was not friendly but wolfish and starving, the teeth long and sharp. And that's when the dread had engulfed her, locking her down in an icy embrace, an ebon fear sucking into her pores and filling her with an almost hysterical panic as she saw that grinning mouth whose smile was mocking and pale and poisonous. She looked into eyes that simmered with a black anti-human hatred, a hatred of the life in her and an almost carnal need to violate her and empty her veins.

That's what she had *really* seen as those withered fingers had reached for her and that mouth had puckered into a shriveled gray blowhole to be pressed against her throat.

Megga lit another cigarette and tried to tell herself it wasn't so, but it was true and she knew it. Maybe she'd always known that's what those things would be like.

Leeches, nothing but leeches.

And if they offered you other things or gave you a glimpse of cold beauty or eroticism or whispered graveyard poetry in your ear, it was only a means to an end so they could feed upon you.

Yet…even knowing the truth of it and feeling the fear still kicking in her belly like a grim fetus…the hypnotic allure of the woman still clouded her mind and whitewashed her brain. Its influence was powerful. It lingered and haunted her skull like a ghost. And what frightened her most was that after Wenda had driven the crone away, Megga herself had become very much aware of how turned-on she was, how she'd wanted that woman to touch her and violate her and penetrate her with those long mottled teeth…and that, more than anything else, had made her go after Wenda, kiss her, tongue her.

She wanted her.

God, how she wanted her.

Her brain rioting with lewd, profane impulses, she would have done her right there on the cold floor. The woman offered death and death was the ultimate aphrodisiac.

Nothing burns so hot as death.

Nothing.

Feeling hot inside, Megga pulled off her cigarette and tried to calm herself. She looked over at Wenda who'd apparently been watching her the entire time.

She was still sharpening the stake and doing so almost reverently like it was a religious experience for her. Megga was all too aware of the phallic shape of the thing. The heat was building up in her and she could barely contain it.

Morris poked at the fire with a stick. "I wonder when they'll come for us," he said.

Megga didn't know but, God, she hoped it would be soon.

24

At first, Doc saw nothing when he opened the door. There was just the corridor leading to the foyer and nothing else. He saw shadows and a clutching darkness pushing out at him that was nearly suffocating. Then he smelled a dark and pungent odor of carrion. He heard a low moaning noise like wind blowing through a pipe. He lifted the lantern high, casting its light out into the corridor and, instantly, panic tore loose inside him with an almost audible tearing sound.

A column of luminous white mist was rushing at him, swirling and fuming like some sort of ghost-fog. It was a seething and hissing helix of corpse gas, bone dust, and sluicing tissue that seemed to be fragmenting, boiling to steam, caught in the suctioning whirlwind of its own churning mass.

And it had a face. A lopsided, upside-down face of pale liquid wax that was melting off the screaming skull beneath…eyes blazing like coals and jaws yawning white like the maw of a shark.

He had time to utter, "Oh my Christ," and that was about it.

It passed right by him in a whitish blur of glacial wind before he could even move. Its flesh brushed against his own and it felt like cold rubber, but seemed to have no more density than smoke. He had an image of a skull-faced wraith rocketing past him like a fired arrow, white hair streaming and body like some loose collection of flapping rags.

The next thing he knew, *she* was standing near the sofa.

Burt had backpedaled and gone on his ass.

Reg was standing behind her with the poker like a knight with a lance.

She stood still as a statue, not even blinking. Doc found that he was rooted to the spot and could not move. It lasted maybe five seconds but to him it seemed like an eternity of suffering.

The woman was an emaciated thing with stick-thin limbs and a head of long, white, luxurious hair. Her flesh was so colorless it looked bleached. There were numerous old scars, ruts, and rough purplish contusions on her body. She had an emaciated, wasted appearance, ribs standing out like the rungs of a ladder, waist like a withered post, pelvic wings jutting obscenely from her hips…all of it covered in a skin that was tight, almost membranous. Her breasts were like plums shriveled in a drought, her hairless vulva like a ghost-white peach.

Doc looked at her, made to say something because in any situation the words just wanted to run out of him.

The woman cocked her head like a listening dog.

Doc closed his mouth.

Her face was sunken with starvation, cheeks hollow, skin seamed and rutted, lips shriveling away from pale gums which sprouted a pair of sharp incisors like the fangs of a viper. She looked at Doc with eyes that were a dun yellow-green, the pupils black specks.

Her mouth yawning open even further, she hissed at him, gouts of drool running down her chin.

He was certain that she would leap on him at that moment, jump him and tear him open with those teeth, oil herself with his hot blood. But she did not want him. Her head revolved slowly on her neck and she fixed her gaze on Bailey who was trembling, trying to contain the whimpering in her throat. If anyone in that room was a victim, it was Bailey. The vampire saw it, and being a predator by nature, recognized it immediately.

Doc moved.

If he had thought about it, considered the dangers involved, he wouldn't have. But he did not think; he acted.

He got between Bailey and the hag as if he were facing her down, placing himself not only in harm's way, but in striking distance. As he did so, a voice in the back of his head said, *just what in the hell do you think you're doing, old man?* And he wished to God he knew.

At the hag's back, Reg brought up the poker to strike. Burt advanced with the axe, maybe emboldened by both of them. If the woman was concerned about being outnumbered and outgunned, she did not show it. Her feral gaze was locked on Bailey who was wide-eyed and shaking, not only paralyzed with horror, but struck mad with it.

The woman put her eyes back on Doc and he felt something shrink inside him.

He saw those teeth.

He could almost feel them impaling his throat, feel her draining him dry with a cold suction. The very idea of it made something like hot wires burn in his chest.

Then she moved.

She turned from Doc and went after Bailey and, again, Doc did not think. He heard Bailey's pathetic moan and the vampire's hissing lust, then he grabbed the hag from behind and pulled her away and back with an irresistible adrenalin-born strength. She twisted and writhed in his grip like a worm, her flesh icy, threadbare like living cobwebs. Her breath was foul and dark and hot. She threw him backwards with comparative ease, his fingers tearing out strips of tissue as he fell.

25

By then, Reg was in motion.

Before the hag could turn, he shouted and brought the poker down with everything he had. It punched between her shoulder blades and erupted from her abdomen. Not a drop of blood came out. The tip of it protruding from her belly was slicked with clear jelly like Vaseline.

Upon contact, upon initial impalement, he felt a surge of cold electricity feed from the woman and run up the shaft of the poker as if he had just speared a junction box and not this writhing horror.

The energy…oddly chill and arcing…drew the warmth from him as if the hag were sucking it right out of him. He smelled awful foul odors, which he knew was the stink coming from inside her. It was the rank smell of unburied corpses, of the rising undead, of darkness, and subterranean crypts.

As the stench blew out of her in gaseous waves, he heard her voice in his head. It was clear and cutting, filling his skull—subjectively anyway—with gushing blood. *RELEASE ME! TAKE IT OUT!* the voice screamed with a grinding, metallic sort of sound. *PULL IT OUT! PULL IT OUT!*

These were the words he heard, or at least the ones his brain deciphered. There were others, all spoken in some thick, guttural foreign tongue, but their meaning was most explicit.

Reg did not pull it out.

He rammed it in further.

The hag let out a guttural, barking sound that was more rage than pain.

She turned around facing Reg who stumbled back, shaking his head.

She shrieked something at him, something garbled and unintelligible that had the tonal quality of screeching door hinges. Then, fangs bared, eyes blazing yellow and green, she gripped the tip of the poker and pulled it all the way through herself until it was free and in her hands. With a snarling, almost braying sort of sound, she threw it at Reg.

For the first time in his life, he was grateful for his natural clumsiness.

As she threw the poker, he backed into a chair and fell over it. The poker thudded into the wall. Not just striking it and chipping out a chunk of plaster, but *burying* itself in there like a fencepost into soft earth.

Doc pulled himself up, noticing that he saw no wound in the woman's belly at all now as if it had closed like a pair of lips.

26

The hag went after Bailey and no one—save Burt—could have stopped her in time. She looked like a white, leggy spider seizing its prey. She leaped up on the sofa and hovered over Bailey. Then she was on her, her head darting into Bailey's throat and Bailey made a sharp, squealing sound as the fangs dipped into an artery, the hag fastening her lips and making a liquid sucking sound.

Doc grabbed her hair and tore her away.

She screamed at him, twisting and clawing at his face and just missing his eyes with her gray talons. She took hold of him and she was unbelievably strong or, perhaps, he was unbelievably weak. The intensity of her shimmering yellow-green eyes tapped his strength. They punched into him like poison darts and he felt everything inside him run like hot tallow.

He heard an audible *hsssssssst* sort of sound in his head that was the noise of his nerve endings shorting out as the electrical grid in his head was shut down by the hag's feral gaze. He stumbled back a step, then two, knowing that he was no longer a sentient being but a breathing, mumbling, mindless machine struck dumb by the intensity of hate in those eyes. He could feel—from what seemed a great distance—his heart beating and his lungs sucking air, but very little else. The effect of the woman's eyes upon him were like a thousand-thousand tiny stinging nettles penetrating his skin, dumping their toxins into him, making him feel numb and rubbery.

He didn't know how long he was like that, microseconds probably, but his dreamlike fugue seemed to go on and on...then, gradually, very gradually, he felt consciousness and feeling returning. It was like a door that had been slammed shut in his head had swung back open...he came out of it with a muted cry, the wind rushing out of him. He breathed in and out, his brain working again after a brief period of oxygen starvation.

It lasted seconds.

And in those seconds, the hag had advanced on him. She moved like a sinister, shadowy blur...a nightmare stick-woman of reaching claws and gnashing teeth and pure, deranged hatred. All he could see was her face rushing at him: the pallid, clownlike grin of fangs and the yellow eyes glowing like candle ends in the hollows of a pumpkin.

She would have had him.

She would have opened his throat and torn out his gullet in a bloody spray, but Reg intervened.

She heard him too late.

He brought the poker down in a two-fisted grip and it went between her shoulder blades again, but this time the aim had been corrected. It slid through her with amazing ease as if her flesh were made of something insubstantial like cheesecloth. The poker pierced her, a good four inches of it spearing through her chest and this time she did not grab it and pull it free. She went down to her knees, jerking and shaking. Her fumbling fingers played at the spike sticking out of her but seemingly without the strength to grip it.

Her heart was impaled.

Doc noticed something extraordinary at that moment: she was younger. The ingesting of Bailey's blood had peeled countless years from her. Her white hair was raven black, shining with blue highlights, just barely streaked with gray. Many of the wrinkles and ruts had been pressed from her face. Her skin was still white, but it was smoother, a hint of color at her cheeks. Even her breasts were fuller, her lips red and swollen with blood.

It was absolutely amazing.

The blood she had drawn from Bailey had rejuvenated her and he could see it happening right before his eyes.

But they had her.

Her heart was split from the poker.

She let out a wild, agonal scream that was high and shrilling...and it was *answered*. From outside the house, dozens of wavering and eerie voices joined hers, rising up into an ear-splitting cacophony that put Reg on his ass and made Burt clutch his ears and drop next to him.

27

The staked hag was a mass of writhing flesh like there were a million vermiform shapes squirming just beneath her skin. A contaminated-smelling steam rose from her...bile and stolen blood foamed from her mouth...her ghostface twisted into something like a Chinese ritual mask carved with upturning eyes, flaring nostrils, and a wide grinning/shrieking/agonized mouth of gnashing fangs. A putrescent slime began to ooze from her skin and she bloated up, swelling with some weird neoplasmic tumefaction until she became a shuddering fleshy barrel of saprogenic foulness that was melting like wax.

And still she screamed.

Though it felt like hot needles were sliding into his eardrums, Doc grabbed up the broadhead axe. Steadying himself, gathering strength even though his head was a drum of shrieking white noise, he swung the axe in both hands. It took off the hag's head...and instantly the screaming died out. Her body collapsed to a wormy heap on the floor and her head rolled into the corner. Within seconds, it was a graying, mummified thing and then the face fell in. The body followed a similar dissolution until it looked like a collection of blackened rags, swirling dust, and pulverized bone. An acrid-smelling smoke issued from the carcass and then it was over.

Just that quick.

It was over.

And it was then that Doc realized Bailey had gone into convulsions.

INTERLUDE #1: PLAGUE CITY

1

Ordek, Hungary, 1827

The city was haunted.

It was a vast, grim cemetery and Jozsef Vajda picked his way from one bone pile to the next, the night wrapping around him and enshrouding him in its depths.

He stepped out of a slouching doorway framed by sooty brickwork and heard his shoes—so worn now—ring out over the damp cobblestones. He was unshaven, dressed in a shabby woolen coat, clutching a bulging flour sack to his breast, guarding it, watching over it as if it were a precious infant. The sack contained food. And in this city and these dire, godless times, food was worth more than mere life.

He thought: *If I can make it home to Elena and the twins, if I can only smuggle this food into our cramped little world and see their faces lighting like stars being born, then I could ask no more of God this night.*

Carefully, he tucked the sack into the folds of his coat with covetous fingers.

He was alone.

Alone with the night which was a black and predatory serpent that had been slumbering away the daylight hours in some nitrous cellar or foul-smelling drainage ditch and was now awake...awake, sentient and malevolently ravenous. It coiled about him, its spiraled length constricting city and country and world and maybe even the cold stars above.

Alone in the womb of breathing night, Jozsef shivered.

Any who watched and hungered—and there were so many in these days of starvation and disease—would know he concealed something of worth. They would smell it, taste its good hungry scent on the air, and take to his trail like hounds on a fox.

So Jozsef practiced stealth.

He moved as the wind would move: in short, quick gusts, gathering himself in darkened boulevards and the grim shadows of moonlight-limned buildings, then rushing forth again, aware and alive and secretive. His were eyes beady and watchful. His nose was filled with the damp night air, which was sharp and unpleasant around him. It smelled of spices and memories, of apples rotted to cider beneath autumn-dead trees, of leaves gathered in cold gutters.

The city was as weary as Jozsef himself.

Not truly alive or dead, emaciated by gnawing emptiness, it stood alone in the enclosing blackness, buffeted by winds, fatigued by struggle, denuded by famine, but still standing, by God, still standing. A dead moon in a graveyard cosmos. Many of its buildings were shells gutted by bombs and never rebuilt. The rawboned corpses of homes, factories, and businesses lie in tenebrous ruin, fleshed out by rubble and described by polluted mists that blew in from the icy river like lost souls. It was a hunting ground of the wicked and the desperate, the hungry and the insane. Here, they were as plentiful as graveworms in moist, corrupted caskets.

But there were worse things and Jozsef knew it.

There were demons on the wind and he could feel them getting closer.

And closer.

2

Beneath noxious membranes of crematory ash, the factories of death ran endlessly into the night, plague machinery rumbling happily, gears lubricated with blood and cogs greased by human fat, rendering the dead into corpse-meal and bone-ash.

The fertile crops of pandemic gave up their graveyard harvest of stiff-limbed forms, and the dead arrived in bales and bundles and ghost-trains. Piled in cadaveric hills, there was no shortage of raw materials: grisly mounds of cold clutching limbs and sightless snow-dusted faces. Supply far exceeded demand.

Men with eyes like blank slate heaped corpses in untidy stacks in the backs of plague wagons until they were crowded with the unburied. Day by grim day in silent funeral processions, the wagons rolled from neighborhood to neighborhood, house to house, collecting the dead for the furnaces of the burning pits, human cordwood pyres that burned bright far into the night. The air exhaled an oily stench of cremation as gray human ash drifted down over the city like December's first snow. The wind smelled of blackness, grit, and vomit.

This was the city of the dead.

3

Wait.

Listen.

Like a rabbit in a wide killing field, Jozsef could feel the talons of the hawk approaching. The crowd smelled what he had and their bellies ached for it and their throats thirsted for his demise, all motivated by diseased brains. Yes, feet running, pounding—men, women, children. They ringed around him like flames, hemmed him in, held him, pawed him, tore at him. Their faces were cardboard skulls pasted with flesh, their stomachs cavernous. Jozsef held tight to his bag of treats as if it were his heart they wished to yank free. He formed his body into a barrier of steel and cement. It was like being in a pen of blood-maddened fighting cocks. Squeals. Grunts. Wicked laughter. Chattering teeth. A sandstorm of famished humanity, blowing and shrieking. Beaten to the ground, never realizing he lay on a bounty of food, the crowd moved on, chased a slat-thin dog into the bony framework of a factory.

Safe now, Jozsef ran off into the night, hid in the sinister shadows of a ruined church, waiting, tensing, wondering in what form invasion would show itself next.

Sucking in a low, sibilant breath, he started off again.

"Good evening, my friend."

Jozsef felt a scream shatter in his throat. His eyes darted about madly, seeing nothing but night and rubble. A wind picked up, making the bare trees rattle like dice in a cup, birthing long, jagged shadows that jumped and played like split-hoofed devils dancing on rooftops. Then he saw a figure—tall, thin, windblown—standing beneath the overhang of a boarded-up distillery. A man, yes, a man, his coat flapping in the breeze like a flap atop a high pole. But there was something strange about him. His form…it angled too much or perhaps not enough, seemed to sway like a narrow dead tree in a sucking mire.

Jozsef looked, his flesh swept by lantern eyes.

"Who…who is there?"

The figure seemed phantasmal, spectral like dark mist that would disperse at any moment.

The figure stepped forward, solid at last. "Jozsef? Surely, I haven't frightened you! Do you not remember your old friend Emil Stanislav?"

Jozsef felt his heart encased in crystals of January ice. Ice that held tight, clung to nerve and tissue like fungi to marble slabs. His breath was shallow in his throat, frosting from his lips. For one impossible, demented moment he thought he could see the gutter ruin of the distillery through his old friend's body. But no, he was solid enough. "Emil? *Emil?* But…no, it can't be you…can it? They said…they said you died…that you wasted away in the state hospital…"

Stanislav laughed and there was something oddly unsettling about that laughter. Like the strangled, retching bark of a sick dog as heard in the small hours of an October night. "Dead? Now, do I look dead? Perhaps my soul has fallen to blight, but this body still moves."

Jozsef let out a long, controlled sigh. "Thank God you're well, Emil."

"What chance brings us together this night, Jozsef?"

"I was…I have been working in the fields outside the city. I have not been home in six days. That is where I go now. To my wife, my children."

"And in that bag you carry?"

Jozsef did not want to admit to it; what he carried was life to his family. "Oh, my belongings."

"You carry food, Jozsef."

"Yes."

Stanislav clutched Jozsef's wrist with hands that were cold as a gravedigger's shovel. But they were good hands, Jozsef thought, callused by a life of honest work. Hands that were strong, sure. Hands that had held babies and caressed lovers. The hands of a saint and a friend.

Stanislav's eyes were dark now like the pathless wastes between dead stars. "I would not take food from the bellies of your loved ones. You know that. Blessed are the ones who can feed their kin in these dark days."

Jozsef looked in his old friend's face, saw how moonlight gathered in hollows and pockets, glowed like swamp gas in draws and runs. He was very thin, wasted even. But the eyes...yes, the eyes were filled with a rapture of life, a semblance of summer days. And in those eyes Jozsef could see memories. The farm on the River Bodrog. Two boys who ran and played and shouted and jumped, always smelling of fresh-cut hay, barley, and crisp cornhusks, their bodies lean with the sinew of muscle and youth, their faces warm and welcome like an August sunset.

"These are not good times for us," Stanislav told him, his voice ringing out like yellow metal on a forge. "Once we were full and fat and happy...and now? Like grapes on a vine, we wither in the name of the Republic, lean and hungry. You...you have no doubt heard stories? Tales? Whispers of strange things?"

Jozsef had. But like fairies sprinkling stardust and witches stirring cauldrons, he paid them no mind. Bad and noisome odors, they persisted, pervaded, were given breath and walked now. Stories of industrial body farms and gray stone rendering plants where the dead were drained of fat and ground-up for bone meal. Of the great, unknown plague creeping forth from some medieval hell that was sweeping the tired, hungry, and destitute into the grave. The great burning pits where their contaminated bodies were reduced to ash. Whispered tales of night-haunters, the undead, and those who had never been born.

One of the stories concerned a tall man who had been seen just after sunset. Dressed in a long patchwork coat of animal skins, his face pallid like moonlight, his eyes blazing red, he stood on desolate street corners with his mouth open, blowing plague onto the wind.

"Superstition," he said. "When life is uncertain, cursed by disease and hunger and sudden death...people blame misfortune on spirits and bogeys."

"How wise you are, my friend."

Uneasy, Jozsef said, "I must get home." He swallowed back deserts and arid vistas. "But Emil...friend, you would walk with me?"

Stanislav was consumed in shadow, his mouth a jagged pumpkin grin, his eyes sterile lunar wastes. "No, I cannot, dear friend. But it is dangerous to cross the city at night. Shrunken bellies and barren minds have created monsters in our mists. Ghouls that would prey on their brethren. You would walk carefully."

"Yes."

"Do you recall the tunnel…?"

"The cellar tunnel?"

"Yes."

Jozsef could remember it. Years ago, there had been an industrial winery where the sweet grapes of the mountains were squeezed into bottles and fermented. The wine cellar beneath was a tunnel that ran some six city blocks, the remains of a medieval smuggler's den, now abandoned.

Stanislav said, "Walk with me, Jozsef. I will lead you to the passage. Then beneath the streets you will go. Follow the tunnel across the city. Proceed to the end and avoid unknown chambers."

So Jozsef walked on and Stanislav accompanied him, two paces back, his footfalls silent as they trod over the crumbling cobblestone lane and its abundant carpet of rain-plastered leaves. Stanislav spoke in a fractured, sibilant voice of things long gone and hopes buried in dark graves. And why was it that his voice reminded Jozsef of shadow-riven country churchyards and disturbed crypts? Of skeletal trees scratching at morose cloud-scummed skies? Of empty cradles and morbid dirges and creaking wrought-iron vault doors? And his eyes. Now, in the raining darkness, they shined with eerie effulgence.

Jozsef did not want to know.

Somewhere, a woman sobbed and somewhere else a dog bayed mournfully. At the passage entrance—like the mouth of slag pit, heaped with mystery—Jozsef paused. Like the winery itself, it had been ravaged by bombs. He turned with a question on his lips, but Stanislav was gone. Like a cherished childhood memory, he had been blown away by time.

But a distant voice channeled through the wind: "Forgive me," it said. *"Forgive me."*

Swallowing, breathing hard, trembling, his head filled with the dank smell of the river, Jozsef slipped down into the darkness, into the echoing void of eternal blackness.

4

The plague brought a silence to the city as rats scratched in the walls of empty houses and wild dog packs haunted gutters awash in corpse-debris. Deserted streets were crowded with the sepulchral monuments of houses and buildings.

If there was a god who watched, then it was some malefic lord of charnel house and mausoleum harrow, its eye the bloated moon above, ghastly and sallow, staring down at the graveyard it had created, infinitely pleased, infinitely sated.

The plague raged on and on.

Sometimes there were crystal-white days of almost unnatural, eerie silence broken only by the moaning cemetery winds sweeping around houses, rattling gutters and ice-slicked rainspouts.

And on other days—

People burst out of doors and climbed out of windows, screaming and beating at themselves in some weird manic blood-rage, tearing out clumps of hair with gnarled fingers and scratching themselves until their blood ran red and hot as the fever boiling in their veins. Shrieking and stumbling around in the snow, massing in some lunatic danse macabre, they were half-dressed, naked, or wearing filthy sweat-stained nightshirts and robes fouled by the black vomit that gushed from their mouths. Singly or clutching one another, arm in arm, mother and babe, father and daughter, they whirled and pirouetted to and fro in a hysterical dance of death, round and round until they fell gasping and gray-faced.

Limbs still twitching, they stared into the sky, lips slicked with bile.

Some were dragged by caring hands back into houses.

Most died where they lay, freezing to death or dropping into corpselike comas from which they would never awaken: teeth chattering and faces steaming with sweat, eyes catatonic and fixed, death hollowing their cheeks and cooling their breath to frost.

5

The wine cellar tunnels.

Haunted by a cloying, palpable damp, they pressed in close. Cold brick, a misting chill, and the stagnant smell of places too long closed-up. Jozsef could hear water dripping and things skittering in the walls. The frost-breath of subterranean worlds hugged him like a sheet stripped from a cadaver. He could hear other sounds, too. Like clawed feet on concrete, paws racing through puddles. From time to time, a baneful melody echoed from unknown depths. He was not alone and knew it. But whether his fellow night-stalkers were furred or pink-skinned, he could not guess.

Listen.

Ten minutes that were ten long, claustrophobic days, Jozsef listened, his ears and their auditory mechanisms perked now to preternatural sharpness. He could hear his blood filling rivers and streams. Air quietly inflating the balloons of his lungs. The steady, neutral hum of neural networks at full alert.

He finally heard a sound and his brain processed it and did not like it.

Breathing.

A shallow, congested breathing somewhere close by. But in that impenetrable, grainy blackness, he could not be sure whether it was in front of him or behind. Fuzz coated his mouth and throat. There was a constricting tightness behind his eyes. That sound…it had a hollow sucking timbre to it like someone breathing into a paper bag.

Keep going.

He could feel debris beneath his step. Rocks, crumbled brickwork, mortar, other things he could not guess. One hand pressed to the chill, sweating wall of the tunnel, he pushed on, refusing to listen, to hear, to acknowledge those sounds that played around him like ghosts—breathing, shuffling footfalls, echoing whispers.

Something like icy fingers brushed the back of his neck and he screamed, running again. Running and stumbling and pulling himself up and wishing to God he had not listened to Stanislav. He fell over a heap of bricks and came to rest in an ice-slicked puddle near some shattered wine casks. Cold, shivering, he did not move. He did not dare to.

Footsteps.

Yes, coming his way now. *Clop, clop, clop.* They came on and brought a freezing stink like that of defrosting meat. When they were but a few feet away, they paused. Jozsef could hear ragged, whistling respiration, something like teeth grinding together. There was a dull shine in the darkness as of two eyes scanning the murk. With a smell now of powdery wrappings, dust, and worm-eaten coffin-linings, the footsteps moved off. Not forward or back, but off to the side. There must've been a passage there.

Fifteen minutes. Twenty.

Jozsef still had not moved. He waited. The footfalls had long since vanished into silence. He stood up, approached the wall, searching for the passage for reasons even he wasn't sure of. His fingers caressed bricks, the seams between, sheared through a netting of cobwebs. He had to know; he had to. Licking his lips with a tongue too large for his mouth, he struck a match, cupped its brilliance. Lurid, darting shadows jumped and lurked: his own. In the flickering orange light, he could see the scattered rubble. The body of a dead rat nearby. Pooled water, slime, filth, and wine barrels. But directly before him, there was no passage.

Who or whatever had passed this way, they had departed through a solid wall.

The match fell from his fingers, ended its life with a hiss at his feet.

He thought: *Some sort of auditory illusion, Jozsef. No solid thing can walk through walls and you do not believe in ghosts.*

He moved on, something in him trembling now, pressed tight into a corner.

Ahead...yes, he was certain of it now, a light, a yellowed illumination.

He approached it warily, soon enough realizing that it was only the moonlight streaming in through a ventilation grating. Its luminescence was gossamer, the color of white lace. He walked into it, his face latticed from the grating overhead. He could smell the streets, a stink of distant thunder and rain. The scant moonlight revealed other things he did not wish to see. To each side, the tunnel was crowded with human shapes. People sitting, backs against the walls. Long dead, they sat there, their hollow, cadaverous faces coveting the glow of the moon. They held skeletal hands, an emaciated lot that had starved en masse down here in the whispering shadows. Men, women, and children: mummies from a catacomb with black holes for eyes. A man in a rotted suit clutched a prayer book. A woman whose eyeless face was flaking away like the dry skin of an onion held a baby whose bones had thrust through its flesh. It grinned up at him, a tiny puckered skull.

Jozsef ran off, staying in the center of the tunnel, needing to be away from that lunatic embalming parlor, away from those staring, ruined faces.

A good distance away, he paused.

Behind him, a clutch of shadows entered the moonlight. Hunched, twisted forms, but small like children. They poured forth, dozens of them, insects from the mouth of a hive. And the sounds they made—high, reedy chatterings and shrill, echoing cries. Their distorted shadows washed through the tunnels in a black tide. Jozsef ran off again. He kept running until there was no breath in his lungs, until his chest ached and his heart strained. On his hands and knees, in that subterranean Golgotha, he wept and begged of God for deliverance. And maybe he got his wish, for the sounds of those pursuing goblins vanished now. Like a polluted river, they sluiced into a different branch, a different passage.

Safety for the flesh, but what of the mind?

Would his sanity ever be a strong and vital thing again? Or would it forever be altered, breached, reduced to some boneless thing that quivered in a carnival jar?

Jozsef rose to his tired feet.

A voice said: *"Thank God, I thought I was alone."*

He went white with fear, gray with dread. "Who is there?"

"My name is Bora," the voice said, that of a teenage girl. She was whimpering now, crying. "I'm lost...can you lead me out of here?"

"Yes. Yes, of course."

Her hand slid into his and he wondered how she could find it so easily when he was entirely blind in the gloom. He could see a vague shape, feel a cold, frail hand in his own. The flesh was damp, icy like the belly of a deep-sea fish.

"Come," he said. "We must go."

They walked together for maybe fifteen minutes while she sobbed. Her scent was of dead flowers and rain on concrete. The smell of desperation, of despair, of hopelessness.

"Have you any food, mister?" she finally asked.

"I...no, only my few meager belongings."

He could hear her teeth chattering. "I'm so cold...so hungry. I don't remember the last time I ate anything. It seems months. Could it be that long?"

"No," he assured her, his tone fatherly. "If you hadn't eaten in months, you would be—"

"But it has been so long, so very long. My father...we had a farm, a big farm. I can remember the vegetables in steaming pots of butter. The juicy racks of lamb, smoked hams and fire-roasted joints of beef. The smell and feel of a kitchen that was well-stocked..."

She went on and Jozsef was quite sure she was drooling.

They came to a gigantic heap of rubble that sealed the passage. But off in a side-burrow, light came from the streets above. Hand in hand, they ran together. An exit. Up the damp, leaf covered steps and into the dank, secret night.

"Thank you, mister," Bora said.

And then Jozsef got a good look at her and he yanked his hand away, shielding his eyes from looking upon that deathmask face.

He saw very well what he'd been holding hands with.

6

As the body count multiplied and staring cadavers were coveted in nearly every house, hideous rumors made their rounds as they always have in the time of plague. People were hanging themselves, slitting their wrists, jumping through windows, sliding the barrels of guns into their mouths, anything to avoid the death that came cloven-hoofed and red-eyed in the night. A seeping viral pestilence. The rumors said people did not just kill themselves, but each other. Mothers strangled infants in cribs and fathers stacked the sightless, blue-eyed corpses of their children in the snow, anything to spare them the distemper of the hungry plague. For death of the pestilence was a horror, but there were worse things. Things beyond death heard whispering on the wind in the dead of night, fantastic forms seen dancing through the snow looking for warmth and scratching at windows for entrance.

But those were stories, old wive's tales and evil fantasies creeping unfettered from the Dark Ages, reborn mouth to ear out of desperation, fear, and communal dread.

But it could not be denied that every day fewer doors were opened to greet the world and fewer shades were drawn to the thin winter sunlight. Like plundered caskets, neighborhoods stood empty. Where once there were the sound of footsteps and life, now there was only the creaking of gates and the scratching of tree limbs on rooftops. And it was not just in the city, but in the farming towns and villages that dotted the mountains: they stood deserted, wind-blown, and monolithic.

The sleep of death was unbroken. It lay over the world of men in a dirty yellow half-light by day, enshrouding it in a silken web of funeral crepe by night. And it was here, in the suffocating stillborn darkness, that shadows crawled and lurked, terrifying shapes ghosting through the night, white-faced, hungry-eyed, cackling a cold evil laughter of resurrection.

7

Pressed tightly against ravaged storefronts and empty plate glass windows soaped with grime, Jozsef saw bodies in the streets, starved things wrapped in rags. But he would not look upon them, would not see. He kept moving, refusing to remember who and what had held his hand in the tunnel. He was weak, he was tired. Surely none of it had happened. He paused at a dress shop, startled when he saw the figures in the windows staring at him and then laughing silently as he realized they were but mannequins. Their dresses were long since purloined. They were angular, dark forms, gaunt as anything that walked the streets this night.

He swallowed.

He realized he was insane now, for as he moved, slinked away, they turned and watched him, pushing lifeless wooden faces against the grimy glass, waxen fingertips tapping, tapping, tapping. Even wood and wax hungered this night.

Jozsef ran through neighborhoods of fallen buildings, empty houses, and weed-choked yards of sprawled corpses. He came around a corner and a crowd waited for him. Small, hunched, evil, they clawed out with tiny white fingers and funereal clown-white faces of graveyard landscape. Human insects, buzzing and needing. He could feel their tomb-cold spread out, filling him with icebergs and snowstorms. And their eyes, dear God, their eyes. Phosphorescent globes of frozen, autumnal moonlight.

As he ran, his mind began to create new systems of classification in its terror. Those who roamed in gangs stealing food, they were the First Level. The Second Level was the dying spread over the walks like dirty laundry. And the Third Level, yes, they had starved to death, but in death, still hungered.

It was demented, but it rang brightly with an element of truth.

He pushed on.

Running, hiding, trapped in some charnel netherworld where the shadows were alive and hungry, where death puppets starved even after the grave, where ghosts prowled and wraiths called him by name, wanting what he had in his sack and the warmth in his body. The night was a blizzard of hollowed faces and predatory eyes. Human hyenas waited to move in on the first smell of a kill, the first heady taste of meat.

He saw things, images that remained even when he pressed his eyes shut. The gaunt, wasted forms...people, but *not* people...that crawled through the rubble, crept up the walls of buildings like spiders on threads. They howled from rooftops and drifted through the sky like threadbare clouds. They slithered from cisterns and fed on cadavers in black, vile slums. Yes, everywhere, stark, electric lunacy. And above it all, a full, bloated moon like a stripped desert skull and below, things with eyes suffused with a necrotic lunar glow.

A block from his home, Jozsef wandered into a shimmering delta of mist that coalesced into a form with a peeled face of papery flesh. He saw cold lamp eyes, a body like a skeletal cabinet, a grinning mouth of carrion. The form drifted above him, caught in a cremated storm of bone dust and bits of cemetery fungi, wrapped in blowing, billowing cerements withered to spiderweb lace.

"Jozsef, Jozsef," said a voice of blank graveyard dimensions. "Jozsef...I hunger so...I starve...I starve, I'm so very hungry..."

Jozsef recognized the form of his mother, dead some seven months now. She floated towards him, whistling and shrieking as the wind blew through jagged rents in her winding sheet, her pipestem body. She moved and hissed and swooshed with the dead whisper of casket satin, the rush of black silk. Her hair was a blowing tornado of meadow grasses, her fingernails the length of yardsticks, blackened and corkscrewed. She danced and drifted in cold ribbons of moonlight.

Jozsef ran off, thinking that even the dead were begging for a few crusts of bread in this empty, gray world of open mouths and growling bellies. By this point, he was caught in some grim neutrality between laughter and tears and he couldn't seem to remember where he'd come from or what he'd seen and maybe, maybe part of him did not want to. He stumbled up the sidewalk, avoiding those with outstretched hands and moons for eyes. He slammed into a woman and spilled them both to the concrete.

He recognized her. "Lydia?" She was Emil Stanislav's wife. "I saw your husband tonight, I—"

"You saw nothing but a vapor," she told him, crossing herself. "My husband has been dead these many weeks."

She trotted away, wrapped tight in her black mourning clothes.

But Jozsef did not care. Wind and leaves in his face, the skull moon leering from above, he found his building, the worn doorway, felt the wood flake beneath his fingertips. Madness still buzzing in his brain, something warm and hopeful moved in him, brought him somewhere he needed to be. An island in the raging sea of insanity.

He looked back once and only once, seeing a tall, cadaverous man dressed in a long flapping coat of animal skins. His eyes were brilliant blood-cherries luminous with spectral light. Grinning, he opened his mouth and exhaled hot pestilence into the wind.

Shrinking inside, Jozsef slammed the door and the voracious beast was held at bay. At last, at last, he found a silence that was not deadly, that did not reach and claw and hunger. Here, the shadows had no teeth.

He moved up the narrow stairway, each creaking step was a childhood melody lost and rediscovered. Home. He was home. And he still had the food, the bulging potato sack of sausages, breads, flour—

The door to his flat.

Oh, old lonesome, time-scarred door with its tarnished knob fingered by too many dirty hands. Jozsef pressed the cup of one ear to the panel…inside there was a stillness of lonely fields and vacant lanes. His skin pebbled, a spider played at the base of his spine. The door was locked. Good…or bad?

He knocked lightly. Asleep, they surely must all be asleep.

"Jozsef?" a voice said, a voice of dust devils and waiting, of time suspended, of yellowed glass and patience. "Jozsef? Is that you?"

It was Elena's voice. Yes, weary. Yes, worried. Yes, fatigued, but surely never conquered. Not that. "Yes! Yes, open the door! Be quick!"

Hesitation. "Have…have you brought food?"

"A bag bursting with it!"

He could hear her coming now, a hissing rustle of shifts. The door was opened. Elena held a candle that flickered with yellow and orange shafts of brilliance. Knife-edged shadows rose up, a parade of magic lantern haunts. The glow consumed her face, threw hollows and worry ruts and sunken cheeks into pools of lampblack. "We have been starving, Jozsef. But that you are home is enough."

And then he was swallowed into the drafty throat of the flat and Elena's bony hands directed him into his chair. More candles were lit, the air smelling of tallow and age and dark spaces. The twins issued from a doorway, swam in shadow. Jolana—fair and blue of eye—and Janos—swarthy with eyes like chips of wet coal.

Along with their mother, they were emaciated, ribs jutting forth, cheekbones thrust from ashen complexions.

The children came to him and caressed him with thin, needle-fingers just as cold as icicles draped from January roofs. Their lips were flower petals pressed in mortuary books and their eyes, depthless catacombs.

Elena said, "Your friend came to see us, Jozsef. You're friend Emil Stanislav."

"Oh no...*nooooo*..."

The children drifted over him and through him like living, breathing mists from tombs. His wife moved in his direction, not walking, not stepping, but pushed along as if by some unseen current. Her skin was white and phosphorescent, her lips like withered roses, her eyes raging vortices of emerald light.

The potato sack forgotten, Jozsef fed his family, and out in the streets tenebrous shades in the form of men, women, and children blew through the lanes like disease germs.

But Jozsef did not know this. For he saw only the rising, glimmering full moons glowering from the red-rimmed sockets of his kin.

The moon in their eyes.

8

In the dim sunshine, the two men paused on the stairwell, both exhausted and worn thin by the things they had done and would yet do. The house smelled of age and misery and poverty. Rats scratched in the walls.

"Well?" said the first man, drawing off a pipe.

"The army has arrested a criminal. A slaver."

"Yes?"

The second man nodded. "Yes. His name is Kosar. He is from Budapest. He was interrogated." The man shivered. "He said that seven boxes of earth were loaded on a Bodrog freighter three days ago. They were bound overseas. England or America, he was not sure."

"Then we are free of Griska and his brides."

"Yes. God willing, they take the plague with them." He shook his head. "It is that seventh box that concerns me. It was said to be as large as a piano crate. Much larger even."

They just looked at each other, fearing to speculate.

The first man emptied his pipe and looked up the stairwell. "Let's get this done then." Taking four sharpened stakes of whitethorn from his bag, he led the way up to the flat of Jozsef Vajda.

PART TWO: GHOST TOWN

1

Wenda was thinking that although she was young and strong in body, inside her soul felt very old like some stained and yellowed—but precious—relic an old woman kept in a high cupboard to remind her of better days. She wanted to be brave and fearless in all things this night, but that old soul of hers was pessimistic with portent of all things bad and baneful. It sensed deathly things on the wind and in the forms of the mortiferous shapes striding through the storm.

Though that awful screeching/wailing had ceased outside, she was still hearing it echoing in her skull and she was scared. She could feel the fear bunching in her shoulders and straining her neck, creeping about at the edges of her thoughts and sliding through her belly like black grease. It was instinct, she knew. An ancient, uncivilized knowledge of evil afoot and the dire threat to not only herself but the members of her little flock.

There was a wolf in the fold and it was moving in closer, slavering jaws opening wider.

Although her body tensed with exhilaration, readying itself for battle, her mind felt old, weary, and wanted to sleep. Her eyelids wanted to shut and it seemed she was staving off exhaustion through sheer force of will and not much more.

But she thought: *You can't sleep this night and you know it. You don't dare close your eyes before sunrise because if you do you might never open them again. Maybe you're tired and maybe those things out there are sending something at you that's* making *you tired. That's what they want. By nature, they're cowards. All predators are. They want an easy kill. They do not want a fight. Why do you think bloodsuckers come in the dead of night? They prefer their victims weak, drugged with sleep, brains cloudy with dreams.*

It makes it so much easier for them.

Fighting off drowsiness, she tossed another log in the fire and Morris jumped. Jumped, but still stared into the flames like some primitive savage who could trust nothing but the light and the heat and blazing coals, his personal anathema against evil spirits. She checked the lanterns and the kerosene in them was getting down. They would need more.

"I wish that screaming would stop," Morris said.

"It has stopped," Wenda told him. "Listen."

"You're right," he said. "What time is it?"

"It's a little after eleven."

"Jesus Christ. Dawn's a million miles away."

An exaggeration, but from where they were sitting, essentially true.

Wenda kept thinking of weak links because she knew that Megga could not be trusted and Morris was a lost cause. He had folded up and he was like a little boy now. She wanted to hate him for that. For being weak when she needed him to be strong. She wanted to shout at him and slap him but that was only her own frustration and fear looking for an outlet and she knew it. Yet, she thought he was a fool. Childlike and absurd. A man in the studio and boardroom where the only real threats were to his wallet, but when it counted he was just a little boy. And because his mind had become simple again, like it might have been when he was seven years old, she knew he was a weak link and those outside could easily trick him. His childlike mind would not recognize the threat. It could be easily swayed, seduced, and corrupted by a greater wickedness just like that of a child who is tempted into the backseat of a car or into a lonely wood by candy and the saccharine promises of a stranger.

In her thinking, there was no greater fool than a man who refused to act like one.

You're being harsh and judgmental, she told herself.

But the truth of the matter was that she could not afford to be anything else. She had been a quiet, shy sort of girl once upon a time. A bumbling and clumsy child. Then, via genetics, she had blossomed into a beauty as a teenager. Something that made her feel even more uncomfortable in her skin as if people might see her and think, *yes, Wenda's a very pretty girl on the outside, but inside she's still a meek and mealy little mouse.* As if they would sense that she was pretending to be something she was not. Like a greasy little mechanic taking a rich man's Jag for a drive, pretending to be a bigshot when everyone else knew differently. Only as Vultura did her personality rise to be the equal of her body. But for all that, she was not conceited and narcissistic. She did not worship her own image and expect others to do the same. She'd had reams of sympathy for others. She was kind and caring.

But right now, that was gone.

She felt almost…pitiless.

Don't be like that. Don't become some soulless thing. If you do that you're no better than those things outside. Morris can't help it that he's weak. Megga can't help being attracted to the dark side.

Megga?

Wenda opened her eyes and realized that, at some point, she had sat down in a chair by the fire and was dozing off.

She looked around.

Morris was still at the fire and Megga…*shit.*

"Get away from that window," Wenda said.

Megga ignored her. She had the curtains parted and was staring forlornly out into the storm. Wenda charged over there. She was going to grab Megga and physically toss her away from the window. But when she got there, Megga said, "Look."

From that vantage point, when the snow quit blowing for a second or two, she could see the front of the federal house that Doc and the others had escaped into. It was surrounded by dozens of shadowy forms. They were all standing out there, just waiting.

Wenda felt a chill run through her that only increased when she saw two children outside the window before her: a boy and a girl. Their eyes were huge and dark like bullet holes in pale vellum. Their pallid faces seemed to glow like moonflowers. They were both grinning, their teeth long and sharp.

"Go away," she said under her breath. "Just go away."

She still had the stake in her hand, so she raised it so they could see it and they both flinched, it seemed, momentarily, understanding exactly what she was going to do with it when the time came. They pulled back into the storm and right before Wenda closed the curtains she saw them standing to either side of a tall, gaunt figure that looked to be dressed in a long ragged fur coat. She saw his face for just a second—white and hollow-cheeked with prominent cheekbones and a hawkish Slavic nose, a trailing gray mustache. And eyes…red eyes burning with a hatred and malevolent wrath that made her feel weak in the knees.

Then the storm buried them and the curtain was closed.

"You saw him didn't you?" Megga said.

Wenda swallowed. "Stay away from the window. You're weak. You're too easily…*swayed* by those things."

Megga sneered at her and sat on the sofa. "If they want to come in, they'll come in."

"If they could, they would. They're looking for an opening and you're not going to be it," Wenda promised her. And when she saw Megga glaring her, she smiled thinly and said, "Don't fuck with me."

Megga looked away.

Wenda couldn't help thinking that once she'd really liked Megga. They'd laughed and had fun together both on and off the set of *Chamber of Horrors.* Now she hated her. She saw her as the weakest link of all and she detested her for it. The only difference between Megga and those things outside was that she didn't have fangs. But that was coming, oh yes, that was coming.

"Man, I gotta pee," Morris said.

Oh great, Wenda thought. *What next?*

2

They had Bailey on the couch now. She'd had some kind of seizure, Doc said, and to whether that was from losing so much blood to the hag or because of shock or both he could not say. She was pale, her throat still dark with dried blood, and when she did open her eyes, the pupils were dilated and unfocused. She was caught in the sleepy post-seizure netherworld of the epileptic.

It would pass, Doc assured them. It would pass.

He doesn't believe that at all, Reg thought.

He had all the faith in the world in Doc. He loved the guy. He was like the cool uncle he never had or the solid, introspective, stone-cool father he never knew. Reg would have crawled naked through a fire ant mound with honey on his ass for him. But, right then, he could hear it on Doc's voice: *doubt.* What Doc was saying he was saying for the purposes of general morale, to keep spirits maybe not flying, but at least from dragging their chins on the ground. He'd been a combat medic in 'Nam. He knew his shit. So when Reg heard the doubt in his voice he knew Bailey was in real trouble.

Doc had bandaged her neck, but they lacked disinfectant. She needed medical care badly. *And maybe a priest,* Reg was thinking.

"She looks pretty pale," Burt said. "How much blood you figure she lost?"

Doc sighed. "Quite a bit, I'm guessing."

"But that...that fucking *thing* was only on her for maybe ten seconds at most."

Doc just shrugged.

Reg was trying hard to disguise the hate he was feeling for Burt right then but it was burning hot through him like shrapnel. When the shit had come down—and man had it come down—Burt hadn't done a damn thing. He'd dropped to his ass with a dumb/confused/helpless sort of look like a little boy who'd heard a voice from his closet and was going to piss his pants and suck his thumb. Even when Reg had rammed the poker through that fucking witch for the second time—*and, man, was that some weird-ass shit or what? Poker went through her real easy like she wasn't even flesh and blood but maybe stuffed with straw*—and they had her, it had been Doc that had picked up the axe and chopped her head off.

Burt had done nothing. Maybe if he had acted like a man that witch wouldn't have gotten her teeth into Bailey in the first place.

"How could that thing suck that much blood out of her that fast?" Burt said.

But Doc just shrugged again.

"Maybe if you'd have helped us, dude, she wouldn't have gotten *any,*" Reg heard himself say before he could stop.

Burt got that wild look in his eyes again. "Meaning what exactly, kid?"

"Meaning you folded up on us. We needed you, *Bailey* needed you, and all you could fucking do was crawl into the corner and hide."

"You better watch your fucking mouth," Burt told him.

But Reg was on a roll and he wasn't about to watch anything. This had to be said, in his way of thinking. "Don't waste your time with that tough-ass shit, Burt. I know what you are. We *all* know what you are now. You're a fucking coward. You're a fucking pussy. You're not even a man."

Burt made a beeline for him and Reg waited, wanting nothing better than to slap him up and beat him down, but Doc got in the way. "Enough," he said. "We have enough problems without in-fighting. What happened, happened. Let's leave it at that."

Burt looked from Reg and then to Doc. "It happened so fast. I didn't have time...I just didn't have time." He waited for acknowledgment of the same from Doc, but Doc would not even look at him. "Wasn't time," he said again, sounding almost wounded.

"We found the time," Reg said.

Burt shook a finger at him and Reg just laughed down in his throat. "Don't bother threatening, man. I know a coward when I see one. I know a little fucking girl."

"ENOUGH!" Doc said. "I WON'T HAVE THIS!"

That took the starch out of both of them; at least temporarily. Doc was mellow as milk, but when he got his back up, you didn't want to be on the receiving end of his temper. Reg had only seen him lose it once on the *Chamber of Horrors* set...but it sent people scurrying under desks.

Bailey opened her eyes. She did not look so good. There were dark circles under her baby blues and she was pale like somebody had pancaked the color from her cheeks. "I'm thirsty," she said. "I'm so thirsty."

Doc looked over at Burt. "Go into the kitchen and see if that hand pump works. Fill a pitcher and bring some cups."

"Out there?" Burt said. "Shit, Doc, you know what happened the last time we opened that door."

"Sure, you lost your nuts," Reg said.

"Fuck you."

"I'll go with you, Burt. I'll even hold your hand, man."

Burt was ready to go at it again but Doc silenced him with a look. "I'll do it. You two watch over our patient and, please, try to act civilized."

Then he was out the door without a moment's hesitation and Reg hoped that yellow prick Burt saw that. Saw how a real man handled himself.

Bailey was looking up at him and *through* him like he wasn't even there. As if he were a sheet of glass, a window, and she was seeing something far more interesting beyond him. Her eyes were huge and glassy, he noticed, and they rarely blinked. He didn't like it at all. He was holding her hand and it was cool to the touch, but there was a dew of fever sweat on her forehead.

"How you feeling?" he asked her.

She attempted a smile that came out looking more like a grimace. "Dreams, weird dreams."

"Tell me," he said.

Maybe she heard him and maybe she didn't, but she went off on her own tangent, mixing up yesterday with today and last week with last month. She was talking about the shoots they'd been on like they were still happening and saying she better call her mom because she hadn't in awhile and she had to get some food for her cat and she was so weak she must have the flu and who was that woman in her dream?

"What woman?" Reg asked.

Bailey moved her lips like she was trying to form a name. "She has the weird eyes. The big weird eyes...she says she can't get younger without me. She wanted to kiss me. On the neck."

Reg heard Burt make a choking sort of sound and retreat.

Then Doc came back with the water. He filled a blue-speckled cup half-way and handed it to Reg. Reg lifted up Bailey's head and brought the cup to her lips. She got a couple sips off it and then her head began to thrash from side to side, her body jerking with convulsions like she'd just swallowed rat poison and not well water. She vomited out most of it, then she settled down, going limp as a noodle, listless and tapped-out.

"It's all right, it's all right," Reg kept saying. "It's all gonna be okay. You'll see. Everything'll be fine."

Her hand was loose now in his, but while she'd had the convulsion she'd nearly crushed it with a strength that was shocking.

"You sure that water's okay?" Burt said.

"It's fine. I drank some myself," Doc told him.

"Then...?"

But Doc would not meet his eyes. "She's got something going on...and I'd rather not put a name to it."

3

Half-dozing in her chair, Wenda thought of David.

She hadn't consciously thought of him in a long time.

She hadn't *allowed* herself to.

David Sellers had been her only true love. A thin, funny man who produced jazz records in New York City. He was the one. She would have spent her life with him. David was manic depressive. When he was low, he could have crawled under a curb. But when he was high…well, look out, he was a world-beater: charming, self-confidant, passionate, boundlessly enthusiastic. About the time they would have fallen into bed together to consummate their relationship, she stopped by his apartment in Albany unannounced.

He hadn't called in two days.

That meant he was bottoming out.

When she went in with her own key, there was a strange odor in the air. Not death exactly, but almost something that wanted to *become* death, if that meant any sense. Which it did later to Wenda, but not so much at the time.

She found him in his rocking chair.

It was turned away from the TV so he could face a blank, white wall. He had laid both of his wrists open and he was painted red with his own blood. Panicking, of course, because Wenda Keegan would not have been Wenda Keegan without some good old hysterics, she started this way, then that, sobbing and moaning and completely out of her element.

There were things you did in situations like this, but she could not remember what they were.

Finally, she called 911.

They told her to get some pressure on his wrists, tie a tourniquet on his arms if at all possible.

She wrapped his wrists in towels very tightly but the blood kept flowing. It soaked through them and her tourniquets—two of David's belts—weren't working so good.

What she remembered most was the blood, all that damn blood, and David opening his eyes once during it all and giving her a look that seemed to say, *Boy, did I ever fuck up things this time.* And Wenda had had a mad desire to tell him, *Yes, yes, you did. You've just fucked up things for both of us and I fear what I'll become if they don't get that fucking ambulance here right now and save your life.* But she hadn't, of course. Her mind was filled with many crazy thoughts but none of them got past the whimpering coming out of her mouth.

As David slipped further and further into the darkness, she clutched him tighter and tighter, trying to hold up his wrists above heart level like they said while squeezing the wounds tightly in the towels.

NO! NO! NO! NO! NO! NO, DAVID! she heard her own voice screaming in her head. *DON'T YOU DARE DIE ON ME! GODDAMMIT, DAVID! STAY WITH ME! STAY WITH ME!*

His eyes half-opened as if he could hear her thoughts, then his head slumped to the side and she knew he was dying. That the beauty and goodness of this man had all but run out with his blood.

"DAVID! DAVID! OH DEAR GOD DAVID! DON'T DO THIS! DON'T DIE!"

But he was dying and she knew it as she sobbed and screamed as the paramedics arrived. As they took him away and her with them, she hoped beyond hope and prayed.

David, David…dear God.

He'd crashed several weeks before. He had hooked up with Public TV in Manhattan to co-produce a documentary on Charlie Parker and the Beat Generation. He was flying high. Then, after sixteen weeks of work, using up every available minute of time, the funding was cut and the doc was canceled. David was inconsolable. He was dragging bottom. Wenda had slowly, patiently brought him back up and he was doing pretty good. Maybe not flying as high as old Charlie "Bird" Parker, but there was hope. He was going ahead with the doc. He was too invested in it to stop by then. He would raise the money himself and sell it to the Discovery Channel or some similar venue.

Day by day, he was his old self.

When Wenda hadn't heard from him in two days, she thought he was deep into the doc.

Then she walked into his apartment after a day of silent foreboding she could not put a name to. When the doctor came out of the ER and told her he was sorry, she barely nodded.

This happened just after graduation from Stony Brook U when she'd been hired on at WKKX, long before *Chamber of Horrors*. After that, she dated no men. She touched no men. She cringed when one touched her in the most platonic way. And on those rare occasions when she touched herself, she saw only David's face. He haunted her mind and lived in her soul and invaded her dreams. And very often, as she fell asleep at night, she distinctly heard his voice say, *Wake-up, Wenny. Wake-up.*

She always did, but he was never there. And the crazy thing was, she hoped he would be. That his death was nothing but a dark, feverish nightmare.

Vultura had helped her enormously.

It had channeled her creativity and given her a purpose, but there never had been any more men. Or women, for that matter. There was safety in solitude and it was all she knew.

4

Wenda, of course, could never understand what it was like, Megga knew, because she had that fine, pure light in her eyes that was reflected from her soul. She could never understand how it was to be carved from death right from the start or how it felt to know the shadows were creeping in on you and the darkness wanted to own you. Those were things that were far beyond Wenda's mindset. She might host a TV show and play a ghoul, but she never understood the dark side or dipped her fingers into the black blood running beneath its surface.

Look at her over there, Megga thought, *with that fucking stake and her silver knife.*

Yes, Wenda had a ferocious look in her eyes like those weapons made her a real world-beater, but she didn't stand a chance. You couldn't fight those outside with a blade and a pitiful slat of wood. She thought she would do the impaling, but the truth was it was *she* who would be impaled. And it would not be easy for her. Those out there were angry and Megga could feel their thoughts like hot black oil filling her skull. They would make Wenda suffer. They would make an example out of her. They would break her in the worst way possible. The attack would be vicious. They would tear her throat out and hang her by the feet and shower themselves in her blood.

Yet, Wenda was so sure of herself.

That angered Megga; Wenda had never been sure of herself before. And now that she was, it was disturbing. It enraged Megga and filled her mouth with a taste like hot steel that she could not swallow down. She knew the undead were going to come and when they did, they would initiate her because they wanted *her* to deal with Wenda, to destroy her, to strip her down to the most basal level of primal fear. She could almost taste Wenda's blood now and that not only sickened her, but excited her. She knew it would be the biggest, nastiest, dirtiest orgasm imaginable and, God, how she needed that right now.

Poor Wenda.

Poor stupid, deluded little Wenda.

The one who stands behind the others.

Yes, Megga had seen him out there and felt the formless terror he always inspired. He was ruthless. He was undying and irresistible. Even now she could hear his cold triumphant laughter and see his white craggy face that had been old when Cobton was new. He had a name and she knew what it was, but she did not dare say it aloud for he might not like that. She did not want to be his enemy. She knew what he did with those that disobeyed or raised a hand against him. He pulled them apart like a boy picking the wings off a fly. He desecrated them and broke them, peeled off their hides and drained them dry. He had filled graveyards with his enemies.

But she could not tell Wenda that.

Because Wenda would say, *then I'll kill him first.*

Megga tried to control her breathing. Tried to avoid looking at the window because he was out there now peering through the curtains at Wenda. And knowing this, Megga could feel the furnace heat between her legs cooking her from the inside out.

5

In the end, Doc did not feel too guilty about any of it.

After Bailey had settled down, Burt announced that he was waiting no more. It was time to make a run for that car. Despite the fact that Reg and he were ready to go at it at any time, Reg had gone with him to scout out the best way which was a window in the back looking out on the square.

Even Reg had tried to talk him out of the idea.

But Burt was resolute: he would do this.

He claimed it was for the good of all but, of course, Doc didn't believe that. In his mind Burt was a sniveling little self-centered weasel. A weakling. And like most weaklings he was quick with his fists because it was the easiest way to prove he was not as weak as he in truth knew he was.

Outside, there was only the snow falling, the wind blowing it around. The storm had abated a bit, but not significantly. As Reg began working the window loose so it could be slid up, Doc tried one more time. "Burt…you don't have to do this."

"Oh, yes I do."

Doc wondered if maybe his motivation was not so much selfishness now but an almost puerile need to prove himself after he'd locked-up when the hag had gone after Bailey. Maybe it was the same thing that drove kids on dares, made them eat a bug under a log or sneak into deserted houses or play chicken with a knife.

Okay," Reg said. "You ready?"

Burt nodded.

Reg shook his head and slid the window up. A blast of frozen air came in like an exhalation from a polar tomb. It was cold in the house, too, when you got away from the fire, but not this cold. Doc could smell something ancient and corrupt on the wind.

Burt swung a leg up onto the sill, pulling his gloves on. He looked at Doc and Reg like some hero in an old movie going into the breach, maybe wishing he had a screenwriter handy to feed him some famous last words. He offered them a thin smile, saying, "I'll lay on the horn when I get around front. Be ready." Then he slipped out the window and landed in a snowdrift. He pulled himself up, brushing snow free and fighting forward into the wind, trudging through the heavy snowfall.

Reg shut the window.

They watched him moving slowly out into the storm, pausing and looking around, then moving off through the courtyard to the fence beyond. The blizzard kicked up and he was gone, lost behind driving sheets of white.

Doc checked his watch. It had been fifteen minutes. "I better get back to Bailey," he said.

Reg nodded, staring through the glass and hoping to get a good look at Burt out there but visibility was down to less than ten feet. Doc left him there, knowing they'd never see Burt again and if they did, it would be bad beyond imagining.

It was his idea and no one else's.

That's what Doc told himself as he made his way back to the parlor. Yet...he felt a twinge of guilt. He always felt sorry for people like Burt. Those that had to prove themselves. Those who lost their nerve when the chips were down and had to overcompensate for it. He'd seen plenty of guys like that in the war and most of them had been much like Burt.

Sighing, Doc let himself into the parlor.

Bailey was still on the sofa, sleeping.

He threw another log on the fire and the blaze leapt up, throwing flickering shadows over the walls. The warmth chased the frost from his bones right away. He lit a cigarette and hoped Reg wouldn't stay out there too long.

Then he saw the wet spots on the floor.

Water?

Yes, it was water. There were droplets of it leading from the window to the sofa as if somebody had come in out of the storm and snow had been dropping from them. *Shit.* He went over to Bailey. Her breathing was shallow, her flesh pallid and moist to the touch. But she was still alive.

But just…

You old fool! They were just waiting for you to leave so they could slip in and feed on her. One of them must have called to her from the window. And Bailey, of course, being weak and delirious had answered. The seduction must have been effortless in her state.

"Yes," she would have said. "Come in."

And one of them had. Maybe Bailey had even opened the window for them.

He felt empty with guilt and remorse. He should have known better. They'd been playing this game God only knew how long. Of course they were one step ahead of him. Of course they waited until he was gone. The hag who'd come into the room earlier had been a mindless, predatory thing, a leech motivated by hunger. But there were others. And many of them would be quite cunning from the centuries.

"Oh, Bailey," he said. "I'm so sorry…my poor child…"

He checked her eyes and the pupils were so huge they were like glistening black onyx, the whites threaded with bloodshot veins. He closed them again, barely able to catch his breath. He had failed her. He had truly failed her.

Her eyes were open again. They were like glass.

"No, Bailey," he said.

She grinned at him.

6

They weren't worth saving. None of them.

This is what Burt thought as he waited near the fence for the wind to lessen a bit and make sure that he was alone because that was the most important thing: being alone. If those things found him out here, his goose was cooked. Cooked? Hell, it was seasoned, hot-buttered, and well-fucking-chewed.

Don't think that shit. Just get to the car.

Sure, good idea. Only now the storm was really kicking up and he couldn't see a damn thing. The snow was up to his hips in places and he was moving roughly at the same pace he did in those dreams he had where he was always running, always fleeing something that he could never quite see (which, he always felt upon wakening, was a good thing). It was just like that. Like his boots were filled with concrete.

He was trying desperately not to think of that thing that had called to him out of the storm after the bus accident. He had to put it out of his mind or the fear would overtake him and he wouldn't be able to think straight. And if that happened, he was going to make a mistake.

Here I am, Burt...right...here...

No, he had to block it. He couldn't afford the luxury of fear. Out here and especially on this night of all nights, a mistake, a misstep could be extremely fatal.

Burt...over here, Burt...I'm waiting for you—

Knock it off!

It wasn't anything but his nerves in the first place. A hallucination. Fear combined with shock produced it. He wouldn't be the first one to have something like that happen. The thing was, he knew, to keep his head, keep his eye on the money and that was the car. Nothing else existed, only the car.

He pushed on further, the snow blowing in his face and down his back. The cold got inside him in a killing frost, the wind trying to drive him not just back but down. Down where it could shroud him in white and keep him like a leg of lamb until first thaw. Snow-devils whipped into him, covering his face so that he had to paw the snow clean so he could see again. His eyes were watering, his nose running. His mustache already stiff with ice. He was very much beginning to think this wasn't such a good idea at all. But he shook that from his head because it would have meant Doc was right and there was no way Burt was going to let himself think shit like that.

Doc was not right.

And neither was that punk Reg.

They were wrong. They were the real cowards because they were afraid to try what he was trying.

Just a few more feet now. With every lumbering footstep, his boots broke through the crust of snow with volume. It sounded like breaking glass to him. The good thing was the wind was so damn loud with its moaning and howling, he doubted whether anyone or any*thing* could hear him.

A few more plodding steps and he made it to the fence, gripping its iced uprights in both gloved fists.

There. The first leg complete.

He sank into the snow on his knees and it came up above his belly. How easy it would have been to wait right there, to sink down in the snow and wait for morning. Let the drift pile up over him like a thick woolen blanket and just close his eyes and wait for the sun. How easy. How perfectly easy. And when morning came he'd get up, brush himself clean, then start that damn Suburu Outback, pull her around front and knock on the door. They'd all be startled, of course. *Thought you were lost out in it,* they'd say. *Driven under or maybe those things pulled you down into their tombs.* He'd laugh at the folly of it all—in fact, he could hear himself laughing right now with a loud, booming sound—and he'd look them in the eye. Especially that bag of wind Doc and his sidekick, that mama's boy Reg. He'd look them monkeyskulls right in the face and say, *Me? Old Burt? Hell, that wasn't nothing but a flurry last night. I just waited it out, caught a couple Zs.* He could just about see the hangdog look on their faces. He could see Miss Fancytits, Wenda Keegan, and that raven-haired Megga standing there. Both looking hungry on account they'd finally found a real man. Maybe he'd have them both at the same time—

Burt cleared his head.

Christ, what was this? A mind movie? A daydream?

He had to keep his shit together here. People died in storms like this. He had to remember that. The snow was moving around him in curtains of white, shutting him out from the world, pulling him down and keeping him here in this pocket of subzero night. He peeked behind him in the dimness and could see his own footprints, but they were filling in fast and losing definition. In ten more minutes they'd be gone, gone, gone.

Snowstorm like this, man, it reminded him of boy's camp when he was a kid. It was up in the Catskills and they had winters up there. Bad winters. They called it Winter Camp and it was a place to ski, snowshoe, skate, and get to know the real outdoors. They sent kids like him there from Brooklyn, the Bronx, and Queens. At night, the winds would scream around the lodge and the older kids would say it was ghosts, snow-ghosts, the spirits of people who'd been lost in blizzards that were always looking for kids they could invite into the storm and bury in the snow. That shit scared Burt. It really did. But what scared him worse was when they said that the caretaker up there, an old needle-nosed Yankee named Orlen Benz, had himself a taste for young boys. Sometimes he took them out to his shed by the creek and they weren't ever seen again. That's what the older boys said. Burt believed it. He thought old Orlen stole the boys away and ate them like an ogre living in a cave. But that's not what the boys meant. Orlen had a *different* sort of taste and maybe one that was even worse. World was full of trash, though, and you had to be careful. Burt's old man had always said that and he knew because he tailgunned on a garbage truck, making the route through Flatbush six days a week. *New York, New York,* he always said. *The town so nice they named it twice. Full of rats and full of lice.* Yeah, that was his old man. One time they'd found a human skull in a garbage can and that was a story for Halloween night. It all started when—

Fuck are you doing, dipshit? Sitting here in the snow gripping the uprights of the fence like a little brat that wants to get out of his crib. Just dreaming away...

Burt's whole body was feeling numb and it was just too easy to want to go to sleep or dream it all away because the snow was like a weave of gray-white, a dream-blanket that wanted to cover you and put you to sleep.

He forced himself to his feet and his knees didn't care for it much at all. His breath came out in billowing white clouds that blew right back into his face along with the snow and wind and what felt like a scrim of loose ice. Jesus. What a night. The fence was one of those old-fashioned types, he saw. Black wrought-iron with lots of fancy metal scrollwork and filigree, sharp ornamental spikes up on top. He had actually toyed with the idea of climbing up and over...but those spikes...sort of thing that could spear a testicle. What a sight that would be.

He pushed through drifts, falling and panting, only staying on his feet because he gripped the fence. He followed it over to the gate. His hands were numb. So were his feet. His whole body was getting stiff from the cold. He needed to get out of these drifts and out onto the road where his legs could do some pumping that would get his blood flowing again.

He looked behind him.

For a moment he saw the looming federal house like some vague gray shape, but then it was gone in the snowfall. The wind kept trying to strip him free of the fence. It was punching into him, slapping him in the face and making him wince. The snow was falling heavier now, thick and encompassing, the flakes caught in a mad whirl around him like a million-billion pissed-off hornets buzzing and circling.

The gate.

There.

He got hold of it and would not let it go. It was mired in the snow, part way open a few feet which would work well. He'd just scoot around it and then climb over the snowbank and the road would be right there in front of him, the car waiting. Easy as pie. He caught occasional, quick glances of the town rising around him whenever the storm allowed it. The buildings and houses were all tall and leaning, dark shadows that were monolithic and crouching like they were waiting to spring on him.

He blinked his eyes. Something moved out there.

He looked again and the snow obscured it.

He thought for sure he'd seen a form out there pulling off into the shadows. He dismissed it. Just the moving membrane of the snow, the weird half-light of the blizzard, lots of leaping shadows created by the blizzard winds and snow.

Yet, knowing these things, a blade of fear still entered his heart. It was not a rational fear where there's an obvious threat or anxiety. This was different. It was bleak and irrational. He could feel it all around him now and it was the same sort of fear he'd felt at Winter Camp when the snow-ghosts cried out at night and made him shiver in his bed. His teeth were chattering. He thought he heard something like a rustling sound moving out there but there was no way he would have heard it in the storm. Yet, he *did* hear it and now he heard it again.

As he began to move around the gate, he stopped, listening.

Listening like an animal.

He could feel it right up his spine and down low in his belly: he was not only being watched, he was being stalked. Something was following him...only it was the sort of thing that made no sound as it moved over the crust of snow. It was silent like river mist and smoke and midnight damp: it came and it went but you never saw it.

Burt was at the point where he was beginning to truly doubt the wisdom of what he was doing. Hell, maybe he *should've* listened to Doc. Maybe, maybe, maybe. But he couldn't go back now because what was stalking him was right behind him and if he retreated now he'd run face-to-face into it...only it wouldn't have a face, of course. Nothing but cold, cruel bone grinning at him, empty eye sockets filled with boiling darkness staring out at him.

What a thing to meet in the middle of a blizzard—

Stop it. Get to that car!

Yes, that was the voice of reason and it should have canceled out the dark ruminations of his imagination and that building superstitious fear within him but it did not. The fear clung to the underside of his psyche like a black spider suckling his soul, growing fat on his terror and the night-juice of his dread.

He got around the gate, refusing to listen any longer.

The wind could do things to your imagination.

The snow was thrown in his face, moving in great shifting blankets of white, the wind pummeling him mercilessly. It was screaming from the throat of the storm in a wailing banshee voice that sounded like dozens of children crying out in abject terror. Yes, that and more: not just the sound of terror, but of agony and death and the formless blackness that waits beyond the pale, beyond the rim of the grave itself.

Panicking, Burt tried to run through the snow and he slipped and went into a drift. He came up swearing at his own clumsiness, brushing the snow free. But swearing silently because he did not want to be heard by what was behind him. He started moving again. The snowbank was right in front of him. It was more than six feet in height, probably well over seven. Morris—or his sponsors—had paid to get the town plowed clean. Burt started climbing up it but it was heard to get a foothold in the powder and he kept slipping back down. God, it had been so easy when he was a kid to scramble up and down snowbanks.

He started up again and slid back down just as quick.

And behind him, a rustling sound.

He turned and saw a figure there at the perimeter of the wind-driven snow, just inside the fence. It was tall and lean, wrapped in a graying shroud. A graveyard angel. It had a hood but no face that he could see...just a hollow that led into blackness. It stood still as a statue. The wind made its shroud flap like a bedsheet on a clothesline, but what was beneath did not stir even an inch.

It did not speak, but a sound came from it: buzzing, as of insects.

He went white with panic. It was the thing that had called out to him in the storm. It was back. It was coming for him.

With a cry, he started climbing again.

The Angel of Death. Dear God, it's the Angel of Death.

He slid down a foot or more and looked back, horror rising in him like bile. The shrouded figure was closer now. It was standing outside the gate. It did not speak. It did not move...yet, it was getting closer. If it caught him, it would enfold him in those arms and bury him in that worm-eaten shroud.

Climb!

The terror unraveling him strand by strand, his eyes bright with lucid fright, he climbed and reached the top. And it was then his boots slipped again on the powder and he began to slide. With a manic cry he reached out for purchase. Boulders of snow broke apart in his hands. Snow was forced up his pants and sleeves. His left boot found something solid and up he went.

The buzzing was louder.

I'm closer now, Burt...so much closer.

He looked behind him.

The Death Angel was at the bottom of the snowbank reaching out to him with hands that were as gray as the shroud it wore. They looked to be flecked with winter-dead lichen. The fingers were threaded with cobwebs as if it had only recently left some ancient tomb. Its cerements flapped, ragged ribbons of cloth or tissue blowing in the wind. He could see its mouth now, its jaws. The graying seamed flesh speckled with mold, the red lips pulled back from yellow teeth and sharp canines. The bloodstained chin from its previous feeding.

Again, it did not move.

It offered its tombstone gray hands, the fingers of which were long and slender, definitely female...its yawning mouth. Like it was caught in freeze-frame, it waited motionless, something carven from marble.

That's when he knew. All those dreams he'd had of escape, of running from something—this is what he had been running from.

Her.

She was death hunting him.

I'm almost there, Burt.

He screamed and threw himself over the top of the snowbank, rolling down the other side into the blowing snow, finding his feet, pulling himself up into the wind that shrieked his name. The road was badly drifted, but he ran forward, tripping, sliding, but refusing to go down. The storm squalled and pushed him back, but he fought on, seeing the car now.

He would make it.

He had to make it.

He turned and the Death Angel was just behind him, reaching out, her teeth on display. They were poised to puncture his throat and she was poised to empty him like an upturned flask. She would drain him and make sure he felt every depraved, grisly moment of his violation.

That steady, droning buzz was even louder, filling his head with tiny wings.

The car.

He saw two forms go running behind it. They looked like children...almost. That stopped him, the snow funneling at him and making him cry out with the cold. It was tapping him. He didn't have much time left.He felt an icy breath at the back of his neck.

He looked back, slipping, and fell. The shrouded woman was inches away, the nails of her bloodless hands nearly scraping across his eyes. His mind filled with a white noise, he crawled on hands and knees through the snow, punching through drifts as the car got closer and closer. He got to his feet and saw huge, shaggy forms perched atop the snowbanks, watching. They were wolves with shaggy pelts, red leering eyes and slavering jaws.

He stumbled away to the car, whimpering now, broken by despair and fear. A seam of yellow madness opened up in his mind that would tear him right open. He reached for the door handle and saw a man standing in front of the car. *Oh, no, not that, not that.* He was tall, almost regal, like a silhouette snipped from the night itself. He wore a ragged fur coat that trailed to the ground. Flakes of snow had collected on it like ash. Malevolence and loathsome evil seeped from him like oil. It was like a palpable curtain of eldritch horror and spectral, primeval terror that shattered the mind like wheat before a scythe. His face was pallid, cadaverous, narrow like a crescent moon, the flesh pitted and scarred as if from ancient battle, the nose prominent and Roman, the ends of his mustache trailing beneath his hard jawline.

There was something unbearably cruel about that face as if it had seen infants thrown into boiling pots and children being skinned, men broken on the wheel and impaled on stakes, woman torn apart by wild dogs and burned alive on pyres. It knew no mercy. It gave no quarter.

Burt stared into it and it felt like he was filled with hot, blowing sand.

The perfectly oval, owl-like, sullen blood-red eyes held him and would not let him go. He could feel the degenerate, diseased blackness flowing from that brain into his own and showing him scenes of carnage and slaughter that were nearly unimaginable...burning cities scattered with rat-picked corpses... lanes flanked with crucified children and adults impaled on stakes and set aflame...maidens violated with fence posts and disemboweled with steel hooks...men quartered by horses and women peeled with knives...the heads of children adorning city gates...the sounds of hooves and clashing steel...streets awash in blood and offal…the air hot and acrid with the nauseating stench of cremated flesh, punctuated by the cries of the damned.

That's what this man was, Burt knew: a mass-murderer.

A sadist and psychopath who unleashed a reign of terror in the mountain wastes of Hungary, putting thousands to their death. Until…until something came out of the night to claim him. He had walked in darkness since.

And he had a name. Burt could hear it reverberating in his skull: *Griska, Griska.*

With his last reserves of strength, Burt opened the car door and there was another one—a little boy sitting there. His moon-white face was broken by an immense and toothy grin, his eyes soulless and blank. The tiny soot-black pupils speared into him.

Burt stumbled away and saw that there were more than a dozen of them ringed around him—mostly women and children, Griska's extended family. Many were naked. Some dressed in cerements and shrouds, but all with those bright yellow eyes and mouths of gray hooked fangs.

He was in a nest of them and he knew he wouldn't escape.

Griska would never allow that.

He's the Pied Piper who calls the flock of lambs to sate the hunger of the Old Mother, a voice in Burt's head told him. *He paves the way so that She might come into the world, refreshed and pure. Gather now, friends, gather in Her name. But do not speak that sacred name aloud, for to pronounce Her name is to summon her spirit.*

Turning, Burt fell into the arms of the Death Angel.

At last, Burt…oh, at last.

She took hold of him, pulling him closer until he could smell the stink coming off her like a morbid perfume: embalming fluid, corpse-slime, and rotting oblong boxes. That constant insectile buzzing was so loud now it was like having his ear up against a hive. She pulled back her hood so he could see her gray rutted face netted in a filigree of cobwebs and know how long she had waited to slake her thirst. Her luminous eyes sucked the light from his soul, the sclera threaded with tiny collapsed red veins.

Her saw her teeth.

The long canines like icicles.

Burt screamed as they sank into his throat and he heard her sucking away his blood with sickening slurping sounds. A hollow opened inside him that would never be full again. And by then they were all on him, tapping him like a keg. Fangs sank into his arms and legs, his belly and groin.

And they drained him.

They bled him white.

Before the darkness took him into silken mortuary depths, he looked up and saw Griska standing there, boundlessly amused, his red eyes glowing like radium, his sharp canines, both upper and lower, interlocked in a grin of almost fatherly pride.

7

It was a half an hour later when Reg showed and from the blank look on his face it did not appear to Doc as if things had gone well for Burt's breakout. Reg walked in, looked at Bailey, looked at Doc, then sat in a wingback chair by the fire, putting his face in his hands.

"I take it he never made it," Doc said.

Reg just shrugged. He didn't seem to have the energy for speech. "Did you see it?"

Reg looked at him through the slats of his fingers. "I couldn't see anything out there with that fucking snow. *But*...I don't know..."

"What?"

Reg lifted up his head, staring into the fire. "I thought...I thought about ten minutes ago I heard him scream. Maybe I didn't. The wind is making weird sounds. Maybe I imagined it...but it sounded like him screaming."

"Don't think about it."

Reg shook his head. "How the hell am I supposed to do that?"

Doc wished he could tell him, but there was no way to wipe it from his mind. He supposed if they survived this entire ordeal Reg would be hearing the screams thirty years from now in his dreams.

He wondered if they were missed by now. It was past midnight. Somebody had to have been asking a few questions and ringing a few bells by this point. With a storm like that out there, though, it was unlikely that the police would make a special run way out here. There was a good chance the highways were closed by now and the secondary roads that brought them to this godawful place were probably drifted over.

If we can make it through the night, we have a chance, he thought. *Even if we have to hike out tomorrow, we're doing it. Another night in this place and we'll loose what little remains of our minds.*

He lit a cigarette as he watched over Bailey, listening to the storm rage, the house creak. This was their cage and there was no getting around that. They had these rooms and floors and not much else. Water, but no food unless you counted the expensive wax fruit in the dining room. The house was much, much larger than most prison cells, but ultimately it was just as confining and just as prone to drive them out of their collective skulls. He needed to sleep, but he didn't dare. It was only Reg and himself now, and it looked like Reg was drifting off so he had to stay awake.

If not to be wary of those outside, then to be wary of Bailey.

She didn't have much time left. She'd simply lost too much blood and it was only a matter of time before she stopped breathing. Then...*then what exactly?* That was a good question. How long before she rose from the dead? An hour? Two? Six? Or did it take a day or two? Doc remembered that in *The Brides of Dracula* it took like seven days. He seemed to recall Peter Cushing saying something like that on *Chamber of Horrors.*

But that was TV, movies.

What about in reality?

He had to suppress a cold, grim chuckle. *Reality? You call this reality? The walking dead?* But unfortunately it was and he had decided some hours ago he would not sit around trying to make sense of it all. That was for later. For now, he would ride it out.

Still...the question remained: *how long? How long did it take?*

Looking down at Bailey he felt the sour bile of fear rise in his gullet and he had everything he could do not to whimper. He breathed in and out, clearing his head. He bunched his hands into fists and clenched his teeth until the fear went away and he could think rationally because never had that been so important.

His mind turned away from darker realms and to Bailey herself.

When Morris had first brought him on board *Chamber of Horrors* and he had met Wenda, he had been amazed at how striking she was. He remembered thinking, *this show will be a hit because of her looks if for no other reason.* When she was just Wenda Keegan she seemed uncomfortable and aloof, but as Vultura she embodied the fantasies of every teenage boy. He met Megga next. She had dark good looks and an almost sinister feline undercurrent that was scary and exciting at the same time. *My God, look at that black hair and that pale skin, those huge intense eyes...like a Goth pinup. The boys'll love her and the girls will want to be her.* Then he met Bailey and, had he been much younger, he would have been smitten. With the blonde hair and blue eyes and flawless skin, she was like central casting's idea of a Nordic prom queen. She was diametrically opposed to Megga in looks and personality. But somehow, someway, they complimented each other: the dark side and the light side, bad and good, moonlight and sunshine. Which was why Morris took to calling them Jekyll and Hyde.

And now, seeing Bailey lying there, so close to death...he hoped when she returned she would not victimize Reg. He hoped she would only go after him because he felt he had let her down and deserved her kiss of death as punishment.

Maybe, subconsciously, you old fool, it's more than that. Maybe you want her to kiss you first and maybe you've always wanted that.

He did not entirely dismiss the idea because the subconscious mind was such a tar pit of base desires and impulses. It was where the animal drives were housed, where the greed and lust and hungers waited sharpening their teeth. It was also where the conscious mind threw all its baggage and repressions that it could not face nor accept. Maybe down there in the basement, *yes,* he wanted her to kiss him. But up in the light where his thinking mind, morals, and ethics ruled the roost, he was only concerned with Bailey's welfare and how he had let her down.

Though he was not aware of it in his physical and emotional exhaustion, his eyes had closed and he was remembering, as a child, the cold farmhouse in Iowa where he grew up. How, each night, his mother insisted that he pray for thirty minutes before bed. To disobey her was to incur her wrath. And to incur her wrath was to get the switch. Sometimes just on the ass when you'd did something bad like the time he and his sister Fran had lit Shaky Papineau's outhouse on fire as a Halloween prank. Their asses had been tenderized red and hurting over that one. But if ma caught you cutting your prayers short, you would know the switch on your back because, according to his mother, you needed to be flogged as Jesus was flogged by Pilate so you would know the suffering of the heretic. Which, even then, Doc knew made no sense but he wasn't about to debate biblical interpretation with his foul-tongued mother. Once she had been sweet like apple cider, then his father left with another woman and that cider had gone to vinegar and its taste had been forever burning and bitter. So, Doc prayed for thirty minutes each night and it was his mother's soul he asked forgiveness for. She who abused his sisters and tormented him because he was the image of his father. His mother had shown cruelties to children which were God's lambs and he figured she would burn in hell for it.

When he left home and went to war, he and religion parted ways. But now, in the midst of this nightmare, he was child again behind his closed eyes and he could hear the voice of a ten-year old Iowa farm boy asking the Lord to deliver them from this horrible place, from this nest of vipers where pale abominations had crawled forth from hell to claim the Earth as their own. And as he prayed, he thought of his flat in Albany, the fine brass bed that he would often fall into, more often drunk than not. The fire flickering, the hoarfrost on the windows. It was like none of this had ever happened. He was home and he was safe and in safety his mind fell back in time to the farmhouse and his mother and his sister, long hot summers of planting and chill autumns of harvest, watching Shaky Papineau stagger from his stillhouse up the hill to his bed after a solid day of drinking, his nerves burnt out like old fuses from corn liquor. He felt peaceful. He was in his bed up in the loft and the fire down in the hearth would throw crazy shapes over the plank ceiling and sometimes he would think they were ghosts come in the night to suck his blood and—

Wake up!

The child inside him jumped out of bed and then the old man he now was opened his eyes, sweating and shivering, and, dear God, he'd been asleep. *Asleep.* That was when *they* came: when you were harmless and dreaming. That's when they crawled in your window and sipped from your throat. Doc rubbed the slumber from his eyes. Bailey was still out, trembling slightly like a dog in a dream. The fire was burning low and Reg was snoozing in the chair and…and what was that smell? That awful smell like dead things washed up to spoil on toxic beaches?

A shadow. Two shadows…

Children.

Two children, the firelight reflective in their eyes like silver coins, shining off their teeth. They had wanted him asleep. They had *compelled* him to sleep so they could do what their kind always did. Doc saw them, a bright white terror exploding in his chest, and he tried to move but it was like he was drugged. He fell from the chair and the sound of it brought Reg awake and he saw them, too. He made a gasping/whimpering sound. The children were gone…*no,* they were crawling up the walls and moving across the ceiling like shadows thrown by the fire. Their shadows crept down the door and disappeared in the vicinity of the keyhole.

Gone.

Disturbed at their play and frightened off.

Bailey chattered her teeth in her stupor.

Doc got to his feet and tuned up the kerosene lanterns until the room was bright with even yellow light and the shadows had been pushed into the corners and under the furniture where they belonged.

You're not welcome here. Go away, just go away...

"They were here, Doc," Reg said, still loopy from it all. "I dreamed...I dreamed there were two kids lost in the storm and they were calling out to me. I found them and held their hands and they were so cold, so damn cold...and..."

"Just a dream," Doc told him, checking his neck and wrists for signs of the bite. He found nothing. "We got lucky. But we won't get lucky twice."

Bailey's teeth continued to chatter.

8

As the tension inside her increased, Wenda felt herself growing rigid. She took one of the lanterns and went to the door. Morris was curled up on the floor by the fire, Megga had fallen asleep in a chair. Now was the time to do things. But she would have to be quick before something happened because something was going to and she could feel it building around her. Whatever it was, it froze her with fear. It seemed to be self-generating and almost electrical. It felt like static rising in the air around her, a negative charge of voltage that was going right up her spine and making the hairs on her arms stand up. It was a cold sort of energy, cold like auroras flickering above ice caps.

Accept it and die, or fight against it.

Yes. She sucked in a breath of cool air and opened the door. There was nothing out there and she didn't really think there would be. Not yet. But soon. Once that energy in the house—or whatever it was—reached its peak, then she would see things. But not before. She went into the kitchen and dining room, gathering candles until she had an armload. She paid no attention to anything she saw out the windows, directing her vision to what was in front her. She ignored the shadows, the funny...*impulses* in her head that demanded she look at the windows and see what was looking in at her.

I will not. You cannot make me.

I will not look in your eyes.

It was working very well until she made to leave the dining room and abruptly dropped a candle. She could have left it, but candles meant light and flame and these things were life and death now. So she set her candles on the table and stooped down to pick up the one she had dropped. She found it quickly enough, but as she stood, her eyes looked over at the window and she saw what they wanted her to see: what looked at first like a blowing sheet that filled her with a stark, childlike terror. But it was no sheet but a drifting wraith clawing at the glass in its blowing shroud, its white face hooked in a grin of defilement, its eyes like glowing moonstones. Whether it had been male or female in life, she could not tell. It was a vulpine ghost and no more.

But the eyes.

It was not easy to look away from them.

That cold electricity she had felt in the sitting room was directed by them. It moved through her veins and across the backs of her arms. It made her fingers and toes tingle. It flowed up into her skull and filled her head with a low buzzing that seemed to rise in pitch every time she tried to turn away from the face and the tapping ghost fingers at the window. There was an unspeakable dominion in those eyes that she did not dare look away from...they were drawing her in and she *knew* they were drawing her in. That was the worst part. They were taking apart her willpower block by block, unmaking it and creating a pocket of blackness in its place that was spreading inch by dark inch and when it was finished she knew there would be no more Wenda Keegan...just a mindless slave, a deadhead zombie that would stumble over to the window and open it.

Fight it...fight it...fight it...

But as those thoughts went through her mind, that awful droning rose up to blanket any defiance. And she knew, somewhere in the depths of her brain, that she either threw that dominance off now or faced defeat.

So she started talking. "What I'm going to do is bring these candles back to the room and I'm going to light it up in there and if one of those fucking things tries anything, I will stick my stake through its black heart."

In her skull, she could hear something like a cheated screech.

Then she looked away, her hands going for the stake and the silver knife on her belt and there was strength in these objects. She could feel it flowing through her, opening her up and filling her with warmth, driving away the shadows in her mind until they had evaporated.

She hesitated no more.

"Where have you been?" Megga asked when she came back.

Wenda showed her the candles.

"You think that's going to help?"

"Light always helps," she told her. Then, almost ritualistically, she lit the candles one by one, dripping wax in puddles to hold them upright. She went around the room and lit five of them. The light was good and it would save on the lanterns which were getting down on fuel.

"We're going to need more kerosene," she said.

Megga grunted. "Fresh out."

Wenda knew there was a maintenance shed or building somewhere outside the town. But there was no way of getting to it, of course. She wondered if there might be kerosene in the house, maybe in the cellar. They were going to need some. If it came to it, they would have to go down below and see.

"We'll be dead by morning," Megga said.

Wenda wanted to give her a good, hard slap across the face because she had it coming, but she didn't. Looking into Megga's eyes she saw something that she had never seen before: vulnerability and innocence. That stopped her. In fact, it deflated her. She had never seen it before and never would have expected it.

Is this the person that's been hiding behind the mask all this time? she wondered. *Is this the real Megga I'm seeing?*

This Megga looked scared. This Megga did not look like the one she knew who courted morbidity, suffering, and angst. This Megga looked like she could be hurt. In fact, it looked like she was suffering right now, fathoms deep in personal pain.

She stood up and walked over to Wenda. Her arms were folded and she would not meet Wenda's eyes. "Something's going to happen, isn't it?"

"I think so, yes."

"All I want is to be is safe," Megga said, her eyes wet. "That's all. That's all I want."

Wenda was moved. She put a hand on Megga's shoulder and gave it a little squeeze. "That's what we all want."

Megga came into her arms then, sobbing, and Wenda could do nothing but hold her. She pulled away slightly at first, but she couldn't turn her back on her. Not now when Megga was finally exhibiting symptoms of being human. Megga held onto her tightly, her face buried in Wenda's hair…then she looked up and kissed her. Wenda pulled back and Megga kissed her again, this time her tongue tracing a hot trail over her lips.

"Stop it!" Wenda told her, pushing her back.

"Why?"

"Because…because I don't like that."

Megga moved in again. "Yes, you do. I see the way you look at me. You want this. You've always wanted this."

Wenda shook her head. "Stop it, Megga."

But she wouldn't stop. She took hold of Wenda and tried to kiss her again and Wenda shoved her back. When Megga fought to kiss her, Wenda slapped her across the face and Megga dropped to the floor.

So that's what this was. Those outside were using Megga again. Probably as a distraction, Wenda figured, and she did not doubt that Megga was a willing participant. She crouched down by her and her eyes were open, staring up. "What happened?" Megga said. "Why am I on the floor?"

Sighing, Wenda helped her up. "I think you fainted."

"I've never fainted in my life."

"Well, you have now."

Megga did not seem to believe her. She knocked aside Wenda's helping hands and sat back in her chair. She looked suspicious like maybe Wenda was up to something and that was how Wenda knew that none of it had been voluntary. Maybe Megga wasn't entirely innocent because she had opened herself up to those things out there, but she wasn't totally guilty either.

Wenda turned.

She heard something. Maybe not with her ears exactly, but with some other finely tuned sense.

Megga said, "What are—"

"Shut up," Wenda told her, pressing a finger to her lips.

She was straining to hear something, *anything*. They were in the house and she knew it. Maybe they had been all along. Regardless, they were here now. The very fabric of the house had been disrupted by their presence. They were out there in the darkened corridors, moving around, gliding forward like midnight shadows, pressing in for attack. Maybe that had been their plan all along: get Megga to seduce her and then in they would come.

Maybe.

"Get over by the fire," Wenda told Megga. "Wake up Morris."

Megga, for once, did not argue. She went over to the hearth and shook Morris awake none too gently. She fed two logs into the fire and the flames greedily rose high, brightening the room but also filling it with countless moving shadows.

Wenda got in front of Megga and Morris with her stake and knife.

They were coming now. She could hear them slithering out there like snakes, silently sliding down floors and over walls and creeping over ceilings. That there were many of them she did not doubt. And at any moment now, the door would burst open and they would fill the room: forked-tongued serpents with massive, glossy midnight-blue bodies, the kind that could wrap up a human being in writhing coils and squeeze them until their guts came squirting out of their mouths.

But that was subjective and she knew it.

She did not really expect snakes. That was a simple phobia of hers. Whenever she was frightened of something, her brain converted the fright into slinking serpentine shapes; a childhood fear.

But these were not snakes gathering outside the door.

She did not know what they were exactly.

Only that they had claws because they were scratching to come in.

9

When the door burst open, Megga took hold of Morris, who was like 175 pounds of rubber: tottering, weak, and pretty much worthless. The fire was hot at her back but she didn't even feel it. Six streamlined shapes came running in, their claws clicking on the hardwood floor. They were wolves...or something much like wolves...but immense and shaggy, their eyes lit red and their bristling hides black and almost oily like they'd been greased with fat. Their jaws were wide, ribbons of saliva dripping from teeth that looked like they were designed specifically to tear out throats and open bellies.

They pushed in and formed a line directly opposite the hearth and the sad trio of defenders who waited there.

Megga shivered, her guts feeling loose. Her nerves were letting go inside her like snapping silken cords and she figured that at any moment she would begin to scream like a little girl. Then she would *actually* morph into that little girl who had been bitten by the neighbor's dog.

She did not like wolves.

She embraced the dark side and the mythic creatures of the night that called it home, but she did not like canine things—dogs and wolves and were-beasts of any sort. Filthy, stinking, stupid animals. Already she could smell the wet-dog, blood-breathed fetor of them, the acrid secretions of their glands that made her blanch inside.

No, no, no, she thought. *If I am to be taken then let it be something with human form. Let me know the hot breath of a lover and cold dead lips against my throat, the benediction of teeth slowly penetrating my carotid, the sucking of lips and the cunnilingual play of a tongue lapping up my blood which will burst free in an orgasmic red tide—*

But it would not be like that.

For in her soul, in the erotic fantasies she'd held hotly in her mind since she was fourteen, vampires were graveyard poets, metaphorical darkly romantic representations of death-love perfumed with comic book Goth necrophilia...but wolves, *werewolves,* were simple beasts, biting and tearing and stuffing themselves with meat. They dwelled in the savage twilight world of human atavism: the primal need to return to the forest and the hunt.

She could not be claimed by these things.

She would throw herself in the fire or beat her brains out against the brick hearth, anything, anything but this.

In her mind, she could see them overpowering Wenda and then coming for her in a night-tide of drooling jaws and empty bellies. She could feel their fangs in her flesh, crunching through bones and licking marrow like cream. Feasting on brain and organ, shearing skin and gobbling throat-meat, chomping down on her groin and smashing her breasts like pale funeral lilies squashed within the pages of a heavy book.

It could not be allowed.

And in her manic terror, she thought: *It was not supposed to be this way...you promised me it would not be this way...you would come to me and take me but not like this, not like this...*

She could feel their minds trying to commune with her own, but she shut them out. They wanted her to snatch up a log and bash in Wenda's head with it, cast that silver blade far away where it could not bisect flesh and form with its foulness.

But Megga did not listen, would not hear. She refused to be the pawn of doglike monsters.

Terrible childhood nightmares crowded into her skull and she saw herself buried alive in grease-furred, animal-smelling pelts. Bitten into and drooled upon as they fought over loops of her candy-red viscera, bubbles of blood bursting from her mouth in a red, sharp scream as a cold snout investigated between her legs. A rough tongue singling out the soft sweetmeats at her groin...then the teeth spearing into them.

But the wolf-things kept trying...trying to get inside her head.

They tried to fill her mind with smoke. Tried to make her see things as they wanted her to see them: not slobbering wolf-males and hot-loined she-wolves, but men and women and, yes, even children. Pallid horrors running on all fours, corpse-things pretending to be wolves for the primeval terror of the wolfpack was so deliciously devastating to the human mind.

But she could not see that.

Her childhood terrors were rich and intoxicating, scarlet wine that filled her and overflowed her and all she could do was...scream.

Scream as they charged forward, padding over the floor to where Wenda waited for them with the gleaming blade of the silver butcher's knife. They had come to feed on her, to strip her to bone and bloody husk, to rip out her womb and savage her breasts and roll happily in her pooling remains—

Megga came to herself, screeching: *"NO! NO! NO! NO! NOOOOOO! GET AWAY FROM ME! GET THE FUCK AWAY FROM ME YOU MANGY FUCKING MUTT!"*

Despite Megga's hysteria, Wenda did not flinch.

She did wither.

She waited for them, the blade ready.

The first one launched itself at her, perhaps as a distraction, while two others pressed in from either flank. Its hackles up, its body a rocket of supernal muscular grace, it came at her. Its eyes glowed a vibrant red, its jaws splitting to reveal the sheath of gnashing fangs...and Wenda met it. She slashed at it quickly with two powerful strokes that laid open its snout and slit one eye into a gummy crimson soup.

The beast roared and stumbled back, steam hissing from its wounds.

At the very second it withdrew, the others came from either side. Wenda put her arm up to block the one on the left and it seized her arm in its jaws. The one on the right tasted the steel of her knife. It slit its tongue open and gashed its mouth. It yelped and fell, the blade scraping over its ribs as it turned to avoid it. The other beast was crushing her arm, but its teeth had not penetrated the sleeve of her thick leather coat. As it saw the blade coming, it tried to retreat but one of its fangs got hung up on the sleeve and Wenda buried the knife into its side again and again and again, crying out with bloodlust as she did so.

The other wolves scattered out the door.

The wounded beast tried to join them, but fell, its legs giving way. It was bleeding and gored, a pink saliva foaming from its jaws. In a final act of defiance, it rose up on its rear legs in a near-human shape, bloody mouth filled with razored teeth…and then it changed back into its vampiric form: a naked woman who had been maybe twenty-five or thirty at the time of her death. Except…it did not *change* exactly or transform like the werewolves on the old flicks they showed on *Chamber of Horrors*. The wolf shell split open like an egg, shearing off into two sections and the woman burst free.

Her phosphorescent white flesh trembled, shivered with a rippling motion, steam rolling from the gaping wounds in her side. The air was pungent with a stink of burning flesh. She made gagging, coughing sounds, stumbling backwards, hands clawing at the air, her vicious canines chomping through her lower lips, eyes white and blank and almost gelid-looking.

She let out a wracking scream of pure agony.

Her eyes fell in and her face sunk into itself like a sun-dried prune.

She crashed to the floor and as she did so, she broke apart into dozens of sizzling fragments that popped like coals in a brazier, throwing off a nauseating yellow smoke as they were reduced to ash. Then there was just a skeleton on the floor, disarticulated and jerking. The jaws of the skull sprang open and she was gone, a wind carrying the ashes across the room, powdering the far wall gray with them.

After that, there was stunned silence for a moment, bits of ash drifting in the glow of the candles like specks of dust. Megga felt stunned and speechless. All her life she'd read about things like that and seen them in movies, but the reality was sickening.

"Oh God," she said. "Oh my God."

Wenda was breathing hard. "Now," she said, "now they know that I'll kill every one of them."

10

As Doc spoke, Reg listened. He was apologetic as hell, pained even, his voice breaking with emotion at his request: "It's more than I should ask yet I must ask it of you. I don't dare leave Bailey alone and if you're not comfortable being here with her, then I surely can't go…"

"I'll do it," Reg said. "No big deal. I can't stand this fucking waiting anyway."

"It could be very dangerous."

"I know."

"They might come for you."

Reg shrugged. "I'll take that chance."

"You're sure?"

"Yes."

Doc patted him on the shoulder. "I'd be more than happy to attempt it myself…"

"No, no. Sorry. But I'm not sitting in here alone with…with Bailey. I don't like how she looks at me when her eyes open."

"Understood."

Reg stuck his trusty poker through a belt loop in his pants, grabbed a lantern off the mantle and went to the door. "It might take me a little while, so don't freak if I'm not back right away."

Doc nodded.

Reg opened the door and looked back once to see him sitting there next to Bailey's outstretched form on the sofa. She was still breathing, but it wouldn't be long, he knew. It wouldn't be long at all and he did not want to be here when that happened. Of course, like Doc himself he really didn't know *when* it would happen or even how it could be, but he knew that it was and it would be. There was nothing scientific to this; it was pure instinct and sixth sense.

He made himself stop thinking about it.

He was on a mission. Doc was trusting him to get this done and he'd do it. They were running low on kerosene for the lanterns. There was only one place it could be stored in the house: the cellar. And that's where he was going.

Swallowing down the fear in his throat, he moved up the corridor past doors that were open—hosting a darkness that was almost organic and brooding—and past others that were sensibly shut. And his mind, wired to his fear like a detonator wired to a lethal charge of TNT, asked him, *what if one of these doors was to swing open and something was to come out at you in a slithering mass of shadows? Something with a face like ivory and lips full and red?*

But he dismissed that right away because if he started thinking things like that he was done for, completely done for.

He passed through the kitchen and paused there in the darkness, feeling the throb of his heart in his chest.

The lantern threw shadows around him and each one, he thought, was going to go for his throat. But it wasn't the shadows that were bothering him. It was something else. Something that sounded almost like footsteps behind him.

His hand went reflexively to the poker on his belt.

He listened. There was nothing.

Then he thought he heard it again: like the slapping of bare feet coming down the corridor.

Despite the chill, sweat ran from every pore on his body. It was steaming in the cold air. The terror was like lightning branching in his belly and spreading through his chest. He told himself there was nothing, nothing at all, that his imagination was getting out of hand, but he couldn't make himself believe it.

He held the lantern up, illuminating the way he had come so that if there was someone behind him, he would see them. But he saw nothing. Nothing at all.

You gotta man up here already. Just do the job and get it done and quit freaking all the time. The more you freak, the harder this is going to be.

True. He could not argue with that. It was sensible.

He found a connecting passageway. This is where Doc thought the cellar would be. Here. Just off the kitchen. Okay. The passage was short and dead-ended. There were two doors. He tried the first one…something letting loose in his chest as he pulled it open. He expected to see fanged night-shapes rushing out at him. But it was just a broom closet with attendant mops and buckets and cleaners. It smelled like Pine-Sol in there. He squatted down and grabbed a metal bucket. If there was kerosene, he'd need something to carry it in.

As he did so, he heard the sound again.

Scampering bare feet like the footsteps of a naughty child sneaking past him.

His heart banging in his chest and his scalp feeling too tight for his skull, he stood up. He was breathing fast as he held up the lantern. But there was nothing. He listened for a minute, then two, as the panic in him rose like mercury.

Stop this shit. You have to stop this shit.

The other door. It was at the end of the passage. Weren't they always at the end of the passage or at the top of the stairs? He'd seen enough horror movies to know that was true. Okay. He moved down there and if he heard sounds he did not listen to them because as afraid as he was he was also starting to get a little angry at his own rioting imagination. If there was something, fine. But if not…then he was ashamed of himself.

He set the bucket down and it clanged in the silence.

He reached out for the doorknob and, sucking in a breath, opened the door. Again, that feeling in his chest…though not as bad this time. Before him was a well-worn set of wooden steps leading down into the cellar which was like some immense pit of blackness. It seemed like the light of the lantern would barely even touch it. Steeling himself, he picked up his bucket and started down, moving slowly and carefully so he didn't trip and tumble down. A broken leg wouldn't do at all. Not in this place. The stairs creaked under his weight and, like the bucket, that creaking was loud enough to wake the—

Don't think that.

Of all the stupid things. He moved down the steps and the light showed him the way. His breath frosted from his lips in the cold. He had the sudden chilling, irrational feeling that somebody was standing right behind him, reaching out to touch him. He felt gooseflesh rise on the back of his neck. If he hadn't known it before, he knew it now: this whole town was haunted and this house particularly. The cellar was a bad place, a very bad place. Being down there, he was that much closer to the black, beating heart of Cobton itself. The knowledge of this was absolute. He could feel it deep inside, in his very marrow—a precognition, prescience, maybe something that man had never really named—telling him that the zero hour had dawned. And that terrified him, made his guts compress into silvery clocksprings.

He stood there, fighting against himself.

The rational man inside him told him to keep going, get it done; the superstitious primitive told him to *run, run, run.*

But he wasn't going to run because if he did that he could never face Doc and he could certainly never face himself. Yet, he was indecisive. In the light of the lantern, he could see his breath rolling out in white clouds.

Behind him…a creaking.

There could have been many explanations for it, the house being so damned old. Old houses tended to make noises. But, at that moment, he wasn't believing it. The old fears were upon him and he could not shake the idea that he was not alone. That he had been followed from the moment he left the parlor. That whoever was trailing him was here with him now.

Only…he could not see them because they did not *want* to be seen.

He opened his mouth with some absurd urge to call out to them, but all that came out was an airless rasping just as dry as needles on aluminum. He took another step down, then another, his heart beating with heavy, muffled strokes as if it couldn't suck up blood fast enough. Maybe that was because his red stuff was thick as tar at that particular moment.

He stopped three steps from the bottom or maybe he *was* stopped.

He could smell it now.

He could smell the thing that had followed him. It carried a dirty, yellow stink.

His breath fracturing in his lungs like crockery, he went down those last three steps to the cellar floor and felt the darkness swim out at him, flood him with its hot corrupt odor, trying to drown him in a rising tide of filth. He held the lantern up. The cellar was huge. Some of the floor was made of flagstones, but much of it was just old packed dirt. Dark dirt like grave earth. The intrusion of light made the shadows pull back, cluster, lurk at the periphery of his vision.

The smell was worse now.

What's bringing that stink in here?

It was a rotting envelope of heat, misery, and something like corpse gas. It smelled the way he thought tombyards, ossuaries, and violated caskets must smell…time and dust and old rot lying cheek-to-jowl in the dank earth. The stench closed his throat to a pinhole and each breath was a knife blade in his chest. It made no sense. Nothing could smell like that in the cold. Things did not rot in the cold, they did not stink; everything was neutral. Yet…he was smelling it. It got so thick in the air bile slid up the back of his throat and he had a mad urge to vomit.

Then it was gone.

As if it had never been.

There was no way it was his imagination. Nothing could convince him of that. Haunted, that's what. Whole goddamn place was fucking haunted. And because it was so, he had to move. He had to get this done before things got worse because they *would* get worse. First, it was the sounds. Then, that smell. Next, he would see it and, worse, it would see him and want to touch him and he knew it, God how he knew it.

The cellar was mostly empty save for some stacked boxes and a few old nail kegs, some shelves stacked with finished lumber, trim, rolls of wallpaper wrapped in plastic, the assorted odds and ends of maintaining a house that had to have been over 300 years old if it was a day. *Guys who lived here originally probably wore powdered wigs, buckle shoes, and short pants,* Reg thought, trying to divert his mind, badly *needing* to divert it any way he could.

He searched around, breathing fast and hard.

There. A red gasoline can. He went over and unscrewed the cap. No, not gas but kerosene. He was in luck. He thought about filling the bucket, but why? He grabbed the can by its handle. It was a five-gallon drum, about half-way full. It was a little heavy, but such was his state that he did not even seem to notice.

Time to get the fuck out of Dodge.

He went over to the stairs (for a moment he couldn't find them in the immensity of the cellar and a hot panic cut through him). He was almost home free now and—

The stairs were definitely creaking now.

Creak…creak…creak.

Somebody or something was coming down them, very slowly, only he could not see them. The steps creaked one after the other. A thick mass of terror settled into his throat that he could not swallow down. It spread out, filling him, making his chest feel like it was clotted with ice. He could not see the thing that had been following him, but he could *hear* it: it made a rustling sound like silk. And he could smell the noxious odor of the disturbed dead it pushed before it. Then he did see something. Not the thing itself, but its breath: as it glided down the steps, it puffed out rolling white plumes of frost-vapor.

Reg stumbled back, tangled up in his own feet and went down. He scrambled back up, leaving the kerosene drum in the dirt and pulling the poker from his belt loop. He would fight. He'd smash it to pulp. Holding the lantern up in a shaking fist, he could no longer see its exhaled breath.

There was nothing.

Not so much as a sound.

He whirled around, looking first this way, then that. It was gone. But as his flesh crept and his heart pounded, he could still smell it. Smell its *nearness*. It was right next to him.

His own breath was coming out in white clouds now, too.

He was gasping, practically hyperventilating.

And as he breathed out, for one quick moment he saw a face take shape in the cloud of his breath...and he let out a short, sharp little scream as something like fingernails traced along the back of his neck.

He swung out with the poker, but there was nothing there.

Only a voice spoken bare inches from his ear. A woman's voice: *"Are you afraid, Reggie?"* it asked. *"Are you good and scared?"*

He screamed again and ran for the stairs and something hit him with considerable force, driving him back four or five feet and putting him on his ass in the dirt. In the glow of the dropped lantern, he could see a form standing at the bottom of the steps.

It was a woman in a bridal gown.

He could see the fine lacework, the pearl beading, the silken train that led six or seven steps behind her. Seeing her, he suddenly wasn't afraid because she was so beautiful...absolutely striking. The gown clung to her curves, the lace at the bosom giving him a delicious peek at the full globes of her breasts. Her hair was done up in red ringlets and set with white orchids and laurel sprigs. Her eyes were green like shimmering emeralds, her cheekbones high, her lips full.

That's what he saw.

Then, blinking, he saw the funeral lilies she clutched in her hands, the smear of blood at her mouth...it had dripped down over her breasts and gown like droplets of cherry juice.

Are you afraid, Reggie? Are you good and scared?

He saw her then as she was, not as he *wanted* her to be.

She clutched flaking dead roses in her hands. A membrane of furry, gray mold had grown up her dress and over her breasts. Cobwebs were spun in a fine lace over her face. They were like a veil he could see through. She raised one gray hand and peeled them away. Her eyes were red and wet like spilled viscera, her face like some yellow-white terra cotta that was splitting open with hundreds of minute cracks. She was grinning with ensanguined teeth that were long, crooked, and sharp.

He let out a cry that strangled in his throat.

She moved at him with a fluid grace that was part mist and part flesh, and all relentless hunger. Her gown was torn and shredded, blackened with corpse drainage and the stains of what she had been feeding upon through the ages, the train graying, rotten, dragging behind her in dusty ribbons and streamers. Rats clung to her. Swollen graveyard rats, squealing and squeaking, hissing and clawing. They swarmed over her, swam in her, clinging to her trailing cerements, nipping at the mold-specked veil that covered her belly.

And in the back of Reg's head, a voice was speaking. Not her voice, but a male voice that was scratching and wizened: *She is the Queen of the Dead, Mistress of Plagues and Pestilence, the split maidenhead of insanity. She isfilth and mud and dirty straw. A doll that walks and grins, the cackling dementia of low, windy places and hollow catacombs. Her flesh is white glass and her eyes are filtered October sunlight. Her tawdry robes are smudged with grave dirt, winding sheets of the buried dead—*

Reg let out a scream at the violation of that cold and forbidding voice.

Then the lantern flickered…the light dimmed.

The woman was gone and he slashed out with the poker here and there, right and left, hearing her giggling next to him. A hand brushed his shoulder, fingers like refrigerated meat. He slashed again, crying and shrieking. He saw those red eyes in front of him, saw them wink out like taillights in the distance. They floated above him, below him. They appeared inches from his face and he struck out again, felt the poker tear through something gauzy like ribbons of obsidian crepe.

Then nothing.

He stood there, his breath coming in a sharp, ragged croaking. Cold breath at his neck, something like a leprous tongue licking his cheek, he ran to the stairs and a cold hand grasped his ankle, yanking him to the floor.

The poker was gone.

He couldn't remember dropping it.

He found his feet and those eyes were right in front of him. It seemed like dozens of broomstick arms and fingers like roofing nails found him and held him, pulling him forward, lips that were cold like the nose of a dog brushing his own. He fought and clawed out at what held him, but it was ethereal and filmy. It tore like wet newspaper and flaked away like crematory ash.

And her voice said, *"Are you scared, Reggie?"*

And then that hideous mouth was so close he could smell the breath billowing from the throat. It stank like black tumors in specimen buckets and smothered babies putrefying in garbage cans. And then those lips had him, sucking his own into that vile mouth of crawling, burrowing things.

The thing that had him was no woman. It was moving and flowing, made of ropes and snakes, flaps and rotting fabric, hot running tallow and dripping wax. It was moist and powder-dry, skeleton and living meat. A fleshy ghost.

And then he was pulled closer and he knew at that frightful moment that if he did not fight, he would sink like a rock into an oozing sea of sucking mud that was the depraved blackness at the bottom of time and sanity.

He threw himself backwards, striking the dirt floor.

The woman was standing before him, reaching out gray stick-like fingers, her ravenous mouth gleaming with teeth.

He grabbed up the lantern, found his feet, and as she tried to take hold of him again, he smashed the lantern over her head, the kerosene drenching her and the flames spreading. She let out a shrill screeching sound, whirling around and around as the flames engulfed her. But Reg didn't wait to see what happened. He scrambled up the stairs and down corridors until he found the parlor and threw himself through the door.

And when Doc went to him, asking him what had happened, he had no voice to answer with.

11

Megga amazed Wenda because of her sheer resiliency. After the attack of the wolf-things, it should have been impossible for her to sleep. She should have been stark awake and dreamless, her eyes burning bright and fearful in her face. But that, of course, wasn't the case at all. She was slumped in the chair, sleeping peacefully. And Morris, well, he was curled up by the fire like a lazy cat. Wenda watched them, almost as a mother watches her children, knowing that it was a hard road they would have to follow and this night went on forever; multitudinous were its evils. These were the things she was thinking about and she could not put them into words exactly...they were more like loose thoughts winging in her head, trying to connect and form a chain, a concept she could figuratively hold in her hand and recognize.

She kept watching them, wondering how they could possibly sleep, and then she knew. They slept because *she* was on guard and they knew it. They knew she would not let them down. Would not let the night-shapes get them.

But you're tired, too. You're wrung out physically, mentally, emotionally. You're squeezed dry right now and you know it. If one of those things showed right now...would you be able to fight it? Would you be able to rise up against it?

That was the question she asked herself and she had no good answers. When she tried to think all she got was silence in her head. Her ability to reason and make sense of just about everything was slipping away, it was lost in the fog of her brain and she could not part the mists sufficiently to get it back. She was tired. God, she was tired. She was sitting in her chair, eyes moving from the fire to Morris to Megga to the curtained window to the door itself. She knew she could not sleep...yet it was past the point where she could do much else. Her hand still grasped the silver knife but she felt no power in it. It was as weak as she was. Crowding into her brain were images of the things outside—a terrifying panoply of blurring white faces and red smiling mouths and huge, ravenous eyes...all of them coming out of the storm, moving in closer and closer.

You can't sleep. You know that, don't you? If they came in as wolves, then they can come in as other things, too, which means—if folklore holds true—that they either do not need to be invited in or, sometime long ago, they were invited in and will strike at any time.

No, you cannot sleep. You cannot.

Yes, she thought as she closed her eyes, I know.

Maybe it was ten minutes later or an hour, but she heard a voice calling to her and she knew it wasn't Morris or Megga. It was the voice of a boy. A little boy. She decided it was a very nice voice. There was no threat in it. First it was singing somewhere far off in the storm, the voice of a little boy lost in the dark woods. Now it was closer, very close.

Wenda, I'm lost and I'm cold. I want to come and sit with you by the fire. I want you to protect me.

She listened to it and tried to answer, but it seemed like her tongue was stuck in her mouth, maybe in her throat. It was caught in some sticky patch of tar and she couldn't get it loose. The boy kept talking, telling her how lost and lonely he was. He was crying. He needed help and she wanted to help him. She was not about to leave him out there all alone. She couldn't do that.

When she got her tongue loose finally, she said, "Just follow my voice. Can you do that? Can you just follow my voice and let it lead you here?"

Yes.

"Good. Just hear my voice and keep following it. You can sit by the fire with us. It's safe here."

Yes.

Wenda listened to her own voice and was amazed at how nice it sounded. She'd always been so self-conscious of it before, but there was no reason for that because she had a really, really nice voice. It was calm, soothing, confident, and loving. Why hadn't anybody ever told her she had such a nice voice...unless maybe they had and she hadn't listened like when they told her she was pretty and something inside her cringed and she quickly changed the subject because her own looks made her very uncomfortable. All she'd ever wanted was to blend in, to not be noticed, but because she was pretty people noticed and she could barely handle their attention without breaking into a cold sweat. Thank God for Vultura. Vultura made everything manageable. You want to look? Go ahead. Go ahead—

I'm getting closer, Wenda. When I'm real close, you'll have to invite me in.

"I will! I will!"

You'll like it, Wenda. It's wonderful to be like us. We live forever. We can run like wolves and fly. We can slide under doors and through keyholes, squeeze through cracks and blow around with the mist. And we can float. We can float high up in the air. Wouldn't you like to float away, Wenda?

Can I come in, Wenda?

That voice. That terrible voice. It sounded like a little boy, but it was no little boy...it was the scraping voice of something malignant and grim *pretending* to be a little boy and not doing a very good job of it. The tone was hollow and echoing like a voice from a buried box.

She heard it again in her mind: *Can I come in, Wenda?*

Then she heard her *own* voice answering it: "Yes…yes, of course you can."

Had that just been a dream or had it been something else? Something worse? Had she just invited something black and crawling into the house? She picked up the knife. The fire had died down and the room was cold, yet she didn't dare get up and feed more wood into it. Her eyes were slipping closed again.

Then a voice: *"Wake up, Wenny."*

David.

She listened to the storm outside the house, blowing, moaning, sounding like what she imagined a banshee would sound like. She listened to the encroaching darkness around her. She could hear the wind whispering down the chimney. The old house was moving, it seemed, it was alive as old houses always are, groaning, creaking, echoing with the ancient sounds of the people who'd once lived there. The hollow thud of footsteps in the upstairs corridors. The creaking of a bed. Hands gliding down stair rails. Muffled laughter in a deserted room. Beams and boards strained against nail heads, windows rattled against casements, rafters that were old and tired with the weight of centuries sighed in the night. She heard all these things and something more that she at first could not identify: a skittering sort of sound. A sound of rats in midnight walls. A clawing, creeping, rustling sort of sound.

Then she knew.

As black fear filled her throat and sealed it shut, she knew very well just as she knew she had invited it into the house. She tried to steel herself for what had to be done, but it felt like she was made of old sticks and limp twine. She could not get her body moving, there was no lick in her limbs.

The skittering sound.

Closer.

Can I come in, Wenda?

She got to her feet and she could hear that voice calling out to her through the dark mists of her dreams. It was telling her she could sit back down and relax because the fire had burned low and it would come to her.

No, no, not that. Never that.

She tightened her fist on the knife and looked around. Megga was still sleeping. Morris had not moved. The candles she had lit were still guttering. She saw Megga's penlight on the table by her chair. Silently, she went over there and grabbed it. She lowered herself to her knees very near Morris.

She made herself breathe.

She made herself ready even though it felt like her belly was filled with a warm, white pulp.

The fire had burned down to a few low flames and a bed of hot coals. The hearth was big. She moved closer to it, cocking an ear. The scratching sound was coming from up inside the chimney and she tried to tell herself it was a bird caught up there or a squirrel frightened by the smoke and heat, but she knew better. What was coming down the chimney was what she had invited in.

The knife in one hand and the penlight in the other, she got her knees as close to the fire as she dared, then craned her neck, leaned forward, and looked up the chimney. As she did so, she clicked on the penlight and it illuminated the black, smoke-stained brick and the pale, naked thing creeping down at her like a spider. She saw the grinning, gruesome oval of its boyish face, how that childhood innocence was corrupted by something vile and noxious. Its eyes were like misty moonlight, its grinning mouth set with sharp teeth that it licked with a black tongue.

Wouldn't you like to float away, Wenda?

She jumped back and tossed two logs into the fire. They were cracked open with dryness; the coals were glowing orange. The logs caught instantly, flames rising up into bright yellow blades of flame that climbed higher and higher as she threw more wood on it.

And up in the chimney, the little boy who'd come out of the grave on this night of blowing wind and falling snow, screeched with an agonized, eerie cry that was part hatred and part angry denial at being cheated out of the blood it had come for. The cry rose up and echoed off into the night like the screech of an owl.

Morris slept on.

So did Megga.

Wenda figured it was all in her mind. Maybe it hadn't happened. But that was wishful thinking and she knew better. She could still her that screaming in her brain—it was white-hot and cutting.

Megga sat up. "What are you doing?" she asked.

Wenda almost started to tell her, then she just shook her head. "Just throwing a few logs on the fire. That's all."

12

"She's barely breathing now," Doc said in an utterly defeated voice that came out dry and tasted bitter in his mouth. He had never felt so utterly helpless and hopeless in his life. This child was dying from loss of blood, from trauma…and there wasn't a damn thing he could do about it. She needed a hospital. She needed a transfusion and only in movies, he knew, did people even attempt such a thing with materials at hand.

"There's nothing we can do," Reg said. It wasn't a question. It was a statement that was almost indifferent in its pain.

"No, nothing. Not a goddamn thing."

Doc needed a drink. He'd never needed one as badly as he did at that moment, but even if he had a bottle…what was the point? It would only accelerate his guilt and self-loathing because Bailey was dying from his own incompetence. This is what he told himself. This is what he believed. If he only hadn't waited around with Reg by the window when Burt had gone.

If, if, if…

He didn't know how much blood was left in her, but it couldn't have been much because she was white as the proverbial sheet. There was not so much as a hint of blush at her cheeks. Where before she had been hot and feverish, now she was just cold. So very cold. Her flesh felt like refrigerated latex.

"What are we going to do, Doc?" Reg asked then. "I mean, really, what the hell are we going to do?"

Doc didn't even have the strength to drag his eyes over to him. Maybe he didn't want to see Reg's face and the desperation cut into it like knife scars. He brought his head down until his forehead rested on his fist and tried to think, tried to come up with something because, really, what *were* they going to do? But the thoughts wouldn't come, the answers were nonexistent in his exhaustion and frustration. He only felt the simple animal need to strike out against something or someone. It made him think of the war, crawling through swamps of the Delta and humping it through the jungled hills of the Central Highlands. He had not understood any of it then. His young mind could not encapsulate the need for war. Maybe it made some kind of vague sense to those who planned it, but on the ground it was incomprehensible. But maybe he understood now. War was born of frustration. War was the result of failed diplomacy. War was what you did when there was nothing left to do: you stopped talking and you started hitting.

That's how he felt now: in his anguish and aggravation he wanted to hit. He wanted to find some goddamn vampires and go Van Helsing on them and ram stakes through chests. *How does that feel, you fucking parasites? How does it feel to be helpless?* Reg, of course, was still looking at him the way the kid might have looked at his father when he was scared, hoping to elicit some sage wisdom and practical advice.

Doc almost started laughing.

Didn't he realize what an absolute oh-my-God pile of refuse his would-be savior indeed was? He was no one to look to for guidance. When he wasn't playing make-believe as Doc Blood he was a worthless drunk. That was the reality of it. The monkey on his back was digging its claws into his throat and screeching in his ears in its need for a good belt of rye whiskey. It would have sold each and everyone of them down the road to get it. It would have handed them over to Count fucking Chocula for a six-dollar bottle of hootch.

But, in character, he said, "We're going to survive, son. Right now, I see only the promise of the dawn and the new day. And we're going to get there, one way or another."

Reg's eyes were wet. But he was *believing*.

God, Doc could see it.

He was believing completely. And Doc knew at that moment if he hadn't before, that he had the gift, all right, the gift of bullshit. If he were an evangelist, he could have gotten Reg to empty his wallet and sign over his house to him. And it wasn't so much that he himself had any special powers of persuasion, it was that he knew what the kid wanted to hear and he gave him the belief he so needed.

"What about…about Bailey?"

"Yes," Doc said, "yes. Well, we'll see what transpires. If worse comes to worse, we'll have to put her out in the snow."

He didn't elaborate on that and didn't need to, of course. Reg had seen the movies—Christ, he worked on *Chamber of Horrors*—he knew what happened to the victims of vampires. He knew very well what they became.

Sighing, Doc held Bailey's cool hand and felt something inside him break open as he made contact. He shivered and shook. Hot beads of sweat ran down his spine, each one a droplet of venom. It was like some malarial fever born of pale green swamps had taken hold of him and he could not shake it. Except, it wasn't that. It was guilt and self-recrimination, disappointment and anxiety. *It'll be over soon, my dear. Soon the big sleep will take you down into darkness.* And even as he thought that, he dreaded the truth of it.

Yes, she would sink into darkness.

But she would not rest.

He remembered, as a child, long before his father had run off and his mother became an acid-eyed, venom-tongued shrew, that she had been a very good mother: caring, calm, loving. When he was sick she used to sit and hold his hand and sing to him. She had a beautiful voice. Maybe not the sort to sing an aria and stun a crowd, but a soft and wistful voice that made a body feel warm and tucked-in, curled-up and content. It was the sort of voice that could summon you from fevers and flus and put you back on your feet as it had him many times. He wanted to sing to Bailey then, to draw her out of a world of graveyards and starving shadows and back into the light.

But he couldn't.

It would do no good.

Because even then, he could feel the dire influence of those outside, those who waited in the storm. He could hear their voices, sweet and singsong and profane. Many voices that were one. It came to him in low pulsations of evil, discordant and invasive. It echoed up from the depths of crypts and cellar-holds. It sounded like whispering satin and coffin-silk, graveyard rats scratching in oblong boxes and lost souls moaning in the dark watches of night. He shut the ghost-voices out and wished dearly that Bailey could do the same. But it was in her, the virus of tombs, the embryo of malignance. And it was growing, gaining vitality as she herself pined away into the grave.

Doc felt for her pulse and it was barely there: weak, irregular.

"She's almost gone," he said to Reg, blinking away the oceans that filled his eyes. "Come say good-bye to her."

"I…I can't. I'm afraid."

"There's nothing to be afraid of. Come over here. *Please.* I don't want her to die alone."

13

Morris had been sleeping for an eternity of darkness and maybe he'd been conscious the entire time. The slumber was like a shroud he wore. One he hid under but could hide under no more. It had been stripped away from him and he had convoluted memories of Wenda and Megga speaking to him, saying things that hadn't made much sense, of heat from the fire baking him, of wolves in a forest: red-eyed, slat-thin wolves hungry for his flesh. It seemed that he had heard and seen things without really understanding them or wanting to. But it had been there, everything that had happened, only he was removed from it like seeing sheets of rain through a window.

What brought him awake and as near to his senses as he'd been in some time was the ghost. The evil ghost with the red eyes.

He tried to tell himself it was a dream. But if it was a dream, then it was a dream of madness, blackness, and a shadowy world beyond the pale of death. No, he was not dreaming. It was the ghost who was dreaming. Dreaming of *him,* dreaming of drawing Morris down into narrow houses and trenches of dark earth where corpse-orchids grew, flowering and fetid-smelling and pulsing white with juices of pestilence.

Morris opened his eyes and saw Megga and Wenda, still on guard, still waiting out the night. His eyes moved warily in their sockets like those of a frightened vole. He had a strange memory of pain and he was almost afraid to move, afraid to do anything but wait there by the fire. He was made senseless and numb by his own fear.

But why the memory of pain?

The ghost. It was the ghost. He had tried to ignore the voice of the ghost and the pain increased; he had tried to completely shut it out and a headache like a hot, bubbling geyser tore through his brain.

That was the pain.

That was the memory of defiance.

He's going to come for me and I know it. He'll slaughter the women and make me watch. Then he'll enslave me.

No, Morris couldn't wait for that. He had to run into the night, into the open arms of the storm, for there he would find sanctuary. Wenda would not let him leave and he knew it. He could see her over there with a sharpened stake in one hand and huge gleaming butcher's knife in the other. Those were her weapons that insured the politics of her office. She wasn't afraid to use them. She was not afraid to kill. She wasn't even afraid to use them on the things outside in the storm.

But he had to find a way out.

He knew what was out there. To them he was prey. They would hunt him down. In his mind he saw himself trying to break free of Cobton, the cold getting inside him, making his blood run like jelly. The white faces pushing in, the smiling mouths of teeth. And the hands. Pallid hands reaching out for him, trapping him, ensnaring him, as he tried to fight his way free. Those people out there would swarm and multiply and bury him alive in groping grave-cold fingers and sucking hot mouths—

No, no, no! I'll get out. I'll sneak out and Wenda won't stop me and those ghouls won't see me and I'll be free, free, free.

Then he heard a mocking, lunatic cackling in the back of his skull. It was an inhuman, incessant, unearthly braying. It sounded like black tides lapping against dock pilings and the squealing cries of wild boars and the yammering bark of rabid dogs opening jaws slavered with white foam. It was the laughter of the evil ghost. Morris could feel its mind entering his own, a creeping shadow network. It infested his brain like writhing white worms that laid hot masses of eggs up and down his spinal ganglia and fouled his neurons with their oozing wastes.

He tried to cry out, but his voice did not exist. He tried to remember warm days and bright suns, things that would drive the ghost away, but it was no good. The evil ghost wanted him to see other things, it directed his thoughts, driving them into the gathering darkness like railroad spikes. *My name. Remember my name and speak it aloud.* Morris heard his voice say it and the ghost was pleased by that.

It was so pleased, it let him see what the others out in the storm knew.

It showed him a series of mountain villages that it had drained dry. The empty houses and overgrown yards, the leaf-blown streets where no feet walked by daylight. The villages which stood empty and thin as their churchyards filled and grew fat. It showed him how the blood had been leeched from these places. When they ran dry as desert washes, the ghost and its worshippers sought new environs where the blood was rich and abundant. They sought new fields to sow their seed and tend their crops of nightmare.

Morris saw a ship at sea, a ghost ship crossing the Atlantic, its sails fluttering rags, its cabin blown with mist...the warped, salt-bleached decks and the shadows that oozed out of holds and casks and crates as the sun sank low. He saw the ghost finding land and leading its followers to Cobton for here was a village with blood running hot and thick in its veins. At night, they fastened themselves to the arteries of the town like leeches and sipped them dry. Soon, the fields lay fallow and the walks unswept, the high houses were silent and the shutters creaked in the wind. Cobton became a deserted village, a ghost town in the literal sense…a tomb of shadows and scratching rats that no sane men visited.

Then Morris saw men, not necessarily sane but dedicated in their grim task. They opened graves and disinterred blood-bloated corpses with staring eyes and florid faces. They drove stakes through the restless dead, pretending they did not see the blood fountaining from chests or hear the screams that came from the lips of corpses. They burned the remains. But they did not find the ghost nor its select community that hid in hollows of night and seams of darkness unknown.

Cobton was shunned and left to rot.

This is what the evil ghost showed him.

It was near to him now and he could feel it.

Like a dog, his hackles raised as its smell, which was that of embalmed things and grinning cadavers puffed with death.

He could see the ghost now: a tall, manlike shape that was more shadow than substance, skeletal and narrow, a blackness blowing out from it like hell itself. Its face was a mask of ashen, carved leather lit by two huge eyes like luminous necrotic moons. It was a cruel face, a merciless face, a cadaverous face of shadow-sucking hollows and bony ridges framed by a drooping mustache, sharp nose, and gleaming bone-yellow flesh. The thin lips pulled up into a rictal grin of violation and a voice like wind blown through a skull said, *My name. Speak it aloud.*

Morris squirmed, fought, but it did him no good.

He would do what he was told.

14

Wenda's voice was so confident and sure of itself it was like a steel blade cutting deep: *"Get away from that window. Do you hear me? Get away from it right now."*

Megga turned, ready to snarl at her…but at the last moment, she acquiesced. She did not like anyone bossing her or dominating her, but there were times to fight and times to do what was asked of you. She turned from the window and looked over at Wenda and wanted to hate her, but found that she couldn't. Wenda had saved her several times now and though she wasn't entirely sure she wanted to be saved, Wenda's concern was touching in its own way. Their safety was a priority with her.

She was ready to fight.

And those outside knew that.

Megga thought they even *feared* it.

"I wasn't doing anything," she said.

"Doesn't matter," Wenda told her. "The way things stand, those things will do anything to get to us. I'm not going to have them using you. I can't allow it."

Megga wanted to look her in the eye and tell her that it didn't much matter *what* she wanted. There was no choice in the matter. The vampires would take them when they decided it was time and she would not be able to fight against it. She had already angered them and Megga could feel it. When the time came, it was going to be very ugly for her.

"If they use me, it's out of my hands."

Wenda's eyes went narrow and dark. "You always have a choice. You can fold up like Morris or fight like me...or you can continue to do what you have been doing: bending over for what's out there."

Megga sat down slowly like she was brittle and might break. "It can be romance or it can be rape when they take you. That's the only choice there is, Wenda. Because they'll get me and they'll get you."

"They won't get me."

Megga laughed. "Yes, they will."

"Is that what they've told you?"

Megga did not say anything.

"Is it?" Wenda said. "I feel them out there same as you do. They try to get in your head. I know that. The difference between you and me is that I won't let them."

Megga laughed again, but inside she was not laughing at all. Her blood was running hot and her ire was up and she wanted to slap Wenda right across the face because, again, Wenda did not have a clue. She wanted to take hold of her and shake her, shout into her face: *YOU won't let them? YOU won't let them? That's because they haven't directed it at you! When they do your brain doesn't work anymore and your emotions short-circuit and you're not sure who you are or what you are and what's right and what's wrong! You stupid, stupid silly little bitch!* But, of course, she didn't do that because Wenda would have hit her. And it wasn't that she was afraid of being hit or hitting, it just seemed like a terrible drain on her energy and she was weakening by the moment. Maybe they hadn't gotten their teeth into her throat yet, but there were other ways to drain someone, other ways to squeeze them out like a sponge. They could drain you psychically until you didn't have anything left to fight with.

It was at that moment that Morris sat up, his eyes looking varnished and shiny. "Griska," he said. *"Griska."*

For Megga, those words were like arrows punching into her, their barbs sinking deep and holding. She sat up, coughing, then gagging, then simply trying to breathe so she did not blackout and hit the floor. Those words. That name. *He's not supposed to say that name. He's not supposed to!* Megga knew the name, she'd heard it in her dreams, but she would never say it. Part of that was the idea of incurring the wrath of its owner and part was a superstitious notion that to pronounce the name of the dead was to summon them.

Wenda was staring at her.

Megga said, "I'm all right."

But she was not all right. That name was still echoing through her skull and stirring things up in there, making a boiling darkness begin to take shape. She squeezed her eyes shut, hoping it would go away but it continued to build and build.

"That name," Wenda said. "Tell me that name. I want to hear it."

Morris just looked at her dumbly. His eyes were glazed, bovine, like he just wanted to chew his cud and be left in peace. "What name?"

"The name you just said."

"I don't know. I was half-awake. I must've been dreaming."

Wenda sat forward now. "Don't give me that shit. Say the name."

Morris was trapped. He looked from Wenda to Megga hopelessly. Megga wanted to jump in, to throw some interference in his direction but she could not seem to do anything but sit there as the darkness moved in her head and her nerves curled like burnt-out wires.

"Say it," Wenda said.

"He didn't say anything," Megga managed. "Just…just gibberish."

Morris would not meet Wenda's eyes and Wenda was fully aware of the fact. She had him and she knew she had him.

Megga felt herself going hot and cold with fever sweat. Morris had spoken the name and that was like calling old ghosts from their graves, only this ghost he had conjured was malefic, cunning, and ancient and she could see its face taking form in her brain: a face white going to gray, skullish and red-eyed, with a thin-lipped, crimson-stained mouth that was smiling and hungry. And she could hear its voice speak, telling her that Morris was weak and he would be broken in the ancient way: disemboweled whilst still breathing, his entrails fed to the dogs, his trunk impaled on a stake. And she would watch, she would be *compelled* to watch.

Wenda was staring at her now. "You know the name, too, don't you?"

"No, no, I…no, I never heard that name."

"They've gotten to both of you," Wenda said. "Then both of you listen: *Griska, Griska.*"

Morris made a whimpering sound and Megga tried not to shake, but she was trembling almost spasmodically by that point. *Do not say the name. Do not speak of it or think of it.*

"It's a Slavic name. He must be the leader of our friends outside," Wenda said, not truly knowing, Megga figured, but intuiting it and having absolute faith in not only her instinct, but what she was reading in their faces. "He must be old, very old. He's the one I'll find. He's the one I'll ram this stake through."

"It won't be enough," Megga said before she could stop herself.

"What?" Wenda asked. *"What did you say?"*

Megga thought she would throw up. Morris was sobbing, openly sobbing like a child that had gotten a good whacking. And maybe he had at that. But why wasn't Griska reaching out for Wenda? Why didn't he bring her under control and smash her, dominate her, make her into a mindless slave like he had with so many others?

There's a reason, a voice in Megga's head said through the fog. *There's a very good reason. What do you think that might be?*

But she didn't dare think. *He* was probing her mind. *He* would know it if she thought things she was not supposed to think. No, no, no, she had to block it out, block it out, block it out, imagine a brick wall like George Sanders did in *The Village of the Damned*—they'd shown that one on *Chamber of Horrors* along with its less impressive sequel—and keep the bad thoughts out or he would read them and make her suffer for her defiance because if there was one thing he detested, hated—and possibly *feared*—it was a free mind.

No, no, no, she would not think it. She *dared* not think of what was different about Wenda.

"Say the name, Morris," Wenda said, feeding on the power of her discovery.

"No!" Morris said through his tears. *"He won't let me!"*

Megga felt a burning white-hot jolt of agony drill into the base of her skull and continue burning right through her brain until she cried out and that voice, that crazy disobedient voice, in her head spoke loud and clear. It told her what was different about Wenda. Wenda was pure. And in her purity, she fed off the light and shunned the dark, refused its attraction. Vultura was just a job to her, a role, there was nothing intimate involved with it. There was not so much as a seam of darkness in her that Griska could crawl into. Morris was easy. He was essentially weak. He was also greedy, self-indulgent, and egotistical. And Megga herself was morose, macabre, and pessimistic. Minds like that were primal and dark and easily mastered. But not Wenda...because...*because* it wasn't just her mind that was pure but her body. She was twenty-seven years old and drop-dead gorgeous but...*but she was a fucking virgin. She had never been touched.* She'd never given in to her animal needs, never connected with the dark side of her primal nature.

This is what Megga knew as she fell out of her chair and hit the floor, eyes rolling in her head. Griska could toy with Wenda, tease her and invade her dreams, but he could never master her unless he sank his teeth into her neck and this not only disturbed him, it frightened him. Wenda was a worthy adversary and he did not like that.

And that's why I tried to seduce her. They wanted me to corrupt her for them. They still want me to. And, yes, I want that more than anything. I want to suck her tongue into my mouth and slide my fingers into her. I want to taste what's between her legs. I want to bite it and suck the sweet juice that runs out.

Trembling, head thrashing from side-to-side, Megga heard a hot-breath moaning escape her lips.

Then...Morris screamed and ran for the door. He threw it open and charged out into the darkness. And Wenda was hot on his trail.

15

Bailey opened her eyes and they were like clear glass, shiny and wet, as if they were covered in the translucent nictitating membrane of a reptile or a bird of prey. Those eyes looked up at Doc, staring right through him like he wasn't even there. Something in the gaze, that was more of a knowing leer, made his heart beat fast and dried up the spit in his mouth.

"Bailey?" he said in a voice weak as a newborn kitten.

She looked like she was going to say something to him, but then her head thrashed back and forth and a clear, watery mucus ran from her nostrils. Her whole body began to move, not just twitching but seeming to ripple with a liquid roll of muscles as if every neuron in her body were misfiring. Her limbs were flailing, eyes rolling, head whipping from side-to-side. It was like the mother of all seizures and in her weakened state, Doc knew she wouldn't last long. Her body alternately went rigid, then loose and boneless. She lifted her head maybe three inches from the sofa and let loose with a vicious and guttural shriek.

"HELP HER!" Reg cried.

But there was no helping her.

It was like she had been invaded by some destructive demon that was intent on finishing her off. As Doc held her, he was amazed at how strong she was, how she moved against him and how he was forced to move with her. The mucus ran from her, drool bubbled from her mouth. Her back arched. Her teeth snapped shut, then chattered wildly. Her lips were writhing worms as they pulled away from her gums and he saw that her upper central incisors had grown narrow like the teeth of a rat, long and sharp.

"DO SOMETHING!" Reg practically screamed.

He was out of his head, pacing back and forth, but refusing to get any closer as if what she had was catchy and Doc was pretty sure that it was. Bailey settled down for a moment and looked up at him with eyes that were hot, burning with what seemed to be lust. Her tongue licked along her teeth, then jutted in and out of her mouth. Under the circumstances, it was appalling.

"Help me hold her!" Doc cried out. *"Goddammit! Get over here!"*

She threw her head back again and let out a broken wailing noise that was high-pitched, nearly deafening. It never truly subsided. It shrilled out of her while her lips pulled away from gums and teeth and her eyes rolled back white. Then it fragmented, becoming something like a hysterical cackling that raised gooseflesh on both

142

Doc and Reg, who, by then, was there with Doc trying to hold Bailey down as tremors rolled through her body. Her head was thrown back on her neck and it was like she was trying to drive it right through the sofa. There was not just drool but pink foam slavering from her mouth by then as if she were rabid. As her body went through an almost serpentine sort of basal writhing, her hands came up, clawing at the air. Doc got one of them down, absolutely astounded at the strength in the limb which he felt could have thrown him clear across the room. Her free hand went right at Reg's face, the nails just missing his eyes and scratching red welts down his cheek.

"Jesus *Christ,*" he said, finally trapping the arm, but learning, like Doc, that grabbing it and then holding on were two different things. It was like trying to capture the whipping tentacle of some huge squid.

The way she was snapping her teeth, Doc was certain she would bite her tongue off. Miraculously, that didn't happen but her spike-like incisors were scraped along her lower lip again and again, several times sinking right into it, and the result was that the mucus and pink saliva blossomed with blood that stained her teeth and ran down her chin. With her head still thrashing, gouts of it flew into the air and spattered the faces of the men who were trying to help her.

Her body jerked with rapid-fire convulsions, then settled back into the sofa. A fine trickle of blood ran from her left nostril. Her face was contorted into some pale fright mask smeared with red. She let out a series of hoarse, barking sounds from her throat. Then she opened her eyes and they were a juicy, opaque red like the bellies of blood-swollen ticks. Her jaws were open, lips pulled back, those terrible fangs ready to strike. She looked up at Reg and made a low, throaty sort of hissing sound like a snake and he let go of her arm, his ass hitting the floor.

"*Oh, man,*" he said. "*Oh my God...*"

Then her eyes and mouth closed and it seemed it might be over. Her limbs went limp and her body, though trembling minutely, was no longer clashing against itself. Her teeth were still chattering and she was a mess from the bloody discharge that came out of her, but the worst had passed. Doc dug a hankie from out of his pants and wiped her face clean of the blood and saliva, which had formed sort of a snotty slime on her cheeks and chin. Her face was burning hot to the touch, droplets of fever sweat exuding from her pores. There was steam rising from it in the cold air and it stank with a morbid foulness that reminded him of warm vomit. It was gagging.

"Is she...?"

"No, no. She's alive," Doc said, feeling for her pulse, which was barely even there. Her breathing was shallow. It rattled in her chest. He could see her eyes moving beneath the lids and jaws working side-to-side like she was chewing on something or trying to form words. He brushed a strand of blonde hair from her face. It was greasy with sweat. "Bailey? Honey, can you hear me?"

Her lips parted with a bubble of blood and her eyes opened.

Doc nearly fell right over.

They had changed again.

The whites of her eyes were a dark red, the color of arterial blood. But the irises were a brilliant milky sort of blue, the pupils like black beads. They looked at him and he felt weak inside. They seemed to spear right into his head and he had trouble catching his breath for a moment. They did not move like the eyes of a human being, but like those of an animal—darting about in the dark, bruised-looking sockets like those of a trapped beast.

Then they closed and it began again.

It was like something in her was fighting against the infection that was taking her over and fighting with everything it had. Her body began to shudder again, then it went wild with convulsions. It went stiff like a piece of lumber, then soft and pliable and quivering. Again, Doc held her and Reg did the same. The contortions were nowhere near as violent this time. She kept arching her head on her neck and pounding it into the sofa. More blood ran from her nose, from her mouth. A trickle of it came from her left eye as if her tear ducts were filled with it. She made croaking noises in her throat. Her teeth chattered and ground against one another.

Her mouth opened and she screamed.

Then she sank back down into the sofa, her chest rising high one last time as she gasped for air...then it sank back down, the breath leaking out of her. One eye was closed, the other stuck half open. She smacked her lips a few times.

A trembling went through her limbs.

Her fingers shook.

Her lips pulled up into a horrible sardonic smirk, then relaxed.

And she went still.

Doc felt for a pulse, put his head to her chest to ferret out a heartbeat. Finally, sighing, he shook his head. Trying to keep the emotion out of his voice, he said, "She's gone."

Reg was shaking, his eyes filled with tears. "What…what do we do?"

Doc wiped his eyes. "Throw some more wood on the fire. Get it blazing high. Then I'll tell you."

16

Amazingly, and thankfully, Bailey was barely aware of any of it. Her mind was oddly dislocated from her body as often is the case in the worst trauma. It seemed, at times, she could see herself flopping about on the sofa with Doc and Reg trying to hold her down like she might float away. But mostly, she was lost in a fog of dreams and disjointed memories. Selling chocolates door-to-door as a Campfire Girl in third grade. Playing softball in middle school. Listening to her mother singing as she made up treat bags for Halloween. Rushing down the stairs as a child, seeing all the Christmas presents under the tree, but being less amazed by them than she was by the twinkling array of lights on the tree itself. But mostly she remembered the sunshine. Running in it, playing in it, glorifying in it, feeling it on her summer skin and reveling in its warmth and purity.

These are the things that went through her head as she neared death and a darkness like black oil seeped up from somewhere far below, spreading a virulent malignance through her body that crowded her out of her own head with primal hungers and impulses until she was no more. And before it consumed her completely, she recognized that she was unclean, she was polluted by the black horror of it. *No, no, not this,* she thought and then thought no more.

17

A split second after Morris ran out the door, Wenda was on her feet. The knife was in her belt and the stake was in her hand. She charged out the doorway into the dimness of the hall, moving more by instinct than anything else.

I've got to get him, she thought. *I've got to bring him down.*

Had she been in a relatively sane state of mind, the wording of her thoughts might have amused her. *Bring him down.* Like he was an animal that had to be brought to earth and killed. But she was not in a sane state of mind. What she was doing was purely instinctive. She had to stop him. She had to get to him before he got outside.

She heard him stumbling off in the darkness.

She went after the noise, wishing she had brought a lantern with her.

He was out of his head and she knew it. He was driven to mania and terror from those things outside getting into his mind. And probably by one in particular: Griska. Even the name left a sickening taste in her mouth. She came out into the entry and a shadow vaulted out at her.

Morris.

He blindsided her and sent her crashing to the floor. Her stake clattered away from her.

"GET AWAY FROM ME!" he cried as he cut away towards the kitchen.

Wenda scrambled around until she found her stake and went after him.

"STAY AWAY!" he said. "STAY AWAY FROM ME!"

He was in an absolute frenzy, it seemed. Tripping and falling, crawling on all fours. Slamming into walls and upsetting things from shelves. Swearing and gasping, punching out blindly, kicking and sobbing.

Wenda raced after him.

She got into the kitchen and Morris, sensing her, jumped away through the archway into the dining room. He was dead-ended and she knew it. She went after him and he made a squealing sound as she bore down on him. He went to the windows and began slapping his hands against them. Wenda grabbed him with one hand and threw him backwards. He stumbled, hit the floor, then was up and scrambling over the heavy oak table before she could get him. She jumped at him as he tried to get back into the kitchen and then they were fighting. He was trying to hit her and kick her and she was doing the same. His fist glanced off her cheekbone at the same time she brought the blunt edge of the stake down on his head.

He made a yelping sound and shoved her away.

She banged her hip against the table, but would not go down.

"MORRIS!" she shouted.

He took off, bouncing his way through the kitchen, scattering copper pots and pans, reviling her with a string of obscenities.

Wenda gave chase again. He was completely fucking loco by that point and she'd already decided that she wasn't going to be gentle when she found him. *I'll bash his goddamned head in.* She heard rather than saw him wing his way clumsily out of the kitchen and she was on his heels. Back in the entry, he saw her and darted back, swinging. She got out of his way and swung the blunt end of the stake again. This time it connected with his fist and made a hollow popping sound as it smashed against his knuckles.

He yelped again and ran.

Wenda wasn't sure what he was up to. He was like some crazed animal trying to bull its way out of a cage. The door was right there and yet he hadn't made a try for it. Maybe, in his confusion, he didn't really know what a door was.

She followed him again.

He cut down another corridor on the other side of the kitchen. This one led to the back door and she knew it. Maybe he was smartening up. Maybe he'd found his way out. She got to him before he got to the door and, again, he turned to fight, going for her throat and slamming her up against the wall near the cellar door and with enough force to knock the wind out of her. Wenda slid to the floor, dazed, and Morris jumped on her. He straddled her, wrapping his hands around her throat. And Wenda knew that while he was many things, he was not a killer. He was being compelled to do this.

Probably by Griska.

He tightened his grip and she could get no air. He was grunting and sucking air through clenched teeth. She could feel his penis against her crotch. It was standing hard, straining against the material of his jeans. And she knew as she saw black dots before her eyes that he was going to strangle her unconscious or beat her down, then rape her. That's what this was about. That's what he was supposed to do.

Wenda brought up the stake and cracked him alongside the head.

Once, twice, three times.

His grip sagged and she twisted, throwing him off. She brought up the stake to beat his brains out. And that's when she heard the shuffling of footsteps.

A creaking noise.

And the cellar door swung open.

18

Once the fire was blazing high and the parlor was filled with warmth and a guttering yellow light, Doc looked down at Bailey's corpse and announced, "We have to get her out of here, Reg. We can't have her in the house. I don't know how long it might take until she...we need to get her out of here."

Reg looked at him and his eyes were just dull. The light had been stolen from them. "It's dangerous to go outside."

"I know, but we'll have to chance it. Otherwise..."

But Doc didn't need to complete that. They had both seen her eyes and her teeth, and they had already had a run-in with one of them—its remains were still in the corner—to know what it would be like if she woke up. She would tear out their throats and he didn't honestly know if he had the strength to fight against Bailey as he had with the hag.

However they decided to do it, it had to be done immediately.

Because he was feeling something out there, something which had been vague for some time but was now gaining substance in his thoughts. Out in the storm, he knew, there was one that was stronger than the others. He could feel it out there, feel it worrying around at the edges of his mind, spreading the seeds of anxiety. That it had power, he could not doubt for now and again its influence seemed to be getting stronger and when that happened, it felt like a gas jet inside of him was being turned lower and lower until it barely burned.

You're woolgathering, that's all your doing.

But he did not believe that. This was not imagination ruling him: it was something else, something out in the storm. Something waiting, forever waiting with an inhuman patience that chilled him to contemplate. Whatever that thing was, Bailey belonged to it now. And it would use her to get at them. He could feel it. She was the bait that would draw them to their own destruction.

"We're going to take her to the front door. Bring the axe," he said. "You open the door and I'll set her in the snow. We'll do it quick. We'll do it real quick."

Reg did not question what had to be done; he accepted. He grabbed up the axe and lantern. As he did so, Doc scooped up Bailey. Holding her dead weight in his arms made something jump in his belly. Although she hadn't weighed more than 115 pounds in life and seemed to weigh considerably less in death, it was the *feel* of her that disturbed him. There was something wrong about it like she had been converted now into a mass of evil. She seemed light in his arms, too light, as if she were now made of some finer, ethereal material than mere flesh and blood.

He told himself not to think about it as he stepped from the room, but not thinking about it was like not thinking about an especially large spider crawling up your leg in the dead of night.

Reg led the way down the corridor, casting fearful glances behind him at what was in Doc's arms.

Doc figured they must have looked like a couple characters in a *Chamber of Horrors* flick: the lantern light throwing distorted shadows against the walls, the grim set to their faces, and the thing they were carrying out into the snow. Like a scene from some old Barbara Steele movie, one of those Gothic potboilers set in a cobwebby old castle. He might have found the image amusing at any other time, but now it was threatening to its core and black to its roots. Bailey's arm was hanging loose and as he walked, it kept slapping him in the leg and that made a cold, sick sort of sweat pop at his brow. He was just waiting for her eyes to open and her teeth to slide into his throat.

As they closed in on the door, Doc could feel the magnetism of what was out in the moaning, hissing snowstorm. It knew what they were bringing and although maybe it found the idea of what they were laying at its feet amusing in some darkly regal fashion, it very much wanted them to keep it. *My gift to you.* Reg reached out to unlock the door and as he did so, Doc felt the strength in him draining away as if it were being tapped by that thing out there.

"You ready?" Reg asked.

"I guess."

But he wasn't ready. God, no. Being here at door was more than just standing at the threshold of shelter and raging storm, it was like standing at the borderland of some malefic black dimension, the intersection of hate and pain and insanity, the crossroads of the nameless and the unknown. It was as if, just beyond that door, lines of diabolic force were concentrated and once he stepped into their field, he would be emptied, discharged like a battery.

He refused to contemplate it.

Reg peered out the window one last time, looked to Doc, and reached for the doorknob. "I don't see anything out there," he said.

But Doc knew it would be nothing that obvious. They would not be clustered and waiting. It would not be that simple. What was out there would not want it to end so quickly for him; it wanted to amplify the pain he felt, generate the maximum amount of terror, suck every drop of despair from him before he knew death. That was part of the game: to make you destroy yourself.

Reg opened the door and the storm came rushing in, the wind throwing snow in Doc's face and sending frigid fingers of chill up his spine. His throat seemed to contract with terror. He was certain that Bailey had shifted in his arms. And he told himself: three, four steps and you can set her down. That's all there is to it. Then you're safe. So he walked out into the blizzard, the wind screaming around the house, the driving snow filled with moving shapes. And a voice in his brain said, *you're never going to be safe again and you know it. He's out here. The thing you fear. He's watching you right now. And you can toss Bailey into a drift and run back inside, but you're only putting it off. He's going to come for you before dawn forces him back into some lair of darkness. You won't be able to stop him. He'll invade the house like a seam of shadow or a river of night. He'll crawl through a crack or ooze down a pipe or flow through a keyhole, but he* will *come and there's nothing you can do about that—*

"Doc!" Reg called. "Just set her down, man!"

Yes, that's all there was to it.

He took two or three more steps and even that close to the doorway, the storm was trying to pull him away and tuck him somewhere deep and cold where he would never be found. Reg was calling out to him again but his voice was lost in the wailing of the storm and Doc knew if he looked behind him, the house would be gone. The snowstorm would have shrouded it from view. He kneeled down and set Bailey in a drift of powder, then stood back up. And as he did so, he felt something build in him like gathering thunderheads. He felt a malign presence near him that filled him with a manic, biting terror. It was palpable and overwhelming. Where before his spine was literally tingling from the menace he felt coming out of the storm, now it was like a cat had sunk its claws between his shoulder blades and was drawing them down his backbone.

He heard Reg's voice.

He turned to go back to the house, but his limbs weren't responding. He felt clumsy and rubbery like he'd been shot up with narcotics. His skull was filled with the rising drone of buzzing insects. That's when he saw the little girl standing not three feet away. The snow seemed not to be falling on her, but *through* her. She was naked, her flesh white as the snow around her. Her hair was a brilliant red that moved in the wind, flying around her head. Her eyes were huge, like glossy black blood blisters that were ready to pop. She reached down between her legs and touched her deathly-white immature vulva like she wanted him to touch her there, too. She reached out for his hand to make him do so. Her voice was pristine in his head: *There's a place where we can lay together. A place where you can touch me. A place where we can sleep together like death—*

And he would have touched her.

God help him, but he would have.

Then something grabbed him and yanked him back and he knew it was Reg, but he still fought because Reg was ruining the most beautiful thing that Doc had ever known. Couldn't he see that?

Reg pulled him back and in his stupor, he could not fight. The girl leered at him, then opened her fanged mouth and made a screeching sound that was the pure stark and desolate wrath of the storm itself.

Then Reg threw him inside and slammed the door.

And once Doc could speak, he looked up and said, "Did...did I put Bailey out there?"

19

When the door swung open, Wenda figured the jig was up. Then a flashlight beam speared into her face and she squinted her eyes against it. She saw a man standing there. "You going to use that stake on him?" he said.

Realizing he was no vampire, Wenda sighed. Morris was just lying there, breathing. "No, I guess not."

"Good. He doesn't look like one of them."

He helped her to her feet and she said, "Who the hell are you?"

"I'm Rule," he told her. "One of the caretakers of this damn place. The only caretaker that's still alive." Before Wenda could introduce herself, he said, "You're Vultura. I'd know you anywhere. I watch your show. It's very funny."

"Thanks," she said, almost automatically. Then she turned to Morris. "Get up. You're coming back with us."

He climbed awkwardly to his feet. The fight was gone from him and he was much the same as he had been before the mania had gripped him: like some wind-up toy soldier with no will of his own. She led Morris back to the sitting room with Rule trailing behind. Megga was waiting there for them. She looked from Wenda to Morris to Rule and raised an eyebrow.

"This is the caretaker," Wenda explained. "He's been...*exactly* where have you been and what have you been doing?" She said this as if it had suddenly occurred to her. And it had. With everything going on, she hadn't really thought to make him explain himself. But now she not only wanted that, but she was ready to demand it.

Rule looked at her, did something with his mouth that was almost a smile. Whether that was to reassure her or not, she couldn't say. There was something very calm and non-threatening about him. He was white-haired, snow-bearded, pot-bellied, wore a set of insulated Carhartt overalls, heavy gloves, and a mossy oak flap cap. But what struck her most was that he was oddly...*familiar*. There was something in his voice, something in his eyes that she remembered.

"I suppose you've got the right to ask that," he said, "and I suppose it would only be fair of me to answer it. See, when this happened, I was setting up the genny out back so you people could have lights for your shoot. Bill was in the car. He was supposed to be getting some cables out, but my guess is he was sitting in the car, probably finishing a chapter in one of his westerns. Bill wasn't the motivated type. Now, of course, he's dead."

"Something came out of the cemetery up there and got him," Wenda said.

"Yes. I heard him scream and I ran out into the square and...well, I'm not sure exactly, but something was dragging him off. Something not exactly human." Rule took off his flap cap and wiped sweat from his face with it. "I was going to go after that thing...then I saw the...the *others* out in the storm. That's when I came in here. I was cut off from the car. I had nowhere else to go."

Megga listened, but looked suspicious. "How did you know it came out of the cemetery?" she asked Wenda. "That's a little specific."

"I saw it," Wenda told her. "In my head." She explained how, when the crone had Megga upstairs, she saw things in her head. She didn't know what they were. Some kind of psychic ripples from the crone herself maybe, but she'd seen them.

"Burt saw it, too."

Megga said, "Burt?"

"When we first pulled into Cobton. Remember? That thing standing in the cemetery. It was no statue of a graveyard angel. It was the real thing."

Rule cleared his throat. "Anyway, I hid out down in the cellar. I figured I'd wait until dawn and get my ass out of here. It seemed the logical choice of action."

"You must have heard us," Megga said. "You must have known we were in the shit."

"I didn't know what was going on and I wasn't about to mix up in it."

"Very brave of you."

He looked at her. "Miss, bravery has nothing to do with it. In a situation like this there are basically two things: death and survival. I was interested in the latter and if you have a brain in that pretty head of yours, I'm sure you'll understand my motives."

Wenda was becoming more and more intrigued by this guy. He was a caretaker of this ghost town, yet he seemed awfully well-spoken. Not that she thought caretakers were idiots or anything, but this guy seemed somewhat against type. And that voice…where did she know that voice from?

As she thought this over, he went on: "Understand that I was against this whole thing right from the start. It was too risky. Bill agreed with me, of course, as Bill was wont to do. I think a lot of the people that live in this vicinity would have agreed with me, too. And if you had grown up around here, you wouldn't be so high-and-goddamn-mighty about it. You'd know the kind of place Cobton was after dark. You'd know the sort of things that have happened here."

"You knew there were…were *vampires* here?" Wenda asked him.

He shrugged. "I knew the stories. I knew this place was supposed to be haunted. I knew people have disappeared out here. I knew it was a ghost town in more than name. And I knew what I saw out here when I was a kid."

"Which is?"

He ignored that, returning to his original stream: "So, we were certainly against it. But the people that own Cobton, the ones that had it rebuilt and refitted it as a tourist trap some fifteen years ago…well, they're not locals. Just history buffs with fat wallets. They couldn't understand why we didn't want to come out here after dark and there was no point in trying to explain it to them. They would have thought we were crazy."

He explained that since Cobton was rebuilt, there had been no trouble and that was because it was only open during the daytime.

The town was period in every way and that meant no electricity. There was no reason for anyone to be out there at night. It had worked out real well until tonight.

"So knowing what you knew, you still came out here?" Megga said.

"I have my reasons. For Bill...*oh Bill*...for Bill it was strictly a matter of economics, Miss. *Jobs is scarce,* as he often told me." Rule smiled for a moment, but it was a wistful smile that faded quickly. "Regardless, we were the caretakers. We took care of this place. We always got out before sunset. We made sure others did, too. Even when this place was being put back together, we hustled the contractors out of here telling them that they couldn't stay after dark because there were no lights and our insurance didn't cover it. It worked. It always worked." He shrugged, then cocked an ear like he was listening. "Besides, nothing had happened in years. A lot of years. But I knew it would. Sooner or later. And maybe that's what I was waiting for."

"You're a real kook," Megga told him.

Rule explained that it wasn't his idea to stay out here after dark. That was something arranged between the historical society and Morris.

"Yet, you and Bill agreed to come?" Wenda said. "Knowing what might be out here?"

"Yes, we did. Bill needed the money...I needed to see what haunted this place."

"What a freak," Megga said, but there was a certain admiration in her voice; she would have done the same.

Rule sighed. "Let's just say that this place has a history of...evil. It was seeded here long ago and its roots run deep. I knew it would give flower again. It had to. Evil is not easily vanquished."

Wenda smiled. She knew then. "Long time no see, Mr. Rule."

"Oh, you remember me, do you?"

"Yes, I do."

Megga looked at both of them, shrugging. "You two know each other?"

Wenda explained that Rule was Dennis Rule, a professor of humanities and English literature at her alma mater, Stony Brook U. She had barely squeaked by in Survey of British Literature II and the Neoclassic period had nearly killed her, Marlowe's Elizabethan tragedies simultaneously confusing her and depressing her. It was only the Restoration Comedies that gave her hope, clearing the slate for Coleridge and Wordsworth.

"Now, now," said Rule, "I thought you showed promise as a critic. You were quite outspoken concerning Raleigh's pessimism."

"I can't believe you remember any of that," Wenda said.

Megga sneered at them. "Well, let's play old home week some other time, okay? We're in enough of a fix here."

Wenda once again had that mad desire to slap her across the face. *We're in enough of a fix here.* That was true, but where did the *we* part of that come from? Megga had proven herself to be unreliable, selfish, and easily seduced by the monsters out in the storm. She was a weak link, a chink in the armor. Wenda firmly believed that she would sell them out the first chance she got and the only reason she hadn't thus far was because Wenda herself hadn't—and wouldn't—allow that. Megga was not to be trusted. Her motives were questionable as were her ethics. She was someone to watch. Carefully.

So Wenda ignored her. "How did you go from teaching Brit Lit to being a caretaker in Cobton?" she asked Rule.

"I retired," he said. "I grew up quite near here so I returned. They needed a caretaker and I have a love of the Colonial Period. Besides, it was something to do with my time. There are other reasons, of course. But in order for you to understand them, you'll probably need to know what happened in this town. How it became a ghost town in the first place. It's a story for a dark night and I guess this one will do..."

20

Let me start out by saying that Cobton was a living, breathing town at one time, Rule began. It was nothing like this museum piece you might have noticed on your way in tonight. There were about 600 people living here as of 1815 with probably a hundred or more scattered about in the surrounding farms. It was an agricultural area that bordered the wild wastes of the Catskills and its fields produced abundant crops of cabbage, pumpkins, sweet corn, onions, apples, wheat and oats. Most of the town was owned by a land baron named Gerrit VanderHoofen who had a huge plantation just south of Cobton. He owned the fields, the forests, the orchards. It may interest you—and amuse you—to know that descendants of this VanderHoofen *still* own these lands. VanderHoofen brought in immigrants as tenant farmers and leased the land to them. From what I've heard, VanderHoofen was a shrewd businessman who would have been rich even by today's standards.

That's your history lesson for the day.

What we're really interested in began happening in 1826, if contemporary sources are correct. This would be the first seed of evil as far as I can tell. Up above Cobton, the land of the Catskills was high, wild country, green and growing and rich. Land cut by deep misting ravines and shrouded in black, impenetrable hemlock forests. Though much of it is second- and third-growth now, you can still get a sense of its mystery and primal fear. The early Dutch and German settlers considered the woods up there haunted and there were superstitions that it was the lair of the Devil, which is probably something they borrowed from the lore of the local Mohicans who avoided the mountains because they were the home of the Manitou and various evil spirits.

I tell you this so you can get a good idea of the people we are talking about: clannish, superstitious, but being an agrarian society probably quite practical by nature. Which brings us to Karl Jorva.

According to an account collected by folklorist Robert Bale in 1897, Karl Jorva was an Austrian immigrant who operated a farm just outside Cobton in the 1820s. Karl and his brother Hugo, along with their wives and children, were among many European immigrants who came to farm the fertile lands as tenant farmers and sharecroppers for the VanderHoofen family. From Cornwall and Germany and Eastern Europe, the immigrants came in waves. But unlike the majority of them, Karl and Hugo raised enough capital to buy their adjoining lands. A rare thing at the time and one that shows that the VanderHoofens were quite progressive in their own way.

Now, both Karl and his brother Hugo were devout Lutherans who read the bible nightly for inspiration and comfort. With a great deal of back-breaking work, Karl and his family cleared the land, raising abundant crops of oats, rye, corn and wheat. Then tragedy struck. His wife, Mara, was stricken with yellow fever and died. Karl was left alone with two growing boys and a teenage daughter. Farm life was a hardscrabble existence in those days and near impossible without a wife. Karl decided to advertise for a mail order bride and was surprised when he received a letter from a young lady in Hungry, Ilsa Stroivecka, who wished to become his wife.

When Ilsa arrived, Karl—being a very practical sort—was not duly impressed. She claimed to be a farmer's daughter, yet to look upon her she was far too frail and thin for the hardship and labor of the agricultural life. Tall, tawny-haired, fine-boned with huge dark eyes and an ivory complexion, she was very beautiful but not the stout, rugged woman he had envisioned who could keep house and children and work the fields as well as any hand.

His misgivings proved correct: Ilsa knew nothing of farming. After the wedding this became all too apparent. Ilsa was quiet and retiring, often preferring to stay in the bedroom where she maintained she was vexed by one illness after another. All expected tragedy, for Karl Jorva was old school. He believed a man's wife was his property to be used and abused as he saw fit. Ilsa could not possibly last. But she did. And soon enough, it was not *she* who bent to Karl's iron will but quite the reverse. Horribly smitten with his "handsome China doll," Karl was soon completely under her thumb and submitted to her every will and want. Even the business of the farm and money were her domain.

Meanwhile, as Karl fell deeper in love, his children—John, Joachim, and Elsje—became increasingly suspicious. They found Ilsa domineering and cruel. She threatened them, often physically abusing them over the slightest infraction of her rules. When ten-year old Joachim fell to his death in a dry well, his brother and sister were certain that Ilsa had pushed him. Apparently, Karl's brother Hugo and his family were also suspicious of this coldly beautiful woman with her stark predatory eyes. And when Elsje turned up missing, questions were asked. There was something decidedly off about Ilsa. It was discovered that she often went alone on midnight walks in the forest, that she not only took the strap to the children but whipped the horses for amusement, and, worse, was seen by the children on many occasions to be eating raw meat or sucking the juices from it.

Perhaps a week after Elsje's death, her corpse was uncovered in a shallow grave in the forest bordering the Jorva farm by Hugo's Alsatian. The condition of the body more than anything worried Hugo, for it appeared to have been partially eaten. Scavengers would do such a thing, Hugo knew, but they did not re-bury the body when they were done. Extremely concerned, Hugo did not report finding the body but covered it and that night, by full moon, secreted himself in the brush along with his eldest son and another farmer. Their moonlight vigil was long and arduous after a long day in the fields, but it did not go unrewarded. Soon enough, a figure came through the trees and began to paw at Elsje's grave. They recognized it as Ilsa right away. She removed the body and to their absolute horror, began to feed upon it, chewing at the breasts and throat.

At this point, Hugo and his company charged from their covert and ordered Ilsa to stop defiling the corpse. According to what the old timers told Robert Bale, Ilsa shrieked and hissed at them, gore dropping from her mouth. When she ran, Hugo raised his long rifle and shot her dead.

There were no charges pressed once the details were made known to the local high sheriff. Such things were best hushed up and forgotten.

But the tale was hardly at an end.

In the coming weeks after his Hungarian bride was buried, Karl—in absolute remorse and denial—began to grow thin and pale. It got so he could barely get himself out of bed at cock-crow and soon the fields were untended, weeds growing up and taking over the rye. Corn rotted on the husk. The wheat went un-scythed. Karl's surviving son, John, began to complain to his Uncle Hugo that he heard the most awful sounds about the farm at night and on more than one occasion he heard a peal of cold evil laughter from his father's room that sounded very much like Ilsa's laughter.

At this time also, children of the local farmers began to complain of terrible nightmares wherein a large white wolf with burning red eyes would come into their rooms at night and lick their throats. When the children were found with puncture marks in their necks, long dismissed superstitions were kindled anew and whispers of the *vulkodlak* and *vlkoslak* began to circulate amongst the immigrant populations, particularly those of Serbian and Czech persuasions.

When Karl Jorva died, having pined away for no apparent reason, and another child died in the same manner, the locals led by Hugo Jorva took matters into their own hands and applied the traditional folk remedies to stop the scourge. The grave of Isla Jorva-Stroivecka was opened and she was found to be "ruddy with life." Although an unpleasant smell likened to rotting fruit emanated from her crypt, she was uncorrupted with no signs of decay. Though pale of limb, her cheeks were rosy, lips plump and "juicy red as if they had been smeared with berries," and her eyes were wide open and staring—"glistening with abnormal vitality", it was said. Those gathered needed no further urging. An iron stake was plunged through Ilsa's chest in the old way to secure her to the grave. Copious amounts of fresh red blood bubbled from the wound and the corpse cried out in a screeching, agonized voice before falling still. The coffin was filled with wild roses, hawthorn, and monkshood—again, traditional remedies to stay the undead—then nailed shut and reburied.

According to Bale, the same was done with Karl Jorva and the child who had been "milked of life." Monkshood, it may interest you to know, is another name for *wolfsbane.*

Now, I call this episode the first seed of evil because after it, things just never seemed right in Cobton. It was like the entire village had gone bad and was slipping closer to the grave day by day.

Things get sketchy at this point, but we do know that the next few years following the Jorva business were bad ones for Cobton. Apparently, blight wiped out the crops and brought about a famine that went on for several years. There are tales of the emaciated corpses of children being stacked in the snow like cordwood. Although the imagery is quite striking, it may just be an old wive's tale. Anyway, as tragedy follows tragedy, there was an outbreak of infectious disease that killed dozens of people. It was then that a farmer named DerGroot got a crazy idea spawned by his fundamentalist religious beliefs and Old Testament fervor. He firmly believed that expiation needed to be offered to the Lord above. The Old Testament is full of blood offerings and ritual sacrifice…some of it involves animals and some of it, humans.

DerGroot was convinced that only the blood of innocents would wash free the stain upon Cobton. Since he had no children and could not offer his firstborn to his god, he offered those of three other families. He abducted them and sacrificed them as burnt offerings. It was said he waited in the woods until he saw a lone child and then he grabbed them, doing it all without so much as a sound, clasping his hand over the child's mouth so there were no cries whatsoever. Then he gagged the child and stuffed them into a potato sack, making off into the woods with them. How he managed to get three in one day is anyone's guess. But, according to tradition, he got them, all right. He took them out into a grove of oaks bordering his property and nailed each of them to a tree before disemboweling them and burning their entrails upon a fire. It was all darkly pagan and fitting, I suppose, since at its roots the Old Testament is a wellspring of pre-Christian depravity and paganistic practices whose origins were born in the darkness of prehistory.

DerGroot was arrested, of course, and duly hanged.

But his wasn't the only shocking crime. A woman named Sarah Goodchild, a rosy-cheeked and pleasant new mother by all accounts, decided to give her baby boy—Jacob or Johanne, depending on which account you read—a bath in the family washtub. What happened we shall never know. Her husband, Peter, went off into the fields to scythe wheat, leaving a giggling baby boy and a happy and contented mother behind. When he came back, the child was floating in water long gone cold and Sarah was hanging above him from a noose of hemp tied off to a rafter beam. Her neck was broken, eyes bulging and tongue hanging from her blackened mouth. Her toes were just brushing the water. The child had been strangled. Presumably, after she'd killed the child, Sarah tied her noose then opened her left wrist and wrote something on the wall in her own blood. What that was, no one dared speak of. It's an unpleasant image, isn't it? Sarah bathing her boy and then, overwhelmed by some strain of madness, strangling him and leaving him bobbing in the water as she tied the rope, slit her wrist, dipped her index finger into her open gushing artery and wrote on the wall before hanging herself.

As they say, trouble comes in threes and so it did in Cobton. Less than a week following the execution of Farmer DerGroot and only two days after the Sarah Goodchild tragedy, suspicions were raised concerning a woodsman named Harrow, Todd Harrow. By all accounts Harrow was an old man by this point, but large and robust from a life spent felling trees in the fresh air. His wife, Regina, was nearly legendary in the village for her baked goods. Each morning she would bring her cart into Cobton piled high with loaves, buns, and pies. They were certain to sell out within the hour. Regina was not known to miss a day. But after she'd missed four of them consecutively, concerns were raised and particularly after the son of a local mason returned to the village claiming he had been chased through the woods by a naked man with an axe. He identified the man as Todd Harrow. The high sheriff went out to the Harrow cabin with a party of armed men and what they found was utterly horrible. Quite naked, Todd Harrow was sitting before the cookstove. Regina's dismembered remains were arranged atop the kitchen table. Todd was feeding her limbs into the stove fire, one by one. Far from being the lunatic that chased the mason's son, it was reported that Todd Harrow was quite calm and relaxed, even hospitable. He invited the sheriff and his men to stay and warm themselves, inquiring as to whether any of them would like a hot cup off coffee. The pot was steaming on the stovetop, heating over the remains of Regina Harrow. What transpired following that is unknown as there are no official records. Rumor had it that Todd was hanged on the spot or gunned down in his cabin. One tale, and a far more imaginative one, claimed that the Harrow cabin was lit on fire and while it blazed, Todd sat contentedly in his chair and burned.

Now these three horrors happening in such a short period of time are alarming to say the least, but it is my belief—and one that is probably illogical and harebrained—that the soil of Cobton and its environs was made fertile for evil by these acts of violence and the Jorva incident.

After that, things were peaceful again in Cobton until late summer of 1828 when a group of foreigners arrived. They were led by a man named Griska. Neither he nor his followers were ever seen, it was said, by the light of day. They situated themselves in an old mill above the town. And it was then that another outbreak of infectious disease began. This plague, however, was much more virulent than its predecessor and by December of 1828, Cobton was a ghost town.

Most of that was never documented for there was no one *left* to document it. What we know comes from rumors and hearsay and tales handed down generation to generation: that a group of local militiamen led by the high sheriff again entered the Cobton Burying Ground the following spring once the ground was soft again. Apparently, the depopulated plague village was not their only concern for it was written that the previous winter there had been a number of sheep mutilated, all of which were drained of blood and badly mutilated. There were also no less than a dozen instances of what was known as the "Cobton Pox" in surrounding hamlets. According to the tales, which were still making the rounds when Robert Bale collected them, the graves of forty persons—men, women, and children—were opened. Save for three, which were decomposed acceptably, the corpses were found to be uncorrupted. They were swollen with blood, ruddy-cheeked, and looked very much like they were sleeping. They were disposed of in the traditional manner by being staked, at which point, all screamed and copious amounts of blood issued from their mouths and noses and other orifices. They were burned in a pyre, it was said, the charred remains interred in a single mass grave in unconsecrated ground. It may be of interest to note, that Griska and his "followers" were not among them.

After that, it seems, there were no more troubles. The town was shunned, of course, and no one dared go there. It was left to rot and fall apart, which it did. So that's the dark history of Cobton. How much of it is true is anyone's guess by this point in time. What I'm going to tell you next I can verify personally—because I was there.

21

Let me preface this by saying that God never created a more reckless and impulsive tribe than boys. And it was in the company of two of them that I visited Cobton. This was back in '57 when I was but ten years old, bright-eyed and naïve and thick-headed, in thrall to my brother Andy who was three years older than me and, in my narrow mindset, the greatest human being that had ever lived.

Andy was one of those kids that comes into this world ready to take it by the horns and conquer it, to squeeze every drop of life from it and drink it like sweet wine. He climbed the highest trees, knocked balls over the fence, beat up bullies, dated the cutest girls, ran faster and jumped higher and spit farther than any kid I had ever known before or since. He was a natural. We've all known kids who are gawky and unsure like colts that need to get their legs under them, but Andy was never a colt—he was a stallion and he was born to run. He was smart, he was fast, he was good-looking, he was athletic, and he was brave. He climbed to the top of the town water tower, he spent the midnight hour in an eighteenth century tomb on Halloween night, he shimmied up flagpoles, swam the deepest rivers in July, built box kites that really flew, and rushed for touchdowns on September nights.

And lucky.

God, that kid was lucky.

He had the Midas touch. Everything went his way. Even things that should have been absolute tragedies turned to gold for him and only enhanced his near-legendary status with us kids. One rainy afternoon he ran across the street without looking and was hit by a car. It should have ended in broken bones and traction at the very least…but not for Andy. He was hit, thrown over the top of the car, rolled down the trunk and…*miraculously*, like a stuntman, he landed on his feet and walked away from it all. Impossible, you say? You didn't know Andy. He was bruised and banged-up, but he was back in school the next day. One year he decided to climb the high pines that enclosed our local athletic field—where one day he would be a star—simply because they were towering and they were there. Here's the problem with that. Just behind the pines there were telephone poles, and strung through the boughs of those pines were the wires. Thirty feet up, Andy reached for a branch and grabbed the hot line. What happened at that point is that he became a ground and 2400 volts shot through him. Well, at the moment he grabbed that line, at the very *same* moment, the limb he was standing on broke and he fell to the ground. There was burnt hole in his palm where the voltage entered him and another at his ankle where it grounded out into the tree. But he survived and the chances of that are probably a million to one.

Just being his brother carried status for me and though I tried very hard to emulate him, I just didn't have it. If it hadn't been for what happened the night I'm going to tell you about, I have no doubt that Andy's sense of adventure would have led him into the Vietnam War and his daring would have earned him a body bag...but who knows? With that luck of his anything was possible. I might add here that, unlike many older brothers, he was not a mean and spiteful creature. He was kind to me, supportive, and was more of a father to me than my real father was. Andy liked having me tag along with him. He seemed to get a kick out of introducing me to people. *"This is my kid brother, Denny,"* he'd say. Andy would have been seventy next month and you know what? I bet he would *still* be introducing me as his kid brother.

But you'll excuse an old man for getting lost in his memories. When you get on the wrong side of sixty like me, it's really all there is. You don't live life; you remember it.

Now...in all Andy's years of daring-do there was one thing he did not even attempt and that was paying a visit to the ruins of Cobton. Even when I was a kid, the ghost stories of Cobton were rife and the name of Griska had not been forgotten: he or *it* had become the local boogeyman. What didn't survive was talk of vampires. I did not know what Griska was. He was just a ghost that haunted Cobton and that was enough. Why Andy decided to visit Cobton in the dead of winter and not summer is a question I can't answer. I went with him as did Bugs Baker, his best friend. We decided the simplest way—well, *they* decided actually—was to follow the railroad tracks that ran from our town and passed just outside Cobton. In those days, the New York Central had a line that crossed the river and Hobart Stream, then sidled up along Lost

Creek for about two miles, swinging away just above Cobton. The tracks were kept plowed so it would be an easy walk.

The night was fairly temperate for February, the mercury barely dipping into the teens. Chill, but not oppressively cold. Not like tonight. Once mom and dad were asleep, we bundled up good in boots and wool socks, long underwear and snow pants, parkas and mittens and scarves. We were ready. We grabbed a couple flashlights and off we went.

Bugs was outside waiting for us. "You bringing the squirt?" he said, indicating me.

"Yeah," Andy told him, "and shut up about it."

Bugs did.

We crossed the town and climbed up the embankment to the tracks and began our walk. Let me say it was a cold and lonely stretch down those tracks. Outside town, the forest pressed in and if it hadn't been for the full moon above, it would have been unbearably black out there away from the streetlights. I can't say how many times I wondered what I was doing during that trek and how many times I asked myself why I was out there and not curled up warm in my bed. I wanted badly to go back home, but it was too late by then and I wasn't about to lose face in front of Andy and Bugs. Just no way. Some things are just more important than your sanity when you're a boy.

By that point, the lights of town were distant. The angle of the tracks and the encroaching forest had canceled them out, snuffing them like the wicks of candles, and the town itself became just a vague glow on the horizon. It was then it began to occur to me that nobody really knew where we were. If something happened, we were entirely on our own. Anything could happen. And that scared me, I recall. That scared me very badly. My imagination was fully activated and showing me one unpleasant scenario after another.

What bothered me the most was the idea that we were slowly being shut off from civilization, from lights and people and safety. We were being led out into a lonely place and I remember wondering if it had been on purpose. If maybe this is the way it happened when kids disappeared without a trace. Maybe they didn't really get picked up by perverts in long black cars or fall through the ice of lonely lakes or get lost in the woods like adults said. Maybe there was nothing accidental at all. Maybe *something* planned it that way, baiting them, drawing them away from the fold, getting them out somewhere desolate so it could do the worst possible things to them. My brain was rioting from all those horror comic books I read. I was seeing malefic forces gathering around us and I was seeing them the way Graham Ingels drew them in *The Haunt of Fear* and *Vault of Horror*...horrible shambling monstrosities that would drive you mad to look upon them (when they decided it was time for you to see them, that was).

I didn't admit that to Andy or Bugs, though.

I didn't want them thinking I was a little baby...but, you know what? *I was.* The night was filled with terrors and I had never wanted my mom and dad so badly as I did then. I kept thinking about the ghost stories we'd been spoon-fed by the older kids about Cobton and what lived there. I couldn't get them out of my mind. I saw them in all their crawling, slinking glory and that only made the night much colder than it already was. The wind was low, but it was sharp and bitter. It pinched color into my cheeks, which were already beginning to feel thick and rubbery like the rest of me.

The tracks were clear of snow, of course. The NY Central used one of those massive wedge plows that came speeding down the tracks and threw snow hundreds of feet in the air to either side. What that did was create what looked like a snow tunnel with huge banks rising to either side. I figured if a train came we'd have been in a real spot trying to climb free.

But no train came.

What we had to fear that night had little to do with trains or anything quite so pedestrian.

We continued on and by then we were a good mile away from home and the night had gotten colder...and darker. The full moon was moving from one bank of clouds to the next. Down on the tracks, our snow tunnel was alive with mulling shadows and we were very much aware of it. In most situations, Andy and Bugs would have been talking nonstop like they usually did. Bugs would be throwing out one bad joke after the other as he usually did. *Hey, squirt, what did the potato chip say to the battery? If you're Eveready, I'm Frito-Lay.* But they were both quiet and I could almost feel the tension coming from them. It was strung thick like webs. I was hearing sounds out in the woods like sticks snapping and branches rubbing together. I knew a winter forest is rarely silent, but I think it was the *quality* of the sounds that were getting to me.

They were almost *stealthy.*

Like something was out there, something was following us, slipping through the tangle of iced boles and snow-drooping limbs, gliding through the shadows. And if I looked, I might see the moonlight shining off its teeth. But I didn't look. I refused to. I was a toy soldier frozen into a perpetual forward stride. I would not give in to what I was praying was just my imagination.

That's when Bugs stopped.

"What?" Andy said.

"I...I thought I saw something," he said and I could tell by the tone of his voice which sounded as hollow as air through a straw that he wasn't kidding. "I thought I saw someone up there...standing on top of the snowbank."

"Ah, you're full of it," Andy told him. "There's nobody out here."

Andy didn't believe that at all. I *knew* I didn't believe it because I thought for just the briefest of instants I saw someone, too...a dark elongated shape watching us. But there was nothing there now and maybe there never had been. Regardless, I was aware of something else: the night had gone unbearably quiet. It was like some drift of silence had fallen over the wood. No sticks cracked. No breeze in the treetops. There was absolutely nothing and it went right up my spine like cold fingers.

"There's the bridge," Andy said.

The trestle cut over Lost Creek and that meant we were almost close enough to Cobton to touch it. We moved on and as we crossed it, the supports and ancient tarred beams beneath us seemed to creak and contract and I had this awful image of it collapsing and us falling sixty or seventy feet to the ice below. But it held, of course. Still, we stopped and it had nothing to do with the bridge itself but what we could see far below in the moonlight. Lost Creek was about twenty feet across down there and even following the spring snow melt it was never more than three or four feet deep. It looked like a white ribbon below us winding away through those dark woods, glowing with moonlight. And there was *something* down there. Something that did not belong. We all saw it and moved as close to the edge of the trestle as we dared.

"What is that?" Bugs asked.

And I, being such a bastion of knowledge and common sense at that age, almost said, *Well, it's just an old post or something.* But I didn't say that because as I looked closer I could see that it was nothing so prosaic. It looked at first like some old, dead and

166

limbless tree poking up out of the ice, kind of crooked and leaning. But as we got a better view of it, I think it occurred to all of us that it was no post, no dead tree, log or stump. It was unusual and weird. Looking down at it made the hairs at the back of my neck stand up. It looked like a man…*almost,* an effigy of one made from rough, knotty poles tied together in a T so that the upright was its body and the crossbar would have been the arms extending straight out like someone being crucified. I knew something like that could not be natural, not in the least, and as I kept staring at it, I got the terrible impression that it was made of bones, crooked meatless bones.

Then something happened and so quickly I would have missed it had I blinked. It was like the crossbar arms moved upward with a creaking sound of old wood until they were perfectly perpendicular with the upright, then they came down and as they did so some wind-blowing cloak fell into place with a rustling whooshing sort of noise and we were seeing the form a man down there. A man standing on the ice with some heavy cloak or coat blowing around him. He was tall and narrow and somehow unnatural. And he was staring up at us.

We should have run.

Wouldn't that be your first instinct? Well, our instincts were dead carp thrown up on a toxic beach, each as lifeless and incapable of action as those fish. We stood there and watched that thing down there, knowing it was no man, knowing it was something malevolent and grotesque that had been waiting for the opportunity we now gave it. Even from way up there we could see its eyes shining red like blood-rubies and we knew this was the last thing kids saw when they got lost in the woods or strayed from the path; the haunter of the dark.

And as we watched, it was approaching the bridge. It was not walking, it was *gliding* forward, floating maybe a foot above the ice, its arms still spread out in some obscene mimicry of the crucifixion. I wanted to scream to snap myself out of it, but my muscles were flaccid, my mind like a marble forever circling a roulette wheel. It felt like everything inside me had gone to putty and I was only vaguely aware of the hot urine running down the inside of my leg.

The thing was rising now.

It was floating up above Lost Creek like a helium balloon and the closer it got, the more real it became and the more I could smell it: a hot, noxious odor of wild fermentation that reamed out my nose and made my eyes water. It was a dark smell like wine going to vinegar, sharp and acrid, with maybe a deadly undercurrent beneath that stank of black wormy soil and funeral lilies rotting to pulp.

That's when I saw the thing really good.

When it was barely fifteen feet below us—rising on its column of fetid air, pushing out a wave of rank heat before it that was hot one moment and glacially cold the next, making our breath come out in great rolling white clouds like cartoon balloons—I really saw it.

Its face was white like that of a circus clown, maybe more gray. A long, narrow face with prominent high cheekbones and a severe Roman nose. The flesh was pitted and pulled tight, like old Papier-mâché that had dried out and split open, fanning out with a multitude of tiny cracks like those you see in old vases. Its hair was long, pulled back in something like a braid, lustrously black, streaked with gray, as was the mustache that hung below the jawline like spikes. It was a Slavic face, unbearably cruel and almost deranged with hatred. But what I saw most as it kept rising was its grinning mouth which split the face like a knife cut, interlocking yellow teeth sharp as fishbones jutting from gums that were black and withered. It was the grin of skull, the rictal grin of a cadaver, the grin of something that lured children into dark woods and sucked the souls out of them like pimentos from olives. And it's eyes…that's what held us, that's what froze us with terror…juicy red eyes that were not elliptically-shaped like human eyes, but huge and perfectly round like those of an owl. They were unblinking, fixing us with a cataleptic stare from tiny black pupils.

That thing which I knew then and I know now was Griska, the bringer of plague, would have had us. He/it would have drained us dry.

But that's when Andy shouted: "RUN! FOR GODSAKE RUN!"

And when I didn't, he grabbed me by the arm and pulled me away and maybe he had seen something we hadn't: there were a dozen of them on the bridge with us, the vampires. They were cadaverous things with bright yellow eyes and smiling mouths of fangs. I saw a few men, bust mostly women and children, many of which were naked. They must have formed some profane family for Griska, his cult of the undead.

Just as Andy pulled me away, Griska had been reaching out for me with long white fingers tipped with black talons like those of a hawk. They looked sharp enough to open arteries. I heard his voice.

It scraped and creaked in my brain like rusting iron: *Take my hand, boy. I am the Maker of Shrouds and the Father of Pestilence. I am He that liveth four centuries past, and was dead; and, behold, I am born for evermore. I am He that holdeth the keys of hell and of death. Blessed are those that would die in the body of the Father.* That's what I heard, a corruption of the Book of Revelation, an ugly and cold violation echoing in my skull. Then Andy pulled me away and Griska snarled at me.

That was also when I saw a little girl standing not four feet from me. She was a pallid thing with flesh the color of tombstones, black braids hanging over her naked skin. I thought for one insane moment that she was such a beautiful, lost child…then I saw the hunger in her glaring eyes and the loops of drool hanging from her chin and I recognized her as what she truly was: an abomination. Her mouth was like a puckered, suckering hole, her entire face seamed and almost corrugated from its appetite.

I saw she was not standing on the trestle, but floating two or three feet beyond its edge like some little death puppet.

Then we were running and as we ran I expected to feel cold dead fingers seize me and fangs like icicles driven into my throat. But that didn't happen. We ran and ran and ran and just above us, on a hillside, was the old mill like a great black monolith, leaning and weathered and creaking in the wind. The town was just below us and it was not the rebuilt Cobton of today but a series of shattered foundations with gnarled trees growing up through them, heaps of broken rubble, roofless structures and bowed walls, a few chimneys like skeletal fingers breaking the loam of a grave. All of it jagged and rising and crowded, ruins frosted by moonlight and drifted with snow.

Then we were climbing up to the old mill, scrambling up the snow-covered hillside like monkeys, knowing we had to get inside. And we did. The mill was barely standing by that point and now it is long fallen, but it still stood then and we forced our way through a rotting plank door and pulled it closed behind us. There were trees growing in there, roots pushing up through the crumbling stone floor. There were great rents in the roof high above and we saw the moon staring down at us, white and bloated like the eye of a corpse.

Andy had his flashlight out and we saw that the center of the floor was gone. Just a collapsed hole that led down into a yawning black pit. I was still half out of my head. I couldn't make sense of much. Andy had pretty much dragged me along behind him. I don't know if it was delayed shock or what, but I couldn't get my brain working. Maybe it was the lingering after-effects of being invaded by Griska...I could still feel his influence just beneath my thoughts like the dragging belly of a reptile. And then, at the door and the walls...scratching. The sounds of paws scratching, trying to find their way in. The sound of teeth chewing at boards, sniffing noses, growls and barks and yapping sounds like there were dozens of wild dogs out there anxious to get at us.

Then it just stopped like somebody flipped a switch.

But it wasn't over. I knew it. We all knew it. The three of us had become connected, wired together, fused in some common circuit of electrical potentiality like we had been plugged into a 220 line. I've never felt anything like that before or since. My own senses were heightened, of course. Fear does that. But this was beyond simple animal fear. It was something else, it was practically arcing and galvanic and it owned me. I shouldn't have been able to see in the dark, but I could. Not just the moonlight spilling in through numerous cracks and crevices of the old mill, but the grain of the wood itself, how certain boards were warped, others splintered, still others coming apart with dry rot. I could even see the ancient square nailheads winking at me like rusty eyes. I shouldn't have been able to see these things so minutely, but I could. And it wasn't only just that, you understand. My hearing was acute, almost painfully so. I could hear not only the triphammer pumping of my own heart, but the hearts of the others, too. They sounded weird like fists punching into soft pillows. That's as close as I can get to a description. I could hear the air in their lungs. Each time they breathed—and they were both, like me, breathing very quietly—it was like the sucking whoosh of bellows. I swear I could hear snowflakes striking the outside of the mill and clouds scudding in the sky. If a moth had flapped its wings, it would have been thunder. Angels dancing on the head of a pin would have shattered my eardrums.

It was crazy...exhilarating, disturbing.

I was numb from the cold, but at that moment I did not feel it. In fact, what I *did* feel was my entire body waking up, every nerve ending standing taut. From head to toe, I was tingling inside and out like a foot that had fallen asleep and was coming alive again with a million-billion pinpricks. I think I achieved, in my terror, something quite near to complete consciousness. Not only was my mind fully active for the first time in my life, but my body. And I swear in that heightened, dynamic, near mystical state, I could hear the panicked thoughts of my brother and his best friend. And I could smell the bitter, sour stink of their fear…and worse, I could smell what was outside the mill. Maybe *they* made no sound and their hearts did not beat as such, but I could smell them and it was a dark, revolting stench that I figured an exhumed casket must smell like. It was blown, it seemed, right into my face, pungent and thick like a green gas of putrescence.

That's when I heard a scratching, scraping sort of noise and knew it was coming from beneath us. In my mind it was the sound of coffin-worms chewing their way into a moldering oblong box. But the reality was something quite different, you see. Andy heard it, too, and edged over near the pit, shining his light down there. I didn't join him; I didn't have to. I saw in my mind what he was seeing in his: a countless number of undead children climbing up out of the stygian darkness. I could see the great black depths below that the flashlight beam could barely reach…the crumbling walls of masonry, the great rusted gears and mangled cogs and millstones cracking open…and the vampires, white-faced and grinning, lips swollen like red worms, eyes huge and empty and shining with a fathomless blackness.

They were coming for us.

And maybe they would have had us but something intervened.

The worst sort of thing.

An old hag came through the door at us…she did not open it, she *flowed* through every crack, seam, and nail hole like a river of ghostly plasma. When she was inside, these ribbons of teleplasm came together and formed the hag: she was a floating chalk-white ghost with a sunken face, a puckered oval mouth, and huge glassy, reptilian eyes like those of a stuffed python. Her stringy gray hair blew about her like reeds, her arms held out before her breasts like the limbs of a preying mantis. Her hands were white corpse-orchids, fingernails black and glossy and at least seven or eight inches long curling back towards the palms. A rustling, propulsive wind came with her that stank of the charnel. It blew the shroud she was wearing into ribbons and streamers as she herself seemed to fragment, breaking apart into motes of phosphorescent dust that were carried along in her wake. That wind blew not only her shroud, but her flesh…it got up underneath her skin and made it flap on the bones beneath with a rubbery sort of sound.

That's what I saw as Bugs screamed and she took him.

It either happened very fast or very slowly; either way, we didn't have the strength to fight her. She chose Bugs and took him, bearing him off into dark channels of night as he continued to shriek at the top of his lungs. She took him down into the pit and as his mind emptied itself, I heard the sound of her blubbery lips fasten to his throat and begin to suck. His screams echoed from great depths below.

That's when Andy took hold of me and kicked the door open. There was no time for anything approaching a good-bye. He simply said: "GET ON THOSE TRACKS AND RUN! DON'T STOP RUNNING UNTIL YOU'RE HOME! GO! *GO!*" I think he might have said other things. At least in my mind I can still hear his voice telling me not to talk to anyone, not to look at anyone, to keep my eyes looking straight ahead and never look back. And you know what? I didn't. I ran with Andy behind me somewhere and I didn't see any vampires besides that girl who was still waiting on the bridge. She called to me but I ignored her. I ran and ran and ran. By the time I reached the bridge, I realized that Andy was no longer behind me, but I kept running anyway. I didn't realize it then, but I know now, that he sacrificed himself so that I could be free. Andy's luck finally ran out. I think...I think a wolf followed me for a time. I heard its padding in the snow and smelled its foul breath, but Andy told me not to look back.

And I didn't.

I never saw this place again until I signed on as caretaker. The idea of coming here made me sick to my stomach, but I came back because I *had* to come back to this awful place where my childhood ended with a terrible screech. None of you may be able to understand that and I'm not sure I do completely myself, but I've been waiting here for things to start up again because I knew they would. Eventually, Griska and his cult would get thirsty. And now they have. And it's only now that I understand why I had to come back...once, before I die, I want to see my brother again...even if he is only a mocking shell.

22

By the time Rule was done telling his story, Morris was curled up by the fire again like somebody's faithful retriever...except, of course, Wenda knew there was nothing faithful about him. If he were a dog, then he was a slinking hyena that needed to be watched very, very closely.

"But you have to understand something," Wenda said. "Your brother, if he's still here, will kill you. He'll kill us. He won't be your brother or the brother to anything living."

Rule nodded. "Yes, I know. But I ran last time and I've been guilty ever since."

"There's nothing to be guilty about. Andy sacrificed his life—and maybe even his soul—so that you could be free, that you could live. Coming back here and putting yourself at risk doesn't give his death the meaning it should have."

Wenda said that and was immediately struck by the incongruity of her lecturing her old lecturer. It seemed absurd. But a lot of things that used to seem absurd were no longer absurd, and a lot of things she never would have said before had wings now and they flew out of her mouth unfettered. There was something quite liberating about that and who she now was.

Megga, who'd sat uncharacteristically silent during Rule's yarning, said, "If your brother comes, he'll be a monster. He'll get in your mind. He'll make you do things. He'll twist your thoughts and turn your own mind against you." She said this like she had personal experience in the matter. "He could make you pick up a knife and slit my throat. You wouldn't have a choice."

Rule nodded. "I think it depends on the discipline of the mind in question."

"You're fucking stupid if you think that. If you think you're smart enough to outwit them or hold out against what they can do."

"Maybe, maybe." He shrugged. "Understand...I did not come here to get bitten in the neck. I have no self-destructive or morbid urges. Perhaps I'm speaking metaphorically. Perhaps what I wanted all along was just to come back here and face my fears. Maybe that's really what it was all about."

"If your brother comes," Wenda said, still clutching her stake and wanting to use it, "I'll destroy him. I'll have to."

"Unless he gets you first," Megga pointed out.

"And you'd hate that wouldn't you?" Wenda said to her and she looked away. "Megga wants to be a vampire. She thinks it's cool to be one of them."

"Shut up," Megga told her.

Rule sighed and looked into the fire. "The attraction is an old one and one of their greatest strengths. They can make you believe they're something other than what they truly are. I know that, Megga, and I think you know it, too. What we're dealing with here is more than parasites, more than just bloodsuckers," he said, a funny sort of steely glare in his eyes. "They're ghosts essentially, hungry ghosts. And there is nothing more dangerous than a hungry ghost. They exist by not only drawing off the life's blood of their prey, but the life energy, I think. When they sink their teeth in your throat it's more than a particularly gruesome and ritualistic mode of feeding, it's penetration, a defilement and violation of your life force. It kills the good things in you and leaves behind a shell powered by basal urges and primitive drives of hunger satiation. You become an appetite, more or less, a cunning, obscene appetite that exists to drain, destroy, and multiply its malignance. That is the core of vampirism, I believe: the hunger, the defilement, the destruction."

"And knowing that gets us where exactly?" Megga said.

He laughed. "Nowhere. You'll excuse an old academic for flights of philosophic fancy."

Wenda nodded. "We've got nearly four more hours until sunrise. If we can make it that long, if we can hold out…"

"They're not going to let us," Megga said.

"She's right," Rule said. "So we can either sit here and wait for it or we can take action of a sort."

Wenda was interested in this. "What sort of action?"

"First, let me espouse another local legend which you might find interesting."

He told them that, according to local folklore, the reason that Griska and his familiars were not located and staked by the sheriff and his raiding party in the spring of 1829 was because they were hidden in a secret vault or catacombs. The location of which was thought to be beneath the old burying ground. Legend also had it that there was a tunnel or tunnels connecting it to Cobton.

"Now, the high sheriff and his men looked for a tunnel that day but couldn't find any," Rule told them. "When I took up as caretaker here I looked, too, and found nothing. I spoke with one of the contractors that rebuilt Cobton. He had heard the stories of the tunnels as well—being from New Hampshire, he referred to them as 'smugglers' tunnels'—but found nothing of the sort."

"What's the point?" Megga asked.

"The point, my dear, is that there *is* a tunnel and I found it tonight. You see, after I saw that thing dragging off Bill, I ran into a house down the way to hide. I went down into the cellar. There's a tunnel down there and it appears that the opening is recent…as if maybe it had been closed a great many years and I imagine it was. That house is two doors down from here." He described the house to them briefly. "It maybe our way out."

"But that's the house where Doc and Bailey and Reg are," Megga said.

Wenda shook her head. "You want us to run over there, risk getting slaughtered, just so we can go into some tunnel that leads to a catacomb? Leads to the very lair of the vampires?"

"Yes," he said.

"Better than sitting here and waiting for it," Megga said.

But she was too anxious and Wenda did not like that. Maybe on the surface she was pretending to be with them and maybe she even believed it, but underneath there was still that fascination with the undead and this made her weak and vulnerable.

"Wait now," Rule said. "Hear me out. First off, if we get to that other house and join up with your friends there'll be more of us. Numbers are important. The vampires like to pick their victims off one by one. It'll give us strength. Secondly, my car isn't parked too far from that house. We could jog over there in five minutes. And thirdly, the legend also says that not only is this vault or catacomb connected to the town, but there's a passage that leads up into one of the old VanderHoofen tombs. If we could make it through the catacomb and up into the tomb and out into the burial ground...we might have a chance."

"In a cemetery?" Wenda said.

"If we make it down to the road," Rule explained, "there's a County Road Commission garage less than a mile through the woods on the other side. It's manned day and night."

"It's suicide."

"Suicide is better than what awaits us here, my dear Vultura," he said.

"Well?" Megga said.

"I'll think it over."

Nobody had really put Wenda in charge, she just took the reigns because they were lying limp. But now that she had, she knew the decision was up to her. As far as she was concerned, she was responsible for their lives. Was she willing to throw them away so easily? The car was one thing...but a tunnel leading God knows where? Maybe into the very lair of the undead? That was insane. *Hide in plain sight,* a voice in her head kept saying, but she didn't care much for the idea of hiding in a secret burial crypt. Sooner or later, Griska and the others would return to it and when that happened, things would get very ugly. She had a pretty good feeling he wanted to kill her in the worst possible way. She had seen him through the window, she had felt the hatred directed at her. He would make her suffer for killing the wolf-woman.

So maybe the catacomb is the best idea if you want to destroy him. Think of the ages of suffering he has brought forth. Think of the joy of plunging your stake into his chest. He hasn't been human in many centuries. He was probably ancient in 1828. Do what Rule wants and kill that sonofabitch. What do you got to lose?

But that's what stayed her.

She wasn't sure whether she believed in the human soul or not, but whatever was inside her that made her Wenda Keegan, Griska would tear it out by the roots.

23

Rabbits and rodents, Doc thought as the delirium tried to eclipse his thoughts once again. *In the end that's all we are and maybe in the beginning not much more.* Scurrying, frightened creatures fearing death that circled high above on wings of midnight plumage, each revolution bringing it closer and closer until its claws were in your back or tearing into your throat. That's what death was. That's what it felt like, he decided.

He sat there watching the fire and listening to the great old house creaking in the assault of the blizzard. The snow it threw against the windows sounded like granules of sand. He knew it was more important now than ever to keep awake, to keep his mind working. It was steel that must be kept sharpened like a blade on a wheel, because the moment he let his guard down, the moment he relaxed, that's when it was going to happen. That's when death would reach out for him.

It's out there right now, that thing that created all the horror we know this night or will ever know. It's thinking about me again, pushing its mind out at my own and I can't let it get inside my head again or it'll start draining my energy away. Each time I weaken, it draws in closer. Each time I hesitate in my resolve, it grows stronger. That is how they work. That is the strength of the undead: by the time they actually come to feed on you, you're too weak to fight. But I will not be too weak! I won't! It's circling me like a carrion crow right now, its buzzard-eyes drilling into me, drawing away my vitality. It's just waiting for the final death rattle of my willpower so it can come crawling in and finish me.

Doc thought about the others—Wenda and Megga and Morris—and wondered if they were still even alive. He faced the unpleasant possibility that they were already dead and only Reg and he remained. But even that wouldn't last. He could feel death creeping in closer and closer. In his mind, he kept seeing the storm out there and feeling the weight of Bailey's body in his arms, the blizzard taking the shape of a pale naked little girl who said, *There's a place where we can lay together. A place where you can—*

"No," he said under his breath. "No."

Reg looked up at him. "What is it, Doc?"

"Um...I was just thinking, son. Thinking out loud. Musing, as I tend to do," he said, covering for his own helplessness. "Sooner or later, what's out there will pay us another visit. According to my watch we've got nearly four hours until sunup and I'm just as exhausted as you are. I want nothing more than to close my eyes, but we can't afford that now. We've got enough wood until dawn, but we might as well arm ourselves. That table over there...why don't you chop the legs off? They'll make for good stakes."

"Yeah...okay. That's an idea."

The fire was burning high, but the kerosene in the remaining lantern was almost used up. Maybe it would burn another hour, but probably less. The wind was howling out there, rising up into a single note of despair and desolation. Doc wondered if he would ever truly feel warm again and decided that he probably wouldn't. He watched Reg chopping free the first leg. Although he was certain that his own life was played out now, Reg was still a boy in his mind. So young, so young. Whatever happened before dawn, he knew he had to somehow save the kid's life. But would that even be possible?

He realized that his lips were moving as he watched Reg and he became aware that he was mouthing a prayer from childhood. Not that he expected God to listen to an old Agnostic like him, yet he prayed and hoped, and as he hoped, he feared. There had to be a way out of this, a way to spare the kid. But if such a way existed, he could not think of it.

He looked over towards the window, past the parted curtains, and saw white faces looking in. He gasped. The girl was out there, waiting for him. He turned away; he would not look in their eyes and, more appropriately, *her* eyes. Never in his life had he felt any stirrings for anything other than mature women, but out there in the storm that child had offered herself to him and he had been aroused by the idea. It disgusted him. More so, it disturbed him. It was a mind game, that's all it was. Those things wanted to weaken him and the girl had been their weapon. She had tapped into some vein of animal need in his subconscious, perhaps, exploited it, perverted it, and in the process filled him with self-loathing. That was how they did it, he figured. They created a crack in your psyche and worked it until it widened, until that crack fanned out and you shattered inside. By the time that happened, they'd already weakened you to the point where you could do nothing but accept what they offered, the cool oblivion of eternity.

There's a place—

No.

— where we can—

I will not listen.

— lay together.

Those words would not stop echoing in his head and he knew there was nothing remotely sensual about them. The tone was wooden and hollow like that of a ventriloquist's dummy…*yet,* there was a seduction he could not deny. It sickened him, yet intrigued him.

There's a place where we can lay together.

A place where you can touch me.

A place where we can sleep together like death—

Sleep. God knew he wanted to sleep and even the idea of lying with that thing in the snow sounded peaceful. Just to close his eyes. And for one moment as he fought against himself and fought against the clutching shadows of his own mind that threatened to zip him shut in darkness, he could not understand why there was anything wrong with the idea of laying with the little nymph from hell.

But, then, as his mind came out of it, revolted by the idea, he could almost feel her next to him…her naked flesh like cold meat, a smell rising from her like gangrenous wounds and infected drainage. This is what she was at her core: filth and perversion, sickness and disease, bile and malignance. And this is what she wanted for the human race—a graveyard world hung in a decaying orbit like a dead fly in a spider's web. A world swinging around a blackened, burned-out star. A world where the cities were mausoleums blown by blizzards of human ash, the towns were mortuaries washed by black rivers of coffin slime, and the only sound was the moaning wind and tombs doors creaking open to expel vampires in fetid, creeping vapors.

He knew in his heart that if these things were not crushed and contained here in Cobton, then they would spread their pestilence to the four winds. It was sheer ugly coincidence that brought him and the others here on this worst of all possible nights; but it was not coincidence that the vampires chose this night to rise from their dormancy. It had been planned that way. This was the beginning. Maybe other cells were waking in other lonely places as well, but, regardless, it was beginning here and now.

On this night.

This was the eve of destruction when the world became a graveyard. And knowing this, feeling it deep inside himself to be true, Doc felt like a small boy on that Iowa farm again listening to the wind blow through the cracks in the loft by night, certain they were ghosts. He wanted to crawl beneath the covers and suck his thumb. And maybe he would have retreated deep into himself, but the wind blowing through those cracks was not wind exactly...it sounded like respiration.

There was something in the room that was breathing and it was neither Reg nor he, but some insidious *other*.

Beads of fear-sweat popping on his brow, he looked around and there was nothing, nothing at all. He could not even hear the breathing now, but he knew that it had been there. Whatever had caused it, was now holding its breath and probably to create the very effect it had indeed created.

"Something, Doc?" Reg said. "You hear something?"

"No...you?"

"Thought I did. I guess not." He came over with a sharpened chair leg. It was oak, about sixteen inches long and sharp enough to draw blood. He handed it to Doc with a bright, expectant look in his eyes like a puppy that had just fetched a slipper and wanted to be rewarded. "How about that?" he said.

"Nice," Doc said, hefting it in his fist. "Very, very nice."

Pleased, Reg went over and started chopping at another chair leg. The noise was reassuring to Doc. It was the sound of life and activity as opposed to the sound of death and silence, which were the music of the tomb.

Doc held the stake in both hands.

He had to be ready now because even despite Reg's chopping, he could hear that breathing again. Maybe it was just inside head, but he did not think so. It was there, all right, and it took more than one set of lungs to produce what he was hearing.

They were gathering.

They were inside the house.

They were making ready and he had to be ready for them. *Hurry with that stake, son. Dear God, hurry with it.* They were getting closer. They were shadows in the corners and behind the curtains, ghosting along the wainscoting and hiding in the patterns of the wallpaper, pooling under chairs. They were here. The things that would soon crawl out of the woodwork.

"Temp must be dropping out there," Reg said, pausing with his axe. "Feels colder than ever in here. You feeling it?"

Yes, oh God yes, my boy, I am certainly feeling it.

"Yes," was all Doc managed to say and it satisfied Reg. He went back at it with his axe. He had turned out another stake and was sharpening the end into a point.

The breathing was louder.

The shadows seemed to be bunching in the room, almost flexing like muscles. Doc was aware of a subtle sound that was quite like the slithering of snakes and another that sounded like fingernails dragged over the walls.

"I thought I heard something," Reg said, his eyes bovine and calm.

"Hurry with that stake," Doc told him, trying to control his breathing. "I think...I think we're going to need it soon, very soon."

Reg went at it faster, his eyes darting around in his head now, looking, searching. Doc watched him as chills went up his back and settled along the nape of his neck. The air seemed heavy, galvanic, as if it were charged with static electricity, and thick...almost like dark liquid as it moved around them.

"Hurry," Doc said.

Then Reg was done and he was standing near the chair that Doc sat in. The lantern was still glowing and the fire was still blazing. Light was thrown in brilliant yellow-orange arcs against the walls, but over near the window there were shadows that it could not dispel. Shadows like black, oozing oil that seemed to come out of the corners and exude from the walls as if the house were a sponge that was being squeezed out.

There were eyes in those shadows like wormholes filling with dusky light.

They pooled and flowed and then rose up until they were not shadows but figures: a few men, but mostly women and children, wasted and starving things like corpses from a medieval plague pit. Some were dressed in rotting, filthy cerements of the grave that barely concealed jutting rungs of rib, others were starkly naked and bled white. A few wore winding shrouds feathered with grave mold and beneath those hoods he saw gray faces threaded with cobwebs. One woman had rats crawling in the moldering shifts of her burial gown. Her grin was that of maggoty fish upon a beach. They looked out at him with eyes that were black and shining like the shells of beetles or luminous and yellow set into faces like pallid moons. A stench of the unburied dead came off of them in a sickening pestilential bloom of the grave.

"DOC—" Reg began, but Doc could not hear him.

He could only see the girl.

Her hair was the most brilliant and luscious red that Doc had ever seen. Her body was immature and undeveloped, but she offered its marble whiteness to him with a blatant sexuality that was ravenous like the hunger of wolves. He could almost feel her teeth sinking into him and scraping against bone while a voice of sugar, dark and sweet sugar said: *There's a place where we can lay together. A place where you can touch me. A place where we can sleep together like death—*

But he would not allow it.

Even though something inside him ran like yellow yolks, he would not allow it for she was the most foul thing he had ever seen and he had only one overriding passion: her destruction. She jumped at him and Reg cried out, but she did not leap, she *drifted*. Like a blown, ghastly ribbon of corpse-white fog, she drifted through the air at him, morphing from that loathsome little cadaver-girl into a woman who was rounded-out and full, voluptuous, sensuous, a fluid muscular grace of hunger, long-limbed, red-mouthed, eyes blazing with carnal appetite.

"DOC!" Reg cried out. *"DOC, GODDAMMIT, LOOK OUT!"*

Doc held his ground, powered by something that even he couldn't really understand. Maybe it had to do with the repulsion he felt for the thing coming to drain him dry, the thing that wanted the world to be a graveyard of bird-picked bones. It was that and maybe an overwhelming need to stand and fight, to destroy the ghoulish infection and if for no other reason than for the memory of the girl herself, what she had been and the horror she now was.

When she got close enough that he could see the searing red jewels of her eyes, he brought the stake down with all his strength and weight behind it. It punched into her like she was made of steam. She screamed, the others screamed, the walls shook and the windows rattled with the cacophonous wailing of the pack.

But it was too late.

She was impaled, speared like a fish, and what he saw then was the same foul little thing from a grave, hissing and writhing, her mouth splitting open as her fangs sheared through her lips. As Doc stumbled back—his hands deadened from some weird jolting electrical discharge that had grounded-out through the stake and into his fingers when it pierced her—he watched her die, he watched her quite literally go to pieces.

He bumped into Reg and seized him in his arms, as if he needed to feel another warm, breathing human being or his mind would deflate like a leaky balloon.

The girl rose up two feet off the ground, her taloned fingers tearing at the stake and succeeding in shearing her own white flesh. It burst open as if from some internal pressure, revealing a pulpy yellow meat that was livid against her bluing flesh. She screeched like an animal being skinned alive, blood blisters breaking open on her body and exploding like rotten grapes. Saliva and blood flew from her mouth in tangles, the pustular pits of her eyes bulging into huge black-red orbs and then falling into themselves with a gushing sluice of slime. The skin of her face became threadbare mesh and pulled off the skull beneath like spider's silk. Contorting and thrashing, she fell backwards, her skeleton bursting free, steaming and breaking apart…but long before she hit the floor something inside her ignited and she erupted with flame and smoke and a cremating heat, crashing down into a heap of smoldering bones that continued to tremble, the jaws of her skull snapping again and again then crumbling away.

And Reg, who was barely on his feet by that point, fell into Doc and Doc grabbed him and shoved him towards the door. "RUN!" he shouted at him. "FOR GODSAKE, RUN!"

And Reg did without further urging.

Doc heard the door slam open and Reg's feet running. The other vampires looked out at him with eyes that managed to be saddened and hateful at the same time. They did not follow Reg; there was no need. Their entertainment was here before them. Eyes wide and gleaming, lit yellow like electric bulbs screwed into their faces, slavering jaws opened, fangs sliding from pale gums, they closed in on him and he waited for it.

24

Reg burst from the door and, in the finest horror movie fashion, tripped over his own boots, hitting the floor like 170 pounds of dead weight. He scrambled to his feet and ran, ran right for the door in his mad flight and was reaching for the doorknob when a voice in his head said: *What the fuck are you doing?*

He withdrew his hand with a strangled yelping sound in his throat.

He couldn't go out there.

They were out there, too, just waiting for him to pull some bonehead move like that. To them, he was prey and like any hunters they were using his own panic against him, hoping he would make a big fat mistake.

No, no, no!

He turned around, fully expecting to see a red mouth and gleaming fangs coming out of the darkness at him, but there was nothing but the emptiness of the old house and the shadows. He had to get somewhere. He had to get somewhere safe. But in his panic, he could not think of where that might be or how he might get there. In fact, he could barely think at all. His mind was clouded with fear. Tears were running from his eyes. His breath came out in a white expanding frost-mist. His heart was pounding so hard it felt like it might explode right out of his chest.

Do something, you fucking idiot…

So he started first this way, then that, approaching corridors and then turning back because he was too scared to go down them. He reached for doors and panicked at the idea of what might be waiting in the darkness behind them. All he succeeded in doing was to bring himself around in a crazy circle until he realized he was facing back towards the parlor. He heard Doc scream in there and he ran for the stairs, trying to jog up them, but tripping and banging his knees in his heavy boots. But he didn't slow down: we went up them on his hands and knees like a hunted animal.

He paused at the top, laying across the landing and gasping for breath.

Outside the storm raged, clawing at the house to get in.

In his fright and manic flight, he had winded himself, expending about five times the amount of energy he might have used if he'd kept his head. Other than his rasping lungs and thudding heart, he was only aware of the sound of the house itself: an immense silence that was so very quiet it was thundering in his ears. *They* knew how to use such silence. It was how *they* cloaked themselves. *They* were coming for him and at any moment he would feel cold breath at his neck and colder lips at his throat. Then they would drain his blood with erotic glee.

He pulled himself up.

Other than the cellar or possibly the attic, he was in the darkest quarter of the house because there were no windows in that part of the upstairs corridor. This is where he had been with Burt earlier and, dear God, he wished Burt were here now. Burt was a selfish asshole, but Reg would have taken him, he would have jumped up and hugged him if only he wasn't so unbearably alone.

Downstairs, Doc was screaming again.

You gonna let those things do that to him? You gonna let fucking Doc die like that? Doc would do anything for you! Doc told you to run because he was sacrificing himself so that you could live!

Reg turned, ready to bolt down the stairs and charge into the fray and save Doc or goddamn well die trying, but he saw a figure coming up the steps at him and his heart skipped a beat in his chest. At first it looked like just a shadow gliding up towards him, but now he could see it was a shape that was becoming a man. Reg blinked and he saw that it was Burt. His face an even bloodless white, his eyes huge and suffused with a dirty lunar glow, his teeth grown long and deadly.

"Hey, Reg," he said in a voice that was screeching and scraping like the blade of a knife dragged over a windowpane. If it was intended to calm him, it had the opposite effect. Burt stopped half way up and just stood there. Reg thought he could almost see the staircase right through him. *"Oh, Reg...do you know what they did to me out there? Do you know what it was like to die like that? Why did you let it happen? Why didn't you help me?"*

Reg let out a squealing sound and raced away down the upstairs corridor. He found a door and slammed it shut behind him, locking it. There was nothing in the room with him that he saw...but that didn't mean one of them wasn't under the bed or waiting in the closet.

Burt was at the door now.

He was knocking with a slow, almost mechanical sort of cadence.

"Reg, let me in," he said. *"I want to show you what they did to me."*

But Reg was not about to do that. He had no intention of doing anything but staying alive...the only problem was that he was now essentially in a cage, a box with no way out and if Burt found a way in, well, there could only be one outcome. But Reg refused to submit. He refused to be something that lay in darkness like a corpse during the day, rising up by night. No, no, no...

The doorknob jiggled. *"We don't need doors to come in,"* Burt said.

And to prove that, he started coming in *beneath* the door like a spreading puddle of ectoplasm, more of him pouring in every second until that glowing white mass began to take on features and Reg saw the elongated mouth and the leering, eyes of morbid starvation.

Then Reg did the only thing he could do.

He picked up a chair and swung it at the window again and again until it shattered and the storm came in, frigid air and snow blowing in. What Burt did then he did not know, because he climbed out onto the roof.

25

As the dead came for him, Doc felt a wind like a glacial whirlpool whip through the room and the windows shattered inward. He saw a shadow rise up amongst the others...one that seemed to be composed of hundreds of bats madly beating their black wings...becoming a cycling vortex of black moths...melting into a skeletal mass that grew up from the floor like a gnarled pillar, a dead tree regenerating its limbs. There was a flapping sound as of a sheet on a line and a great cloak seemed to unfold and envelop the shadow. When it parted, a man was standing there, a tall and gaunt man wearing a flowing hide coat, the black fur of which was threadbare and ragged, standing out in spokes with frozen blood. His hands were amazingly pale, blue-veined, the fingers long and slender with tapering yellow nails that looked sharp as razors. Doc could imagine fingers like that—sure, practiced, surgical—poking through bowels and muscles and delicate tissues to remove malignancies.

But the man was no healer and those fingers did not take away pain, they inflicted it.

The other vampires were not moving now. In fact, they had frozen in place like graveyard statues. Only their eyes were alive, shining with diabolic hunger.

At that moment, Doc was beyond simple fear. His heart did not seem to beat and his lungs did not seem to draw breath. He stood shivering, nerve endings feeling plucked like the strings of a lyre, his blood settling low as if it feared to be drained.

The figure before him had not moved. The wind still rushed around it like a gust from a tomb. The walls shook. Bits of twinkling broken glass spun in dust-devils.

In Doc's brain, there was something like music, like scratching violins and stringed instruments played with sawtoothed files. The sepulchral figure before him stared down at him with a frightening elemental wrath, his eyes a brilliant liquid red going to purple like wine stains. They looked into Doc, drilled into his skull, with absolute and irresistible dominance. He felt things breaking apart inside him, shattering and splintering, black universes opening up and swallowing him, retching him body and soul onto the barren faces of dead worlds where slithering shadows crawled into his head and ate him alive from the inside out.

Then the wind died and the walls stopped trembling and Doc heard a voice in his head. A ranting, enraged voice, one nearly deranged with anger. It at first sounded like German, then Latin, then a dozen dialects he had never heard before until becoming a flat, almost guttural Slavic tongue.

Doc did not know what kept him on his feet because it felt like all the blood had drained down into his knees and his head was spinning. He looked into the eyes of the figure before him and felt weak inside. The man had long, poker-straight black tresses spilled over his shoulders. Streaks of brilliant white came from each temple and feathered out into gray. His long drooping mustache was of the same color. His face was long and waxy, the chin sharp and the nose hawkish, the nostrils flaring. The skin was the sickly yellow-white of leprosy, stretched tight over the skull below. There were deep pockets of shadow beneath the high cheekbones, filling the hollows of the sunken cheeks themselves. The face was set with minute wrinkles and cracks like an old photograph. It seemed to have the texture of spun cobwebs. It was grotesquely corded as if there were roots growing under the skin.

Doc knew who he was: this was the boogeyman from the charnel pits and he would make the world into a graveyard. The boogeyman had a name and Doc knew it. It trembled on the tip of his tongue. "You..." he said. "You are Griska. You are a Magyar."

In Doc's head, Griska began to laugh with a hysterical cackling, breathing out clouds of soot that winged in the air and became death's-head moths. A stink of wild fermentation blew out from him. His mouth split open like a knife cut, his teeth pearly white, the central incisors narrow, long, and hooked like those of a pit viper. In Doc's head, there was more than laughter, but a choir of anguished children behind each syllable. Too many voices, too many dialects, but all of them lorded over by a screeching, hideous male voice: *Behold, I stand at the door, and knock. Give unto me that which is mine. And give unto Her that which is hers.*

Griska wanted some kind of offering, some sort of sacrifice...but one offered to him *by* the victim. That was the greatest depth of corruption and the greatest joy for a thing like him: to be given a life, to have it laid before him by the victim's own hand.

But Doc refused.

He wanted to shout his defiance at that smug ghoul, but Griska seemed to know. He knew the flavor and the taste of defiance and did not care for it. In Doc's head, his voice said, *Martyr*. A wind seemed to blow out from him and Doc felt it take hold of him with hurricane force, lifting him off his feet and driving him ten or twelve feet through the air until he impacted with the wall. His boots were three feet off the floor, but he did not fall. The force held him and that force was generated by Griska himself. Throughout the room, the walls were creaking and groaning and Doc soon saw why: nails were being ejected from them. No, not ejected but *pulled* free by the same force that held him, pressing him against the wall with such might he thought his guts would be forced out his mouth.

But that didn't happen; the nails found him instead. His left arm was forced up and out until it was parallel with his shoulder. His right arm followed suit until he was held there in some grim parody of the crucifixion. Then the nails were flying.

The first one he felt more than the others. It made a sterile whiteness explode in his head.

It went in through his right wrist like a spike, through muscle and tendon and artery. It brought pain. Unreal, white-hot pain. The second nail filled his belly with needles, bringing a fevered numbness and a cold running sweat. The third nail brought a sweet and muddy revelation, a distorted sense of mystery, exaltation, and dark desire that ran from his wounds in a red, flowing sap.

Doc screamed until his throat was raw.

Hanging there, impaled by three nails—one in his right wrist, one in each of his ankles—bleeding and gasping and half out of his mind, he felt a fourth impale his left wrist and the crucifixion of the martyr was complete, he knew.

But he was wrong.

It had only just begun.

The other vampires parted and the wall behind them was suddenly not webbed with shadow, it was vibrant, gleaming, and he could see *beyond* the woodwork. He could see the lathing beneath it and each individual brick as if the entire wall were energized by some sort of radiant energy. It was bright and getting brighter, the mortar between the bricks glowing now as if it were infused with atomic radiation. A blurry, white form was coming through, a roping and snaking mass like a nightmare squid or jellyfish, something ethereal and transparent pushing itself into human form.

The luminous form solidified, became female, a specter in ragged, graying robes that flowed and drifted in unseen currents. But what Doc saw most were eyes that were silver and red, imploding star-fire and flickering carnival lamps. Their light was cold and pulsating and he withered in it.

No, no, no...not this one...please, not this one...

The shrouded figure approached him and he heard a buzzing like a storm of hornets coming at him. It was inside his head, a constant almost feverish droning that seemed to turn his mind inside out. He could hear Griska speaking to him. The words were beyond him, but the voice eternal and undying as he hung there, crucified, a martyr being washed clean in the florid bounty of his own blood. It was hot and wet, smelling of dirty pennies and black covetous sin. And, oh dear God, the beauty that was the pain that was the beauty, all the poisons and toxins finally running from him in hurtful, cabalistic rivers. This was the time of the draining, the emptying, wherein his soul was finally and ultimately purified in a flux of bubbling red venom.

The Death Hag.

The buzzing was louder now and then louder still.

Shivering and bleeding, his ears ringing with that constant buzzing, Doc shouted: "PLEASE PLEASE ANYTHING ANYTHING..."

Griska was cruel, vicious evil given form and he was puppet master to the others; but this thing, this hag, she was their prophet, Doc knew, as she came for him, his mouth dry and his throat constricted like there were a pair of hands squeezing his windpipe shut. The world went out-of-focus, teetering madly this way and that like something reflected in a funhouse mirror. He blinked his eyes, tried to shake that dizziness out of his brain...and the Death Angel reached for him.

A low, bestial growl sounded from her throat as she gnashed her teeth. She was so thin, she was practically diaphanous. There was a veil of membranous cobweb-skin over her face like the caul of an infant and he could clearly see the contours of the skull beneath. The caul sheared and the face beneath looked mummified and ancient like straw-dry wicker, spread out with hundreds of wrinkles and diverging lines. The lips were seamed and the teeth gray and pitted, overlapping fangs. They were vulpine, dog-like, but the sound coming out of her throat was the squealing of pigs.

Doc looked into her eyes. They were yellow bleeding into red into pink into red until there was no iris or pupil, just those two moist red orbs, each swelling from their sockets, wet and glistening like fresh blood.

He waited in frozen silence as a burning, stagnant heat swept from her, a torpid, gagging heat of malarial swamps and raging viral fevers. Something like inky bile was running from her mouth, her nostrils, dripping to the floor from orifices hidden by her shroud. She arched her back and vomited a stream of buzzing hornets at him. They lit in the air like drifting motes. A thousand of them drilled into him with their stingers and he screamed out a red mist of blood...

And inside his head, there were white, searing shockwaves of pain. It was like a thousand separate red-hot pokers were spearing into his brain, each one burning its way deeper and deeper, setting off pinpoint eruptions of agony that came together in a rending, blinding white explosion that tossed him screaming into the blackness. His nervous system had been overloaded, overdosed, pushed far beyond acceptable levels where consciousness could hope to be maintained. This was the cumulative effect of countless stingers punching into him and injecting their toxins into his tissues. It caused immediate systemic crash.

When Doc felt himself returning to the land of the living, bare seconds later, he was immobilized. It had very little to do with the nails piercing him, fixing him to the wall and everything to do with the absolute terror thrumming through his system.

He could not speak.

He could not feel.

He could not see.

He could not hear.

For a few moments, his neural slate was blanked and he just hung there from the nails, bloody and damaged, then he opened his eyes.

Baptismal.

Yes, that's what this was. Others were inducted into her obscene cult via the bite, but not him. He would be baptized and made an example of.

She would accept nothing less.

The other vampires swarmed in now, lapping up the blood that drained from him, suckling his wounds and creating new ones as they bit into him.

Griska stood there, watching, grinning like something that devoured children in a dark wood. In Doc's head, he said, *Now, here comes the Mother to put you to bed...Martyr.*

Doc was dizzy from the loss of blood, from pain and trauma, his eyesight was blurring. But he could feel, he could sense, he could know what was coming now. He could smell *her* bouquet, the smell of mass graves. He could feel *her* touch which was that of crawling, maggoty things. Her voice was scraping darkness, screeching metal, and the screams of eviscerated children, cooing at him.

The Death Angel opened her shroud and gouged out a strip of gray rib meat with one black nail.

Doc would not look, *could* not look. He was too weak to fight. He could only accept that which was offered, the putrescent meat and bile that were pushed into his mouth. He screamed himself into darkness as his tongue licked and his teeth chewed and his throat swallowed, his soul rotting to carrion.

For this was Her Body and Her Blood.

This was communion of the damned.

INTERLUDE #2: THE VURVOLAK

1

Cobton, 1828

Hysterical and raving, the infected trooped out into the snow of the village square in ghastly death-trains. They danced and shuddered with idiot splendor, their dead-white faces split by mortuary grins and welded into grisly rictuses. They tore at themselves with knotted fingers, their blood steaming into the snow in mindless sacrificial offerings to the sepulchral gods of boneyards. Their voices screeched and shrilled into the night, echoing off the barren, idiot face of the dead moon above. Others, a great many others, lay chalk-white in beds, pining away as death leeched the life from their very veins.

They died in numbers.

But they did not stay dead.

2

It was a night of howling black wind and breath turned to frost, so they stayed close to the fire. Katya would not allow them to leave it. She told them that in warmth and light there was safety. Against what? But those were the things Katya did not like to talk about so she cleaned the kitchen, sweeping and mopping the flagstone floor, knowing that evil spirits lived in dirty places and she would allow no such spirits here. Not in the home of her daughter and her precious grandchildren. Pausing with her broom, Katya watched the children closely—Michael, Anna, and the infant, David, sleeping so soundly in his bassinet—and crossed herself, knowing that children were always the first, always the first.

"Mashalla," she said under her breath in her native Albanian tongue: *As God wishes.*

"What did you say, Grandma?" Michael asked her.

"Just talking to myself, child. Muttering, muttering." She looked at him there by the fire and thought he was the image of his father. The poor thing. "Old ladies talk to themselves and young men must pretend they do not hear."

Michael smiled and turned back to the fire.

The children were afraid and she knew it. Their father had left with the other men before nightfall yesterday to track the evil to its source and none had returned. And they would not return…not as men. Now her daughter had gone out to fetch the priest so he would come and bless the house again. It was a reasonable act, Katya knew, given that her husband had not returned, but to go out on a night like this. The wise course would have been to stay so they could guard the children together.

That's foolishness, Mama, Etonya had said to her before she left. *I do not believe in such things. Those are old stories. Cobton is ill…but not with that. You must forget the old superstitions.*

They have served us well thus far, Katya told her.

Mama…please. Don't say those things before the children. You will give them nightmares. They are worried about their father and I am worried about my husband.

Katya nodded. *You* should *worry about your husband. He has not come back. He may return tonight and when he does, he'll go for the children. They always go for the children and you know it. They kill the thing they love best. The plague is upon this village. You have seen the signs. You know what is happening. We are all in danger, terrible danger. The Vurvolak—*

I won't listen to that! I do not believe in such things!

Then why do you go for the priest?

Enough, Mama!

But for Katya it was not enough. She knew things. She had seen things that others had not. She had seen the plague of the Vurvolak before. And it was here now. *They say three old men are missing. You know whom I speak of, child. The three who gather in the summer outside the town hall, telling their stories of the old country. They were wise—they knew the Vurvolak was among us. I was with them when they opened its grave on the hill. I was there when it cried out—*

Enough!

Etonya would hear no more of it. This was a new country and a new life and the old ways needed to be left in the old country. Katya could not talk sense to her. Yes, this was a new country and its ways were simple and naïve. What better place for evil to take root than in a place where no one would believe in it? Etonya refused to admit these things, but Katya could see the fear in her eyes. She knew her daughter believed and was afraid for her children. Why else go out at night into the storm to fetch the priest? She was terrified that her husband would come back and terrified of what he would bring with him. She had been gone nearly two hours now. The church was only twenty minutes away. Etonya should have been back long ago and it was Katya's fear that she would never be back, that out there in the cold depths of the storm she had found her husband or *he* had found her.

Katya crossed herself and began sweeping again.

The wind was moaning outside, rising up in what seemed a dozen shrieking voices filled with hate and torment and death. She would not listen because if you listened, she knew, sometimes you would hear your voice being called. She swept faster, chasing away every last speck of dust even though it was hard to see properly with only the firelight and the glow of the oil lamp. She did not trust herself to be inactive. She was old and she was tired. If she sat down, she might fall asleep. That's when they would come. That's when they always came…in the dark watches of night.

Katya heard the children whispering.

"What is this about?" she said. "Are we telling secrets?"

Anna giggled.

"She's telling crazy stories," Michael said.

Katya was interested now. "What sort of crazy stories?"

Anna said that her schoolmate, Stephen, claimed that his sister stood outside of his window at night. But she had been dead a week and it could not be.

"Those are awful stories," Katya warned her, shivering, "and we will not listen."

She knew the family Anna spoke of. They had not been heard from in days. People said the plague had claimed them and Katya knew it was true, only that the plague was of a far different variety than people thought…or would admit. Cobton would be a graveyard soon. If the plague was not rooted out by traditional means, there would be no one left before long. The signs were everywhere. The men came with wagons during the long white afternoons and carted off the dead. Sometimes entire families were put into the grave, but no one would listen to Katya when she told them the bodies must be burned to ash. She was a crazy old foreign woman and what did she know with her old wive's tales?

But she knew because she had seen it before.

Today in Cobton there had been very few in the streets. Doors were bolted, shutters were closed. It was December 1st. Snow fell and blew up the lanes, tree limbs creaked in the wind. Even in winter, the village was a busy place. Children played in the streets and wagons came and went, women gossiped in doorways and men drank at the inn. But today it had been noticeably silent. The only voice of the village was that of the wind as it moaned down empty avenues and narrow alleyways, skirted the snow-heaped rooftops.

It was the silence of the grave.

There had only been one wagon out and the pounding hooves of its team had been like thunder booming. The wagon was piled with the dead. They were taking them up to the burial ground to be interred before the ground was locked hard with frost. They would not listen. Katya had tried again and again, but they would not listen to common sense because she was a crazy old woman.

She had seen rats in the village.

Great voracious swarms of rats that poured down into the streets from the old mill on the hilltop that no one would visit now. They claimed it was too much of a climb in the snow, but there were other reasons only they would not speak of them. Yet, it was curious how when the sun began to set and the long shadow of the mill was cast over the town like that of a cemetery monument, the villagers went out of their way not to be caught in that shadow as if its touch meant death.

When people began to die of the wasting sickness with no discernable cause and the rats ran free in the streets, it could mean only one thing, the very thing Katya had lived in terror of most of her life: the coming of the Vurvolak. The rats were not too active in the daytime, but at night they were bold, sweeping over the town in a hungry, dirty horde, eating anything they could find. Even dogs and stray sheep had gone missing now. Their lair was up in the old mill. It should have been burned to the ground, but no one was brave enough to go up there to root out the source of the pestilence. So the rats bred and their numbers swelled which was bad enough in and of itself, Katya knew, but up there, in the dark bowels of the mill, she feared what slept with the rats and came out only at night.

"When will Mama be back?" Michael asked.

"Soon, very soon now, my child," Katya lied. "You will see."

But, oh, your mother is my daughter and I love her, but I do not think I want her to come back now. I do not want her to bring into this house the thing she has found out there. Katya crossed herself again. The children were hungry and the pot of barley soup on the stovetop was making their stomachs growl. But they could not eat. It was an old Albanian custom that food must not be touched when a priest is expected, not until he himself sits and sups. To break with custom was to invite dire catastrophe, Katya knew. If custom had been followed in Cobton as it should have been, the village would not be a corpse in search of a grave now.

"Can we eat soon?" Anna asked.

"Oh yes, very soon now. Very soon."

Tonight, she would make preparations. She would not sleep. She would hang a bag of salt around the throat of each child and recite a psalm for protection against evil. She would anoint the doors and windows with holy water and keep the fire burning high. She would keep the door barred and nothing would enter, not unless it was invited.

And I will never invite them! Never!

Oh, but maybe you won't have a choice, old woman. You have spent your entire life believing in the unbelievable, fearing the unknown, and embracing the impossible, thinking you could guard against these things with your superstitions and old customs and folk magic. But maybe what you failed to take into consideration is that the Vurvolak have their own sort of magic and it is a cunning and diabolic magic. A magic that is black where yours is white. They are of an ancient seed and possessed of dark abilities you cannot guess at. Once they feared you in their own way, but that was when you were young, pure of mind and pure of body, but now that restless stream of strange blood within you has dried up.

You cannot hope to withstand them.

They want the children as they always want the children. It's where they always begin their cycle of contagion. They will feed on the children. Your grandchildren. They will empty them of blood and life and soul and turn them into walking shells, predatory ghosts that exist only to spread the seed of evil—

Katya shut it out of her brain. She would not think such things. She would not let herself walk down that path for it led into the black heart of a forest she would never, ever escape from once its black spiking branches enclosed her. No, she *could* fight them and she *would* fight them.

And as she thought this, she heard a momentary peal of braying laughter that was strident and absolutely inhuman. *Stupid old crone, silly cauldron-stirring old fishwife...did you think we had forgotten you? Did you think by leaving the old lands that you would not see us again? That we would not come for you in the end and profane all that you hold sacred? That we would not turn this village into a cemetery as we have done with so many others? Your son-in-law searched for us and we welcomed him. He stands at our side now. Your daughter went to look for the priest and she found him...or perhaps, he found her, drinking deep of her sacramental wine until it flowed in hot coppery rivers down his chin. And we'll have the children. Each, in turn, shall be milked. Then you, old woman, then you. You shall sleep with the rats. For tonight the Vurvolak comes...*

Shivering, Katya went over and warmed herself by the fire with the children. Its heat could not dispel the chill deep inside her marrow. David began to fuss in his sleep, so she rocked his bassinet gently. These were her riches and her precious jewels: the children. She would fight to keep them safe and free of the ghosts of the night.

"Papa's not coming home, is he?" Anna said, her eyes misting.

"Oh yes, child, he'll be coming and your mother, too."

Michael's lower lip was trembling. "They're dead."

"No, no!" Katya said to them, hugging them close to her.

"Stephen said the dead are coming back and—"

Katya clutched them both tighter. She would not listen to such things, she would not let their innocent mouths be tainted by such awfulness. She could not allow it. She held them there before the fire, repeating an old saying from her childhood village: "Ssshhh, my children, for tonight the Vurvolak comes. It comes for your daughter, then for your son..."

3

And sixty years before...

Thump...thump...thump.

The soldiers were working down in the churchyard below Katya's window, doing their grisly task that all knew but must never be spoken of. It was the sound of hammers upon stakes.

There were other sounds, too, but she shut her ears against them.

The plague was spreading and the elders of Haidam were worried, adults living in terror for their families. Two villages not far away had become ghost towns now and the elders would not allow it to happen to a third. They called in the army and the business of exorcism, overseen by the village priest and a military surgeon, went on most of the day.

Katya's father assisted them.

She heard the stories he told mother by the chimney corner at night when he thought the children were sleeping. Katya crouched on the stairs and listened. Having already cleaned out the burial yards of the other cursed villages, the soldiers knew exactly what to look for. They searched amongst the graves for tiny holes that the Vurvolak used when leaving at night, issuing forth as ghostly mists before becoming corporeal for the seeking of blood. They found twenty-five graves that were suspicious. Upon opening them, they discovered that while seven of the cadavers were sufficiently decayed, eighteen were in a most unnatural state. "There are tests to be made," father said to mother. No one wished to defile the dead unnecessarily. They looked first for livid puncture marks upon the throat or wrists. Once these were found, a cursory examination was begun. The fingernails of the Vurvolak often grew long and sharp, as did the canines or central incisors. The surgeon checked for this. Other telltale signs were the staring, cataleptic eyes, cheeks ruddy with life, or a bloated overfed appearance to the corpse itself. The Vurvolak often chewed at their shrouds in the grave or scratched at the lids of their coffins. These things must be differentiated from those of premature burial, father says. Some of the corpses were floating in coffins filled with blood and there was no mistaking what they were. Others required more than a general physical examination: the surgeon, using long needles, pierced suspicious bodies. If blood ran in combination to the above symptoms, then the cadaver in question was most certainly a Vurvolak.

But there was only one sure way to know.

And Katya had seen proof of that, peering through the shutters of her window at what was happening far below.

She was told to keep her shutters closed. Everyone in the village not employed in the work in the churchyard was told to do the same. This was not a spectacle to be watched, but a most dire and grim affair and the army would arrest any who thought otherwise.

Thump...thump...thump.

But Katya had to see. She opened the shutters only after she heard a most awful scream. She looked down into the churchyard below and saw dozens of exhumed graves with great piles of black earth next to them. Two soldiers wrestled a coffin from the ground and brushed soil from it. The lid was pried open and even from her vantage point, Katya could see the corpse in the box...it was bloated like a barrel and shining red with blood, a distended human spider fattened from its feedings. The surgeon and the priest examined it and, shaking their heads, stepped back, and two soldiers step forward. One had a stake and the other a heavy mallet.

Katya knew she must not watch.

She must not see this.

But she was unable to look away and she begged God for forgiveness for her iniquity. The mallet was swung and the stake struck. There was a moist, meaty sort of sound as it impaled the body. A fountain of glistening red blood shot up into the air in a gushing spout, splattering the soldiers. The effect was instantaneous: the body writhed and thrashed. She saw its ensanguined hands clawing at the air, flailing and fighting. The mouth opened with a horrid, rending scream that echoed off amongst the graves.

Thump...thump...thump.

The stake was driven clean through and the corpse no longer moved. One of the bloodied soldiers took an axe and chopped the head free. The surgeon stuffed something in its mouth and then the head was returned to the box. The priest made a blessing over the coffin as it was filled with wild roses and nailed shut.

Another coffin was unearthed and opened.

The examination was made and a stake was placed against the breast of a woman who had once been Katya's schoolteacher. The stake was hit once and the corpse nearly leaped from the box. It seized the hand of the soldier holding the stake and as he cried out in horror, the corpse bit into his hand. Three soldiers took hold of it as the stake was pounded through. The scream of the dead woman echoed in Katya's brain for many days.

She closed the shutters.

Trembling, dizzy, a hot-cold sweat running down her face, she dropped to her knees on the floor. Every fear she had known as a child came back to haunt her now. They bunched in her head, cackling in her ears. She had seen them now. The Vurvolak. The stories were true. They were not just ghost stories to be told by firelight. Mother always laughed about the Vurvolak when Katya told her the wild tales she had heard...most of them from Grandma Mirajeta...but maybe, just maybe, mother only laughed so she did not scream.

And perhaps, mother did not know everything after all.

Mirajeta was much older and wiser than mother and knew many things. It was she who covered all the mirrors in the house when she learned that the graves were to be opened. Mother did not stop her and chide her for being superstitious. She just looked away. Mirajeta said the mirrors had to be covered for those lying in the churchyard would try to contaminate the living through them. When they saw their destruction coming, they would seek the reflections of any living person in a mirror and make them a Vurvolak.

The night of the exorcism was a bad one.

Mirajeta told Katya that the Vurvolak would seek retribution for the destruction of their brethren and that she, Katya, would be in the most danger of all. Katya was thirteen. Her menses had begun. A menstruating virgin had a power that could shake the world, Mirajeta said, if only it could be directed. Was it not true that a virgin in menses could turn wine into vinegar or make horses miscarry or blight the harvest? Or that a girl in such a state could wither flowers and curdle milk within the cow? And as they could do such things, so could they be devastating to the Vurvolak, Mirajeta explained. A virgin in menses would know the locations where the Vurvolak hid during the daytime and who their leader was. They would not be able to control the mind of such a girl. With a stake in her hand, she was deadly to them. And they knew it. They would want to kill Katya, to make her like them, as punishment for her father helping the soldiers and because of her power, which was derived from the fact that she was ripe but uncorrupt.

So that night, the shutters were locked and the windows bolted. Fires burned high in hearths. Mirajeta placed a linen bag of salt around Katya's throat and drew another circle of salt around her bed. A wax cross that had been blessed on Ascension Day was hung above Katya's head. White roses and hawthorn branches were strung up in the corners. Mirajeta sat in a rocking chair and prayed in a wavering, eerie voice throughout the night.

Nothing would silence her.

Not even when, just after midnight, the Vurvolak gathered outside the house in numbers, drawn from every crypt and moldering secret grave for miles to stand there beneath the pale light of the thin-edged moon, sending their minds out to those in the house, compelling them to open doors and windows and, more importantly, to invite them in. Katya, shivering and sobbing in her bed as Mirajeta recited a curious combination of Christian psalms and apotropaic folk charms, felt their minds reaching out for hers, scratching at the walls of her psyche like dogs trying to get in.

She would not let them.

But that didn't mean they could not send images into her head.

They showed her that this night they were bringing more than the plague of the Vurvolak to the village, but the plague of death, the Black Death. She saw things that would happen in the next days or weeks—the bodies of villagers set with bleeding red blisters, faces shriveling, bodies bursting with morbid infection, bile and yellow drainage running from open festering sores like hot tallow. She saw the villagers stricken and mad, dancing in the night as fevers shook their bodies and lunacy ripped their minds open. She saw them spread out in loose-limbed corpse heaps, rotting dead things being gnawed by plump graveyard rats and pecked by carrion crows.

She could stop it.

She could save them all.

She only had to sacrifice herself and invite them in.

But she would not, so they besieged the house, clawing at the shutters and scratching at the doors with fingernails grown sharp from pawing at the lids of coffins. They pounded at the door, screaming throughout the night. They shouted obscenities down the chimneys as they cavorted on the rooftop.

In the morning, they were gone.

Katya told her father where they went because she could see it in her mind...the ruined, war-scarred abbey in the mountains. He and the other village men rode to destroy them. But even then it was too late for the Vurvolak had blown their hot plague breath into the houses of the village all night long and the signs were everywhere: moths. Death's-head moths, Sphinx moths...they gathered in the village by the thousands, clustering on the façades of houses and covering windows so that no sunlight could penetrate within. They darkened the sky in swarms. They were three inches thick on the ground. Everywhere, they fluttered their wings and crawled and crept, emitting their mournful and sibilant cry.

Mirajeta was beside herself, fully admitting that her charms and prayers and talismans were helpless against this incursion of death. These were plague moths, they were the harbingers of ruinous pestilence. Did such moths not gather in numbers in battlegrounds and killing fields? At gallows and gibbets and places of execution? Did not they not seek the charnel house and tomb? And when they gathered in a village, did not the plague soon follow? These were the questions she asked.

The family was moved that day to Ostrava where Katya's aunt lived.

Within two weeks, Haidam was a sunwashed corpse with the dead sprawled in yards and streets, hanging from windows and lying in doorways. And by night, the Vurvolak walked.

4

"But first on earth, as Vampyre sent,
Thy corpse shall from its tomb be rent;
Then ghastly haunt thy native place,
And suck the blood of all thy race..."

"What is that Grandma?" Michael asked. "Was that a poem?"

"It means nothing, nothing," Katya said. "I'm just an old woman jabbering on."

But Michael did not believe that any more than he believed that she was the confused old woman she pretended to be. She was old, yes, but wise. She knew many things, but liked to act (at least to Michael and the other two children) that she knew nothing. But he most of all saw through that. Being the oldest, she had told him much more than the others, things he knew his mother had no patience with.

They whiled away many a rainy afternoon, Katya and he, with funny anecdotes, silly stories, and a wealth of Old World superstitions concerning the village she had grown up in. Katya, for example, would not allow a dog inside because it would scare off the angel that protected the house. She thought it bad luck to trim you fingernails after dark or look into a mirror after midnight (the mirror in her room was always carefully covered at sundown and uncovered at first light). She would cross the street if she saw a black cat and would spend the rest of her day moaning over her prayer beads. If someone went on a journey, nothing must be touched in their room until they returned or it invited disaster. Spilled salt meant conflict in the household. Whistling indoors invited poverty. Witches could not cross streams because the water washed away their charms. She was a great believer in spirits, both good and bad. A house must not be swept on Fridays for it would cast good spirits out. Water left uncovered overnight in a glass was a sure way to invite a spirit into a house and pouring hot water down drains would enrage the spirits living in the pipes and they would curse the household. She taught Michael that evil spirits lived in dirty, desolate places and that pebbles in a child's eggshell rattle would drive them away. She believed completely in the evil eye and infants had to be covered amongst strangers so it would not be cast upon them.

Your mother thinks I'm an old woman whose brain has gone soft as porridge with age, Katya told him one afternoon while they dredged up a bucket of water from the old mossy-stoned well. *But listen to me, my child, and pretend that I am not your aged grandmamma, not some fool old woman with bleary eyes and a bad back. Pretend that I am your school chum and playmate telling you tales in the schoolyard wood. Things you must listen to and take to heart, yes? When I tell you there are unseen things in this world, you must believe me. When I say there are nameless horrors that creep in the shadows and foul abominations that crawl beneath the cloak of night, you must hear me and believe. I do not say it to frighten you, but to warn you. To keep you safe.*

Most of her folk beliefs involved death.

If someone died in bed, the mattress must be burned. Mirrors must be covered for seven days after a funeral. And when you left the graveyard following a burial, you were never to look back over your shoulder at the grave or the ghost of the deceased will think you want it to follow you home.

Although Albanian by birth, Katya's family had moved to Moravia—in what was then part of the Habsburg Dynasty and would later be called Czechoslovakia—and settled into a tiny village called Haidam on the border of Hungary in the Carpathian Mountains. It was here, that her own Albanian folk beliefs were combined with Moravian and Hungarian traditions. She told Michael that in Haidam, when someone passed away, their body must be brought to the cemetery in a roundabout fashion so the ghost could not find its way home again. That in a house of death, the blinds must always be pulled and shutters closed for if a body lying in wake was struck by moonlight it would come to life for five days, standing in the corners, staring at its family and drooling. Death by consumption was particularly dangerous, she claimed, for if the body was not buried face-down and its coffin filled with garlands of wild roses, the consumption would wipe out the entire family, one by one. One needed to take special care with suicides as well. The corpses of such had to be washed in running water to cleanse them of evil influences and the graves of suspected witches had to be pierced with needles so they could not rise up to torment the living. And after someone died of a wasting illness, all children must sleep with a sprig of hawthorn on their headboards and must never look out windows after midnight or they would see the deceased begging to be let in.

Katya told him that on St. George's Eve, all doors were locked in Haidam at sunset for it was a terrible time when witches, warlocks, werewolves, vampires, and other malignants walked the earth freely in search of prey. Houses were garlanded with wild flowers, garlic, and thistles. Wild roses were hung over thresholds and crosses of tar painted on doors. Only the village priest and the church bellringer were allowed out at night. The latter to ring the church bell until dawn and the former to bless the village and tend to a great bonfire called a Need-Fire, which drove away the foul things that stalked by night.

These were the things Michael's grandmother told him and believed in absolutely.

Just as she believed in the Vurvolak.

5

When she discovered that the old men were wise with their years, Katya told them her suspicions about the strangers who lived up in the old mill above Cobton. Belic, the Serbian, was not surprised nor were the two Szarka brothers, Vidor and Endre. Their suspicions were the same as Katya's. She had often sat talking with the three of them, sharing memories of the old country. The Widow Varga was with her usually, but now the Widow Varga had died...only a week after the death of her nephew, bearing the signs of the old sickness.

"She is as those up in the mill," Katya told the three old men. "She comes for her family at night and then she will come for me. Then she will come for you."

And as she said this, Katya wondered if what they said was true: that for the Vurvolak, the blood was the life. That as they drank it, the blush of youth returned to their cheeks and a woman of, say, eighty, might walk again as a girl of twenty. Was that possible? Twenty...twenty. She imagined herself as a Vurvolak, filling herself with the sweet blood of children she lured off into the woods, enriching herself and sipping their vitality away like a spider with a web of juicy flies. First, she was a bent-backed, scarf-headed old woman, her mouth trembling and gnarled hands reaching out...but soon enough she walked tall and straight, her eyes blue and clear as the mountain streams she bathed in as a child. Her hair flowed around her, her skin smooth, white, and unblemished, her lips a succulent blood-red.

And, oh, there was the seduction: to walk as a girl of twenty again, to feel the bloom of youth as you bask in the heat of your own blood.

But Katya knew better. The Vurvolak were not pretty, they were not handsome: they were grotesque and obscene, rotting to blackness within. They were like dolls or puppets—empty inside. They were crafty and sly. They might appear beautiful and flaunt carnal invitations, but they were wolves; forever hungry, forever circling their human livestock. They would give you what you wanted most. They could be your lover or friend or protector, they could even wear the face of the one you longed for most, but they were dead things that came alive as the cool moonlight played over their graves. And it always ended the same way: with the puncture marks in the throat and the sound of sucking mouths.

"One night soon," Katya said to the old men, "you will hear the wind at your window, but this wind will scratch at the shutters and ask to be invited in."

While the Szarka brothers crossed themselves at the impact of her words, Belic related an incident that happened many years before when he was a boy. There was a peasant named Kradjec who had fought in the war then returned from the front to his family's farm outside Vrsac. It was said he was ill and fatigued from battle, carrying a pox he had picked up in Silesia. A week after returning, Kradjec died in the night. He was buried without the holy Sacraments in a pauper's grave because the priest was a coward whose family had perished of cholera and feared the same. Two days later, Belic told them, the ghost of Kradjec was seen walking through Vrsac. The peasant farmers said that he appeared to them in the form of a large black wolf with red eyes. It would look in their windows at night. It had ravished a teenage girl and carried off a boy into the forest after sunset. They found the boy's body later...it was twenty feet up in a gigantic black oak, a limb speared right through the chest like the lance of a knight.

"But that's not what had killed him," Belic enlightened them. "It was something else, you see. He was, quite literally, BITTEN to death. Oh yes. They found the teeth marks and punctures in him...dozens and dozens of them. Something had slowly bitten him to death as cat kills a mouse. Kradjec also killed several sheep by tearing out their throats and sucking their blood. Within a week after his return from the grave, his family had all died after complaining that he visited them at night. The illness made them weak with fevers and night-sweats, an uncontrollable trembling of the limbs."

"I have heard such stories," Vidor said.

"The elders claimed Kradjec was a Vulkodlak," Belic said. "It was decided he must be destroyed."

Since he was strong and large for his age, Belic was one of the locals that went to the grave of Kradjec and exhumed his coffin. He said Kradjec was not corrupted in the usual manner. His eyes were sunken and his nose had fallen in, giving him a most horrid skull-like appearance, but other than that he was quite robust for a man who had lain in his grave for some two weeks. The corpse, in fact, was bloated, the cheeks florid, the lips swollen and juicy. There was blood on his mouth and hands. A stake of whitethorn was driven through his chest and at that point, Kradjec rose up, screaming, bright red blood gushing from the wound. It spurted from his eyes and nose. He vomited a great volume of it from his mouth. As he screamed, a cold draft rose from him that was dank and clammy like air that blows out from a tomb long sealed.

"It was the draft of death," Belic said. "I saw birds drop from the sky, dead. A dozen sheep were said to have keeled over. That night there was a caul over the face of the moon. I smelled death that day...not decomposition, mind you...but the true blackness that is death."

The others watched him as he gathered himself. He packed his clay pipe and a put a match to it, puffing out clouds of smoke.

"Before the stake was driven all the way through," he told them, "Kradjec cried out in a voice that was not his own, telling us things he could not have known in life. Dirty secrets and half-lies...terrible things about friends and lovers, families. I will not repeat the filth he spewed, but he told me when I would die and how I would die."

Belic said before that hammer came down again, Kradjec's face inflated like it was filled with gas and a strange sort of decay overtook it until most of the meat was clean eaten away. His flesh was a riot of popping sores that ran with black ooze like the juice squeezed from an inky cap mushroom. Within seconds, he split open like roasting meat and they could see the skeleton beneath which was horribly alive with some unnamable vitality. As he cracked open—Belic likened the process to a turd that has dried in the sun for a month—gouts of yellow fluid poured out of him once the blood was gone and that fluid was undulant with grave maggots. By that point he looked like a mud-and-straw scarecrow bursting its seams. His face had fallen into a central vault-like pit and his clawing hands hung with loops of skin that dangled like holiday ribbons. The fingers were gray and spongy as they gripped the sides of the coffin, exploding into mush.

"The stake was driven in the rest of the way and Kradjec...he was just gone," Belic said. "The clothes he wore just deflated and there was nothing but a few scraps of bone, blowing gray ash, some black ooze...and hundreds of carrion beetles filling the casket. God help us."

Vidor wiped sweat from his face. "He...he told you when you would die?"

"He did." Belic nodded. "And it will be soon."

Endre, the elder of the Szarka brothers, said he had heard— though not witnessed—such things in Hungary. A woman who had returned from death had fed on her own children. She was dug up and brought out into the forest. She was disemboweled and her head was cleaved free. Gouts of blood flowed from her. Even headless and gutless, her body fought and clawed for some time. According to local custom, her heart was removed, severed into four pieces and burnt separately.

Katya said, "There is one among us who has brought the plague of the Vurvolak."

"Griska," says Belic.

"That is what he is called: Griska." Katya looked from Belic to the Szarka brothers. "He is said to be here. He is said to be up in the old mill. But who has seen him? Who has known him that still walks in daylight?"

Endre stared at his own knotty hands. "Was there not a Bela Griska of history? A Magyar who commanded a peasant army of 400, which held out against over 100,000 Ottoman Turks for many months? Is my memory correct?"

"It is," Vidor told him. "A fierce warrior to his enemies, a butcher to his own people. But it could not be the same Griska...not after these many centuries."

Endre shrugged. "So what are we to do?" he asked.

"I think you know," Belic said.

"We go to the grave of the Widow Varga," Katya told them, knowing they were in agreement. "We open it and then...we see."

It was hard work for old men, but Belic had spent his life as a carpenter and it was he who did most of the work. The coffin of the Widow Varga was opened as Katya prayed and a hot breeze of putrescence blew out at her. This was the only sign of earthly decomposition.

"Oh, Ivanka," Katya despaired, looking down at the corpse. "It is true."

The Widow Varga had been an old woman with threadbare white hair, a face seamed by wrinkles...now that face was smooth, unmarked and unblemished, her hair lustrous and dark. Blood was slobbered from her mouth and down her throat. Her teeth had grown long and sharp and her eyes, forever staring, were huge and dark like the depths of a pond.

"Don't look away, my darling," she said with a voice that was like velvet caressing Katya's brain. "Just look in my eyes, my dear Katya. You are wrong, so very wrong about it all. You know that I love you, my good friend. I would not lie to you. I want you to look deep in my eyes and remember what it was like to be a girl. A beautiful girl, long-limbed, round-hipped, and full-breasted. A girl men wanted and women admired. Reach out, Katya, reach out and touch me and I'll give you your youth back. Then together we'll crush these doddering old fools. Reach out, Katya...touch me...touch your old friend..."

Katya began to do just that, caught in the web of what lay in that box.

"NOOO!" Endre cried. "SZORKANY! VURDERLAK!"

Then Katya blinked her eyes and what she was looking down at was not the youthful, beguiling figure of Ivanka Varga but a tomb-hag. It looked like some worm-eaten crow in ragged skirts, something made of scraps and rags and yellow rungs of bone, its face scabbed, leprosy-yellow, and set with cavernous black eye sockets and a mouth like a mantrap with gnashing teeth. As she breathed, moths winged from her throat and a stench blew from her like green carrion.

Katya's heart had stopped and when it began beating again, she thought the casket was filled with immense spiders that were shiny black and leggy, hundreds of them tangled together, jaws dripping venom and eyes like glossy red pearls. At any moment, she knew, they would explode free and engulf her.

Belic swung his axe and the Widow Varga burst like a seed pod as it cleaved her chest open. Blood that was bright and dark cherry-red gushed up and she sank away in it for a second before emerging, a haggard red effigy looking like a woman turned inside out and being birthed from herself.

Katya saw no more; she passed out.

When she came to, Ivanka Varga was on a pyre of sticks and hay. The flames engulfed her and she writhed and made a moaning sound but that was it. Blackened and smoldering, she split open with plumes of oily smoke...and a dozen flaming rats tried to escape the pyre but were killed by the old men. The smoke became a swarm of corpse flies that blazed to ash, then a rising cloud of death's-head moths. None escaped the flames. Every bit of her burned until there was only a charred mass flaking away.

"It is done," Belic said.

The surprising thing was that throughout the entire process, no one down in the village of Cobton came to investigate.

But Katya did not find that surprising at all.

6

Vurvolak, do not knock this night. You cannot come in. You are barred from entry, Vurvolak.

These were the words that Katya heard in her head again and again as she waited before the fire with the children, holding them tight and waiting for her daughter to return...which was the thing she now feared the most.

She knew there was a pot of barley soup on the stove and the children were so very hungry, but still she waited for the priest. There was beef in the soup, a rich hot stock that would warm them all. She could smell it and feel it sliding down her throat as she spooned it into her mouth. But she could not eat. One was not supposed to eat until the priest showed. It was disrespectful to do otherwise and a serious breach of tradition...but the children, the poor hungry children. They needed to eat.

Thump...thump...thump.

That was the sound from the Haidam churchyard when she was a child: the sound of stakes being pounded into the chests of the undead. Why did it echo in her head after all these years? Why would it not leave her alone? It was so long ago and she had been so young like a flower just spreading its petals; now she was old and tired and worn, withered to the stalk.

The Vurvolak will come for you, old woman. You were there when Belic and the Szarka brothers destroyed the Widow Varga. That was a crime against the Vurvolak. They will now destroy you. Just as they wanted to destroy your father for helping the soldiers in the Haidam churchyard so very long ago.

You must stay awake.

You must be forever on guard this night.

But it was not so easy when you were old and your blood ran slow and cold like molasses and you had spent so many, many years on guard, watching the shadows for what might lurk there. Nearly eighty years now. That was a long time. How many others had died from one calamity and one pox after the other, but still Katya lived and breathed in her old, pain-addled body. How many winters she had shivered through, how many bright spring mornings she had seen and how many starry July nights. There was a weight that came with the years and she could feel each pound pressing down on her, straining her over-labored skeleton. She was fighting to stay awake but she feared she had already slipped into dream.

Thump...thump...thump.

Katya realized her eyes were closed, but as she tried to open them there was pain in her skull. It was like her eyelids had been tacked shut and she had to tear them open to see, but the pain, the godawful pain...it was in her head like red-hot needles piercing her brain. The more she tried to wake, the more the pain increased. But if she surrendered to it, the pain lessened and it was easy and soft like falling into a feather bed before a roaring fire.

Thump...thump...thump.

Why do I hear it again and again? This is what she wondered and although the rational part of her brain told her that there was a very good reason for it, she did not want to know. It was so much easier drifting off. She wanted rest and quiet with no more pain, no more suffering. Yet...she knew she must wake up. It had never been as important as it was now.

Thump...thump...thump.

She clawed her way to semi-wakefulness and that's when the pounding stopped and she heard a voice that was sweet and pure as she had once been sweet and pure. It was an almost cooing sound and it said, "Yes, come in."

Katya came fully awake. "NOOOO!" she screamed. "DON'T LET THEM IN…"

But it was too late because they filled the room like wraiths, vaporous things made of black swirling mist coalescing into shadowy eldritch forms with clown-white gloating faces, red lips, and hollow eyes. Michael screamed as three or four hags took hold of him, their mouths going for his throat and his wrists. Katya screamed again as she saw the priest standing there with his pallid, bloodstained face. He was holding Anna's hand. Anna's father was in the doorway. His eyes were red ice, his face smooth white wax. Katya grabbed a burning stick from the fire and advanced on the one she knew was Griska, tall and vulture-like with the narrow face of a starving rat. He did not back away. He stood there in his long animal fur coat, his face merciless and sadistic in its pleasure. His skin was sickly sallow yellow, his eyes huge and staring and liquid red.

He grinned like an exhumed skull, his teeth long and sharp jutting from pale, puckered gums. *"You are meat,"* he said in a voice which was more like the snarl of a rabid wolf than the voice of a man. *"Meat for the dogs and meat for the rats."*

He reached out to her with a long-fingered hand whose nails were ragged and sharp, grave-earth packed beneath them. He began to cackle and as he did so, his tomb-breath blowing hot and putrescent in her face, Katya felt her heart in her chest: *thump…thump…thump…*

She swung the burning stick at him as he reached out and gripped her heart symbolically, yet so very literally that there was an eruption of pain in her chest like she had been kicked.

Meat, he had said and *meat* she most surely was.

The burning stick never even got close to him.

He fixed those black-hot burning devil's eyes upon her and Katya was crushed, shattered, and split apart by hatchet-like blows of invisible force. After a dozen of them, she was bleeding and raw and broken…but Griska kept at it with a manic lunatic glee until she seemed to implode in a storm of luminous gore. She came flying apart…head nearly spinning off her shoulders, limbs dropping away, viscera corkscrewing from her rent abdomen like pink, fleshy worms unwinding in manic, seeking flight...and then her dismembered husk and its attendant tissues and appendages and organs did not fall to the floor but were held aloft in a spinning meat-colored, whirlwind of blood-mist.

And though her sensory network was ravaged beyond repair, Katya heard it once again: *thump...thump...THUUUUMMMMP.*

It was the sound of her heart exploding to red pulp.

Before her sight was gone, she saw Etonya, her own daughter, lift the infant David from his bassinet. The child was squirming and crying as his dead mother peeled his swaddling blankets free like a wrapper. Etonya held the plump infant high for all to see and then sank her fangs into his soft white throat.

PART THREE: THE CATACOMBS

1

They're waiting for me to make some kind of decision, Wenda thought as she stared at the kerosene lantern, knowing that soon it would be empty of fuel and they would be down to Rule's flashlight and Megga's penlight. *I have no hold over any of them, yet they're empowering me with the decision. Do we take our chances here in this room and hope for the best or do we do the very thing the vampires would not expect and make a try for that other house?*

"The longer you sit there woolgathering," Megga said, "the less our chances of survival are. You need to make a decision already. Are we going or are we going to sit here and wait for it?"

Megga, of course, was baiting her and expecting some sort of reaction so Wenda gave her none. She just watched the lantern and tried to sort it out in her own mind, ignoring Megga as if she hadn't spoken at all. Mostly, what she was trying to do was to get a grip on her own conflicting emotions. They were rioting in every possible direction and until she got them under control, she was going to be no good. She needed to get back in the zone, the Vultura zone, where she was confident and cool and always did the right thing at the right time. Unfortunately, at the moment, she was feeling too much like plain old indecisive, panicky Wenda Keegan and not enough like her alter ego.

You have to get it going again. You have to lead and you know it.

But that's where the trouble lay. She did not want anything to happen to Rule or Morris or even Megga, but she feared—as Wenda Keegan—that she would make the wrong choice. If she got these people killed, then their lives would be on her hands, and maybe on her soul, and she did not like that, she did not like that at all.

"Well?" Megga asked her.

Wenda looked up at her. "Well, what?"

"Are we going to do something or what?"

"It's under consideration."

Rule cleared his throat. "It's not a decision to be made lightly. In the final analysis, we're in grave danger regardless of our actions. Yes, we might die and become like them if we wait here…but on the other hand, if we try a breakout and luck does not favor us, it'll be all the same, won't it?"

Megga looked exasperated. "I'm not waiting. I refuse to wait."

Wenda stood and went over by the fire. "Oh, shut up already."

She did not expect what came next. Megga charged at her, hooked her by the elbow and spun her around. Before Wenda could do much more than be surprised, Megga took a swing at her. She'd reached her breaking point so she bunched her fist and sent it at Wenda's face. The blow was struck out of rage, so there wasn't much control behind it. One of her knuckles caught Wenda's cheekbone, the force of it carrying Megga herself around in a semi-circle. Wenda responded instantly, jumping forward and shoving Megga hard before she could regain her balance. Megga hit the floor, flipping herself onto her back to make another try at it, but Wenda was on her by then. She straddled her, gripping her by the throat with one hand and bringing the stake up with the other like she was going to impale her right then and there.

"Don't!" Rule cried out.

Megga had a foam of saliva on her lips, her teeth clenched, her eyes wild and stormy.

If I kill the bitch here and now it'll probably save us a lot of trouble down the road, a whole lot of trouble.

"So do it!" Megga challenged her. "Fucking stake me!"

But Wenda had already loosened her hold on the stake though she still gripped Megga's throat. No, she wasn't about to do it, but the absolutely insane thing was that the vibe she got off Megga was that she seemed to *want* to be staked…as ludicrous as that seemed. She was practically hungry for it and that in itself was as scary as anything Wenda had thus far encountered. Was it something suicidal and self-destructive in her or was it something more? A lot of writers liked to toy around with the pop psychology idea that the stake through the heart of a vampire was something more than impalement but a symbolic sexual penetration. All the Freudian overtones aside, Wenda nearly believed it at that moment because Megga wanted it.

"Please," she said.

But Wenda got off her. There would be no penetration and Megga looked disappointed.

That's when Morris, who seemed oblivious to everything but his primitive fascination with the fire, turned and said the most absurd thing: "Don't hurt her, Vultura. She's under contract the rest of the season."

Megga didn't seem to see the humor in it, but Wenda started laughing. It came rolling out of her and when it subsided, she said, "Okay, Morris. But when this season is through, fire the bitch. She can go back to working the drive-thru window at Wendy's with rest of her Goth tribe."

Which was spiteful, of course, but true.

Megga pulled herself from the floor and sat down in her chair, lighting a cigarette with a visibly trembling hand.

Wenda rubbed the welt on her cheekbone and tried to make sense of it all. Several times tonight, Megga had openly come on to her. Now she had attacked her, then was nearly reduced to tears when she wouldn't shove the stake into her. She was acting like some pissed-off, jilted lover. How did you explain any of that? There was a weird sexual undertone to it. Megga was moody by nature. She was argumentative, confrontational, sarcastic, bitter, angry…and tonight she'd displayed all these things, as expected. But the eroticism was not something Wenda had seen coming. But it was there. It was still there. Even now as Megga sat brooding and smoking, she would look over at Wenda with her dark eyes and the seduction, the appetite in them, was there.

Maybe this is how she copes. Maybe this is her version of a nervous breakdown. Maybe the stress and terror and anxiety are finally forcing her out of the closet and she's confronting feelings she always had about me.

But it was nothing that simple and Wenda knew it.

She'd never had any doubts in her mind that Megga swung both ways or that her almost obsessive devotion to Bailey was more than just sisterly, but she did not believe that Megga had been harboring the hots for her. It just didn't wash. There was something there, something going on, but she had the intuitive feeling that it had more to do with the psychic influence of those things outside than with any hidden, deep-set yearnings.

The good thing was, it felt like Vultura was back.

And Vultura was not real happy with Megga the Graveyard Girl. She was filled with disdain and something quite near loathing for her. Not only was Megga not to be trusted, she had morphed into some crazy and nicely fucked-up bitch with highly questionable sexual desires…if wanting to be staked was any indication.

Wenda kept watching her and as she did so, a series of images began to pass through her head. None of them, she thought, were of her own making. She was channeling images from Megga's mind and she knew it. She saw children taunting Megga as a child, calling her *Creepy Meggy,* because while other girls played with dolls or poured over issues of *Tiger Beat*, Megga walked around with books of macabre cartoons by Charles Addams, old well-thumbed horror comics like *Tales from the Tomb* and *Witches' Tales,* and decorated her room with posters of cinematic ghouls like Bela Lugosi, Christopher Lee, and Reggie Nalder. In fact, her first true sexual experience had been auto-erotic as she masturbated at thirteen while watching a vampire flick called *Subspecies.* An attractive teenager, but disenfranchised, friendless, and antisocial, she snuck into cemeteries at night and masturbated while pressed up against headstones and vaults. Bailey represented something to her. Bailey was everything she was not. She was a purity that Megga needed to corrupt. When Bailey did not do what she was told, Megga would slap her again and again until she drew blood and then, overcome by the sight of it, she would lick it off her lips and seduce her.

Was that the nature of their relationship?

Was it some sadomasochistic thing?

Wenda could not be sure. She was certain that the images of Megga's childhood and teenage years were correct, but the Bailey-thing was murky and she could not tell whether it was true or some suppressed fantasy.

Finally, Wenda turned away because she began picking up images of herself. Of Megga licking blood from her. Of biting her in a place she would never care to be bitten.

But as she tried to shut it out, it was like maybe Megga herself had turned the volume up and she could hear her voice plain and clear: *You don't have to be afraid, Wenda. You never have to be afraid of us. All those stories and movies are all utter crap and there are no such things as vampires. It's a silly word of Serbian origin. Meaningless. We prefer more descriptive terms like Vurderlak and Vulkodlak, Vorvolakas and Vurvolak. We exist*

*between reality and dream, light and shadow, life and the grave.
Take my hand and I'll show you things you never knew existed. I'll
take you places undreamed and to worlds untenanted. I'll take you
beyond the pale of death and to the Other Side and back again. I'll
make you young and beautiful forever. Just let me touch you. Let me
put my hands on you. Let me put my lips on you—*

Wenda forced it out of her head because she knew then it was
not Megga at all, but something using Megga like a sort of relay
station. And as she realized this, she could still hear its voice calling
out of the night, rising louder and omnipotent, a buzzing and hissing
and thoroughly inhuman voice. It was growing angry and impatient.
It did not like to be ignored. It could do things that would make her
sorry and as it described them in detail its voice took on the whining
petulance of an angry child, a rotten little brat that was not getting
its way.

Then she knew.

Somehow, she knew.

Because underneath that awful voice there was something else, a
stinging sort of pain born of fear because it could not corrupt her
and this frightened it. She had something. Something it was afraid
of...only she did not know what it was and if she hoped to live
through the night as a living, breathing human being and not wake
up tomorrow night as a slinking graveyard rat with a black and
depthless hole where her soul had once been, she had better figure
out what it was.

What made her special.

What made her different.

And, most importantly, what made them *afraid* of her.

"What is it?" she said aloud.

Megga looked at her, blinking.

"What is it? I have something they don't like and you know what
it is."

"You're losing it," Megga said, sitting on her little secret golden
egg of knowledge, refusing to lift her flanks so that Wenda might
get a look at it. She would not tell and maybe that was because she
was afraid to.

"Well?" Rule said, maybe sensing another confrontation and
wanting to steer things clear. "What are we going to do?"

Wenda turned from Megga. "You think our best bet is to try and
get out of here?"

He shrugged. "I suppose I do."

"Okay. Let's do it. Let's go out there. Let's see if we can get the drop on them." She looked over at Megga. "You're hot for this, so you can lead the way. There's the door. Lead us out."

Megga got up, keeping her distance from Wenda whom she clearly did not trust. Still looking back at her, she went over to the door and reached for the knob. And as she did so, there sounded a knocking from the other side.

2

When Reg got out onto the roof, he realized in his white-edged terror that he had nearly forgotten about the storm, the raw immensity of it, the glacial chill that blew like needles of ice straight from its whirling gut. But as soon as he stumbled out into the snow, it found him. It screamed in his face and sent frozen currents of air up his back. The wind seemed to hit him from every direction like it wanted to squash him flat. The snow was coming down heavy. It blew in his face and spun around him in white tempests. It was about two feet deep as he inched along on all fours so he could climb to the roof next door.

When he'd made it about ten feet from the broken window, he turned and looked back. The shadows and flying snow obliterated everything. He couldn't even be sure where the window was now.

He trusted in his instincts and kept moving.

The pitch of the roof was low and the snow itself gave him good traction as he moved along. The blizzard raged around him, a primal and angry force. It moaned and howled and if somebody had shouted five feet from him, he doubted whether he would have heard them. He didn't dare try and stand or even rise to his knees: if that wind got hold of him, it would toss him right off the roof and to the street far below. Better to stay down low where it couldn't get a grip on him.

He was trying desperately not to think of Doc.

Trying desperately not to remind himself that he had abandoned Doc.

Later. There would be time for guilt later.

He sidled up to the edge of the roof and it was just as he'd seen it out the window earlier with Burt: these houses were all packed in tight and getting from one roof to the next would be easy enough, though not without danger.

He knew he was only two houses away from where Wenda and the others had gone. If he could cross the next roof he'd be there and then he could kick a window open and get inside.

Brushing snow from his face with fingers that were already numb inside his gloves, Reg moved precious inches closer to the edge of the roof. The house next door was a different type and it had a steeply-pitched roof. Not only that but it was about five feet lower. The gap between them was maybe two feet, which wasn't much in good weather...but tonight, in this goddamned storm, it was like jumping from one icefall to the next on Mount Everest. This is what held him back.

You got a choice to make, man. You can go back and face those things or you can sit here and freeze to death. In an hour you'll be like a frozen steak. Or, you can jump to the next roof and pray you don't roll right off it.

"Fuck it," he said under his breath.

He got up in a crouch, kicking the snow away from him so he had himself a good launching platform. He counted to three, sucked in a breath, and then sprang like a cat. He didn't fly like he would have without all the heavy winter gear on, but he spanned the roofs easily and landed in the snow of the one next door and what was utterly amazing to him was that when he landed, despite the pitch, he landed solid and sure.

That wasn't so bad.

But that thought had barely passed through his mind when the snow beneath him gave way and he felt his boots skidding over iced shingles and he was sliding with no way to slow his descent. He let out a cry that was lost in the storm. He kept sliding, picking up speed, his boots dislodging columns of snow that swept up and over him, much of it going up his pant legs and up the back his parka. Then he struck something solid that groaned, but held. A rainspout, a gutter...he didn't know what it was but it was all that saved him.

For the longest time he did not want to move.

He didn't *dare* move.

He could see his skid-marks in a perfect unbroken trail above him and he thought if it hadn't been such a fucking tragedy, it might have been funny.

He just wanted to lay there and be safe. But the snow up his legs and back was unbelievably cold and his limbs were going as numb as his fingers. It was getting so he couldn't even feel his face. Fatigue was on him and the urge to close his eyes and just sleep was almost overwhelming. But he remembered from high school Health class that this was one of the signs of hypothermia. He needed to get out of that goddamn wind and warm himself, or before long he would start thinking crazy things and begin making irrational choices.

Like roof-crawling in the winter isn't evidence of that.

He started climbing again, moving very slowly, worming his way up the face of the roof to the ridgeline above. If he could get up there, then the crossing would be a lot easier. It took him at least fifteen minutes to do it, pushing himself up carefully until he could get his hands on the ridgeline and then on something else, maybe an old lightning rod. He pulled himself up until he was sitting on the ridgeline, legs to either side, gripping the lightning rod—because that's what it indeed was—and hanging on for dear life as the wind tried to strip him free. He felt like a sailor in a storm-tossed ocean, each gust of wind like a wave crashing into him.

Now and again, the blizzard would lift momentarily like a veil and he would see all those rising rooftops around him, some higher, some lower, most of them sharp and jagged like black volcanic rock reaching up into the maelstrom of the snowstorm. Then the veil would drop and he was a man alone again. An explorer who'd sunk his flag at the South Pole and was done in as he gripped it in the wrath of the polar night.

He knew he had to keep going.

The idea of just waiting and freezing to death wasn't an option. Not after what he'd already been through. Everything, as he saw it, was now about survival.

Still gripping the lightning rod, he pulled himself around it and sat on the other side. So far, so good. Now it was time to let go and shimmy down the ridgeline to the next roof. Although the idea wasn't exactly intriguing by that point, it was the only option available, so he let go, crouching down, and started moving.

He hadn't gone very far when he smelled something hot on the wind.

Something that stank of death.

It didn't belong out there and he knew it. Out in the subzero depths of the blizzard, the world was pristine and white and odorless. Still, the smell came out of the storm at him like a channel of putrescence.

He held onto the ridgeline, in absolute denial that he had smelled anything at all. It was an olfactory hallucination, he knew. That's what Doc would have called it. *You see, my boy,* he could hear Doc saying, *that odor cannot exist, for in plummeting temperatures like these when the mercury is hanging well beneath freezepoint, there can be no bacterial action and with no bacterial action, the smell of death cannot exist.* Oh God, how Reg wished Doc were there to put things into perspective for him. He'd know what to do. He'd know how to handle this. But Doc was dead and...and...*I let him die, Jesus Christ, but I let him die*...Reg was on his own and no one could help him. No one at all. So he clung to the ridgeline, shaking, teeth chattering, his blood seeming to cool in his veins like the waters of a creek going filthy and dark with silt.

He was not alone.

At the very edge of the roof, he saw something like a black and gnarled tree that looked very much like a woman. He could almost feel its roots sliding into him and feeding on the hot vein of his mad, swooning terror. As he watched, blinking away flakes of snow, it spread black wings, throwing out limbs, and a gray shroud that flapped in the wind.

Although he could not see beneath the shroud, he knew it was a woman and he wondered if it was the one Burt and he had seen outside the window earlier.

She stood there like she was made of something ethereal that the wind simply passed right through without touching. There was a crust of snow atop the ridgeline about four or five inches deep. She should have sunk right through it, but she stood atop it like a ghost.

And she was moving.

Not walking, but *drifting* in his direction and he wanted to scream. But when he tried, all that came out was a soundless breath of forced air. He was numb all over, his limbs thick and his fingers like sausages. He felt watery and weak inside like his guts were melting. And still she came on, drifting forward, her shroud blowing around her, that smell coming with her. The shroud blew aside and he saw part of a face like a gray leather mask and a frozen grin of teeth. She reached out for him, rustling like silk, her fingernails long and sharp like rapiers. She was a corrupted thing that would eat his soul and slit his throat and lap up the hot red life that ran out. The closer she got, the more of her face he saw until it was fully revealed like a skullish puzzlebox opening. It was seamed tombstone gray, bloodred eyes like exploding stars. Her flesh seemed to glow like a lantern, her mouth filled with hooked, overlapping fangs like those of a shark.

"Please," Reg heard his own voice say, cracking in the cold.

But there was no mercy to be found here. Inside his head, he could feel her already taking him. A channel had been opened and he could see into her mind, which was a seething nest of primal appetite, a scorching black desert void of well-picked bones and blowing sand. Beneath the shroud, he saw her body and it was made of dozens of voracious, slat-thin graveyard rats that would bury him in teeth and scraping yellow claws.

When he did manage to scream, it was far too late because she hovered above him, her winding sheet flying around her in all directions and showing him sights he did not wish to see.

But before she fed on him, before physical violation, there was psychic desecration as what was in her skull filled his own like dozens of dark and screeching mandrake roots crowding out his own thoughts and reducing them to abstractions. She was feeding on his soul, biting into it and tearing out great bleeding chunks of it. The pain was not physical, but a spiritual defilement that was beyond agony.

He fought against her…or something in him did.

His fists struck out and his fingers clawed at her, but she seemed to be no more substantial than a fogbank. His hands found flesh that gave way, bones like polished marble, furry things that clawed and bit and drew blood. She grabbed hold of his hair and yanked his head back, burying first her face in his throat, then her teeth…which were like icicles sliding into his carotid.

3

Megga heard them cry out to her not to open the door, but she threw the lock and gripped the knob and not even Wenda was fast enough to stop her. Her original impulse when the knocking began was that finally, at last, they had come for her to slake their thirst and satisfy the bone-deep hunger within her. *At last, at last.* But what made her throw the door open with excitement was not that but a voice that said, *"Please let me in…hurry."* And that voice belonged to Bailey.

Then the door was open and Bailey was standing there and for one moment that came and went too fast for her mind to properly analyze, she saw an image of another woman with yearning eyes and a vapid grin…but then that was gone and it was just Bailey.

By then, of course, Wenda had grabbed her, but Megga fought free. *"Let me go! You fucking let me go!"* she cried out.

Then she had Bailey and towed her into the room. Bailey gasped, her breathing fast and her words almost garbled: *"They got Burt...they got Doc...they took him...we ran...I think they got Reg, too..."*

Megga led her over to the fire and Bailey went down on her knees, holding out her smooth white hands towards the heat as she shook and whimpered and Megga held her.

"I'm so cold," she said. "I'm so cold."

Rule and Wenda just stood there. Megga could feel the suspicion coming from them in dark waves, but Bailey was back and she didn't care what they thought. Fuck them and their suspicion.

After she had warmed herself for maybe five minutes, Wenda approached her cautiously. "Tell me again what happened."

So Bailey did, staring into the fire and sobbing out her story which was neither better nor worse than anyone expected.

"You're okay. You're with us now," Megga told her, holding onto her and feeling a chill coming off her that was almost unnatural.

Rule got the door closed and said, "Maybe we ought to put off our plans for awhile until we see...see what this is all about."

Megga glared at him. "What it's about, you idiot, is that Bailey's back and she's the last of our friends that are still alive. What else *would* it be about?"

Rule just shook his head.

Wenda, as always, kept watch.

Morris was sitting by the fire, too, but he edged away from Bailey little by little as if he did not want to get too close to her.

"You're sure no one else is alive?" Wenda asked.

"No. I don't think so. Oh God, why is this happening?" She buried her face in Megga's shoulder and cried. "Why?"

Megga held her, noticing with rising ire that Wenda and Rule kept giving each other little looks that were apprehensive and skeptical. They did not believe that Bailey *was* Bailey and if they didn't knock it off, Megga decided, she was going to grab that stake from Wenda and beat them both silly with it. Point being, she herself was not naïve. She knew any number of things might have happened to Bailey out there and if somebody had asked her to place a bet on who might have survived from Doc's party, her money wouldn't have been on Bailey.

But she was here and she seemed unharmed. And that was enough.

That had to be enough.

4

The feeling Wenda was getting off of Bailey was sheer poison and it was coming in through her pores, making her sick deep inside. She did not, of course, believe for one moment that what was sitting by the fire was Bailey. Everything was wrong about her. It wasn't just the idea that she had survived a run, alone, through the storm and to this house, and had somehow gotten through the front door which Wenda knew for a fact was locked. It was more than that. Just as she had with Megga, Wenda was picking up vibes from her. It was not contact with her mind exactly—when Wenda tried to make that happen as it had with Megga all she saw was a whirlpooling, hollow blackness—but something else that made her shrink inside, a sort of spiritual depravity that blew off Bailey in rank, sickening waves. And the more she tried to get a sense of it, the worse it became until she was smelling, in her mind alone, a stench of tombs and charnel vaults, places where great age and decay slept together cheek-to-cheek.

But, for all of that, Bailey was acting much *like* Bailey.

She was weak and submissive, crawling under Megga's wing like a baby bird in need of succor as she always did. And Megga responded in kind by becoming increasingly protective of her. If she were animal, Wenda knew, Megga would have been displaying a clear threat posturing: *Don't you dare touch what is mine, don't you think about hurting her or I'll scratch your fucking eyes out.* If Bailey was what Wenda thought she was (and she was nearly convinced of *that*), then this was a card she was going to play. This was a wedge she would drive firmly between Megga and Wenda herself, like they needed anything more to separate them. She would play on Megga's sympathies and if Wenda tried anything, anything at all, she'd have more than a very cunning bloodsucker to deal with.

This had to be approached carefully.

They had all been through so much now. Wenda knew that Megga could not really be blamed for her protectiveness of Bailey. Bailey had always represented a normality, a clean and easy purity that she herself lacked. So she was clinging to her and even more so than usual because having Bailey back gave her something to fight for, something to believe in, and a reason to want to survive this nightmare. And, in essence, that was good to see, except that it was horribly warped considering that what was among them was not Bailey but an absolute monster.

Rule was standing at Wenda's side, but even he was confused about the turn of events. He was suspicious and he certainly wasn't going to turn his back on Bailey or her mother protector, but he was clearly confused.

While Megga rocked Bailey in her arms like a sick child, Wenda circled around behind them. She had the stake in her belt and the silver carving knife with its immense blade in one white-knuckled fist.

"Bailey," she finally said. "The front door was locked…how did you get in?"

"What?"

"You heard me."

"Knock it off, Wenda," Megga said. "For God's sake."

"It wasn't locked," Bailey said, speaking into Megga's shoulder. Her voice was innocent and cooing like that of a little girl.

"Yes, it was."

Bailey looked over Megga's shoulder now and her eyes were filled with a blank hatred and there was no denying it.

You've got her, Wenda thought to herself. *You've got her on the ropes, you've got the bitch cornered. She's going to show her teeth. Get ready.*

"Answer my question," Wenda said, pressing her farther into that corner.

"Why don't you leave me alone?" Bailey said and there was venom in her voice of the sort the *real* Bailey would have been incapable of under any circumstances.

Megga was sneering at Wenda. She was getting pissed and she was about to act. Only she never got the chance because something else intervened. Wenda heard a scratching sound and a rat came scurrying across the floor. It was the biggest rat she had even seen: a swollen thing easily the size of a tomcat with greasy gray fur and glaring red eyes.

"What the hell?" Megga said.

Wenda heard Bailey giggle.

And then—

5

"AAAAAAHHHHHHHHHHHH!"

The scream came out of Megga's mouth and it was purely involuntary. She did not know where it came from, only that it felt like something had reached down her throat and dragged it out. When she felt it coming, then heard it…she was momentarily shocked. *Fuck is this? What the fuck is this?* Then something seemed to snap in her head and it felt like her heart was going to pound its way right out of her chest. "AAAAAAHHHHH! YA-YA-*YAAAAHHHHHH—*"

There was a rush of absolute pain through her body that felt amazingly like she was bound in ropes that were yanked tight and twisted with such force she was certain her ligaments would pop, her bones would break, and her guts would be forced from her mouth in a fleshy surge.

Then the pain was gone and with it, her free will. She tried desperately to get her mind to think properly and her body to obey her commands, but it was like it had been kicked to the curb or maybe right out of her skull. She was no longer at the helm. She was a passenger. Her body was a machine that was being remotely operated and she could do nothing about it.

Her anger at Wenda for doubting who and *what* Bailey was completely overwhelmed her. She jumped to her feet and went right at Wenda with black murder in her heart even while inside, she cried, *No, no, no, no, don't do this you can't do this what the hell are you doing?* But by then, she was in motion and Wenda—the new impervious, fearless Wenda—actually shrank back in terror at what she saw.

"BITCH! BITCH! DIRTY NO GOOD INTERFERRING CUNT!" Megga heard her voice cry out. "IT WILL NOT BE ALLOWED! *YOU* WILL NOT BE ALLOWED!"

Wenda stepped back a few more steps as Megga came on. "What the hell are you doing? *Megga! What the hell are you doing?*"

But Megga could not have answered that question even if she had been able because she really didn't know. Her body, her mind, her very being had been hijacked…she was a dancing puppet, a grinning marionette, a wind-up toy soldier, a deadly doll programmed to kill. She was trapped inside her own body with no control whatsoever. She could hear her heart pounding, the rush of blood in her veins, air being sucked into her lungs… but each time she tried to so much as influence a single finger, there was a neutral humming and nothing more.

She dove at Wenda.

She wrapped her white-knuckled hands around her throat.

"MEGGA!" Wenda managed, but that was it before her windpipe was squeezed shut.

Megga had her. She had the bitch and she was going to kill her…but long before that happened, she would do the most awful things to her, violate her in the worst possible ways, squeeze the goodness and purity out of her, and leave her as an empty shell that would fill with a blackness that would rot her to her core.

The cunt would suffer.

She'd cut out her tongue.

She'd tear off her tits with hot pincers.

She'd shove a burning log between her legs and—

Crack. Wenda fought back with pure venom. She slapped her in the face and punched her in the head. And when that didn't work, she brought her knee up right between her legs with everything she had. Megga squealed and fell away and Wenda punched her in the face. Inside the mockery of her own body, Megga shrieked with pain.

But her body and the raging mind came right back for more. *"DIRTY RUTTING CUNT! SUFFER! SUFFER! SUFFER! HOW YOU WILL SUFFER!"* And before Wenda could fend her off with blows, Megga had a hold of her again. The two of them grappled as Rule tried to pull them apart and Morris moaned and Bailey giggled.

As the battle went on, Megga thought she knew who had hijacked her body.

Then she was certain of it.

Carrion.

A stink of carrion.

She could smell it inside her mind as if she were trapped in a rotting casket that was slowly sinking in graveyard earth. Griska. It was his smell: carrion, embalming fluid, a noisome stench of rotting hides. His voice was speaking to her, an oily and reptilian hissing. He warned her that defiance would bring dire consequences. Her entrails would be yanked out and fed to mad dogs while she was still alive. Then, he would drain her dry, embalm her, bathe her in the blood of her friends…but she would not be dead. She would feel every last agony and indignity. He would shove dead mice up inside her while graveyard rats devoured her from the inside out. Her eye sockets would be nests of squirming maggots and swollen, juicy spider eggs would fill her mouth, each bursting forth like a white grape to fill her mouth with skittering, leggy horrors...only she would not be able to scream because her lips would be sewn shut with threads of her own gut.

Megga screamed soundlessly...as her body fought with Wenda.

They knocked over a chair and slammed into the wall, finally crashing together to the floor and taking one of the drapes with them. They fought and clawed and punched, rolling on the floor and tearing at each other. Megga tore out a clump of Wenda's shiny red hair and Wenda nearly ripped an ear off her. Then Wenda had her. She forced Megga onto her belly and rode astride her back, one arm circled around her neck in a fierce headlock.

"NO! NO! NO! NO!" Megga screeched as she raged and gasped, her body thrashing. *"YOU MUST BE PUNISHED MUST BE BROKEN MUST BE SEEDED WITH FILTH HE SAYS SO IT IS HIS WILL—"*

Then, incredibly, Megga went limp as a rag beneath her, going out cold. Her head thumped against the floor and she did not move.

"You...you killed her," Morris said.

"No...I didn't," Wenda breathed.

Still panting, she turned Megga over. Megga's eyes were open, but they were rolled back white in her head. There was a jumping tic in the corner of her mouth. Her entire body was trembling.

"Looks like she had a seizure," Rule said.

And Megga supposed she would have thought so, too, yes. She linked up with her mind and her body responded. She blinked her eyes. Licked her lips. She was sore everywhere. Laying there on the floor, hair hanging in her face, blood seeping from one nostril, she said, "Sorry, Wenda...it wasn't my choice..."

Wenda just scowled at her. There were red scratches like warpaint over her left cheek, blood on her mouth. "What are you talking about?"

Megga only wished she could explain.

6

"Shit," Rule said, trying to back away as a rat lunged for him.

Wenda tried to aim a kick at it as it passed her and missed.

The rat stayed on target and when it was inches from him, he caught it with his boot and sent it spinning end over end with an enraged squeaking. It rolled over and came back up, coming at him again.

Rule tried to get out of its way and tripped over his own heavy boots and went down.

Wenda tried to kick it again, her boot glancing off its flanks, and only succeeding in propelling it right at Rule.

"GYAH!" he cried out as it scrambled up his leg.

He flipped over and the rat hung onto his overalls by its claws, which were pawing furiously like it was trying to dig its way through them. He got to his knees, then climbed unsteadily to his feet and the rat still hung on. Not only did it hang on, but it climbed him like a cat up a tree. And it was only his forearm that kept it from his face. It bit into the sleeve of his overalls and hung tenaciously there by its teeth. He swung his arm back and forth, trying to throw it.

At first, Wenda wasn't sure what to do because she'd coveted an unnatural fear of rodents her entire life.

Then she moved.

She reached out and grabbed at the rat, feeling her fingers sliding through its oily pelt and then her fist gripping its hairless, snakelike tail. Inside, she cringed with revulsion…just the feel of that tail. It was like a writhing muscular cord, worming against her hand.

Then another rat showed.

And another.

Both were easily as big as the first and both went right after Wenda.

She let out a scream and released the tail of the first rodent. She kicked one of them aside and the second scrambled up the leg of her snowpants, its teeth nipping at her knee, trying desperately to break through the heavy nylon.

But by then, Wenda cringed no more.

She seemed to remember that she had the knife in her hand. She slashed it against the rat's spine. It squealed and hit the floor, its backbone laid open. As blood sprayed out of it in a mist of droplets, its head swung back and forth in one direction and its hindquarters in another.

Then the other rat closed in.

Still dazed from the kick she'd given it, it came on with little grace. It went right for her ankle and she kicked it again. It rolled over, then sat up on its haunches, hissing at her. Its eyes were shiny red and absolutely unearthly. She was reminded of the juicy cores of squashed cherries.

"WELL, COME ON!" she shouted at it. "COME AND GET SOME!"

It needed no further urging.

It shot through the air with amazing speed, looking like a flying squirrel as it fired itself at her. What she did then she did with pure instinct. She saw it coming and swung the knife in a vicious arc that split the rat in half. It let out a weird, trilling sort of squeal, each section hitting the floor, the legs of both still trying to run, to scramble, to do anything they could to get at her.

Somewhere during the process, Rule had shed his rat right at the wall and when it tried to rise up, he smashed its head to red goo with his boot, bringing it down half a dozen times. He now did the same with the upper quarters of the bisected rat.

Wenda turned, gasping, and Rule did the same.

They saw it at the same moment and it stamped its indelible impression of stark horror on their faces simultaneously: rats, more rats. The room was filling with them like a spigot had been turned on or a pipe had burst. They filled the room in scratching, red-eyed hordes. They hung from the curtains and crawled along the baseboards and tumbled down from the walls. They swarmed up over the furniture and scrabbled right over the top of one another. They brought a horrid, deathly stink of submerged coffins and cemetery ooze, dripping and dark places where yellowed bones were wrapped in moldering shrouds, spiders spun their webs in silent dusty corners, and corpse-fungi grew in moist white sheets up stone walls set with the brass nameplates of the sleeping dead.

They not only filled the room, they overflowed it.

7

Although Morris seemed oblivious to just about everything, he was not oblivious to rats. They were three feet deep on the floor, a surging, squealing, squeaking ocean of them. It was like they had abandoned a sinking ship and he were an island. They swarmed over him in a dark wave, clawing and nipping, driven into some primal rage, needing to bury him alive.

He could have attempted escape.

But he didn't.

He squatted down as they ran over him, fighting for space atop him, allowing himself to be submerged in the stinky, swollen, lice-hopping sea of vermin. One moment he was there, the next jump a dark hump buried by rats.

8

"Jesus Christ," Rule said.

Jesus Christ, Jesus Christ, Jesus Christ.

His voice echoed around inside Wenda's head like it was an empty metal drum and the disturbing, downright frightening thing was that the words themselves made absolutely no sense. It was the good old King's English, as they said, but it might as well have been Low Latin or Sanskrit for that matter; her brain could not process it. It felt as if she were being sucked into a black hole at the back of her head.

What the heck is going on here? What's happening to me—

The thought was left uncompleted as knives of agony slashed through her mind, scissoring her thoughts, making her brain feel like it was dropped into a pan of boiling oil.

She cried out.

She screamed…but nobody heard it. She was under attack but it was of a very intimate, private nature. She felt her herself being drawn back into the shadows and she knew without a doubt that Griska was responsible.

She saw lips.

Lips smeared red with blood.

They were at her mouth, licking, sucking, then moving down to her throat, nipping at her jugular. But it wasn't her blood that they wanted, it was something more, something of far greater importance. The lips moved down. She could feel the needle-like teeth behind them dragged over her breasts, the mouth drawing in her nipples like it wanted to suck them free.

The icy tongue left a cold, beslimed trail as it sought lower regions. Across her belly, licking at her navel, then at her thighs, moving between them. A darting tongue stabbing inside her. There was no pleasure. It was abrasive like the tongue of a cat, long, thickening, seeming to swell inside her as it lapped her pussy like a bowl of water. The teeth teased and nipped before biting into her vulva and making the blood run like sweet wine. Her entire vagina was seized in the mouth, the teeth and tongue alternately biting and suckling. It was like she was being devoured.

She screamed at the violation.

Cold laughter echoed around her.

And the voice, rasping and foul-breathed in her face: "Now you are ruined, virgin. Now you are despoiled and made weak. Now you walk in darkness."

Wenda fought because he *took hold of her.* He *had raped her with his mouth, laid her raw and made her bleed, and now he would complete the act, consummate it, fill her with his cold, dead seed.*

Screaming, she fought with everything she had. He was a wolf-thing and a dog-thing, snarling and biting, the blood-oiled fur of his rancid-smelling hide coat rippling with vermin, with crawling and worming things. His face was September mist and his eyes were cold yellow marrow grease. His breath smelled like plundered tombs.

But he was too powerful to fight.

His jaws darted in and snakelike fangs impaled her throat, going in deep, piercing her jugular while the tongue lapped up the blood and awful sucking sounds filled her ears. She could feel that ravening mouth working her neck like a suction pump, drawing her blood out, draining her, emptying her, the teeth worrying at the soft red pulp of her throat.

Then she belonged to him.

A slinking, parasitic whore that draped her bleached body over his sarcophagus by day and waited only for night when the lid would open and he would look upon her, piercing her with the glistening bloodstones of his eyes.

But she was no friend or lover.

Not even a worshipper.

She was sacrifice. He gutted her and pulled her apart, yanking out organs in meaty masses and entrails in bluing coils, his long delicate, perfectly white fingers shining with globs of yellow fat and bone grease which he deftly licked off his fingers. The jewels he plucked from her gut he stuffed unceremoniously in canopic jars. The hollows within her were filled with spices and chemically-scented desert sand, oils and dark fluids and exotic embalming jellies.

She was a mummified thing, stuffed and mounted.

And when he needed something to torment, he put her back together so he could violate her once again.

Wenda came out of it, gasping.

Mind games, nothing but mind games. Horrifying and even devastating, but ultimately only games. The cruel pranks of a mischievous child. Griska knew he had to break her in order to break the others.

You won't break me. Maybe I fear you, but when I find you, I'll tear your heart out with my bare hands, leech.

The rats were pushing in.

Her breath catching in her throat, she waited for them, knowing there were hundreds of truly appalling ways to die and her death would be in the top ten. It was as she realized this and the rats made ready for the slaughter, that she saw Bailey make her move.

9

When the rats went after Rule and then Wenda, Megga was struck not only speechless but motionless. She sat there by the fire with her mouth open and tried to think of something to do and could not come up with a thing.

"Stay by the fire!" she told Bailey and Morris.

She tossed a few logs into the blaze and the fire burned higher and brighter. Then she grabbed a blazing log and made to get to her feet. But what stopped her was Bailey. Even over Rule and Wenda's shouting, she heard Bailey giggling with a sadistic sort of amusement like a young serial killer who had just eviscerated a puppy, discovering the sheer primal joy of death for the first time.

She looked over at her. *"Bailey?"* she said.

Bailey was grinning at her, her eyes huge and pale yellow like twin dead moons rising over the airless void of a lifeless world, her mouth pulled into a red-lipped and predatory grin of spike-like fangs. A stink that was cold and harsh like the meaty smell of an unwashed corpse came off her.

Megga realized it was her breath.

"Pretty Megga," she said with the rasping, raw voice of an old hag, *"let me kiss you."*

Megga screamed.

Bailey had never been Bailey and somehow she had known that, but refused to believe. Denial was so much easier. What lived inside of Bailey's skin was coming out now, breaking free like some hideous reptile coming out of an egg. She reached for Megga with a hand that ruptured open as if from internal stress and another hand came out, one that was a pale blue-gray, the nails long, yellow, and dirty, graveyard earth packed up beneath them.

The Bailey-thing smiled.

Its grinning mouth was an atrocity. It was not remotely human. It was the grin of a child-eating ogre, a primeval monster, a night hunter and soul-eater. Bailey's lips inflated like balloons, going black and flaking, pulling back to reveal a horrible, crooked dentition of discolored teeth stained from numerous feedings, black grit packed between them. There were so many teeth and so gnarled and overlapping were they, the mouth could not close…they filled it like roots will fill a buried water pipe. They were all sharp, but the canines were especially long and especially sharp, like glistening ice-picks.

Megga tried to back away from her.

A horror, a monster hiding under her skin the whole time. I held that thing in my arms. I embraced it. I protected it. I let…dear God…I let it nuzzle its face up against my throat.

Rats ran over her, but she was impervious to the revulsion that might have once caused. Now there was just the thing before her pulling itself out of Bailey's skin, revealing itself. Its face broke free of Bailey's own and it was a pallid mask set with wrinkles and ruts, huge hollows beneath the cheekbones, the eyesockets like black vaults. And the eyes themselves…they were a bleary, diseased yellow threaded with pulsating red veins swollen like engorged bloodworms.

"My pretty Megga," said the evil beldam, leering at her, the teeth jutting from her mouth dripping with foul secretions. "I could just eat you up…in fact, I *will* eat you up. I'll kiss you the way you want Wenda to kiss you and in the place you like best. The place you used to kiss Bailey. I'll kiss you and kiss you and suck you up until you're dry…"

Megga was not sure if she had actually said any of that or if it was just some horrid imagery in her mind that her brain had translated into words. Regardless, the paralysis that held her there at the beldam's mercy broke with a nearly audible *snap*…and she pulled away.

The beldam laughed with a shrill, grinding sound.

She was a cadaverous hag with a face like the crumbling, powdery linen of a mummy that hung in flaps. Her reaching fingers were poisoned roots. The rats swarmed up and over her. They crawled through her silver-white hair and through the ragged crow-black shifts she wore. One of them hung from her cheekbone by a flap of face meat and a dozen hairless, fetal rats, squirming with placental slime, hung from her throat, suckering with their flabby

233

pink rodent's mouths. The beldam plucked one bloated sewer rat free of her breast and shoved it in her mouth. She did not chew or taste…she sucked it down her throat with a gulping, gobbling sound, the scaly tail flickering over her lips before disappearing entirely.

"Now, pretty Megga," she said, her voice cloying and sweet. "As I sucked in the rat, now I'll suck in you…"

10

"GET AWAY FROM HER!" Wenda called out, kicking at the rats that pushed forward in greasy, flaccid ranks. "GET THE HELL AWAY FROM HER!"

Her voice was barely even audible above the squealing and squeaking of the rats themselves. Yet, her voice *was* heard. Megga looked over at her and the beldam snarled at her and Wenda could almost hear her voice: a dry, scraping, semi-human version of a rat squeal. *Stay out of this, you pretty cunt! This one is mine! This one is promised to me!* And the thing was, Wenda knew she would never get to Megga in time. The rats were gathering, bristling, ravenous and blood-hungry. They would never let her reach the beldam before it was too late.

But if I don't, Megga will be little more than a graveyard rat herself…something sleeping in a narrow, dirty box full of crawling vermin.

The rats seemed to sense her intentions. A cresting wave of them pushed in her direction and she saw then that these were no ordinary rats…they were monstrous abominations, mutations that could only have come to term in bone-strewn, sunless subterranean graveyard passages. They were fungous and flabby, mold-caked things with pelts bristled like those of wild hogs. Their snouted, slavering mouths were hung with narrow yellow teeth, eyes rabid and fixed…but almost human.

They would tear her apart and she knew it.

But she did not back down.

As they came, she made ready to do battle.

The beldam looked over at her with eyes like the eggs of blowflies.

Too late, too late, too late, pretty cunt. She has been claimed.

The beldam seemed to be growing more grotesque by the second…her face corrugated and ancient like the trunk of a centuried oak, set with hollows and seams so deep they looked like they had been carved with a knife. Her eyes were wide and yellow and bulbous like they were trying to push free of the pink, flayed sockets that held them. Tiny black pupils darted about.

And her mouth.

That crooked, grinning mouth of fangs.

She was going to tear out Megga's throat and there was no way to stop her.

11

Megga tried to throw herself back but she fell into Morris who let out a perfectly bovine sort of *"Ooomph"* sound and then the beldam had her. She seized her by the arms in a grip so powerful, Megga knew she could have snapped her forearms like dry twigs had she chosen. Even through the sleeves of her parka, Megga could feel the invasive grave cold of the beldam's hands that didn't even look like hands by that point…but gnarled blue-gray claws, the knuckles of the fingers like the twisted knots of old hemlock trees and the fingernails like the black claws of a bird of prey.

The beldam pulled her forward.

Megga screamed.

A tongue that was narrow, glistening and black like that of a giraffe licking at soft fruit came out and slicked across her lips. It was cold like thawing meat. Megga had expected many things from the vampires. In her mind and hot-blooded Goth fantasies, she had been seduced by them countless times. But never had she imagined it would be like this…so absolutely devoid of heat, of desire, of eroticism. That was the stuff of women's romance novels; the reality was ugly and cold: she was being licked like a dog licks a shank of meat before he bites into it. She was being *tasted*.

Megga screamed again.

At the sight of the thing that held her…its smell…its feel. At what it was about to do to her which had very little to do with romance and very much to do with rape. Grinning, the beldam's jaws opened wide so Megga could see just how long those teeth were that would soon sink into her throat.

"NOOOO!" she cried out. "I WON'T LET YOU! I'LL TELL HER! I'LL TELL HER WHY YOU'RE AFRAID OF HER! I'LL SHOUT IT OUT EVEN IF YOU RIP OUT MY FUCKING THROAT!"

The words came out in a flurry and they actually stopped the vampire woman. For a few fleeting moments she looked confused, maybe even fearful if such a thing were possible with a face like a leathery fright mask. But it didn't last. They were all afraid of Wenda because she was incorruptible and Griska most of all because he knew the threat she posed. But it didn't stop the beldam for long because she was basically just a hungry animal with no true sense of self-awareness of who she was or what she *had* been before this horror overtook her.

So she raged.

She snarled.

She hissed like a snake.

She was angry at Megga for confusing her with things she did not necessarily understand. Things that got in the way of the feeding. Still gripping her arms, she threw Megga to the floor and crept over to her.

As the beldam's shadow fell over her, Megga knew she had seconds.

Threatening her with Wenda hadn't been enough. It had saved her throat for a few seconds but that was all. The vampire made ready to strike, her ragged claws tearing into the material of Megga's parka, her scabrous face hovering over Megga's own, a ribbon of pink drool hanging from her lips. She looked like a human vulture and smelled like one, too... stinking like something that slept with the dead and fed on their bones in cobwebbed crypts, plucked eyeballs from crusty sockets on lonely dark highways.

From somewhere that seemed impossibly distant, Megga heard Morris cry out, but the beldam's eyes had her. They held her. She was transfixed by them. They were haunted tombs, black sink holes, shattered nebula sucking in light, life, and sanity, leeching the room of anything decent and warm.

The beldam had her and she knew it.

She would have fought if there were something to fight *with*.

But she was drained, emptied, laid absolutely bare on some essential level and there was no fight in her. She breathed and her heart pumped and her nerve endings tingled madly, but other than that and the fact that her cells still divided, there was nothing. She was a juicy slab of red meat waiting to be fed upon.

Then a voice.

It came from somewhere. A silver needle in her head, piercing and poking, bringing pinpoint eruptions of pain but also a fuzzy sort of awareness. It wanted something from her. It *demanded* something from her and although it was not Griska's voice, it had nearly as much immediacy and power behind it.

Megga! Fight! Fight! Don't just lay there!

Her eyes blinked and she saw the beldam hovering over her. She had no idea that only bare seconds had passed since she'd been thrown to the floor. Time was elastic and formless in her head.

I said fight! Fight! Fight!

Oh, but I can't, don't you understand that I can't?

She wanted to, she wanted nothing better than to obey that voice. She felt her limbs coming to life and her blood flowing, then her muscles bunching, but it was too late because there was no way she could avoid those teeth coming for her throat. She could already feel the cold breath of sepulchers against her neck.

That's when the beldam screamed.

She let out a cry that punched into Megga's head like an awl. She turned and Morris—*Morris* of all people—had grabbed the burning stick from the fire that Megga herself had dropped. He had it in his hand. He jabbed the burning end into the beldam's hair and flames rose up on the side of her head along with twisting plumes of smoke. The air was filled with the nauseating stench of her scorching hair. The beldam rose up to take care of Morris and he stuck the burning stick right in her face.

As the vampire screamed again, Megga rolled away and climbed drunkenly to her feet. She saw legions of plump sewer rats gathered around, squeaking and rubbing their forepaws together, their serpentine tails rattling on the floor.

The beldam took hold of Morris and tossed him aside.

He struck the wall next to the hearth and went down, dazed. The beldam turned towards Megga again. Having tasted her, she was not about to concede defeat. She was going to milk her dry and bathe in her blood. She screamed with a wrath that was deafening.

Megga, rats or no rats, made to run and she almost got away, but then a hand grabbed her shoulder blade and pulled her back. Off balance, she tripped and fell sideways, landing on a dozen rats that squirmed and squealed beneath her. Then the beldam reached down and gripped her with a cold and slimy hand, yanking her to her feet like she was weightless.

There was no escape and as the vampire brought its face in closer, offering a sunken grin, it said, *"Isn't this what you wanted, pretty Megga? Isn't this what you've always longed for? Haven't you always wanted to sleep with the rats and the worms in dirty, foul, low places?"*

Yes, yes, yes, Megga realized, as she tried to pull away from the creature and found that she was mired like a mammoth in a tar pit.

It was true, it was all true.

She'd always wanted to be among the undead, to sleep in dark beauty and sip at soft white throats as midnight thunder clashed and boomed. It was the need to be dangerous, to be offbeat, to be the vamp that made every man burn with heat and every woman smolder with jealousy. Not one of the many, but one of the *few*. But now that she was faced with the reality grinning sardonically behind the fantasy and it had unmasked itself, showing her the true and malefic nature of itself, she wanted nothing to do with it. This was deadly, this was eternal, this was a hideous death-in-life.

The hag moved in for her kiss and her sup.

Megga heard Wenda cry out. She saw the lips of the beldam and she did not recoil from them because there were red and plump and succulent, the face behind them young and high-cheekboned, eyes blue and deliciously Nordic. It was Bailey and Megga needed to see no more: she was pulled in and she opened her mouth so that she could put her tongue in Bailey's mouth.

But Bailey screamed.

Screamed because Morris was attacking her again. With that same burning log, he was beating her savagely about the head and when the beldam—because, dear God, it *was* a beldam again, embalmed face and lurid grinning mouth and glaring, beady rodent's eyes—made to lay him open with her claws, he swung the log again and she slapped it out of his hands and took hold of him.

He might have cried out.

He might have screamed in abject terror.

But all Megga heard as the beldam's jaws seized his throat was a sound like a tongue sliding into the juicy pulp of a plum.

Before she could be stopped, the beldam drained him. She lifted him off his feet and sucked at his throat with a wet, slobbering sound. Not just feeding on him, but gulping his blood, guzzling from his throat, slurping the red sap until it ran down her chin and pissed from every orifice and Morris, his bloodless face and glazed eyes staring up at the ceiling, seemed to shrivel in her death-grip, making a sound almost like an aluminum beer can crushed by a fist.

She tossed him aside.

And Megga…uplinked as she had been with Wenda…felt every second of his defilement.

She felt the vampire seize him as if it were seizing her.

She felt the iron grip of its clawlike hands. Then, and worse, she felt its cold face pressed up to his warm, pulsing throat like the muzzle of a wolf. The lips felt like raw meat. The vampire let loose with a growling, hungry sound, its saliva spraying against the side of his throat…and then the teeth went in. Like surgical steel scalpels they perforated the skin of his neck and punctured the jugular beneath. They slid in, then out, in, then out, assuring that the vein was open and would stay open so the mouth and tongue could do their work.

It was agonizing.

The impalement was explosive and resounding to his nerve endings, it made waves of white-hot agony rip through his head.

Then…nothing.

Maybe there was an anesthetic quality to the spit of the vampire and maybe he just sank into darkness from the sheer trauma. Like the suctioning mouth of a leech, the vampire's lips fastened tightly to his throat in an unbreakable seal, gulping down the dark, rich flow of blood, filling itself, gorging itself until he was like a spring that ran dry and his veins collapsed and his heart fluttered in his chest and stopped cold and dead.

A dozen bloated rats twining her legs like hungry cats, the beldam turned on Megga. She had taken in too much blood and she was swollen with it, engorged like a leech. It ran in scarlet rivers from her mouth and nose, it filled her eyes until they looked like huge yolky blood-eggs. The front of her filthy, ragged burial dress was dyed red with it and it ran in a stream from between her legs and pooled on the floor. She stood there, an ensanguined human sponge.

But it wasn't enough.

She would feed again.

She was gluttonous for it and she'd fill herself until she popped like a water balloon. As she came for Megga, she was bloated like a blood-fattened tick.

Her right foot left a bloody print on the floor. The blood-ova of her eyes were luminous like fissionable materials. Her voice made a hissing, gulping sort of sound as it tried to talk through the hemoglobin that gushed from her lips. One breast had worked itself free of her cerements and it expunged droplets of crimson milk.

Megga did not try to escape.

The rats were all over her, crowding on her body like maggots on carrion, not feeding, but encompassing her, enveloping her, burying her in their greasy, lice-hopping pelts and flabby, warm bodies.

The beldam came for her and there was nothing that could stop it.

12

A rat flew through the air like it had been shot from a gun and hit Wenda full in the chest. She almost went over, the air forced from her lungs with the impact. The rat that hit her hung on by its teeth, which were sunk into the front of her parka. She knocked it free by bringing her fist down with a strength that even amazed her because she distinctly heard and *felt* its spine snap.

It dropped writhing to the floor.

Another stormed in, sleek, glossy black, and about the size of a Rottweiler puppy, it seemed. As she kicked it, five or six others took its place. One of them climbed her leg and bit into her thigh. She grabbed it by its hairless tail, yanked it free, and swung it with everything she had towards the wall. It hit hard and fell to the floor, back legs kicking.

More of them bit into her legs, right through her snowpants.

One got on her back and bit her ear.

You won't win, you dirty crawly little bastards! I won't let you! I will not allow it! she thought as she waged war on them, plucking them free, tearing them free, crushing and stomping and smashing them as more poured forward to fill the gap. *Don't think I don't know what this is about! Don't think I don't recognize this as the diversion it's supposed to be! But it won't do any good!*

She fought with horror and repulsion and rage. The rats climbed her legs and jumped on her back and tangled their claws in her hair, yet still she fought. She tore them free and kicked them aside, smashing them beneath her boots and laying them open with the silver butcher's knife. They kept coming, crowding forward in ranks but she was not about to go down beneath them and she knew they weren't strong enough to take her, not unless her own fear overcame her.

The knife.

They feared the silver blade.

When she hacked one with it, a dozen more skittered away in terror. She knew very well what was going on with Megga and

Morris, but the rats kept her from doing anything about it and she supposed that was why they had been sent.

As one bit into her cheek, she ripped it free and snapped another's neck as it nuzzled into her throat. She killed a dozen and still they came, but when she swung the knife they scattered like wheat chaff before a scythe. And this became her strategy, though she hardly had the time to recognize it as such. She kept the others at bay by swinging her knife in arcs. And while she did so, she tore the other ones free, punting and stomping at them. She ripped a final one from the back of her parka and charged forward, the rats retreating in waves.

Splattered with ratblood and ratmeat, she reached Morris just as the beldam finished with him and bore down upon Megga.

Except the beldam was no beldam…soaked in blood and stinking of it, she was younger. Her face was smooth and unlined, her eyes bright, her hair a luscious shade of red. Coils of it were plastered to her face with sticky venous fluid.

She did not see Wenda coming.

Not until it was too late.

Megga was dazed and out of it, barely on her feet by that point, probably in shock from what she had just seen and what was about to happen. While Rule fought the rats with a poker from the fireplace, eight or ten of them hanging off of him and more leaping at him all the time, Wenda went after the beldam.

Outside the house, at that very moment, there rose a howling discord of dozens of disembodied voices screeching into the night. It was a cacophony of anguish and fury and incarnate hysteria.

Wenda brought the knife back in both hands like a sword. She swung it. The beldam caught wind of it. She turned, whirling around, blood spraying from her. Droplets of it spattered against Wenda's face.

The beldam snarled.

She screamed in wrath.

And the blade came around with irresistible force, every ounce of strength and weight Wenda had bringing it to bear. It entered the hag's throat just beneath the jawline and split her neck like black oak, cleaving her head free which spun end over end, landing in the hearth, right in the blazing heart of the fire, casting flaming sticks and glowing coals over the floor.

Decapitated or not, as the flames engulfed it, the head did not scream in agony, it *laughed*. Ablaze and filling the room with a most appalling stench, it laughed with a high, shrieking sort of sound, breathing out clouds of gray ash. *"I SHED MY SKIN, DID I NOT? I WORE THE BODY AND FACE OF THE TENDER ONE, DID I NOT? SHE IS THE LIAR! THE LIAR! WENDA KEEGAN, THE UNTRIED ONE! HER BUD HAS NOT BEEN BURST AND HER ROSE IS UNPLUCKED AND HER MAIDENHEAD NOT YET SEEDED! SHE SHE SHE—"*

The voice raged on and on, a crusty and deranged shriek that rose to a high treble until the words no longer made sense and then the head, blackened and blistering, screamed. The mouth opened like the sooty throat of a chimney and the scream was that of a chainsaw ripping into a dead tree. The sound was loud, deafening, and everyone covered their ears. But it was not just in the room, but in their heads, grating and rending and shrilling like saws biting into steel plating. A wind rushed through the room, lashing and blowing and it stank of fetid meat and burning hair.

And through it all, the headless body did not fall.

It stumbled about, clawing out with its hands, seeking flesh to rend and lives to take. From that of a curvaceous, rejuvenated woman, it had expanded with the blood it leeched, bloating until the buttons of its rotting burial gown popped free one by one. It was like the living trunk was filled with helium. It became a flabby and vile puppet that bounced and contorted, convulsed and writhed like a marionette. But as the head broke apart in the heat like an eggshell, the trunk grew rigid and trembling, mottling with purple spots of fungi, then splitting open and oozing a milk of blood and a foul gray necrotic slime as it began to first fragment and then putrefy, becoming an especially grotesque and ambulant corpse that finally stiffened and went still, tipping over like a felled tree and smashing into a stew of gut-waste, organ-matter, and powdering bones on the floor.

By that point, Wenda was down on one knee, physically ill with the smells that burst from the thing in rapid succession: a green and maggoty putrescence followed by stink of rotting fruit and mildewed linen, then a desiccated and dusty smell of attics and planks splitting apart with dryrot. There was a final enveloping smell of great age like wormy books flaking on shelves...then nothing.

The head in the hearth snapped and popped, but it was a sterile thing by that point like a melon whose juice and pulp had been boiled from it, leaving only a burnt, splitting husk behind.

The rats were nearly nonexistent.

Most had fled back to wherever they had come from, vanishing like ghosts at dawn. What few remained were injured and Rule, bitten and clawed, his overalls scathed with scratches, was hunting them down and smashing their heads open with the fireplace poker. He seemed barely aware that there was anything else in the room but himself and the rodents.

13

Wenda stood slowly, looking around.

Morris' leeched corpse was curled up like a road-struck dog and it would have to be attended to, she knew, before it woke up and started causing trouble. Because it would. Sliding the knife back in her belt, she stepped around the remains of the beldam and helped Megga to her feet. She looked like she was in shock. Wenda took her over to the fire and tossed in the last few birch logs they had. Next, they'd burn the furniture if they had to. The flames burned high and bright and warm. Wenda could feel the fatigue in her limbs, but the night was hardly over with.

Megga just stared into the hearth, the blaze reflected in her dark and glassy eyes. Wenda dug in one of her pockets for her cigarettes, found the remains of her pack, lit one up and shoved it between her lips. She had no idea whether it was the proper thing to do or not, but it was all she could think of. It was the first thing they did in old movies.

Rule sat in the chair behind them. He was breathing hard. "That's only the beginning," he said after a few minutes. "They won't let us live to tell the tale. They can't. Their survival depends on us becoming like them so we can't bring people to burn this place in broad daylight or hunt them down."

Wenda made a grunting sound, but had little energy for anything else.

Megga seemed to realize there was a cigarette in her mouth and her addiction took charge. She blinked a few times and then began dragging off it, blowing out clouds of smoke. "She gave up the secret."

Wenda just looked at her.

"She gave up the secret," Megga said again. "Before the head stopped moving…it gave up the secret."

"What secret?" Rule said.

"The secret of Wenda."

Wenda said nothing; there was nothing she could say. What Megga said or, rather, the importance of what she said was not lost on her. She could still hear that awful voice in her head. *Her bud has not been burst and her rose is unplucked and her maidenhead not yet seeded.* Those were the words and Megga had known it all along because those things had been in her head right from the start. It was true, of course. Wenda was a virgin but it was not something she went around admitting to or shouting from the rooftops. It was simply a personal choice. One that was possibly archaic by today's standards, but one that had always seemed right for her...particularly in light of certain events in her life.

"So that's the secret?" she finally said. "They're afraid of me because I keep my legs crossed?"

There was a bitter sarcasm there, but she couldn't help it. Somehow she'd been hoping for a little bit more. Some secret strength she never knew she had. She wanted to be able to shout *SHAZAM!* and go on her merry way kicking undead ass. But virginity? *That was it?*

"It's ridiculous," she said.

And it was.

It was the craziest goddamn thing she'd ever, ever heard.

Because she hadn't wanted to be a virgin. God no, she hadn't really wanted that, but...but...but...*but David died. He died and I miss him and I'm still in love with him and I can't help myself.*

"You're incorruptible," Megga told her. "Don't you see the power of that? Of purity? Of goodness? There's more to becoming a vampire than just getting bit in the neck. That's only the physical part. The spiritual and psychological part is offering yourself and taking part in your own destruction."

"Excellent," Rule said, very much approving. "Wenda is our own Athena, our warrior maiden. Her strength is her virginity. It's the wellspring of her power and its virtue cannot be sullied. As Athena defeated Ares, the god of warfare and bloodshed, so shall our Wenda defeat Griska, the lord of the dead."

"You two are getting a little mystical for me," Wenda admitted.

"It's not something you need to think about," Rule said. "If it's true—"

"Oh, it's true, all right," Megga said.

"—then it's something that exists whether you believe in it or not. It does not require your cooperation or your belief. It simply *is.*"

Wenda didn't bother responding to that because, realistically, how could she? It was a completely irrational idea. Maybe Megga was right—it seemed possible in some crazy way—but it was contrary to everything Wenda had always believed in, honored, and practiced in her somewhat narrow view of reality. She wanted to debate the very idea, but debating it was like debating the existence of a superior being. Faith was faith and belief was belief. They were states of mind and no matter how much empirical evidence you threw against it, the faithful remained faithful and she knew she'd never convince Megga that it was pure fantasy.

And particularly since she wasn't sure that it *was* fantasy at all.

There was something within her, something inside her, some well of strength that she'd never tapped into before this night. *And who are you by this point to be clinging to worn-out tenets of what's real and what's not? What's possible and what can never be? Maybe yesterday you could get away with rationalizing, but not now. Not after what you've seen this night. There are dark things in this world, horrible things that skulk and hide in the sunless corners and now you have seen some of them. You have seen true evil...is it that hard to believe that maybe in you there is true goodness?* But, yes, it was. Just because she'd never had sex? The very idea seemed ludicrous...then again, so did this entire visit to Cobton.

Wenda slumped forward, letting her face fill her hands. God knew there had been many times when she viewed her virginity as a weight around her neck and many occasions when she could have gotten rid of that weight. But she hadn't. It wasn't always a conscious choice either. Fate and circumstance constantly got in the way. She'd had relationships with men...and every one of them dissolved into a comedy of errors. They'd each devolved into chaos long before the bedroom was reached.

Like David, for example.

She blanched at the memory.

But was all that purely a matter of stupid, annoying coincidence...or was it the hand of something beyond herself constantly intervening, saving her for this night, keeping her blade sharp and her virtue intact so she could do its bidding?

"I wish it had been me," Megga said, pulling furiously off her cigarette. "I just wish I had been the one. God, all my life I wanted to be special. I wanted to stand out. I wanted to be one of the few and not one of the fucking many. Maybe if I'd have known I might have kept my virginity past my sixteenth year. But you know what?

I doubt it. I'm not like you, Wenda. There's always been kind of a...a seam of darkness in me. I fall too easily. I give in to temptation and vice. It's like second nature to me to be self-indulgent and weak. I'm not strong. Not inside where it counts. Not like you."

"I've never been strong either," Wenda admitted.

"Before tonight."

She sighed. "Yes, before tonight."

"If Doc was here, he could explain this to you and it would make sense," Megga said. "You know it would make sense."

"Doc?" Rule said.

Megga explained who he was and, more importantly, *what* he was. "He's really a fascinating guy," she went on. "He's one of these people that have immense talent and intelligence, you know? But for some reason, nothing ever really comes of it. He should have had his own show in Vegas or been a movie star or a bestselling author or something. He's special. But he ended up working on a midnight horror show with us. Why? That's what I always wondered: *why?* You see all these talentless bums in life that become rich and famous through pure hype and groveling self-promotion and then there's guys like Doc that truly deserve it, but fate turns a blind eye towards them. Why is that?"

But no one had an answer.

Wenda was aware at that moment that Rule was watching her. He had not said anything in some time since his comparison of her to Athena. Even in the dimness of the waning lantern and the shadows reaching across his face, she could see he was looking at her. More so, she could *feel* him looking at her. He had something on his mind and she just hoped like hell it had nothing to do with warrior maidens and virginity.

Without prompting, he said, "I'm thinking about the nature of evil. How it establishes itself, how it is fertilized like a crop, generated and ultimately harvested. The idea of spiritual evil is pretty much archaic in our modern society, but I think the three of us know that it in fact exists. I've never doubted it. I've always seen it as a force of nature like wind, rain, fire, and storm...an elemental force and certainly one of the oldest, something that no doubt predates our little world here by an unfathomable amount of time." He had their attention and saw it. "I spoke earlier of evil being seeded in Cobton and causing a blight here that continues to this day. You probably thought I spoke metaphorically in a sense, that my mind was too mired in the classics to consider this problem rationally…for after all, what do I know about Cobton except what I found in the old archives and heard as the twice-told tales of old-timers? Other than my visit here when I was young that cost the life of my brother…what evidence do I have to support my theory that this is an evil place that attracts evil deeds and evil entities like a magnet attracts metal filings?"

"We've seen all the evidence we need," Wenda told him.

He nodded. "Sure. But have you considered the epicenter of this evil? Because there is one and it's down in those catacombs I spoke of. It's there, I think. It's festering and malignant and it needs to be cut out at its source."

"So we're back to that?"

"Yes. It should be done. What's down there has to be destroyed."

"Griska," Wenda said.

He shrugged. "Maybe. And maybe I'm talking about something even *worse* than Griska. Something that has taken habitation here and regenerated evil again and again."

"And what is that?"

But Rule admitted he did not know. Only that he could feel it as he'd always felt it in Cobton. That it existed, he did not doubt. No more than he doubted that it was now rising up for some reason to spread and multiply, to germinate its foulness. "I think we're on the edge of something…something large in scope and complex in nature. Call it a blueprint if you want. Something Griska might have had in mind when he first came here. To establish Cobton as a vampire colony and then spread that pestilence far and wide. Whether by coincidence or design, we happen to be here when this evil of his is just coming to term. We're in the not-so enviable position of being able to stop it or at least cripple it before it goes too far. I think we need to take advantage of that. I think we need to destroy Griska and his flock and the silent malignancy that empowers them before they spread their wings cross this county, this state, this country, and maybe this whole damn world."

Wenda looked disturbed by the idea. "And how do we do that?"

"By going down into those catacombs and destroying them."

"We'd better wait for dawn."

But Megga shook her head. "They won't let us live until dawn. If we're going to do something, we'd better do it soon."

14

Megga was trying to make Wenda see how important it was that they move on this, but Wenda, of course, was too worried about risking their lives. She would have risked her own in a minute—and had—but she did not like being the caretaker of other lives. It scared her and Megga knew it. She was too cautious, too conservative. And that would cost her. That would cost all of them because Megga was somehow tuned into the undead outside and she knew they were gathering now. They knew what was being discussed inside the house and they knew it was a threat to them. Rule had somehow ferreted out the truth of there being another who stood behind Griska.

This was something Megga herself had not even seen in her mind.

But it was true.

It was real just as she now knew the vampires were indeed massing to spread out of Cobton, to carry the plague from town to town to town. It was an ancient plan and they would not be interfered with.

Though she knew how dangerous it was to open her mind to them, she did so, casting about outwards for the one mind whose intensity and dominance could not be doubted: that of Griska. It was out there burning like a hot ember and she could feel its heat, feel herself drawn closer to it like some suicidal moth flying closer and ever closer to a flickering candle flame.

She thought she was reaching out for Griska, but the opposite seemed true. Her mind was sucked into some black vacuum with force and urgency. She was not in control. Heat waves blew over her from the searing ember of the vampire's mind.

Come, little one. For certainly you are welcome here in this place.

Like a thumbtack driven into a wall, her consciousness was firmly affixed inside that of Griska. She thought with *his* thoughts and looked out through *his* saturnine eyes. His mind was a buried tomb of hot wind that carried a multitude of anguished voices, perhaps the leeched souls of his victims. It was a place of rank contamination and seeping venom...like waking up inside of a black carcinoma, an infesting, parasitic malignance. But for all of that, for as appalling as it was, as much as it made her *essence* feel violated and submerged in filth—and it did, like drowning in a narrow casket of black mud—it was also...*absolutely incredible.* She saw through not just one set of eyes, but *dozens*. At first it made no sense. Her brain could not contain it all or hope to process even a fraction of it. It was like watching fifteen or twenty TVs simultaneously and hoping to follow the action and plot on each screen. It all came at her in a jumble of noise...but slowly, patiently, she was able to focus her view so that she looked into each set of eyes individually.

It was...amazing.

She saw the house through the storm and realized she was looking through the eyes of Griska's brides and children out in the blizzard. They watched and watched and did little else. She knew that he could look through their eyes, but they could not look through his. It was because he was the leader, the progenitor, the all and everything. He was the...the *master,* just like in those creaky old vampire movies they showed on *Chamber of Horrors.*

But it wasn't just through their eyes that she could see.

It was through the beady eyes of rats that scratched in the walls and nested in the cellar. Through the bleary eyes of a spider hiding in the corner of the sitting room. Through those of bats hanging in the attic. An owl that swooped over the rooftops of Cobton. And even from a fly on the mantle woken by the warmth of the fire. She looked through its multi-lensed eyes, seeing a stunning, nearly hallucinatory panoramic view of a world of giants: Wenda and Rule and even herself. Gigantic monstrosities, distorted and wavering as their images jumped from lens to lens.

Then she heard a voice that shattered all of it like the glass of a mirror.

The virgin.

The virgin.

That damnable virgin.

She must be culled, she must be felled.

The Mother fears her.

The Mother...the Mother that is as much filth as the virgin herself is purity.

Yes, the Mother, the Queen of the Dead.

Megga's mind was filled with images of *her*...maybe not who she *really* was, but a series of subjective images.

Yes, yes, yes, Megga understood now.

She was the one that stood behind Griska. *She* was the source and the wellspring that Wenda could dam.

And as she realized this, Megga knew that Griska had invited her into his head so she would know. It was vitally important that she knew. Her job was to demoralize the others, yes, but to corrupt Wenda at all costs so her soul was no longer white sugar but dirty soil writhing with crawling things.

Fell the virgin. Desecrate her so that I may make sport and spectacle of her violation. That I may lay her well-used and well-plucked rind at the feet of the Mother.

Then Megga was back in her own head and the connection was severed like a plug pulled from a socket. She was alone in her head and she knew what had to be done. If she wanted to walk side-by-side with the Queen of the Dead, then she knew very well what she must do—

"Megga!"

That voice, that shouting, droning voice.

"MEGGA!"

She snapped out of it and Wenda was standing over her, shaking her by the shoulders. Megga wanted to kiss...no, she *needed* to kiss her because that was the beginning of seduction that was the beginning of desecration. She reached out for her and Wenda slapped across the face. She slapped her again. And again.

"Bitch!" Megga cried out, shoving Wenda away.

"Snap out of it! We have to go now," Wenda said. "Something's happening. It's happening...right...NOW!"

Wenda kept talking, but Megga could not seem to understand what she was saying. She understood the slapping just fine because that was pain and she reacted like any animal would to it. She looked at Wenda whose eyes were wild and desperate. Wenda wanted to escape, she knew. She wanted them to run out of there to...to begin the hunt. Wenda had murder in her heart, more so she had *extermination* in her heart and she wanted Megga to follow along.

Megga shook her head from side-to-side.

No, no, no. What Griska had promised her was not this existence she'd known all these years which was one of struggle, hopelessness, and inner turmoil, rebellion at all of the above, but something savory and mellow. Something sweet like a warm chocolate dissolving in her mouth, the sugar buzz firing innumerable endorphins in her head. A feeling of peace. A feeling of belonging and being not alone, but part of something bigger. She could already taste that chocolate in her mouth...the sugary, almost orgasmic satisfaction of it as hot red liquid chocolate filled her mouth.

Blood. Not chocolate, but blood.

Megga wanted to taste it and swim in it. She wanted to drown in it.

"ALL RIGHT, GODDAMMIT!" Wenda shouted at her. "IF YOU WANT TO STAY, THEN STAY!"

Good, she was going away. Thank God, she was going away.

Megga blinked, then blinked again.

Now she could see what Wenda feared. What sent her running with Rule in tow.

They were coming through the walls.

The vampires were crawling out of the woodwork.

Wenda had slammed the door shut as she departed. Now tiny white threads were sliding beneath it and crawling up its face like climbing ivy on a fence. It was impossible, but she was seeing it. Now those threads were thick as tree roots. They grew in great profusion, growing and clustering, taking on the general form of a human body. Yes, now the roots were branching into rootlets and slender tendrils and wire-fine fibers. Megga was seeing a near-perfect human form made of those knotting growths. Now they were melting into a whole. Dirty, gray, straw-like hair rose from a head like a nodding white puffball. A jagged depression became a sardonic, grinning mouth of long, sharp teeth. Yellow eyes winked open.

Everywhere.

It was happening all around her. The vampires were not entering the room as mists or shades or even wolves, they were *growing* themselves into it. Fibrous bodies were assembling on the walls, tendrils climbing and writhing, whipping and joining and knotting like puppets made of white yarn. They grew up out of the corners, from beneath the baseboards, creeping cords winding around the edges of the window casements like creeping masses of fungi. A gray fibrous mass fleshed itself out in the chair Wenda had been sitting in and Megga found herself looking at a little girl who kept counting her fingers, licking the white palings of her teeth.

As the vampires bloomed about her like graveyard orchids, the door swung open and Megga gasped, thinking, *thank God, thank God, Wenda's come back for me, she's come back to save me from myself.* But it wasn't Wenda. It was another woman. She walked with a soundless, light step. She was naked, long-legged, the hair drifting from her scalp so blond it was nearly white. But there was something wrong. Something terribly wrong and Megga knew it.

She saw that as it walked its skin seemed to billow and flutter like a balloon fed by a gas jet. And as it got closer to her, she could see minute cracks in the flesh that the light passed clean through.

In the back of her head, she heard her own voice. It was the confused, fearful voice of a little girl. *This isn't right. Something just isn't right here…*

The woman moved closer as the other vampires took shape along the walls. She walked with a strange side-to-side sort of motion, making a kind of rubbery sound of the sort a blow-up doll might make if it was to walk.

Then Megga saw what it was.

Not a vampire exactly. Not even a woman exactly.

As it got closer, she could see it had no eyes, just black holes in the face. It smiled a big, lunatic, moony sort of grin. There were no teeth behind the smile. In fact, there was nothing. It was hollow. The light from the fire caught it, shining through the holes of its eyes and the cavern of its grinning mouth…and there was nothing inside it.

It was a walking skin.

A human peel.

And as it got closer and something bunched inside Megga in feral terror, she could hear its voice in her head. A scraping, scratchy sort of voice that had very little volume and very little substance: *I shed my skin, did I not? I wore the body and face of the tender one, did I not?* Yes, this was the beldam that they had killed. It had shed its skin to wear the likeness of Bailey. It was dead now…but its skin was very much alive. It came after Megga like a sock without a foot in it, a living membrane, a walking pelt.

It needed a body to attach itself to.

It would wear Megga's.

When it reached for her, she screamed. She tried to push it away, but there was no true way of fighting it. Her hands pressed into it and it gave instantly, hot air rushing from the mouth. And then it was on her. It did not grip her so much as it *affixed* itself to her, sticking to her hands and adhering itself to her face. She could feel it moving on her, sliding over her and consuming her. It was appropriating her, assimilating her, ingesting her.

Megga was on her feet, tearing and clawing at it.

The casing had all the substance of a pair of nylon stockings. Yet, it clung and moved, gluing itself to her. She stumbled, staggering this way and that, finally going to her knees before the fire. She knew what had to be done and she did not hesitate. Before it completely webbed itself to her, she shoved it into the fire. As she herself was singed, the skin shriveled, blackening and curling, the whipping blond hair igniting. The skin screamed with a hollowed, empty sound like a shriek coming from a pipe. As it blazed and Megga cried out from the pain and the stink of burning hair, she pulled it free. On the floor, it curled up like the sloughed skin of a snake, blackened and smoldering, great holes melted through it. It tried to creep away before collapsing in a smoking, crackling heap.

Then Megga ran.

The vampires did not try to stop her. They touched her with icy fingers and hissed inside her head with voices like leaking steam valves. *MEGGA MEGGA MEGGA MEEEEGGAAAAA.* She shut them out. She pressed hands over her ears. She would not listen to it. *PLEASE MEGGA MEGGA MEGGA OH PLEASE OH SWEET DEAR MEGGA MEGGA MEGGA MEGGAAAAAA.* One of them was growing from the wall right next to the door like fingers of woodrot trying to imitate a human being. It fattened and fleshed out, lifting its faceless clumped head to her.

She hit it.

She hit it with a balled-up fist right where its face might have been and it...*exploded.* Like a stepped-upon fruiting body of fungus, it came apart like a juicy, black tomato, spilling foul yellow ooze that leaked in rivers.

Then she was through the door.

She was out of the house.

She was in the storm. It took hold of her in frozen hands, gripping her, squeezing her, throwing snow in her face and shoving icy air down her spine. Crying out for Wenda and Rule, she plunged headlong into the night, frantic and half-mad. When hands reached out and took hold of her, she screamed.

15

As soon as they stepped outside, the wind found them.

Holding Rule's hand, Wenda and he walked side-by-side into the blizzard. If something were waiting for them out there—and, no doubt, *something* was—then they would face it together. Head-on. She was aware of the forms standing out just beyond the periphery of the storm. They got no closer. Not just then. She could feel the cool emptiness of them. Not human beings. Not things with souls. Just animate hunger. They were breathing hides and no more.

It wasn't far to the Georgian house where Doc and the others had run after the incident with the bus. That all seemed ages ago now. No more than forty feet, but never had that distance seemed so long as it did at that moment. Antique houses rose up around them in the blizzard like ghost ships coming out of sea fog, phantasmal and weird.

"We're in incredible danger," Rule said.

And, yes, Wenda figured they were at that. But what choice had there been? With dawn getting closer and more subtle modes of persuasion failing, the vampires had dropped all pretenses and simply forced themselves into the room. Something which was either an act of desperation or a herding maneuver to force them out into the storm. Either way, it worked.

They pushed on through the tomb of the blizzard, clutching hands tightly, waiting for it, tensing, expecting to be attacked at any moment. But they weren't. In fact, nothing happened until Megga burst out of the storm, screaming their names. They took hold of her and they were three. It wasn't much with what they were facing, but it was something. Megga, of course, was nearly out of her mind, gibbering and stuttering over what she had seen and what had touched her. She wanted them to know, to understand, to feel the depths of her horror…but in the end she just fell silent. Words could not convey what was in her head.

They found the Georgian within minutes.

It was tall and somber, its multi-paned windows filled with darkness. But the worse part was that the front door was wide open. That did not bode well. Wenda smelled an almost sweet, unnatural sort of odor coming out at her. She knew what they would see and what they would find would not be good.

They all knew it.

Regardless, no one suggested that they turn back.

Wenda led them in. She carried her sliver-bladed knife in one hand and a kerosene lantern in the other, lighting the way. Megga was behind her with empty hands and a hollow heart. Rule came last. He carried his flashlight, but he didn't waste any batteries shining it around. The lantern would do. Wenda led them towards a doorway that was open. They could see the low flickering of a fire beyond it.

Rule felt something pull up inside him as they reached the doorway.

He knew whatever was in there would be horrible and it was what the undead wanted them to see. He followed Wenda in there, practically dragging Megga behind him. He thought she might be in shock. When she'd first found them in the storm, she wouldn't stop blabbering out her torment. Now, she wouldn't say a word. But as he pulled her into the room with him, he could feel how she drew back. She knew there was something in there that she didn't want to see.

It was a parlor.

The fire in the hearth had nearly died out. Wenda raised her lantern, casting light around and he turned on his flashlight, panning the room and soon wishing that he hadn't. There was a body tacked to the wall, crucified with nails, and it was an absolute obscenity. Not only was it swollen and puffed purple-blue like every bone within had been broken, but it looked like it had nearly been turned inside out, bowel and organ and gut pushed out of the rent body cavity, dripping and seamed with yellow fat. But despite the carnage, there was barely a drop of blood to be had. Rule could imagine why. In his mind, he could see the vampires crowded up to the dying man, suckling him like piglets at the milk-swollen teats of their mother.

Megga made a slight squealing sound in her throat, but she continued to stare. Sickened, Rule clicked off his flashlight and turned her away from the atrocity.

"Its Doc," Wenda said, her voice edged with defeat. "It's Doc."

Rule sighed. "If he's…like this, then I doubt the others survived."

"Burt, Reg, Bailey…oh Christ."

Megga pulled her hand away from his own and dropped her weight into a chair. Rule knew she had given up. If Wenda gave up too, they were done. He could fight to the death and it would do no good. His death would be an amusement for Griska and his legions. Nothing more than amusement.

"We have to get down to that tunnel," he said. "There's no time to waste. Dawn is getting close and they're going to get very desperate."

Wenda was staring at Megga. She looked forlorn. Empty.

"Wenda…we don't have time," he emphasized.

She nodded. There were a couple stakes on the floor. No doubt they had been manufactured by Doc and the others. She took them, slid them through her belt with the others.

And Megga screamed.

They looked over at her. Both were still having trouble getting the image of Doc out of their heads. Wenda opened her mouth to ask Megga what in God's name she was screaming about, but the words never came out.

Rule saw what she was staring at.

It was something that did not look especially threatening...*cobwebs*. At least, what he assumed were cobwebs. White crepe-like tendrils dangling in the air, several of which seemed to be dropping over Megga. They looked, absurdly enough, almost like Silly String. Megga brushed them away from her face. In a frantic rush to get away, she hit the floor on her knees and Wenda pulled her away.

Cobwebs?

No, they weren't cobwebs and he knew it. He expected only the worst and he was not disappointed. In the time it took him to realize there was something seriously fucked up and Wenda pulled Megga to her feet, the extraordinary was occurring: much like Silly String, the cobwebs were filling the air. A network of them was coming from the direction of the ceiling, it seemed, attached to the chair Megga had been sitting on by several thick white cords like the anchor strands that held a spider's web in place. It happened very quickly.

Rule backed away with the others. In his mind, the stuff looked like ectoplasm.

"We better get out of here," Wenda said, her voice sounding dry like it was blown with sand.

The cords came together with a sliding and whipping sound, breaking apart into threads and filaments, interweaving and crisscrossing until it looked like there was a great living net in the room. But that quickly thickened as the ghostly white threads knotted together, taking on a ropy near-human form as the rootlike growths had in the other house. They fleshed out in seconds and there was a featureless female shape drifting above them, still connected by myriad white fibers. The woman looked like she was made of pale phlegm, roiling yellow gas, and tresses of coiling bloody tissue. A grinning face emerged. A set of swollen breasts. A mounded pregnant belly as if she had died in childbirth. Rule could see the faces of unborn children trying to push through her skin which was like gray lace.

"WE HAVE TO GET OUT OF HERE!" Wenda shouted. *"NOW!"*

Rule realized then that he had been seduced by the impossibility of what he was seeing: a living cobweb woman. He hadn't been able to look away from it. He would have waited there, he knew, until she came for him, until she buried him alive in her webby, seeking mass and drained him dry drop by drop. Even then, threads of web were snaking through the air in his direction.

"Come on!" Wenda shouted.

Rule led the way out. He slammed the door shut, leaning on it, breathing heavily, realizing how close he'd been to sacrificing them all. But it wouldn't happen again. He would not allow it.

At least, that's what he kept telling himself.

16

It was cold and dark in the house. Now that she had been away from the fire for a time, Wenda felt numb inside. She wondered if she'd ever feel warm again.

Rule led them on down corridors that probably made perfect sense by day, but at night were a complete maze. But he knew the way. Despite the horror that was behind them in the parlor, he moved them slowly and efficiently, scanning the way ahead carefully with his flashlight.

"It's a game," Megga said.

She hadn't spoken in some time, so both Wenda and Rule stopped and looked at her. Her eyes blinked rapidly in the darkness. "It's a game," she said again. "That's what it is. We don't stand a fucking chance. They're toying with us, letting us think there's hope. At the last moment, they'll snatch it away from us when they're done letting us run the maze like rats."

"There's always a chance," Rule said.

Megga laughed at him. "They're destroying us even now, planting seeds of fear and indecision in us. They're ancient and cunning. We're hopeless and week. They are the children of the night, the—"

"Just shut up," Wenda told her. "We don't have time for your uber-Goth drama."

Megga just shook her head. "You don't understand. They already own us. They can claim us anytime they want."

"They own *you*. That's all they've ever owned. And they've used you to cause trouble again and again. Quit being so fucking weak. We don't have the time for it."

Rule led them on again and Wenda found herself wishing that Megga had not found them, that she'd stayed back in the other house with her own kind. She would have been a happy, morose little vampire by now. Wenda didn't like thinking things like that. It wasn't in her nature…or it hadn't been before tonight. The last thing she wanted to do was to sacrifice one of them to the walking dead, but her patience with Megga was simply bone-dry.

"Okay," Rule said. "The door is just around the bend."

When they got there, he did not open it. He considered it carefully. He looked over at Wenda as if to say, *ready?* She nodded. He grasped the knob and threw the door open. He explored the darkness beyond with his light. He saw nothing move on the stairwell.

Wenda felt the tension drain from her. Nothing had leaped out at them. That was a plus. Even so, the adrenaline surging through her system would not completely release its grip on her.

"Let's go," she said, feeling the press of shadows behind them. "I think they're coming."

Rule swallowed and led them down the stairs, his breath puffing out in the flashlight beam in white clouds. There was death below and he could feel it.

17

By the time they reached the cellar floor, the vampires were coming down the stairs.

Rule picked them out in the beam of his flashlight: seven or eight ragged figures that seemed to be as much mist and smoke as they were flesh and blood. One moment, they seemed perfectly corporeal. The next, they lost solidity and the light seemed to shine right through them, illuminating the stairwell and little else.

He needed little more inspiration.

Moving sure and quick, he grasped Megga's hand and towed her away deeper into the cellar, Wenda at their side. Despite the winter chill, the darkness felt damp. It seemed to crawl around them. Sounds bounced and echoed and it was hard to know if they had made them or if it was the vampires.

Rule did not believe it was the undead: they were unbearably silent. They made no more sound than patches of moonlight traveling across a midnight lawn.

The cellar was used for storage and it was crowded with dark shapes and menacing shadows. Boxes and crates, stacked lumber, old apple baskets and stone jars, nail kegs and aluminum milk jugs.

He found two more kerosene lanterns that he had filled not a week before. He gave one to each of the girls and Wenda abandoned her nearly empty one.

He knew his way through the maze because he'd been down in the cellar dozens of times in his job as caretaker. Much of the assorted junk down there, he had brought down himself. As he led them through it all, quickly as he could, he thought: *You won't get these girls because I will not allow it. Maybe I'm old and I'm weak and I'm approaching the end of my years, but, by God, I'll fight. You know I'll fight. We all will. Dawn's coming now and if you don't get us all, if you fail and leave just one of us alive, that one will hunt you all down and stake every goddamn one of you. You know it's true.*

He led them on, very aware that the vampires were closing in. No matter. If they wanted to attack, they would attack. They didn't because they were afraid of Wenda and the power that arced inside her. They knew its strength and they feared it, feared it as all creatures of the night feared the first rays of golden, pure sunshine.

He led them around some shelves, an ancient wood boiler, and to the far wall of the cellar. The walls were fieldstone that had been quarried in the early days of the 18th century. Before them, a massive section was missing. This was the opening of the passage and it was like a black hell waiting for them. Behind them, the vampires were making themselves known with a low hissing that was their voices.

What if Megga's right, he thought as he stepped into the opening. *What if this is all a game? What if they're herding us down here on purpose for the death blow?*

But he refused to dwell on it. In his heart, despite his misgivings, he still thought this was the right thing to do. He honestly believed that.

Megga and Wenda joined him in the passage. It was large enough to walk upright in. As Rule's light illuminated it, they could see that it canted downwards in the distance.

Wenda wrinkled her nose. There was a low, animal stink blowing up at them. It smelled hot and salty like curing hides.

Rule led the way again. They had no time to consider whether this was really what they wanted to do or not. Their instincts had brought them here and they would have to carry them through. As they moved down the claustrophobic tunnel, the stink seemed to thicken in the air until it was nearly gagging. It wasn't decay exactly, just age, advanced age combined with the stench of wet pelts, rotting straw, yellowing bones, and old blood, as well as something sharper, stronger. If contamination and defilement had an odor, this was it.

Maybe fifty feet into it, the smell seemed toxic like poison gas. A dank, damp, cloying smell permeated the walls.

Keep going! Keep going! For godsake, don't think! Just move!

Yes, that was the thing. He moved farther down the tunnel and it continued to cant ever downwards like they were heading into the lower regions of hell. And maybe they were. What struck Rule as being more than a little odd, was the fact that the air seemed *warmer.* It should have been at least as cool as that of the house, but the temperature most certainly had risen. Not warm enough to shed coats, but noticeable. It was like they were probing deeper and deeper into the evil body of Cobton, approaching the hot-blooded mass of its pumping black heart. At any moment, he expected dozens of glowing eyes to open before them.

As he tried not to think, he also tried not to listen.

Their shuffling footfalls were echoing all around them, amplified and resounding. Now and again, he thought he heard the reptilian hissing of undead voices or the squeaking of colonies of rats. It all amazed him, as they moved farther down beneath the town, that something like this could exist in the first place. Who had channeled it out?

Had it been the vampires? He couldn't conceive of that. They didn't strike him as being industrious beyond the getting of blood. Leeches did not dam rivers and vampires did not dig tunnels.

No, this had existed before. Perhaps part of it was artificial, though much of it was probably natural. Maybe it *had* been a smuggler's den at one time. He didn't suppose he'd ever really know. All he knew for sure was that they were going somewhere, getting closer to something. And whatever that was, he could almost feel it reaching out for them…the bigness of it, the starkness of it.

Megga stopped. "I heard giggling."

"Just ignore it," he told her.

"Giggling," she said in a dreamlike voice. "Children giggling."

They pushed on for what seemed at least another thirty minutes to the point where they were all beginning to doubt the sense of what they were doing, if they hadn't before.

Rule thought: *A river. This is a dark and winding river like the Styx that will lead us to the land of the dead. We're trapped in its running current and we couldn't get out of it if we wanted to. Like corpuscles in narrow veins, we're being carried towards the heart of this abomination. We will see things no one ever has and lived to tell the tale. Our deaths will be legendary in their suffering, but we will die with grim revelation in our eyes.*

Then, as they began to seriously lose whatever sense of motivation they'd had, the tunnel opened up and they stepped into a huge cavern. There was no doubt in their minds that it was a naturally hollowed-out limestone cave. Rule figured they had come down easily seventy or eighty feet beneath the town. This was the secret, storied chamber where Griska and his followers hid while the high sheriff and his boys had destroyed the blood-slaked townspeople in the cemetery above.

"Look," Megga said. "Look where we are."

As a historian and something of an antiquarian, he was fascinated. If it hadn't been for the very obvious threat, he could have explored around down here for days. But if he was intrigued, Wenda was not. She was on a mission. She saw closure and this is the place where she would find it.

"Let's go," she said, leading them on with her lantern held high.

18

"We're under the graveyard."

The ceiling of the cavern was at least forty feet above them. In the beam of Rule's flashlight, they could see thick, tangled tree roots poking out and what looked to be caskets that must have settled deeper into the earth through the years. Some looked poised to fall and others already had. Apparently the subsidence had been going on for some time because there were dozens of shattered coffins around them that looked like they had exploded upon impact, casting bones, partial skeletons, and withered broken things in rotted cerements in every direction. They had to step around them, over mounds of earth strewn with femurs and jawless skulls, avoiding the shards of earthen boxes.

Given time, the entire cemetery above would come crashing down into this charnel pit.

Let's just hope that's not today, Wenda thought.

In the light of the lantern, she studied the faces of the others. Megga seemed to have shrunk inside her own skin. Her eyes were fixed and glassy. She didn't look up to swatting a mosquito let alone fighting what they would have to fight. And Rule…his eyes were vacant, distant, the eyes of an old man that just wanted to close. He would fight, but he was already pretty torn up from the rats. This is what Wenda had to fight with. These two. She had to put them up against a merciless engine of wrath, something that took human lives almost casually. Something of immense power, immense hate, and immense evil.

Dawn is approaching and the undead know it. They'll be more cunning and more desperate than ever. But maybe in their haste, I'll find their weakness.

She led Rule and Megga on through the cemetery, waiting for death to come on night wings. Her head was fuzzy. She felt a curious mixture of dread, exhilaration, and disorientation. Her time-sense was completely askew. Had all this only happened tonight? Was it really only a matter of hours since the bus crash or was that something that happened days or weeks ago? Her own life before Cobton had lost focus. *Chamber of Horrors,* Vultura, the Graveyard Girls, Doc Blood, the cobwebbed sets, the weekly routines, the tired old movies…it all seemed like it was part of someone else's life now. A story in a book. A documentary she'd seen years ago. It was gone now. There was only the knife in her hand and the stakes in her belt.

This was all that remained…other than the concentrated night-smell of the undead which was the stink of death and dissolution, the spiced, unpleasant odor of a bricked-up root cellar where onions rotted to mummified peels and tomatoes boiled down to a black slime of putrescence. That's what she was smelling. A dark, vomitous odor of disease and pestilence, succulent human fruits rotted to cobs and vinegar-stinking drainage.

The odors filled her, revolted her, yet steeling her to what must come next: not killing, not extermination, not even something so sterile as eradication, but a process of cleansing and decontamination.

She studied the shifting shadows ahead, her flesh prickling with a chill that was beyond simple air temperature. Though there was abject silence ahead, a great soundless lagoon of it, she sensed motion, a delicate shifting of the ether very, very close to her. She swallowed, pushing forward, almost daring it to show itself.

And then it did.

Rule gasped.

Megga moaned.

Wenda took one faltering step backwards, then met it head on.

A woman rocketed forward out of the darkness, her face twisted in a wolflike mask, eyes a dun yellow, fangs jutting from her mouth like sewing needles. She reached out with hands that were like the claws of an owl.

Wenda slashed at her with the knife.

She cut the air before her with fierce side-to-side strokes, feeling the blade tearing into the mass of the woman, cutting through ghost-mesh that seemed to have no more solidity than wood smoke. The result was instantaneous: the woman screamed, her voice booming like thunder, and it cycled through the tombyard, echoing and echoing as the vampire seemed to collapse into a funneling column of phosphorescent corpse-gas that was sucked away into the darkness.

Breathing hard, Wenda said, "Come on. We keep going. Nothing stops us now."

She walked forward, upright, proud, and almost arrogant in her defiance. She would not stop. Her stride was sure, her way was set. She would cut deeper and deeper into this nightmare until she found the black beating heart of it and then she would smash it to jelly. She was tired. She knew she was tired. Quite possibly, she was not thinking right...yet, the energy inside her that forced her forward was so very, very sure of itself. It was like a plug seeking an outlet so the electrical circuit could be complete, one with itself.

Behind her, bunched together, she could feel Rule and Megga, the tenseness that was now part and parcel of who and what they were. She could feel it right up her spine. The vampires were gathering around them now in the darkness, flocking like moths around streetlights. The others were aware of it. They were terrified. Even Megga. The fear crawled beneath her skin in sickening waves. Wenda pushed forward, ever forward, stepping lightly and surely amongst the ancient tombstones and shattered crypts. They were like a trio of flies trying to sneak through the lair of a funnelweb spider.

Hesitate and they'll drain you dry.

The fact that they hadn't yet spoke volumes. They would in an instant if Griska gave the word, but he would not sacrifice his family unnecessarily. What was inside Wenda concerned him. He felt its power, recognized its threat. He would do nothing, not until the time was right, not until the odds were stacked in his favor and Wenda had every intention of never letting that happen.

She sensed a low, warm wind beginning to blow from somewhere directly ahead of them. What she sought would be there and Griska would try everything he could to see that she did not reach it.

It was then that the vampires showed themselves.

19

Megga felt her mind returning a bit at a time. It seemed as if it had been locked away in cold storage, but now it was thawing. She became aware of how sore she was, how tired, how absolutely beaten. Yet, Wenda pushed them on and on in some personal, suicidal quest that she herself did not completely understand.

She has to be stopped.

Megga flinched.

It was Griska's voice.

He was in her head as he had been in her head most of the night. There was some tenuous thread strung between their minds now and she did not have the strength to sever it. He wanted her to stop Wenda. No, he *needed* her to stop Wenda in any way she could. He showed her the delights that would be hers if she cooperated, how she would walk the night for eternity as some dark maiden, a consort of the damned.

But he showed her what refusal would bring as well.

He showed her an image of herself laying on a blood-soaked mattress as dozens and dozens of vampires traumatically impaled her, sinking their fangs into her legs and arms, her throat and face, her breasts and belly, her thighs, her vagina, spiking her again and again until her blood leaked out from literally hundreds of punctures.

Cooperate. Kill the virgin. Strike her dead.

And she wanted to tell him that she was not strong enough, that even if she attacked Wenda, Rule would stop her. Stop her long enough for Wenda to punish her for her transgression.

But Griska didn't care about that.

His voice, his consciousness, rose up into a shrill, insectile buzzing noise that made her feel weak and nauseous, blind with stupidity where she could not gather a single thought.

Why not Rule? Why not him? That's what she wondered when it passed. Why didn't Griska make Rule do what he wanted? Why was she the one that had to initiate this?

Because you're dark at your core and your soul is corrupt, she heard a voice say in her head. It was not Griska's voice; it was her own. Somehow, that made it all that much worse. *The undead didn't channel into Wenda's head or Rule's. They knew who their kin was. They instinctively recognized you as one of their own. This is what you wanted, isn't it? All along, haven't you wanted this? Well, here's your chance. Make your move. Betray your friends and you can live forever.*

"I can't," she said under her breath. "I can't do that."

Rule had his light in her face. "What did you say?"

Megga shook her head. "I...I don't know."

The words had barely left her lips when she felt dizzy, as if she might pass out cold. It was like all the blood in her body rose to her head like an elevator car. She stumbled into Rule and he held her up. She could feel the vampires around them, the incessant droning of their thoughts, the fierce and unwavering loyalty to Griska...and, yes, something *beyond* Griska. Something else. Something darker.

Wenda was speaking to her, saying something, but the words made absolutely no sense. She could feel Rule's arms supporting her. She blinked. Then blinked again.

She saw a cemetery...not the tomb wreckage from above they'd been stepping around and over, but a necropolis of the highest order. Graves, mausoleums, huge ornate crypts, chapels honed from black stone. She was in a burial ground of great honor, a place where the gods buried their own. Creeping fingers of mist blew about and the atmosphere was vile and decadent...and for Megga, it was like coming home after a long absence. This was the place she had seen in her dreams, the epicenter of her morbid Goth fantasies. The grounds were oddly landscaped, lying over hill and valley. Immense, winding stone staircases wound amongst the vaults and sepulchers. Wicked, blasted trees sprouted up from the evil ground everywhere, their blackened boughs reaching to the sky like slashes of darkness.

This is what I've always been looking for. This is my place. My home. My retreat from my boring, banal existence. Oh, to die here.

To lie on a stone slab or be interred beneath the ground, resting uneasily beyond a tomb gate enveloped in creepers. Cobwebs and black silk, carven candelabra and scratching graveyard rats. The rain of dust and mute centuries. Oh, dear God, dear God...

This place had been waiting for her all this time, anxious to welcome her home and wrap skeletal arms about her, to hold her in worm-eaten shrouds and moldering shifts. She was a prodigal daughter no more; the wretched wastefulness of her former world was distant memory, a piss-stained newspaper blowing away in the breeze. She was happier than she'd been since the days she'd nursed at her mother's teat. There was that same level of comfort and satisfaction. She only wished there were inhabitants here, a family to accept her and embrace her as part of their order.

But wait...as she stared across the weedy, tombstone-jutting marble wastes about her, the dead *were* coming to greet her. Reedy things. Wraiths. They seemed to be composed of equal portions of protoplasm and colorless gas. They were human in general form and appearance, but obviously not people as she knew them. *Ghouls? Vampires?* She couldn't say, but that they welcomed her there was no doubt.

Their eyes were glistening orbs alight with brilliant shades of amber and sunset orange. They moved in closer, surrounding her with an icy ambience. Death had freed them of their clothing and Megga saw only transparent nakedness all around her. Their bodies were enclosed by some bizarre gaseous envelope that acted as a membrane, holding the form they wore in life. Inside this, she could see their dormant anatomies and aged bones, among other, more freakish things. Streamers of ectoplasm blew around them and in them as if moved by some secret wind. They ringed around her, dancing, singing wordless songs that reminded her of howling October winds. Their hollow-cheeked faces were clown-white as if sculpted from some colorless, flaking marble. The song they sang was joyless, their grave-molded lips devoid of smiles. A young girl moved in, as if for a kiss, and then passed through her. It was unpleasant like nothing Megga had ever experienced. Sensations of cold, dampness, and insanity slid greasily through her at the contact. She felt oddly violated, but there was no true word for souls sharing the same physical space for a split second.

But she knew.

They only wanted to worship her. That's all they asked. She was their queen and they wanted to worship at her feet, her own host of revenants. They touched her, swarming around her, moving within and without her. They only wanted to know if she would be their queen and her lips formed one word, *"Yes."*

20

Rule felt the coldness, the dankness, the chill of the grave coming off of Megga and he took hold of her. He shook her. He didn't know why he felt it was necessary, but he did it anyway until her eyes seemed to focus again.

"What?" she said. "What are you doing?"

"What are *you* doing?"

"It's so beautiful," she said. "I've never seen a cemetery like this before. It's absolutely perfect in every way."

He looked over at Wenda. What cemetery? What the hell was she talking about? The bones and shattered coffins around them? Was that it? But if so, exactly what was so perfect about it?

"What are you talking about?" Wenda said, growing very suspicious.

"The cemetery," Megga said, offering the both of them a nearly unspeakable grin that made something in Rule's belly roll over. "It's like something out of Poe."

He did not know what she was seeing, but he had no doubt she was seeing something...something that Wenda and he could not. Maybe it was a hallucination or a waking dream and maybe she was just out of her head...and who had better right? But even as Wenda grew tense, he did not dismiss it. Chances were, Griska was showing her something she wanted to see, amplifying not only the seduction of the dark side but her own coming destruction. Then again...who could say? Maybe she *was* seeing something that they couldn't. Maybe she was psychically channeling something.

Twenty-five years earlier, when his mother was dying of lymphoma, he had watched her rotting away in a hospital bed. She was so full of drugs that she was incapable of a coherent thought, let alone a coherent sentence. One day the charge nurse said, "She keeps talking about some man she's seeing." She dismissed it, of course, as a drug-induced hallucination. But as Rule had held her hand, his mother had opened her eyes, which seemed very bright for the first time in many, many weeks and said, "Oh, I'm so glad he's back. Isn't he just the most beautiful man? I can't wait to begin our journey." She died the next day. Of course, being a guy who had taught literature for years, he was haunted by it. His imagination nagged at him. Was it just a hallucination or had she indeed seen Death?

And he wondered the same thing about Megga right now.

"Let's get moving," Wenda said. "We don't have time for this."

Ah, Little Miss Practicality reminding him that it was important to be practical when in the business of vampire slaying. He liked that. He could see it in his head. *When killing vampires, one must be practical.* If he still had his office at Stony Brook, he would have had that lettered on a card to hang on the wall.

They moved on and suddenly Wenda halted. "Wait," she said. "There's something."

He opened his mouth to ask her what sort of something...and a wind came blowing out at him. He couldn't conceive of where it might be coming from, but it was there. It came with a high, shrilling, wasplike buzzing that was so loud he had to cover his ears. Gust after gust punched into him, separating him from Megga. He hit the ground, tried to stand, and was knocked down again.

Hell is this...what the hell is this? What—?

He still held his flashlight and nothing could make him let go of it. He didn't want to imagine the absolute, cloistering blackness of this place or how he might wander, lost and alone, in it until the vampires found him and fed on him. In the beam of his light, the wind was filled with flying debris: dust, clots of dirt, what might have been finely ground powdered bone and human ash. It blew in a wild, raging tempest. He could barely see anything. He thought he heard Wenda cry out or maybe it was Megga. There was no way to be sure.

Drifting about the perimeter of the light's illumination, he could see vampires like black death's-head moths circling ever closer—their stark white faces and grinning red mouths, eyes like yellow, red, and silver starshot.

He crawled slowly towards where he thought he had been when the wind hit him. The dust-clotted beam of his light found nothing but heaped black earth, fingers of frozen meltwater, and stray ice-locked bones. He was most assuredly alone and that's what Griska had wanted from the beginning, the very beginning. As Megga had said, a game, it was all a game. *They're toying with us, letting us think there's hope. At the last moment, they'll snatch it away from us when they're done letting us run the maze like rats.* Yes, yes, yes, that must have been true all along. Griska had wanted them here on his private killing grounds and he had fooled them into thinking it was their own idea.

"WENDA!" Rule cried out. *"MEGGA! DEAR GOD, CAN YOU HEAR ME?"*

But it was pointless.

Not only had the wind separated them and blinded them with its cycling debris, it was howling now like blood-maddened wolves, baying and shrieking. All means of communication between him and the others had been taken away, one by one. They were trapped down here in these monolithic catacombs, this rat-crawling lair of the undead. Horror crept inside him, chilling him, filling his brain with nightmarish imagery.

And the wind increased in intensity.

21

Whereas the sudden windstorm had knocked Rule on his ass, it propelled Wenda forward to a place that she knew she would have found eventually. She was no longer under the cemetery now; that was far behind her. She was under the town itself, pushed into secret channels of night and nameless chambers of charnel silence. Her internal clock told her that daylight was probably less than an hour away and she could sense the desperation, the *fear* the undead held for the first cleansing rays of dawn.

They want closure on you. They want you finished by then. Griska must finish you. It is his job to protect them. He has to stop you before...before...

She wasn't sure. Certainly, before sunrise. The idea of her living past that hour was a horrid danger to them. They knew very well what she would do. Yes, that was part of it...but there was something else, something bigger, something far grimmer. A secret, a divine mystery that she was not to know of but she knew all the same.

The other that stood behind Griska.

He had to keep her away from whatever it was, even at the cost of his own existence.

Holding her lantern high, ever aware of the dark sweet smell of putrescence thickening around her, Wenda moved ever forward over the hilly terrain, amongst heaps of earth and low hollows filled with frozen pools of water. There were bones littered about and most looked quite old, but she saw other debris now, too. Bricks and huge, shattered stones, blackened beams and heaps of rubble.

She stepped around massive rusted gears half-buried in the earth and staffs of twisted iron, ancient rotted planks that looked like they had been dropped from far above.

And they had.

She was under the old mill that Rule had told her about. Somewhere above would be a shaft leading up into the ruins. Up there, the air would be glacially fresh and cold. Down here, it was a buried mausoleum. The vampires were all around her and she knew it. Mostly, they were discorporeal things, shades and phantoms, hissing masses of mist and white smoke through which burning eyes and blood-red mouths could be seen.

She was very close to the epicenter now and she knew it.

22

Using a stone, Rule pulled himself to his feet and the wind seemed to slow and die out. A figure stepped out in a gore-stained parka that was filthy from years of sleeping in the dirt and beneath dank piles of autumn leaves. Its face grinned at him, except it wasn't a reflexive action of muscles but more like the white vellum of the face had been torn.

You came back, eh, squirt? We've been waiting for you a long time.

It was Bugs and with him was Andy, his brother Andy. Staring at them with his mouth open, it was 1957 again and he was ten years old. He felt small and weak and utterly in thrall to them, which, he supposed, he truly was. Their faces were like death-swollen toadstools, greasy and shining.

I think he's scared, Andy.

He is.

Let's see how scared he can get.

Rule stood his ground as they moved slowly in on him, but it wasn't out of machismo or some self-destructive seam of bravery, it was because he felt rooted to the spot, rooted by terror. Maybe the skin he wore was that of a sixtysomething ex-lecturer of humanities and English lit, but inside, down deep, he was a ten year old boy who was scared stiff. He was still in awe of his brother, but mainly of the abomination he had become.

Andy stepped lightly in his direction, the flashlight making his face glow like the mantle of a deep-sea squid. His eyes were huge and yellow, the color of drainage leaking from an infected wound. His lips were threadbare, split by seasons of cold, the teeth discolored, fangs mottled. He reached out with a hand much like the crooked roots that grow from the bases of ancient oaks. The fingers were spidery and limp.

That's it, Andy. Scare him to death. Scare that little fucking pimple to death.

Rule tried to lick his lips but they felt like burlap. This was not Andy; this was a dead thing from a grave. Andy had been wonderful and amazing, kind and sweet and bigger than life. But this…this *shell* was an animate doll, a living mannequin, a mocking puppet carved from coffin pine. There was nothing inside it but a vast, black, whirpooling nothingness.

Let me have him, Andy. Little fucker left us here to die. Let me show him what that was like.

The real Andy would have—and *had*—fought like ten tigers to protect his kid brother back in the dim days of the 1950's. He would never have let anyone harm slight, bookish Denny Rule. Now, however, he sacrificed him easily, willingly, and with a cold, inhuman mirth.

Go ahead, Bugs. Show him your stuff.

Bugs was more than ready. What happened then was shocking and weirdly hallucinatory, but it seemed that somehow Bugs unzipped himself like a garment bag…and inside he was empty save for the furry, oily bodies of rats. What seemed dozens of plump rats pressed together to keep warm. They came out of him in a flood, pouring, creeping, surging, and Rule was drowning in them as their teeth bit into him and their claws laid his flesh open. The rodent waters rose higher and higher and he was going under, he was going to suffocate on filthy, flea-hopping rodent pelts.

Andy, Andy, no please Andy don't let him—

He opened his mouth to scream and a rat wedged itself between his lips.

23

Wenda stopped.

This was the place.

This is where they wanted her to go and where she knew she *had* to go.

This was their lair.

There were coffins all around her…crude plank boxes and oblong packing crates jutting from the earth, lids sprung open in trenches in the ground, others scattered on the low hills of dirt around her. In the lantern light, she could see the bloody handprints and smeared red-brown fingerprints on the insides of the lids from being pushed open by the leeches when they arose for midnight feedings. But they all looked old, impossibly old, stains decades old. Rule was right: they had come out of dormancy this night. The very night that Morris arranged for the shoot. If that was karma, then it was karma of the fuck-you-and-yours variety.

Breathing hard, trying to keep the fear in her guts at a manageable level, she set the lantern down and pulled out one of her stakes. She waited with the knife and stake for what came next. She did everything in her power to appear bored, unconcerned, unimpressed...as if facing hordes of the undead was something she did monthly like menstruation, whether she needed it or not.

It was a ruse and she knew she was failing at it, but she did her best to put that out, doing it as Vultura and not Wenda. Now more than ever, she needed that mask to hide behind. The truth of the matter was that the fear she felt was huge and crushing. It ran cold fingers up her spine, slid slivers of ice into her heart, and filled her throat with sour-tasting bile. The fear was palpable and it owned her. And it was only magnified by the atmosphere of the catacombs, which was one of depravity and foulness.

Still, she waited.

She did not call out to the others; she figured they were dead so her mind refused to consider them. She could hear something like a distant wind, a faint dripping, little else but the throbbing of her own heart. She was aware of the fact that not only was the atmosphere becoming more virulent, but the stink was rising, a vile combination of dankness, age, and rot.

The rats were steadily gathering around her. They came in waves, bringing their sewer-smell with them. At first they hid in the shadows, their beady eyes appraising her with simple animal apprehension, but the more that arrived, the bolder they became. Now they were Roman citizens filling the Coliseum, squeaking and boisterous, shifting and hissing, rows upon rows of them on the ground, ranks crowded atop the mill wreckage, clustering on timbers like magpies on telephone lines.

They had not come alone.

Up above where tree roots dangled like spidery fingers and sections of the mill hung from the earth precariously, bats roosted, stretching their wings and making chittering sounds, shitting down upon the rats beneath them.

They're gathering for the show.

Wenda did not believe for one mad moment that they were intelligent enough to know what any of this was about. They were under the dominion of Griska and he brought them here in numbers to increase her unease. She did not doubt the sheer power, the inflexible authority of a mind that could do such things, but at the same time she saw weakness in it. Though the vermin offended her, she knew it was all drama, stagecraft, an attempt to undermine not only her drive and willpower, but to terrify her.

And she wasn't about to say it wasn't working.

In fact—

The temperature of the air dropped suddenly as something began to take shape around her. Except, it never really did take shape properly…it was a smoke ghost, a monster of the mist, something insubstantial like cold fog and hot wind that spun around her in a graveyard whirlwind. She saw white, white hands reaching out for her, a severe Slavic face that seemed to be dissolving to steam, two lurid red eyes…but all of it was constantly moving, constantly reshaping itself, constantly seeming pass through the four states of matter, gas to solid to liquid and, possibly, even plasma. It seemed to throw a field of energy around her that was burning hot then freezing cold. It was Griska, an ectoplasmic monstrosity, and she was caught in his tempest.

She could not get away.

She couldn't even fall to the ground.

He spun her around, dragging her inside of himself and spitting her out, lifting her and dropping her as her head spun with vertigo.

Let me

Let me

Let me in.

She wanted to scream and cry out, but she had no voice. He was peeling away the Vultura mask so she was simple, trembling, terrified Wenda Keegan, defenseless and hopeless. He was in her mind, circling around the edges, tormenting her, telling her how she was weak and he was strong, how if she did not submit her death was going to be ugly and of long duration. He would take her apart bit by bit, slit her open and let the rats feed on her internals while she screamed her sanity away.

The smoke gained substance and she saw something like a massive, membranous wing strike her, sending her plummeting into the dirt.

She tried to get her limbs working again as she crawled away from Griska's vortex, but he pulled her up again and spun her around and around. She could feel something cold and wet licking her throat. It must have been his tongue. Then lips brushing her throat...repulsive, flabby lips like two blood-swollen leeches mating.

His mouth battened to her own and sucked the air out of her lungs.

Now it felt like a dozen lips were on her, tasting and teasing, gently sucking. As she wavered at the edge of reason, she knew if she did not fight and fight right now, all was lost. He would break what was left of her will and then drain her dry.

She could feel the knife in her hand.

Miraculously, she had not dropped it.

The stake was gone, but right now it was the knife that mattered and she knew it. It was an extension of what was inside her. With a silent cry breaking from her lips, she slashed and hacked at what held her. The blade slit it open, shredding it like cheesecloth, tearing it free from her like sticky cobwebs.

Griska instantly weakened.

She reached out and tore at his mass, gripping ribbons of snaking tissue in her hands that tried to go gaseous as she tore at them. She ripped. She tugged. And as she did so, she slashed. Her left hand, the hand that tore at him, was pierced by what felt like dozens of cold needles that made her fingers go numb. It went right up her arm, but the attack worked. He stopped spinning her. He ejected her from his mass and she heard a wailing, enraged scream that was his pain venting itself.

The stakes.

On her knees in the dirt, her head still reeling, she fumbled for them in her belt, but there was barely any sensation in her hand. She dropped one, then another. By then, Griska had her again. He lifted her into the air and tossed her. She struck a moldering, warped casket, but she did not drop the knife. She made to slash at him and he threw her twenty feet like a dog worrying a chew-toy. She hit the ground, the wind knocked out of her.

Don't let him, don't let him, don't let him...win.

But he was winning and she knew it. Her defiance had surprised him, maybe even shocked him, but he had dealt with many like her during the long, gray procession of the centuries. He knew how to break her and he would. As she made to slash him, it felt like a hundred hornet stingers punched into her, each piercing her and delivering its injection of venom. He tossed her and she rolled through the dirt. Her entire body felt numb now, frostbitten and senseless. The Griska-thing hovered over her, blowing around her, readying itself for what surely would be the death-blow.

Just lay here, she thought. *Lay cool and easy. Play dead. Get it? Like when you were a kid, play...dead.*

When she saw Griska's cruel face pushing out of the noxious mist just inches from her own, she brought the knife around in a savage arc, slitting it from forehead to chin. It parted like cool jelly. She slashed and hacked at it. *"HERE!"* she screamed at his melting face. *"HOW ABOUT THAT? AND THAT? AND THAT? HOW DO YOU FUCKING LIKE THAT, YOU GODDAMN PARASITE!"*

Griska shrieked, folding in on himself and then mushrooming back out. Trying, it seemed, to control his shape, but having trouble as Wenda kept stabbing him, bisecting him with that damnable silver blade. He howled with agony and wrath. He had underestimated his opponent and now he was paying for it. And though he was still not strictly a corporeal being—part mist, part flesh, part boiling steam—he was wounded.

He was gored.

A foul smelling vapor hissed from his mass, a rain of watery brown-red blood going to the blackness of India ink. He still tried to attack Wenda with dozens of sucking mouths and jabbing needles, but it was half-hearted and almost pathetic, like a wounded dog trying to bite. Feeble, weakened.

Wenda got to her feet and slashed at the bleeding ghost, gutting it and tearing it open. Her onslaught was fierce, but so was his retaliation. Something like a fist was driven into her temple and she was pitched to the ground. Shaking it off, she sat back up and something hot and acrid-smelling struck her full in the face, blinding her, sending her reeling with its foul odor. She brushed it from her face and it came again, a hot stream of...blood.

He was pissing on her.

He was pissing blood onto her.

When he stopped and she cleared the burning liquid from her eyes, he was standing not five feet from her. In his shaggy black hide coat, he looked like a human buzzard standing there and he smelled like one, too. The putrescence that filled her nostrils was not his odor—that was dry, dusty, and aged like a worm-holed book rotting on a shelf—but the stink of his breath, which was that of something that had been chewing on carrion.

But he was damaged.

She saw that much.

The other vampires had gathered now with the rats and they were all moaning with a high, eerie sibilance as if they could feel his pain and his...shame. He stood hunched over, enhancing his buzzard-like appearance, and Wenda knew she had damaged him with the knife. His face had indeed been slit open, the gash, perfectly bloodless, ran from the crown of his skull to his chin, perfectly splitting his hawkish nose. In fact, one side of his pallid, scarred face had slid down perhaps an inch, giving him the look of a reflection in a broken mirror and making him all that much more grotesque. His visage was narrow, bony, and rodent-like, spattered with blood, clumps of hair missing from his head, his flesh almost scaly, the teeth jutting from his mouth sharp and hooked like those of a pit viper. One eye was destroyed, gashed and popped like a blood-cherry, oozing a red-black juice down his craggy, graying complexion.

He brought up one hand and touched his face.

The fingers were remarkable white, remarkable long and oddly delicate, the nails ragged, yellow, and filthy.

With a thick accent, he said, *"You dare...you dare...you dare touch me?"*

Wenda wanted to tell him that, *yes,* she had dared and she would now dare to destroy him completely because time was on her side and dawn was approaching fast now. But he fixed her with his remaining leering red eye and held her like a bug on a pin.

As she trembled, he came for her.

24

Wenda heard the vampires begin to wail again with that unearthly, eerie sound of mourning. And it was not because Griska was coming to fix her, to empty her like an upended jug. No, it was because something else had shown up on the scene...a bunched, crawling thing that seemed to be primarily composed of rats, crawling, squeaking rats.

She knew it was Rule.

The rats had been sent to destroy him—and they were doing it, all right—but there was more fight in his ornery old body than Griska and his ghouls had counted on. The will to survive at his core was a flame that could not easily be blown out, like one of those trick birthday candles.

He pushed through the ranks of rats.

Some parted, some scurried, others attacked him.

But they certainly couldn't stop him. He still clutched his flashlight in one raw, red fist and the rodents that had bitten his skin away had not been able to make him let go of it.

Dear God, he was swarmed with them. They were in his hair. They were hanging from his face by their teeth. Small ones had worked their way up the legs of his Carhartt overalls and down the back. They were gnawing at him, scratching and tearing at him. What she could see of his face was a bloody ruin. Between two bloated rat bodies, she could see one eye peering out as if from the depths of a shaggy cave. He reached up and tore one rat from his face and then another. He coughed out a blob of blood.

"GET AWAY FROM HER, YOU FUCKING LEECH!" he shouted. "GET THE FUCK AWAY FROM HER!"

Wenda knew then that, somehow, he had sensed the fix she was in and nothing, neither vampires, rats nor witch-winds, were going to stop him from reaching her side and lending assistance, even if that meant forfeiting his own life, which she was certain he had pretty much done.

He fought to his knees, then his feet and it was the utmost physical battle to do so. Rats fell from him and he peeled more free with his left hand, hammering at them with the butt of his flashlight. But for those that fell, others climbed him like a tree. He put his light on Griska and Wenda noticed that the beam partly illuminated the ghoul and partly shined right through him like he was made of some transparent material like cellophane.

Rule took two, then three faltering steps backwards, fighting the rats that were quite literally eating him alive. Wenda could hear their jaws working, teeth scraping against bone, as they glutted themselves with his flesh. Yet...he staggered forward, his voice cycling out of his throat in a screeching tirade: "YOU'RE ALL DONE! YOU'RE ALL FUCKING DONE! THE SUN WILL RISE SOON...AND...AND YOU'LL FRY IN IT...EVERYONE OF YOU FUCKING BLOODSUCKERS..."

Wenda wanted to go to him, but she knew it was pointless. The fact that he had made it even this far was practically supernatural. He dropped to one knee as the feeding frenzy continued, falling face-forward, his body writhing and shuddering with awful contortions. Gradually, it stopped moving. The grim silence was broken only by the feeding sounds of the voracious graveyard rats. They bit and chewed and tore. Even their savage appetites could not breech the material of his Carhartt overalls, but they still got at him and soon he was no longer visible, mounded by the rank, squirming hides of the rats themselves that dipped their blood-dripping snouts into him again and again.

Maybe Griska had let Rule get that far to immobilize Wenda completely, but, again, he had underestimated the hate that raged inside her. So when she jumped to her feet and rushed him, he was scarcely ready for her or the blade in her hand that came streaking in a silver blur at his face. He ducked back, holding up a hand to shield himself. The blade easily severed three fingers off his left hand that fell into the dirt and writhed like waxy, white earthworms.

He let out a bellowing roar that was more wolf than human.

An inky blood dripped from the finger stumps. He clawed out at Wenda, but by then the blade was coming again and this time it pierced him just left of the sternum and again he roared, but with such volume and manic fury that rats went squealing away and bats filled the air in panicked flight. The ground seemed to shake. Clods of earth fell from the roof overhead.

Wenda was amazed how very easily the blade went in.

It was not like she was jabbing it into meat and flesh, but into something far more insubstantial like perhaps a heap of threadbare linen. But her aim was off and she completely missed his heart, though the pain she caused him was not only evident, but considerable. The handle of the knife, upon entering the cage of his chest, grew burning hot in her hand and the blade seemed to shine. She smelled something like burning hair and meat. His rodentine face and scabrous flesh drew back from the screaming fanged pit of his mouth.

Then…Griska exploded.

There is no other word to describe what happened at that moment. He literally erupted. He seemed to blow apart into a thousand black, winging fragments that became a swirling, rushing, maddened swarm of bats that flew right into Wenda's face and covered her body, tangling in her hair, biting and nipping as she fell backwards to the ground.

"Gah!" she cried out, quite involuntarily. *"Oh God, get em offa me, get em offa me!"*

She slashed at them with the silver blade and each bat it bisected blazed up with orange fire, dropping away into a melted, black rubbery ball. Her other hand tore at wings and snapped little bones and twisted little heads free.

But they were everywhere.

She couldn't seem to fight her way free of them. There had to be easily thousands as she first thought. She twisted this way and that, trying to throw her way free but it seemed like more pushed in all the time. She knew in her fright that they were not trying to bite her to death. Such a thing was impossible. No, they were going to bury her alive and when she screamed out for breath, they would fill her mouth with their plump, furry bodies and lodge themselves in her throat until she could not draw a single breath.

She stumbled about, some insane and surreal bat sculpture, still fighting, still pulling them free, still smashing their little bodies and slashing them into flaming bat debris as they engulfed her in a squeaking, pulsating black cloud of beating wings and nipping teeth.

I won't! I will not submit to you, Griska! I will not give in and you will not stomp me under! I will fight and fight and fight—

And fight, she did.

They hit her from every conceivable direction, battering her and punching into her, thumping and nipping and cutting. They roosted in her hair and covered her body and went at her eyes. Still, she smashed them and cut them and with each little death, the swarm weakened. Blood was running down her face, steaming in the air. It was her blood *and* the blood of broken bats. Her body was an envelope of pain and the constant beating of those wings pushed her mind closer and closer to complete collapse.

She slashed one last time deep, very deep, into the heart of the swarm...and they withdrew. They abandoned her in a whirring cyclone, flying off in a twisting column that disappeared into the shadows.

And that's when she saw something extraordinary and disgusting beyond description.

Griska was gone now.

He had flown off *as* the swarm to lick his wounds. The other vampires were in the air, wraiths that winged and drifted about. But they had no interest in her, they had another objective.

And it was standing not too far away.

At the very edge of the light, she saw it.

The Death Angel.

That's what it looked like and that's what it had to be. A tall, gaunt form covered in ragged, graying, mold-speckled cerements that seemed to hang in ribbons and tatters and discolored bolts. It wore a hooded shroud and she could not see its face. But she could see its mouth...red-lipped, filled with long, gnarled teeth set in black gums. So many jutting teeth they were like stalactites.

The Death Angel. The Death Hag.

One by one, the vampires became corporeal and offered their throats to her. She put her puckered lips against them, drawing off a taste of the blood they had taken in. She was a great glutted leech, but she always wanted more and they always gave her more.

Well-fed, her mouth red with blood, the Death Angel advanced on Wenda.

The vampires moved off, drifting, then breaking apart like ash on the wind, becoming a black-winged swarm that flew off and away.

The Death Angel was a graveyard statue, unmoving and silent. But each time Wenda blinked her eyes, she was closer and then closer still, raising up gnarled hands, extending thorny black talons that were like those of a barn owl.

Wenda had a knife and a stake, but they hardly seemed enough against this thing. Just about anything would have seemed inadequate. Her mind was caught in a web of primal dread, circling back and forth, back and forth, but finding no way out.

A cold wind blew off the Death Angel. It was the terrible, unnatural cold of tombs and graveyard barrows. Forget the undead, forget Griska, Wenda knew, this was the real one, the ancient and undying one, the Mother of shadows and the Mistress of Plagues. A ravening, lewd pestilence given form and intent.

Then, in the sullen depths of Wenda's mind, the Death Hag spoke with a ragged, grating sound like a wind from low places and hollows blown up through a drainpipe clogged with sediment.

Bow down before me, the voice demanded. *Give unto me that which is mine. Make an offering of it, virgin. I want to see the blood run. From your throat. From your eyes, your mouth, the hole between your legs. Give it unto me.*

Wenda shook with terror. The flesh at the back of her neck had gone rigid. The makeshift weapons in her hands were clutched tightly, knuckles white. She was feeling raw, superstitious terror. That most basal and ancient of emotions. The thing coming for her leeched the strength from her body, filling her with despair, death-phobia, and a bleak paranoia. She blinked and the Mother of Hags was closer, bringing a thick mephitic stench that was equal parts decay, dust, excrement and vomit.

The Death Angel was seven feet tall if she was an inch, sheathed with ice. Ice that was cracking apart, shattering like safety glass. Beneath it, she was a thing of rotting shrouds and threadbare cerements, a ghoul wrapped in a winding sheet that was tattered and blowing, the fragments crawling around her like swollen graveyard worms seeking flesh to despoil. The hood slid back inch by inch and Wenda saw an amnion of undulant, threading cobwebs that tore open like fine mesh to reveal a face that was oblong and narrow, seamed and split like pine bark, the mold-speckled flesh so very gray it seemed blue. The teeth were gnarled yellow ivory tusks. One eye was hidden by the webs, the other a bulging egg-sac the color of sour buttermilk that sheared open as if covered in a thin membrane, revealing a juicy, blood-engorged orb like a gelid pupa giving forth larva.

Wenda screamed with atavistic terror.

25

She tried to backpedal away, but her legs got all wobbly and she went down on her ass, her stomach roiling in hot waves, cold sweat poring down her face. Her insides had gone to liquid rubber and dry heaves rolled through her.

The Death Hag was right on top of her.

She heard a snarling, guttural noise that was not even remotely human and then beaded and rat-skinned hands took hold of her and tossed her with ease. She thudded against a casket with a sprung lid. As she turned to face the Mother, teeth nipped at her, claws tore rents in her parka. She was seized and shaken and slammed back down on the coffin, the air whooshing out of her.

She tried to crawl away and she slipped, falling inside the rank dirt of the box and the Death Angel hovered over her.

Wenda let out a scream as she waited for those claws to open her throat and disembowel her...but that didn't happen. The winding sheets fluttered, pulling back, exposing an emaciated body that was pocked with blotches of fungus, bloodstained and meat-spattered. A row of distended, pendulous tits ran from breast to abdomen. There was a great ulcerous hole between the legs that dripped bile. The body began to split open between the breasts, yawning like a black mouth, revealing cone-shaped shafts of cobwebs that seemed to be in motion, threads and fine hairs leaping from their openings. They looked much like the funnelwebs of spiders.

Wenda cried out as the webs blew out at her, coming from the funnels and from the gaping mouth of the Death Hag herself. They covered, netting her, winding her up in fibers of sticky lacework that felt like strands of undulant phlegm. It poured out of the Mother, gradually cocooning Wenda until she could barely move and barely breathe.

At the edge of sanity, she remembered the silver knife in her fist.

She slashed at the webs, severing them, slitting them open until she could fight free. The hag screeched with a cheated, angry rage. But still Wenda cut and hacked like an explorer in the jungle with a machete. She stabbed blindly out at the Mother and felt the blade pierce flesh that was much like webwork itself. The Death Angel screamed again and this time it was an agonized, wailing sound.

Wenda knew she had hurt her and she would hurt her again.

The Hag Mother circled around her slowly, slowly, no more pretense of cemetery marble. She was flesh and blood, grotesque and incarnate, filled with wrath and blind hatred. Images flooded into Wenda's mind: the bloated spider-witch smacking her lips as she lapped the blood from her torn throat; the hag gutting her and wearing her bloody skin, dyed red with stolen life.

The Mother's sheets were still open and it looked like somebody had taken a drill to her, bored holes through her face and neck and chest. But that wasn't it at all. She was honeycombed like a beehive, or maybe a hornet hive in this case...her body tunneled with little waxen-looking chambers from which a seeking storm of yellowjackets now flew. Dozens and dozens of them, legs hanging limp under those yellow- and black-striped bodies, stingers juiced with venom. Wild and surging, they filled the air in a droning cloud, descending on Wenda who met them, slashing at them with her knife. They stung her face, her hands, they got up the sleeves of her coat and down the back.

But she would not relent.

Crying out, she charged through them and saw the Death Hag reaching out for her with thorny claws. She jabbed with the knife, slicing and slitting, laying the hag open, piercing several of her breasts that popped with an inky, sewer-smelling discharge.

The Death Angel made a squealing sound and came at Wenda.

A sickly yellow pallor emanated from her, the color of disease and infection unchecked. She towered over Wenda, an undead, inhuman atrocity. The hood had blown free of her head and she had trailing black-and-gray locks greased with human fat. Hornets crawled in her scalp and lit from her mouth. Her eyes were huge and glossy black, the pupils a leering, burning red. Her face was that of a witch with jutting chin and hooked-nose, but it was not truly a face as such…just a nest of buzzing hornets *pretending* to be a face. She rose up in a maelstrom of flapping rags and tawdry robes that glistened like oiled hides. Her fingers were reaching sticks, hornets freely passed through great gaping holes in her hands and wrists.

Wenda stood her ground, terrified but unflinching, smelling the mortuary perfume of the Queen of the Dead which was a stink of embalming fluid, suppurating wounds, the rancid blood of swine, and funeral lilies rotted to a soft white pulp.

When the hag raised her long, skeletal arms, her robes and rags parted and hanging beneath were dangling bones and tanned limbs, a blossom of curled hands and…*chains.* Dozens and dozens of rattling chains. They all ended in hooks. Many of them had the impaled bodies of butchered infants skewered on them. From her yellow, braided, tumescent flesh, spikes emerged like the thorns of rose stems.

She looked like a living Iron Maiden ready for sacrifice.

Hornets peppering her face, Wenda hacked at her with the knife, she cut deep, the blade scraping against fungal bone. The hag shrieked and laughed and screeched. The meat and bone that had been carved free were caught in her whirling vortex and reabsorbed.

Wenda felt her mind splinter like deadwood, felt all that she was shatter like fine crystal as the Death Angel pulled her in, vacuuming her into that cyclone of thrashing ropes and rags and bones and spikes that was the Queen of the Sacred Rot.

Hornets stinging her, webs encasing her, Wenda felt her strength ebbing. She cut and hacked…but it was no good, just no good. She could not fight against this thing. No living person could.

Fight, you have to fight. You have to find her weakness and exploit it. You must. You must. You must. Think of Doc and Bailey, Reg and Morris and even Megga in all her insipient weakness. Think of the legions this fucking monster has sucked dry. Think of the babies she strangled in cribs, the children she defiled by moonlight—

Wenda fought with a primal scream ripping from her throat. She stabbed with the knife and clawed at the hag with her fingers into

283

flesh which was like a nest of crawling worms. She fought with strength and agility she did not know she possessed. The Death Angel's red pupils swam in a gummy soup of ebon mud, sucking Wenda's mind from its housing, turning her brain to sauce. A raging furnace-heat blew off of her, carrying a stink of ash pits and funeral pyres. She was a hood of infection, a throbbing pink waste, a river of polluted slime and casket-ooze, something that might have been shoveled from a slaughterhouse floor. Piercing needles and dry rot, stinging hornets and exhaled carapaces.

Wenda felt the spikes press into her skin, felt the hag's arms enfold her, felt all those dead babies and mummy hands come alive, clutching and pulling at her, little mouths biting and trying to suckle her.

But mostly she saw the face of the Death Hag.

It was like the fissured bark of dead trees, the flesh hanging in bulging, blowing strips like cured hide. The lips were black and cracked open, the mouth opening and opening and opening, gnarled yellow-and-gray teeth long as fingers. They moved in to shear her face from the skull beneath, to tear her throat open.

And then—

Then the Death Angel mutated, shifting into a pulsating mass of threadbare gray fur, a bat thing with a long and slithering serpentine tail, perfectly hairless, that wound her up like a hangman's noose, constricting her tighter and tighter. Its swollen teats were pressed against her. It spread immense, leathery, membranous wings pulsing with arteries as big around as Wenda's own thumb. Its head was bullet-shaped, the brow backward sloping, the skull exaggerated, translucent red eyes set in craggy draws, the face noseless and streamlined, the jaws set with teeth like knitting needles.

Wenda was done and she knew it.

She went limp in its fearsome grip as claws like ice-tongs held her securely. The Death Hag was following the swarm now, retreating with them. They had left earlier and now she would scent them on the wind and fly to the lair where Wenda's death would be slow and hellish. The Death Angel flew through the catacombs, dipping and diving, and finally rising up, up, and up through the shaft beneath the mill that Rule had spoken of. It would lead into the world above.

The Death Hag soared upwards with incredible speed.

As Wenda teetered on the edge of consciousness, something clicked in her brain. She knew the Mother's weakness. It was all-too obvious: *arrogance.* She was too arrogant to believe in her own death or to think for one shivering moment that the weak little virgin she carried like an owl carried a mouse had completely out-thought her, out-maneuvered her, and turned her colossal, ancient ego against her.

The Death Hag never guessed this until the sheer velocity of her flight carried up the shaft and above the ruins of the mill…right into the blinding rays of the rising sun. It was only then she roared with hate, with pain, with a maniacal wrath that soon became a weak, tortured mewling. The storm had blown itself out and the sunbeams were like red-hot pokers spearing through her, impaling her, bisecting her, bursting her open with flames and smoke and sizzling rot.

She let forth a freight-train howl that was deafening. It made the world tremble. She began to quiver, roll, tremble, wriggling and squirming like a bag of snakes as she fell earthward, leaving a churning contrail of smoke in her wake. As Wenda fought free of the incinerating mass, the Mother's body became a sculpture of wicker and cane and clawing sticks crackling apart and then nothing but searing rags and blazing ropes, wings unraveling like dirty yarn…all of it caught in her own foul blasting wind. A skein flaking and fragmenting and unwinding until she was a vile pocket of smoking, sucking air, a storm of refuse, ash, dust, bone fragments, and chattering teeth. A single red and bleeding eye looked out with a cheated, glaring hatred as it orbited her monsoon of charnel refuse and howling slag like a dead moon.

By the time her remains crashed back to the floor of catacombs and Wenda was thrown free, singed and hurting but alive…there was nothing but a smoking, popping wreckage of splintered bones and broken wings, the flesh melting off the convulsing blackened skeleton below like hot rubber.

The burning skull broke free.

It cracked open like a chestnut from the heat.

The face flaked off.

The jaws snapped open one last time.

The remaining eye burst from its orbit as flaming ejecta.

One gnarled claw hand reached up…then clattered to the ground, breaking apart.

The Death Hag's shell collapsed into itself and went to fragments, then powder and blowing dust.

Dissolution was complete.

Wenda gagged at the smells that blew past her: putrescence, burning hair, cremated bones, moldering hides.

Then nothing but a ghost-odor of immense age rising from the litter of the hag.

Then…silence.

Except for a voice in her head, singing: *Ding dong, the witch is dead, the wicked witch is dead…*

EPILOUGE: PURIFICATION

1

You're the last one.

They're all dead: Mole and Reg, Megga and Bailey, Morris and Burt...all fucking dead. What do you think about that? What do you honestly feel about all that?

In the catacombs, Wenda sat there by the lantern, looking at the bones and makeshift coffins spread over the hills and mounds of earth, some having slid down into trenches and hollows. She felt numb. She felt as if she had taken so much abuse—physical, psychological, and spiritual—in the past twelve hours that she would never be able to feel again. She was dead inside and unfeeling outside.

"What now, Wenna?" she whispered. "What now?"

She didn't bother answering that one because she fully well knew what came now, what was next on her agenda. The job was not done. Somewhere down here, Megga and Bailey were sleeping in boxes waiting for sunset. Maybe some of the others, too. They would have to be destroyed. If not, they would keep coming for her. She didn't believe for a minute that she could put enough distance between herself and them to stop it. Maybe it would take weeks, months, maybe years, but one night they'd come knocking at the door, thirsting for her.

It won't be just your friends either. There's another one here. A bringer of pestilence like the Death Hag. You must find him. You must stake him.

She thought about the vampire swarm.

After the Mother had siphoned off some of their blood, they had left. They had escaped. The Death Angel had seen to that. She sent them off to seed their evil in the world at large. *Off, my children. The virgin is mine and I claim her. Afterwards, I'll join you.* Maybe it wasn't anything quite like that, but some message must have been passed. Now they were gone and the Death Angel would never join them. But where had they gone? Their boxes were still here, filled with black earth…wouldn't they need them? Much of the old legends were true and Wenda saw no reason why this part of it wouldn't be, too. After all, why shovel dirt into them in the first place?

Still the question remained: Where had they gone?

There was no doubt that they had come out of dormancy this night after many decades of sleep. They had risen up as part of some plan forged long, long ago. It stood to reason that they had a secondary location set up somewhere, maybe an old barn, a disused building, a sewer system or an abandoned warehouse. Chances were, they had a caretaker, too, who was part of the plan. He or she must have found a new hide for them. And it also stood to reason that they probably had many hides. She would have to find them. Somehow.

But that would be for later.

Thinking it over, she was surprised that they hadn't had a caretaker here, some blind and obedient muscle to deal with intruders. Or maybe they were just too arrogant for that.

Chamber of Horrors was extinct now.

The entire crew had been wiped out. There would be many, many questions. If Wenda went back to what remained of her old life, she would have to answer them. Unless she didn't go back. Unless she lived on the lam and hunted them down, staking vampires in cellars and attics, dragging them out into the sunshine in lonely places.

Bailey.

Megga.

"Oh dear Christ," she said under her breath, tears breaking hot against her cheeks.

She gathered up her stakes and began.

2

Bailey was easy to find.

She had made no real effort to hide. She was in a simple trench cut from the earth. She still wore her snow gear. One pale hand rested against the side of her grave, the other was curled at her side. She was lovely even in death, even with the pallor of the tomb on her face. Wenda stood there, looking down at her, her guts crawling with a slow and uneasy nausea. Staking a stranger was one thing, but this was something else.

Suck it up. This is for Bailey. This is the least you can do. Look at her. She'll make a pathetic vampire. She'll be no good at it.

That was true. Wenda knew it was true.

Some would have natural cunning and animal instinct that would survive death. Some were probably already black at their core. And some would be efficient simply because they were efficient in all things. But not Bailey. She would make a mess of things because whatever slight tendrils of humanity remained in her would be revolted at what she had become.

Looking down at her, Wenda was sure of this.

The process of vampirism destroyed the warmth and poetry in their souls, replacing it with animal appetites and drives, leaving a great hollow within them. But she could see the self-revulsion, the self-loathing imprinted on Bailey's face. That's what had survived: the shame of what she now was.

Wenda found a heavy iron gear about the size of a dinner plate that would work just fine as a hammer. She unzipped Bailey's coat, placing the stake to the right of her sternum.

"I'm sorry, sweetheart," she said. "I really am."

She brought the gear down with everything she had on the head of the stake, pushing it in maybe three inches. Bailey's eyes fluttered open and stared. She looked surprised, but not unpleasantly so. The next hit with the gear drove the stake all the way through. Bailey gasped, her lips trembled. Then she closed her eyes and began to look very much like a corpse.

In the next hour, Wenda staked Burt and Morris.

She could not find Reg or Mole. Doc had been butchered so he was dead enough. Walking around in the dankness, lantern held high like some graverobber on the late show—or *Chamber of Horrors,* for that matter—she finally found Rule. The rats had killed him. There was no doubt of that. But while she had battled with Griska and the Death Hag, his body had been dragged off. He was hung upside down and drained. Wenda cut him down and staked him, even though it seemed a bit superfluous.

Megga was not far away.

She slept in a box with the lid closed. Obviously, she had reanimated because there was a smear of blood at her mouth. She made a beautiful vampire as Wenda had figured she would. She had stripped away her snowpants and parka and was only wearing her Graveyard Girl costume, a black and ragged dress that showed lots of leg and plenty of cleavage. The vampiress every teenage boy lusted after. She even had her hands folded over her bosom like one of Dracula's brides. Nobody could play it to the hilt like she could.

There were two stakes left.

Wenda repeated the process, placing the stake just right of the sternum next to the round of one breast. She didn't bother apologizing about any of it to Megga because she figured for the first time in her life, Megga was happy. Content.

"I'll miss working with you," Wenda said. "Your sarcasm always made me laugh."

It was probably a very stupid thing to say, but it was true. It was the truest thing she could say about Megga. She brought the gear down and Megga came awake, screaming and thrashing, as the stake pierced her heart. Blood bubbled from her mouth and the stake entrance wound. Her hands flailed at Wenda. She hissed and spit, her fangs piercing her lower lip. Wenda hammered the gear down two more times…and she settled back into the box. With her hands hooked into claws, the blood splashed over her porcelain-white face, her mouth contorted in agony, Megga did not look to be in peace (like Peter Cushing always said on *Chamber of Horrors)*, she looked like she'd died in extreme agony.

Wenda stumbled away, senseless, dizzy, spattered with blood. There was a screeching white noise in her head. She was shaking and trembling, mouth unable to stay closed. It was like some delayed reaction to shock and trauma.

She went down on her ass and held herself, rocking back and forth.

This is the right thing, this is the right thing, she thought. *I know it's the right thing and I have to do it. I just have to.*

That made her feel scarcely better, but it seemed to clear her head. She wanted to stop. She wanted to get out of there. She needed some kind of closure, but there was one last thing to do. She looked amongst the crates, searching, searching. It took her some time, but she was guided by an inner directional sense that led her, in a roundabout way, exactly where she needed to go. The route took her past the remains of the Death Hag—which looked very much like a dozen different animals melted into a common hole: a rent wing, a bony vertebrae, a fan of claws, a desiccated rat tail the size of a python, a cloven monstrous skull—and through the wreckage of the mill that had fallen from above. She crawled under mangled iron gears, over shattered rafter beams, around piles of stone and heaped planks.

When she found a heap of boards hastily pulled together, she pulled out her last stake.

3

Wenda tossed aside the scraps of wood, dug some soil free, and found herself looking down into a passage that looked like the entrance to a prehistoric barrow tomb. She lowered her lantern down at arm's length. The tunnel dropped down about eight feet and then curved upward, disappearing into the darkness.

Clever. Very clever, leech, but it won't save you.

Sucking in a breath and ignoring the survival instinct that told her to get out, that she had beaten the odds again and again, she lowered herself down into the hole. It smelled dank, moist, and dirty down there like underground pipes clogged with human grease and rotting animal matter. The passage was low and she crab-crawled its length until a pit opened up before her, banked with black soil. It dropped down maybe five feet and down there was a single oblong packing crate. Its lid was smeared with ancient bloody handprints, what looked to be scraps of tissue and clumps of hair. The lair of a human rat.

She slid down there and sat before the box on her knees.

This was it.

This would be the last one.

Oh no, you're wrong. The swarm left and you'll never rest until you track it down and stake every one of them. You can already feel it inside you, the need to destroy all of them. Almost like the choice has been taken away from you as if you are no longer in control of your destiny.

And, God above, it sure seemed that way.

But that was for later so she tucked it away in the back of her mind and gathered her strength. She had to be vigilant and strong now. Any sign of weakness and he would exploit it as he had done for century upon century. Things like him never died because they were too cunning to die.

She set the lantern atop a stone so the light would be good and even for what she had to do. She set the silver blade next to it and took the last stake out of her belt. Then, with her free hand, she worked her fingers under the lip of the lid. Right away, like making contact with some high voltage line, she went stiff. Her belly rolled. Her hair stood on end. She was filled with a curious thrumming energy that made her feel weak, beaten, a heavy inexplicable anxiety feeding through her.

She shook it off.

It was only powerful if you believed it was.

She flipped the lid free. It landed in the dirt.

And screamed as a flurry of bats came winging out, circling around her, and flying off.

Griska was there, wrapped in his ragged hide coat. It was patched with mold, tufts of black fur spiky with dried blood. It looked like the wing of a buzzard. Bats crawled over it, others suckled at his throat. Two long white fingers were hooked around the edge of the box, the nails of which were dirty, splintered, and clawlike, dug right into the wood. The other three fingers of the hand were missing because she had chopped them off herself. He was still badly damaged, his face divided by the cleft she had slashed, one side set down lower than the other. His graying, scarred face was filled with hollows, ancient punctures, the left eye now a blackened scab, the right wide open, bleeding red and owl-like. His lips were pulled back from his hooked, pit viper teeth. They were stained pink from his feedings, black crud packed between them, the gums mottled like those of a wolf.

That single juicy blood orb of an eye was staring at her.

Its gaze drilling deep inside of her like a hot needle.

But Wenda was no fool. She'd watched the movies and she had read the books. Studious by nature, she had studied the undead in detail to prepare for *Chamber of Horrors* and various public appearances and signings. She knew what Griska was doing, how he was probing at her mind. How, had she not been a virgin of all things, he would have invaded her brain, drowning her mind in blackness until he owned her.

"No," she said, her voice dry and scratching. "No, it won't be that easy for you. You're powerless and I know it."

Gripping the stake in both hands, she brought it down with considerable force. A force strengthened by the memory of her friends and how they had died and how this repellent leech had taken her life away from her.

Griska screamed with a wild, hysterical screech of agony and desperation. His hands flayed at her, his head shook from side to side, his teeth gnashed, bats crawled from folds in his coat spreading their wings.

She brought the stake down again and again and again, shearing through his chest, cracking rib bones, ripping open his black beating heart, splitting it, rupturing it, mutilating it until it would beat no more. His final scream blew into her face with a stink of hot decay.

Blood burst from his cloven chest, it spouted from his mouth and nostrils, it squirted and sluiced from him, his remaining good eye popping like a red bubble. Wet and stinking with his drainage, Wenda fell back and away, her hands and the sleeves of her parka a brilliant crimson right up to the elbows. Griska squirmed in his bloodbath, writhing and twisting and shrieking. Bats flew free of him, hornets poured from his mouth in buzzing swarms. The box jumped and shook. His feet kicked out the lower panel, his clawing fingers cut trenches in the wood.

Then he sank in the steaming and bubbling blood. He tried to rise from it one last time like some hideous, jerking puppet. He was more skeleton than man by that point…bony digits scratching at the box for purchase, teeth chattering madly, his fleshless face hanging with strips of tissue, his scalp set with sparse clumps of hair. Then he sank back down, drowning in his own filth and ichor.

And that was it.

He was done.

By the time Wenda looked down inside his grave, the blood was evaporating, leaving nothing behind but what looked like fragments of bones, clotted dirt, and a floating white seam of fat. The air stank horrendously. It was as if every moldering casket in a cemetery had been blown open at the same time.

That was it.

Nearly out of her head from trying to breathe in that vaporous envelope of hot corpse gas, she scrambled out of the pit and back up the passage, crying and whimpering, Griska still screaming in her head like a banshee. She crawled out of the hole and didn't stop moving until she found a ray of sunlight filtering through the mill wreckage above.

She had left her lantern below.

Once she had gathered herself, or as much as she would ever be able to, she didn't bother trying to retrace her steps in the darkness. She started climbing, using the fallen beams and stones from the mill. It was dangerous and more than once she nearly fell, but after about twenty minutes she made it to the mill. The air up there was fresh, unbelievably fresh after the charnel pit below.

She fought her way through snowdrifts that came nearly up to her waist in places and made her way down to Cobton below. It was as she stood in the snow, looking over at Rule's car, very close to where Burt had been killed, that certain practical matters began to occur to her.

There would be questions. Many questions.

The only thing she could do was create more mysteries. With that in mind she went around front of the Georgian house where Doc had died. His corpse was still in there. Upstairs, she found two more kerosene lanterns and she emptied them downstairs until the walls and rugs of Doc's tomb were quite saturated with fuel. Something breaking inside her with a nearly audible crackling, she lit the place up with a match. The fire consumed the room, rushing up the walls and licking at that fine, dry woodwork, tasting the curtains and engulfing the furniture. It was her hope that the entire house would fall into the cellar so that the passage to the catacombs would never be found.

I'm sorry, Doc. So sorry. We all loved you so much.

4

The keys were in Rule's car.

It started instantly and it wasn't until she was driving past the wrecked bus in the Subaru, that the pain and trauma of it all began to take hold of her. She gripped the wheel and shook, but she did not slow down and she did not stop. She didn't dare. Even in four-wheel drive, the Outback was just making it through the snow and drifts. The heater felt good. She was cold to her core and hadn't realized it.

She thought of the undead.

She thought of cells of them waking up across the country, across the world. In her mind she could see them reaching from the shadows: pallid horrors, long-armed, grinning with red mouths. They would have to be stopped. They would have to be tracked down and destroyed wherever they were hiding. She wouldn't be the only one. She knew that. Others would shrug off their disbelief to do what had to be done. She only hoped it would be in time.

"I'll find you," she said. "I'll kill everyone of you."

Two miles down the road, it began to snow again. The Subaru slowly vanished into a white wall of snow, shrinking away, becoming a dot and then vanishing altogether.

—The End—

NIGHTMARE OF THE DEAD
VINCENZO BILOF

In a world of war and mayhem, a twisted nightmare of undead cannibals begins.

The outlaw Neasa Bannan uncovers a horrifying conspiracy engineered by the psychopathic mastermind behind the Confederacy's deadly flesh-hungry weapons. A homicidal gunslinger and a brotherhood of killers emerge out of Neasa's tragic, blood-soaked past while the living dead ravage the land.

With the fate of the country in the balance, Neasa must decide: save the Union from the undead menace, or surrender to Saul's vision of ultra-violence.

www.severedpress.com

ICE STATION ZOMBIE
JE GURLEY

For most of the long, cold winter, Antarctica is a frozen wasteland. Now, the ice is melting and the zombies are thawing. Arctic explorers Val Marino and Elliot Anson race against time and death to reach Australia, but the Demise has preceded them and zombies stalk the streets of Adelaide and Coober Pedy.

www.severedpress.com

The Coalition

When the dead rose to destroy the living, Ron Cutter learned to survive. While so many others died, he thrived. His life is a constant battle against the living dead. As he casts his own bullets and packs his shotgun shells, his humanity slowly melts away.

Then he encounters a lost boy and a woman searching for a place of refuge. Can they help him recover the emotions he set aside to live? And if he does recover them, will those feelings be an asset in his struggles, or a danger to him?

THE STATE OF EXTINCTION: the first installment in the **COALITON OF THE LIVING** trilogy of Mankind's battle against the plague of the Living Dead. As recounted by author **Robert Mathis Kurtz.**

www.severedpress.com

MACHINES OF THE DEAD

The dead are rising. The island of Manhattan is quarantined. Helicopters guard the airways while gunships patrol the waters. Bridges and tunnels are closed off. Anyone trying to leave is shot on sight.

For Jack Warren, survival is out of his hands when a group of armed military men kidnap him and his infected wife from their apartment and bring them to a bunker five stories below the city.

There, Jack learns a terrible truth and the reason why the dead have risen. With the help of a few others, he must find a way to escape the bunker and make it out of the city alive.

www.severedpress.com

JUDGMENT DAY

Dr. Jebediah Stone never believed in zombies until he had to shoot one. Now they're mutating into a new species, capable of reproducing, and the only defence is 'Blue Juice', a vaccine distilled from the blood of rare individuals immune to the zombie plague. Dr. Stone's missing wife is one of these unwilling 'munies', snatched by the military under the Judgment Day Protocol.It's a new, dangerous world filled with zombies, street gangs, and merciless Hunters desperate for a shot of blue juice. Has the world turned on mankind? Is Mortuus Venator the new ruler of earth?

TIMOTHY
MARK TUFO

Timothy was not a good man in life and being undead did little to improve his disposition. Find out what a man trapped in his own mind will do to survive when he wakes up to find himself a zombie controlled by a self-aware virus.

NECROPHOBIA

An ordinary summer's day.
The grass is green, the flowers are blooming. All is right with the
world. Then the dead start rising. From cemetery and mortuary,
funeral home and morgue, they flood into the streets until every
town and city is infested with walking corpses, blank-eyed
eating machines that exist to take down the living.
The world is a graveyard.
And when you have a family to protect, it's more than survival.
It's war.

www.severedpress.com

Zombie Fallout
Mark Tufo

CURRENTLY IN DEVELOPMENT WITH

Illuminandi Media

ShaedStudios.com

www.ingramcontent.com/pod-product-compliance
Lightning Source LLC
Chambersburg PA
CBHW030532270626
47155CB00024B/2763